CW01095537

Born in Stoke-on-Trent and educated in Sandbach, Cheshire, Nigel Macbeth taught for seventeen years in the Potteries before moving abroad to teach children of British Forces personnel in Germany and Gibraltar.

He retired in 2004 after thirty years teaching. He has been married to Trish for thirty-two years. They have one daughter, Melissa.

'The Right Cause' is his first crime thriller.

THE RIGHT CAUSE

Nigel Macbeth

THE RIGHT CAUSE

Vanguard Press

A CIP catalogue record for this title is
available from the British Library.

ISBN 978 1 84386 399 1

*Vanguard Press is an imprint of
Pegasus Elliot MacKenzie Publishers Ltd.*
www.pegasuspublishers.com

First Published in 2008

**Vanguard Press
Sheraton House Castle Park
Cambridge England**

Printed & Bound in Great Britain

Dedication

To the two women in my life.
Trish, my wife, and Melissa, our daughter.

18th December

The room was just how he imagined it would be.

Desk, slightly away from the wall, two chairs on either side, carelessly pushed into whatever position they finished in. Strip of magnolia paint, half covered by a grey filing cabinet, detaching itself from the wall. Brown door, closed now, offering little in the way of welcome, except perhaps for its long, thin pane of glass that allowed the occasional glimpse of the outside world.

The desk was bare, the chairs were wooden and the window, high on the wall above, had been covered by a sheet of plywood, which, on closer inspection, was five millimetres thick. Enough thickness to keep the light out.

And it was cold.

Ben rose from a chair, the one he'd been told to sit on when he first arrived, and wandered over to the radiator. Leaning against it, he realised it was barely on. It probably needed bleeding, but he had neither the tool nor the inclination to do it. He made a mental note to tell someone.

He began to pace the room, slowly at first and from end to end across the length, but after a few minutes, he began to vary his route and his speed. He played a game of touch: touch the chair, then touch the wall, then touch the magnolia paint that was falling from the wall.

Perhaps the drink was still within his veins, but he hadn't drunk enough to cause delirium or drunken behaviour. The exercise was just a way of getting warm in this godforsaken interview room in a police station in Manchester.

He'd never been in such a room before, but he'd seen enough of them on television or in movies, to know what they were like. New York, London, Paris, Bangkok, it didn't matter where the room was; it was always the badly furnished, badly decorated, same. Ironically, he found comfort in the familiarity, despite the circumstances.

He even felt he knew what would happen next, if the movies were to be believed.

It did. The door swung open and in walked two gentlemen, smartly dressed, one in more expensive clothes than the other.

"Hello, Mr Price," said the better dressed one. He raised his hand and Ben felt himself instinctively grasp it and shake it. "Sorry to keep you waiting. My name is Sebastian."

"I'm Ben," he replied. The moment was smothered within a surreal atmosphere. He had never, in all the movies, seen a police officer shake hands with a suspect, not before the interview anyway. He'd expected two men to come through the door, one well dressed the other not so, good cop bad cop, high flyer downtrodden, and that's what they looked like. But within two seconds of seeing each other, they were shaking hands and on first name terms.

"And just to complete the formalities," said the second man, "I'm Delaney. Never had a first name, never wanted one." Delaney didn't shake hands. Walking past Ben, he lifted something from his pocket, attached it to the end of the radiator and began to turn. There was a loud hissing sound which lasted for ever and then a gush of water as it hit the wall. The strip of magnolia paint wafted with the force. "Why are these rooms always so bloody cold?" he asked no-one in particular.

"Please, Ben, take a seat," said Sebastian. He waved his hand in the direction of the chairs. Ben felt obliged to sit. It would have been bad manners not to do so. Delaney leant against the radiator and Ben wished in some way, it had been he who had done the asking. "Take a radiator," he would have said and Ben would have obliged, gladly.

The seat was colder than he remembered. He felt the muscles tighten in the base of his spine. He shivered involuntarily, probably from the cold, but he wasn't sure.

"Ah, that's better. Coming through now," said Delaney. Ben could imagine him anywhere in the world, strolling into the room with his bleeding key, heading straight for the radiator and making himself comfortable.

He looked around and saw that Delaney had lifted the bottom of his coat so that he could half sit, half lean against the rim of the radiator. Arms folded, his smile lit that small section of the room.

Sebastian, on the other hand, chose to sit opposite, on a chair identical to Ben's. He was impeccably dressed. He was, of course, wearing a suit, but there are different ways to wear a suit. It fitted perfectly, as did his shirt, white with the thinnest of pin stripes, and his silk tie, Windsor knotted, suitably central. He crossed one leg over the other. His shoes were beautifully polished. His hair, expensively cut, flopped slightly forward so that occasionally he pulled it back from his forehead.

When he spoke, it was with quiet authority, well spoken, but not too clipped. There was no need to emphasise what was already obvious. Sebastian had had a privileged upbringing, but had the good nature to be polite to one and all. His parents' product; they must have been proud of him.

So, Ben thought, what the hell was posh, privileged Sebastian doing in a cold police station in Manchester? The two didn't go together.

Delaney, on the other hand, was made for this room. He too was wearing a suit, well cut, but it just didn't sit right on his more rounded body. His tie was loose at the neck and the top button of his shirt was undone. Ben doubted whether he could have fastened it. It wasn't that he carried too much weight, it's just that Delaney and clothes didn't go together.

No matter what he wore, he would still look the same. Suit, sports clothes, pyjamas, they would all be worn, but only as a necessity. He was well dressed, but in a careless fashion. He didn't care what he looked like. He was interested only in the practical things in life like radiators that needed bleeding. If something needed doing then he did it. The job was the job. And that was all that mattered.

First impressions can be misleading, but in this case, Ben thought he was right. Over the next few weeks, he would learn many things, but one thing in particular. First impressions never reveal the complete picture.

"So, Ben, I suspect you know why you're here," said Sebastian. It was not a question, but it required an answer.

"I think so," Ben said. A pathetic reply, but he'd decided, when he was sitting alone with only the cold to keep him company, that he didn't want to give too much away. After all, he'd done nothing wrong. He was a witness, not a participant, although the way he'd been handled and put in the police van and had the door slammed on him didn't suggest that. He'd checked for injuries, but it wasn't rough enough to result in that. It wasn't what you would call pleasant either.

Hands held behind his back, not handcuffed, he'd been brought through the side door by the plain clothes officer who'd rushed him down the corridor to the brown door, told him to sit in that particular chair, closed the door and stared at him through the pane of glass to see if he was behaving himself.

He was. After a few return trips, he must have decided that Ben was not a terrorist or suicidal or a suicidal terrorist and made no more visits. It was a cold night and a constant supply of hot tea from the canteen must have been more appealing.

According to Ben's watch, which was not always the most reliable, he'd been left to freeze for forty minutes before testing the radiator and starting his 'touch' training regime, so Sebastian was right to apologise for keeping him waiting, even though the words sounded like meaningless protocol.

"Well, go on then. Tell us." Delaney's voice came from the warmth behind him. Ben suspected that, if he cared to look, the words were not even accompanied by a trail of breath circling its way towards the ceiling, so thawed had Delaney become.

"Well, it's really simple. I'd gone out last night," offered Ben.

"On your own?" asked Delaney.

"Yes."

"Unusual."

"Yes, I suppose so."

"Billy No Mates?"

"Not really. Just wanted to go out on my own. Not a crime is it?" Ben admonished himself for getting irritated so early in the interview when he had nothing to hide.

"No, it's not a crime," said Sebastian. "Quite like to do it myself from time to time. Keeps the options open."

"Options?"

"Yes, you know," answered Sebastian. "Whatever the choice. Girls. Boys. Paid. Unpaid. Nice to have options."

"No. No. It was nothing like that. Just a quiet drink on my own."

"Was that drink or drinks?" Delaney asked.

"Well, I suppose it was drinks. Only a couple though."

"More like four and a half, actually," corrected Sebastian.

"No, you've got it wrong there."

"No, Ben, I'm afraid we haven't." Sebastian's tone had lost some of its friendliness. It was still remarkably polite, but now there was an edge to it that suggested to Ben that he might not be here for a friendly chat after all. There was something more to it than that.

Sebastian stroked the hair from his forehead, caressed his tie, ensuring that it was perfectly central, flicked a shred of fluff from the right thigh of his trousers with the back of his little finger. And he let his words linger.

Ben retraced his steps. The Black Bull for a swift one. It was quiet, too quiet for a quiet drink on his own. A stroll down the road, more into town now. The Crown for one, but then there was that hippie with dreadlocks hanging over his face and rings in his nose who insisted on gabbling about Glastonbury and how it was one hell of a trip to sleep under the stars with your back against the mud and someone pissing on you. You couldn't get much closer to nature than that, he'd said. Ben thought they didn't have much in common. He finished his drink, made his apologies and left. The Oasis, where the corner seat brought calm, despite the music pounding from the other side of the bar. A slow pint, another half finished and then the drunken girl, scantily clad in summer clothes in December, who straddled him without warning and rotated her hips against his groin before he flung her to one side and left with her foul mouth and filthy laughter ringing in his ear. The Dragon, where he feared for his life, drank quickly and left, followed swiftly by a brawling mob spilling out onto the pavement and sending him crashing against the lamppost.

And then the police arrived.

Four and a half drinks. How could Sebastian have been so bloody precise?

"You're an intelligent man, Ben," he said. "Model pupil. Excellent examination results. Conscientious student. Good degree. Rapid promotion and now an advanced skills teacher. This is quite some C.V., Ben"

Ben began to feel uncomfortable.

"And there's more. Popular with the kids. Popular with the staff. Popular with the inspectors. Good sense of humour. Local football team. Nine handicap golfer. Everything at your feet, Ben."

Delaney cut in. "So, why the hell were you on your own, drifting from pub to pub, drinking yourself silly, getting involved in a pavement brawl? Becoming a habit. Doesn't sound like an intelligent man to me, Sebastian."

"I've had problems," Ben heard himself saying.

"Problems?" Delaney threw as much sarcasm as possible into one word. "We've all got problems laddie."

"Not like mine," Ben said.

"Tell us then. We're here to help you." Sebastian reached forward, rested his hand on Ben's arm, left it there. Despite his reassuring tone, his friendly touch, Ben didn't believe him. Couldn't believe him. Four and a half pints. How could he be so bloody precise?

And Delaney? Delaney and his 'drifting from pub to pub' and his 'drinking himself silly' and his 'becoming a habit'. How did he know all that? It was only the brawl on the pavement that he could have known about. And then he'd got it wrong. Ben was an innocent bystander.

"I was an innocent bystander," Ben said. "I'd gone into the pub for a drink, downed it quickly when I saw trouble brewing, got outside, only to be followed by this mob who shoved me against a lamppost. I didn't know them, didn't want to."

"Amazing what you can get involved in when you've had a few pints," said Delaney.

"I wasn't involved in anything." Ben could hear the pleading in his own voice as Sebastian's words re-emerged: well respected, always had been, always tried his best, always did what was right. What would happen when this came out? Ben knew that recently he had been finding work more difficult. The concentration and enthusiasm that had come naturally to him had waned and that had not escaped the notice of his boss, but now, with this, there would be good reason to question whether he could continue. Had everything changed because some drunken mob had shoved him against a lamppost?

No. He couldn't blame the drunken mob. Everything had changed before that. Before the gyrating, foul mouthed girl. Before the dreadlocked, pissed on hippie. Before he had walked out of his house, everything had changed.

Sebastian interrupted his thoughts. "I believe I know the answer to this next question, Ben, but I'll ask anyway. Have you ever been in this situation before?"

His mind was scrambled, unable to understand a simple question. What situation was he talking about? Surely he didn't know about Ben's dreams, his reckless ideas, his nightmares. The constant desire to kill, take another human being's life. It was not psychotic, not wanton. This was individual, personal. There was only one man Ben wanted to see dead and until he was, his mind could not be at rest.

He was pulled back to the present. "Have you ever been inside a police station before?" asked Sebastian.

"No. No, I haven't."

"Interesting, eh?" asked Delaney.

"I could think of better words. It's not you sitting here being accused of something you haven't done."

Sebastian spoke quietly. "But Ben, you haven't been accused of anything. Other than a night out on your own. And that's no crime, is it?"

"And what about your partner there?" Ben threw a nod of the head in Delaney's direction. "He mentioned the pavement brawl. I think 'getting involved' were his exact words."

A smile brushed across Sebastian's perfect features. He didn't allow his teeth to show, but it was a smile nevertheless. "Mr Delaney can sometimes get ahead of himself, I'm afraid. But there was no accusation, no charge levelled at you, Ben. Just a recounting of the facts. Getting involved doesn't mean being responsible. There are many things

17

we get involved in but have no control over, no responsibility for. But they happen and we can't deny that. You can't deny that, can you? You yourself said you were 'shoved against a lamppost.' I think those were your exact words. That sounds pretty involved to me, Ben. Not responsible. Just involved."

There remained that even tone to his voice, a measured response to win Ben round again, set things straight between them, renew their friendship. He allowed the silence to continue, broken intermittently by the shuffle of Delaney's shoes as he shifted position on his radiator.

"Four and a half drinks. How could you be so bloody precise?" Ben asked.

There was that smile again, the one with no teeth showing. "You are an intelligent man, Ben." He found another piece of fluff on his trousers, this time a little lower, close to his polished shoes. He curled it up between his forefinger and thumb and then allowed it to drop to the floor. Immediately, he leaned forward and picked it up. Standing, he walked over to the plastic bin in the corner of the room and watched as the fluff drifted down to rest on its base. He took a handkerchief, perfectly folded, out of his pocket and brushed his forefinger and thumb. Re-folding the handkerchief and placing it in his pocket, he rested his shoulder against the door, covering the pane of glass.

"Ben," he said. "Mr Delaney and I have a proposition for you."

*

His grammar was perfect. Most people would have succumbed to the lazy 'Mr Delaney and myself' or even 'Mr Delaney and me' which would, of course, have been drastically wrong. Take Delaney out of the sentence and it would not have made sense. 'Myself have a proposition for you' or 'Me have a proposition for you.' Whereas Sebastian's 'I have a proposition for you' was perfect.

Ben couldn't help but notice. It was the first thing that hit him. It was the teacher in him, he supposed.

Sebastian's words sank into Ben's befuddled mind. Delaney and Sebastian had a proposition for him. What the hell did that mean? "Proposition?" he asked.

"Yes."

"What kind of proposition?"

Sebastian took the lead, whilst Delaney remained in the background warming himself on his well bled radiator. "August this year. Emma Parker walks into a police station in Liverpool. She claims to have been raped behind a club by one man while three others watch. There is slight bruising to both wrists, as if she has been held down, and a love bite on the left side of her neck. She is very, very distraught. The back of her clothing is dirty, with a few smudges of oil smeared around the shoulder blade area, consistent with movement whilst on her back. The front of her clothing is clean. Her story is quite believable to the young constable who deals with her. This is supported by a more senior officer who has had vast experience in this abhorrent aspect of human nature."

Ben hears the details, they register, they stir his memory. The name, Emma Parker, is implanted in his mind. The mention of her name causes his heart to race and his blood to freeze. She was the catalyst to his plight, and yet she was as innocent as Ben is now. An innocent bystander.

Sebastian continued. "Emma is examined by a female doctor, who confirms that recent intercourse has taken place. She also suspects that a criminal assault has occurred, although, in comparison to many cases, the injuries are minor. I doubt if Emma Parker would have called them 'minor.' There is an investigation. Four soldiers are interviewed, one of them admits intercourse but denies rape. There is full army co-operation and police decide that there is no case to answer, no prosecution. Emma is not pleased. It didn't help her cause that she was out celebrating her twenty-first and was extremely drunk. There is nothing wrong with that, but when drunkenness leads to staggering from table to table flirting with everything in trousers, sitting on anyone's lap, snogging anything in her path, mounting the stage and pole dancing and then twirling her forefinger at the aforementioned soldier, leading him out of the side door into the alleyway, then all of this does not strengthen her case. The club manager offers all this in a written statement, also stating that at one point, Emma was almost evicted from the club. It must have been bad. No-one ever gets evicted from that club. Statements from the other three soldiers concur with the manager. They were the only witnesses to the alleged rape. Their statements confirm intercourse, but no rape, supporting their colleague. This is not surprising."

The incident destroyed Emma Parker's life. Ben had held her in his arms and she had cried until she slept, her head resting on his chest. He had lifted her and placed her gently on the settee. Her mother had brought a blanket and Ben had placed it over her. He could see the pain through her closed eyes and the blame she attached to herself etched on her face. She was innocent of any crime, except perhaps naivety and who amongst us has never been guilty of that?

As he left her sleeping, safe in the company of her tender mother, Ben hoped that, given time, she would be able to live her life again. Perhaps she might even be able to accept her innocence, although the process would be long and the memories deep rooted.

"But Emma gave the police other information, didn't she Ben?" Sebastian waited for an answer. Ben suspected he never expected one. "Emma was very clear on the detail. She told police that during her rape ordeal, she heard her friend, Lynn Thomas, calling for her in the alleyway. The soldier's hand was covering her mouth, so she could not respond, but she did see Lynn over the shoulder of her attacker. One of the other soldiers turned and saw her. Lynn ran for help. The soldier followed. Later that night, Ben, Lynn Thomas was found dead in her crashed car at a known traffic blackspot. She had not been drinking. There was no evidence of any third party involvement. The coroner passed a verdict of accidental death." Sebastian took a break before continuing. "None of this is news to you, Ben. You know the rest."

Sebastian was correct. Ben knew the rest.

Every last detail, every statement, every lie. Emma identified Sergeant Jimmy Buller as the soldier who ran after Lynn in the alleyway. He denied he had ever left the scene. He said he was with the other men all the time. He gave a detailed description of the sexual activity that took place, according to the men, who unsurprisingly agreed with each other, down to the last detail. It was as if they were reading from the same page. Which they were. He could even describe in detail the recent tattoo that Emma had around her genitalia. How would he know so much detail if he had not been there, he asked. He remembered how he thought it was more beautiful than his wife's, who just happened to have one in a similar position. And then he smiled.

"If only I had not had so much to drink," Emma had said, "Lynn would still be alive."

Of course this was true, but she was not responsible for her own rape and Lynn's death. She was the victim, not the perpetrator.

And if Ben was willing to accept this, then hopefully Emma would. After all, Lynn Thomas was Ben's fiancée. They had planned to marry in the spring.

*

Sebastian continued. "It festers Ben, doesn't it? It just won't go away. It lies there, deep in your brain and you know that even if the kids at school take your mind off it for a while, when you're on your own at the end of the day, the first thing that comes into your mind is Lynn. And the second thing you think of is Sergeant Jimmy Buller, who did, quite literally, get away with murder. You don't blame the authorities. They did their best. The evidence just wasn't there to prosecute. You don't blame them, just as you don't blame Emma. You blame one person only. And the more you think about it, the more you go over the events, the more you think of his sickly smile, the more you know he's guilty. And he's got away with it."

"He's a bastard." Delaney moved from the comfort of his radiator, pulled up a chair and sat next to Ben, on the end, resting his chin in his fingers and his elbows on the table. Sebastian uncrossed his legs and moved them under the table, now that Delaney had crowded their space. He remained upright, back against the chair, but looked a little uncomfortable. He crossed his legs again, this time left over right, and turned his back slightly away from Delaney.

21

"Sergeant Jimmy Buller," said Delaney. "Twenty years experience. Three tours of Northern Ireland. The Balkans, the former Yugoslavia. Iraq. You name it, he's been there. His written record is exemplary. And that's not all. His men would go through anything for him. Whether that was out of respect or fear is not clear. Private Jonny James died for him. Stepped in front of a bullet meant for Buller. Got a gong for it, but that's not much good when you're dead. Buller spoke at his funeral, even cried. Never been seen before."

He was painting an impressive picture of a man Ben despised. He could see why people found it difficult to believe that this paragon of the British Army could have been involved in Lynn's death. Could Ben have done all the things he had done? The institutional bullying, the training, the crawling through mud layered with sewerage, the throwing of kit in his face because one collar was ironed worse than the other, the humiliation of marching time with a mattress on his head because his bed wasn't perfect, harried and prodded at every move by some sadistic swine of a sergeant who knew what he felt like when he was young and recently recruited and wasn't about to make it any easier for anyone else.

The wars. The killing. The mass graves. The diggers, standing idly to one side, silent, having revealed the grim truth. The families, thousands of them, devoid of men, men who were now lying beneath Jimmy Buller's feet, bundled together, limbs detached or akimbo. Their wives and children crying, endlessly.

The answer was simple. Ben knew he could not have gone through all that, could not have witnessed what Sergeant Jimmy Buller had seen, could not have done what Jimmy Buller had done.

But neither could he have stood and watched as an innocent girl was raped. Neither could he have followed her friend and murdered her.

"But there are doubts," continued Delaney. "There's no denying that he would be one man you'd want to have beside you when the orders came to fight, but to soldiers like Buller, it's just a legal way of satisfying their blood lust. Their killer instinct is accepted, even encouraged, in the military, but in civvy street it becomes unacceptable. Why do you think so many of our homeless are ex-military? They've done their duty, served their purpose and they're cast aside to fend for themselves in a society that abhors their being. The job they do is essential, but that doesn't mean that I have to like them personally or have them living next to me, that's the attitude people take. Talk to most professional soldiers and they'll tell you that going to war is like footballers playing in the World Cup Final. They've done all the training and now is the chance to prove themselves. It's their World Cup Final. Most soldiers feel this way. But there are doubts about Buller. He's different."

"Can I just interrupt for a moment, Mr Delaney?" asked Sebastian.

Delaney didn't mind. He turned his hand upwards and angled it in an 'after you' gesture. Placing his hands on the table, he rose from his seat and made his way back to his radiator. There was a creak of the radiator, a kind of greeting for an old friend, as he resumed his half sitting position. Ben didn't look round. He didn't have to. He could imagine him, arms folded, jacket undone, a ripple of stomach protruding over his belt. He would adopt a disinterested pose, yet listen to every word spoken.

Sebastian turned towards Ben, crossing right leg over left. He flicked his hair back with his hand. He smiled. No teeth. "At this point, I think I need to tell you something about Mr Delaney." There was no response from behind. Ben could only conclude that Delaney was quite happy to let Sebastian talk for him, and about him. Either they trusted each other, or they had planned this moment, or they had played this game so many times that the script was no longer necessary.

Sebastian continued. "Mr Delaney was an undercover operative in Northern Ireland at the height of the troubles. His brief was to infiltrate the Irish Republican Army, the IRA. To say that he was successful is an understatement of immeasurable proportions. He was able to save the lives of hundreds, maybe thousands, of civilians. But the most remarkable fact about Mr Delaney is that he survived. When the troubles were winding down, he vanished. The IRA, an extremely well organised group of people, some would say terrorists, used everything at their disposal to find him. He was, to them, one of their own. They still believe that. Eventually, they accepted and mourned the passing of their comrade. Remarkably, so did his contact on the British side. Mr Delaney, to all intent and purpose, is dead. No record of him exists. It is as if he never was."

He flicked his tie so that it hung between the lapels of his open jacket. If everything he said was true, and Ben had no reason to doubt him, then the brawl on the pavement outside the pub earlier that evening was becoming more of an irrelevance to this intimate gang of three sharing secrets in a police station in Manchester.

Sebastian continued. "Delaney, of course, is not his real name." He lifted his hand in a gesture to Delaney, who returned to his seat. Ben found himself staring at, almost studying, his face. There was no sign of expression, no sign of pride, no acknowledgement of what had been said, no arrogance, nothing. His impassive face had been what had kept him alive. If Buller was a hero, then what words could describe this man. Unassuming, single-minded, reticent. The Americans would call him a National Treasure, in their inevitable self indulgent way.

Delaney placed a brown, insignificant folder on the table in front of him. "You can look through that all you wish, Ben, but you will find no evidence of what I am about to tell you." It was the first time he had addressed Ben by name, apart from 'Billy No Mates' and 'laddie.' Perhaps, Ben thought, he was warming to him. "That's Buller's service record so far. Bloody impressive, I can tell you. But before you start changing your mind about this guy, let me tell you a few truths about Sergeant Jimmy Buller."

And he began his tale of discreditation. "Iraq. Intelligence warned of a roadside bomb. Buller was there, saving local lives, shouting them to safety, pulling them away from danger. A little too roughly, perhaps. Two Muslim girls, in their teens, had their veils ripped from their faces, exposing themselves within their own village. That's how they would feel, Muslim girls, without their headscarves. Exposed. Naked. Buller knew this. He'd been to the lectures, told about respect for the culture, the softly softly approach, the battle for hearts and minds and building bridges. He'd been told about sensitivity. Buller doesn't understand the meaning of the word. When the explosion occurred, the girls were safe, the other side of the road, crouching behind a wall. Their eyes were smiling, grateful to the soldier who had saved their lives. He'd done a good job. And then he couldn't help himself. A quick glance around, a grab for their face and the shredding of their dignity. These girls were fifteen years old. They'd never trust a British soldier again. A swift investigation concluded that the veils had become detached when Jimmy Buller was saving their lives. He never even noticed it had happened, he said, so busy was he before, during and after the explosion. Two days after the explosion, he was accompanied by his Commanding Officer to the girls' home. They refused to meet him. He had destroyed their dignity. He had seen them naked. He apologised to the father, recounted his version, issued a further apology and left. The girls were killed in crossfire twelve days later. They refused to move when British soldiers tried to help them."

Delaney stood. He stretched his back and raised his arms in the air, letting out a long sigh. Turning his back on Ben, he strolled towards the door and continued. "The Balkans, the bit once known as Yugoslavia. Buller, along with two squaddies under his command, was escorting three prisoners to temporary barracks where they were to be interrogated. The truck they were travelling in was attacked by Serbian troops. Buller's reaction was automatic. Bursts of fire from the back of the truck brought an even more intense response. The truck swerved off the road and rammed into a tree. The engine was still running. Buller jumped into the cab and found the driver bleeding heavily from both legs. He pulled him out of his seat, reversed the truck out from the tree and drove to safety, while his colleagues were blasting away in the back. Sounds simple, but it takes some doing. But there was a problem. When he arrived at the barracks, steam bursting from the radiator, bullet holes lining the tarpaulin cover, there were no prisoners to interrogate. They were dead, shot to pieces. Tests proved that they were killed by AK-47s, weapons that are not standard issue to the British Army. It is interesting though, that the squaddies escaped unharmed. Not a scratch. Even stranger, they were firing from the tailgate with the prisoners closer to the cab, on the floor. The fire was coming from directly behind the truck. Now you tell me how heavy fire can bypass two soldiers in firing

25

position, causing no injuries at all, and kill three prisoners lying on the floor."

Ben could not answer. His experience of warfare was limited. He had no knowledge of what happened in war zones, apart from the news summaries and sometimes he queried their impartiality. He had no evidence, it was just a gut feeling. He knew what bullets could do, how people died, but he had no idea who was guilty, who was innocent and the technicalities involved. Delaney was talking about a different world which Ben had, fortunately, been able to avoid.

Sebastian remained at the table. He appeared relaxed. He could have been watching the weather forecast, the way he leaned his head to one side, listening to every word. Detached, but involved.

Delaney returned to the table, but remained standing. "Northern Ireland. The IRA was not in one of their more pleasant moods, despite the growing feeling within the Province that a deal was in the offing. One of their members suspected his wife of having an affair. Now the IRA is not known as being the most moral of groups, so this would not often cause discussion at one of their meetings. The member would usually be told this was not their problem, just get her sorted out and not waste their time. But at this particular meeting, there was much discussion. You see, the member suspected that his wife was shagging a British soldier."

Delaney sat down, causing Sebastian to uncross and cross his legs again. For the first time, he looked at Ben and Ben at him. Into his eyes. For the first time, Ben saw an acknowledgement that he was there, that what he was saying related in some way directly to him. That he was here for Ben's benefit. "I think you can guess where I'm going with this one. It happened more than you think. Troops calling at a suspect's house, finding nobody there, except the wife, a bit of a connection, a follow-up visit and if her husband's been away for some time on IRA active service, there may be a chance. Don't believe the fallacy that all wives were committed to the cause."

"What happened?" Ben asked. "Was she punished?"

"You could say that. Poor lass was found hanging from the beams of her local Catholic church. Perhaps surprisingly, the IRA was not involved. They were having their meeting at the time of death. I know that for a fact. I was at the meeting. Suicide was the verdict, but the husband didn't think so. Normally, the IRA would take matters into their own hands, but it was April 9th 1998 and guess what, the next day the Good Friday Agreement was signed and that was just a tad more important than some unfaithful wife."

Ben had heard of the Agreement. Who hadn't? But 1998 was a long time ago and he could only vaguely remember some of the details. He was certain that justice for victims, past and present, was part of it. If this was true, then there would have been an investigation into the woman's death.

Delaney read his mind. "I know what you're thinking. Good Friday Agreement. Creation of Human Rights and Equality Commissions, comprehensive review of criminal justice and policing arrangements, money allocated to the victims of violence. All true, but in reality it could be a bit one sided. If the Provos or the IRA had killed or maimed a member of your family, then there was a case. If British soldiers were involved, it took a whole lot longer. Look at the Bloody Sunday enquiry. Still going on, despite countless so-called closures. Anyway, the husband wasn't that bothered. The irony of it all is that he was shagging the wife of a fellow IRA member at the time. He didn't push for justice. Too many irons in the fire."

"So, suicide it was then," Ben proclaimed.

"That's right. You're getting the hang of this, laddie. Personal involvement breeds self-preservation. Sometimes that means that the truth remains tightly hidden. Sometimes it means someone gets involved. Personally."

Delaney pushed back the chair. The feet scraped across the ground, causing Sebastian to grimace. Ben was a bit too numb to react at all. He got the impression that Delaney had almost finished and that it was soon Sebastian's turn.

Delaney was right. The laddie was beginning to get the hang of this, even though the laddie understood very little of what was going on.

"Talking of irony," Delaney said, "did you know that Serbia's only arms factory, Zastava, last year signed a contract with US based

Remington Arms Company to provide twenty four thousand weapons for them. The oldest gun maker in the States collaborating with a Serbian company in an arms deal. Perhaps the contract will be reciprocated at some stage. Then we won't need to worry about AK-47s shooting at our lads, it will be Remingtons. Long live the Special Relationship."

"Okay, Mr Delaney, I think you can get off your soap box now." Sebastian turned towards Ben, uncrossing and crossing his legs as he did so. Delaney began to rise, but hesitated as Ben threw a question at him, somewhat naively.

"How do you know all these things, Delaney?"

"You forget, laddie. I don't exist. And it's amazing how much you can find out if you don't exist." Ten minutes ago that would have been the end of it, but now, with a renewed confidence, Ben needed more.

"But the question was how? How do you know all these things?"

He sat down again, as if his body couldn't quite take his weight all on its own. Weary, Ben supposed. "Iraq, the Commanding Officer. Yugoslavia, the driver of the truck. Time has a way of raising consciences. People are more willing to talk when there will be no recriminations. Ireland, I did my own investigation after I vanished. The British Army had no reason to link Buller with the suicide of a woman in a Catholic church, the police had no inclination to, the husband had other things on his mind and the IRA had Sinn Fein to worry about. But it was Buller who was involved with the woman. Buller's wife told me after they separated. It's not all she said. It wasn't the first time he'd strayed. 'Habitual' was the word she used. 'Abusive' was another. 'Ask the kids,' she said. Living with fear must be the most terrible thing. How many women has he abused? How many women has he killed?"

Delaney lifted the brown folder and tossed it across the desk. "Iraq, Yugoslavia, Ireland. You won't find any proof in there. But there are doubts, Ben. You have to agree, there are doubts."

*

28

Delaney reclaimed contact with his radiator. The creak was a little muted. Ben noted that the room was warmer now. The radiator, like its occupant, had done its job and had now faded into the background.

In the quiet, while Delaney rested and Sebastian watched, Ben tried to assimilate what had happened to him. He'd gone out for a quiet drink, drifted from pub to pub, wanting to be alone amongst the crowds. He'd been in a police van, a police station, a police interview room. He'd met two strangers who seemed to know everything about him. He'd heard stories from Iraq, the Balkans and Northern Ireland.

Alton Towers made an entrance into his thoughts. He remembered his annual trips with his mother and father. Through the gates, he would dash towards the Corkscrew and stand as upright as a small boy could do against the measurement chart. He waited, at attention, for his parents to catch up with him, daring any other child to move him from his spot. For two years, their answer disappointed him, and he had to content himself with the Green Grasshopper.

On the third year, he'd reached the required height and dragged his mother off to the queue. Dad said he'd rather watch. The truth was he just didn't like heights. He was the bravest, kindest, most considerate man Ben had ever known. He would take on the proverbial wall for him, but the Corkscrew and he were not natural playmates. His face told Ben that his pleasure was in seeing Ben's pleasure.

That first ride of ecstasy thrilled every muscle, every bone in Ben's body. He was twisted, turned, thrown around every corner, every corkscrew. The skin on his face gravitated to areas it had never visited before and then returned to its original place, elated by the ride, grateful to be back home.

Ritual became tradition. Even when he became a teenager, even when he was a student, even when he qualified as a teacher, he would make the journey, stand at the measurement chart and take his ride. Even when the Corkscrew was overtaken by scarier, more dangerous rides, even when Dad died, too young, even when Mum could no longer take the battering and the bruises, he would ride his favourite ride.

And then, one year, it was gone, as was his childhood, at the age of twenty-five. That year heralded Ben's final visit to Alton Towers. He

29

was never able to ride the Corkscrew again, but tonight he felt he had come close.

He was battered and bruised, yet strangely energised, by the events. He was beginning to feel almost comfortable in Sebastian and Delaney's presence, but still fearful of them, fearful of the unknown. His thoughts returned to the present.

"Why am I here?" he asked.

Sebastian responded. "How does a brawl on a pavement sound?"

"Sounds like an excuse to me."

"You're absolutely right. An excuse to get you here alone with us."

"But, why?"

"A proposition."

"Ah, yes, the proposition. I'd almost forgotten about that amongst the fogs of Iraq, Northern Ireland and the rest. I'm listening."

"Mr Delaney and I are what you might call organisers. Through our experience and background, we can deliver foolproof solutions to, shall we say ... circumstances ... which should have been resolved, but have not. We plan things to the final detail and whatever we plan will work. We're good. We find this easy. It's what we do."

"But what has this got to do with me?"

"A little more patience please. It's been a long night, I know, but you'll see. All will be revealed. Let me make this very clear, Ben. What we do *not* do is get involved ourselves in the final delivery. That is the sole preserve of the group or individual with whom we work. The option is open to that group or individual to accept the plan and continue, or reject it completely. We produce the plan. It will work. We will not change the plan in any way whatsoever. All things will be taken into consideration. We will know, having met the client, what he, or she or they, will be capable of and what will be possible. If the client rejects the plan, there will be no recriminations. Mr Delaney and I will disappear and will never be seen again by the client. If the plan is accepted, we will be with the client all the way to a successful conclusion. Then we will disappear, never to be seen again."

"Sounds like that Millionaire game to me. You see the question. You know the answers. You just have to pick the correct one. With you, there are only two possible answers: reject or accept."

"Exactly, Ben."

"But, I ask again, what has this to do with me?"

"We can organise the death of Sergeant Jimmy Buller."

*

'Oh, shit.' Ben's immediate reaction was 'Oh, shit.'

Not 'I must be dreaming' or 'They must be joking' or 'Was it possible?' or 'Are they capable?' Ben knew this was not a dream. It was reality, they were serious, it was possible if Sebastian and Delaney said so and they were very definitely capable.

They had taken Ben on a trip along the fringes of their lives and their confidence and demeanour had convinced him that this was no bragging contest. He never doubted that what they said was what they could do: that the murderer of his beloved Lynn could be killed. That which he desired more than anything else.

And then, perhaps, he could get his life back on track. They had presented him with a chance to escape from his abysmal existence. He would no longer need the drink to forget. He could read of the death of Sergeant Jimmy Buller, war hero and serving member of Her Majesty's Forces. He could buy the papers, make the scrapbook, immerse his sorrow in Buller's demise. And live again.

"What are you thinking?" asked Sebastian.

"I'm thinking 'Oh, shit,'" Ben replied.

Sebastian understood. "A natural reaction, Ben. You've wanted this man punished since the moment Emma Parker singled him out from the group of soldiers. You looked into his eyes through the two way mirror. You saw no remorse. None. You hated him. The hatred is still there. We can see it in the way you move, dragging yourself from home to work and back to home again. Every day, you teach and you arrive home unaware of what you have taught. Every night you drink and you are unaware of what you have drunk. And now, we're at that point, Ben.

31

That point that you thought you'd never reach, or have the opportunity to do so. You have to decide. Do you want us to organise the death of Jimmy Buller?"

There was only one answer to that question. It was an answer that Ben despised himself for. To desire the death of another human being was despicable. It was against everything he believed, everything that had been instilled into him by parents who would be appalled by his thoughts. The bile rose in his throat. With an effort, he forced it back as he had done many times before.

Ben knew his parents had never been in his position. They had never had the one they love snatched from them in a treacherous act by an evil man. Even after his father died, there was never such grief, never such hatred, never so many revengeful thoughts. Heart attacks are different from murder.

He hated these feelings of his. Almost as much as he hated Sergeant Jimmy Buller.

Sebastian continued. "Only one man can make the decision, Ben."

"The answer is yes," he replied. "I want you to organise the death of Jimmy Buller."

"I know it's against everything you ever believed in. It's a difficult decision. I admire you for making it."

Ben looked across the table. Sebastian had the look of a man who believed his own words. He understood Ben's thoughts, his dilemma. And yet he was wrong. "It was not a difficult decision, Sebastian," Ben said. "It was an easy decision. I want him dead. I want it done as quickly as possible. Then I'll have to live with my decision. That may be the difficult part."

Sebastian nodded. Ben suspected he had delivered a similar speech many times before and had received both positive and negative reactions from his clients, as he called them. He believed Sebastian when he said that clients heard and saw no more of him after their decision. This was no virginal case. Ben was no guinea pig testing out a theory. Ben knew that Sebastian was good at this. He knew he would be successful.

"Let me enlighten you, Ben. Maybe I can answer a few questions, the seeds of which are germinating in your mind." For the first time since entering the room, he pushed his chair aside, with barely a sound, stretched and walked, slowly and deliberately. "We work for a group of people who believe in British justice, but accept that it has its failings. Sometimes, through no fault of its own, the correct resolution is not found. The guilty walk free. Sometimes before the case reaches court. That is where we come in. And here we are. In a grandiose sort of way, I suppose we are righting the wrongs of the system."

He was wearing a proud smile. His teeth were gleaming white in perfect rows. He was more relaxed now, although Ben had never thought of him as being tense before. There was a naturalness to his walk, his talk, his humour. He had let himself go a little. He continued. "We are exceptionally well paid for what we do. I suppose that comes from being perfect. We have never failed. Don't worry about the cost, Ben. All our fees are paid for by our employers. You are simply the client. If you like, you are the provider of justice."

It was a strange term to use, but Ben accepted it. He himself felt more relaxed now that the reason for Sebastian and Delaney's presence had become clear. The anxiety of the original arrest had passed and, although he was now involved in something more serious, more sinister, he felt more comfortable with it. More comfortable with being involved in murder than with a brawl on a pavement? It didn't make sense.

It had helped that Ben had made his decision quickly. The cards were on the table and the game was about to be played. But games need rules and, as yet, he hadn't been allowed to know them.

Sebastian leaned against the door, throwing his muscular body in front of the pane of glass. Ben heard the radiator sigh behind him. "All was going so well," Delaney said. He sat down at his chair, nonchalant, with his elbow on the table and his cheek in the palm of his hand. "But now I need to be the bearer of tidings that may be good, but are quite possibly bad. There remains one outstanding situation to be resolved. As you have heard, Sebastian and I are the organisers. That means that someone else has to deal the blow. The provider of justice, if you like. And that's when all this becomes personal, Ben."

Delaney sat at the end of the table. He remained silent.

Sebastian was motionless.

To express no words, to show no reaction, is a difficult thing, but it was second nature to Ben's new found friends, his enemies. They were patient men. They had had to be to survive.

Delaney, lying in a ditch, machine gun in hand, waited for the army patrol. He had arrived in the early hours. He had watched the dawn break, seen the sun rise over the mist covered countryside of South Armagh. The Chinooks had swooped low over their heads carrying rations and replacement ammunition to the heavily fortified barracks of the hated British Army.

Local farmers blamed the myriad of masts covering the landscape, vital for communication said the army, for producing high levels of radiation, causing an increase of deaths in sheep and stillborn calves. Their claims had been ignored, treated with disdain by Commanders and Government. Delaney sympathised with the farmers, but he had a job to do.

He had already been in position for three hours and not a word had passed between him and his colleague, a man suspected by the IRA of being a collaborator with the British Army. Delaney's mission was simple: confirm or reject the suspicion.

He confirmed it with a single bullet through the heart at close range. Enemies were satisfied. One less fanatic for the British Army to deal with. The IRA believed Delaney without reservation. The traitor had to die.

Life was full of irony.

Delaney was comfortable in the silence. He could remain silent for as long as it took. Sebastian was more restless, crossing and uncrossing his feet at the ankles. But he was impressively resilient. He was waiting for Ben's reaction. He could wait for as long as it took.

"So, this is what you mean by getting involved? Personally," Ben said.

Delaney dropped his head in a nodding gesture. "That's right, laddie. You see, Sebastian and I, we've got nothing against Buller. He's never done us any harm. He doesn't know us and we don't know him. Okay, I think he's a bastard who has caused the unnecessary deaths of fifteen people. And that's just the ones I know about. Some of those deaths were during conflict, so that may be acceptable, the pressure these guys are under, but the vicious nature of some associated deaths can never be tolerated. He's a murderer many times over. I know that. But he's never done anything to me. Personally."

"I need to get this clear in my head," Ben said. "Two minutes ago, you were asking me to sanction - that's not too strong a word is it? - sanction the death of Jimmy Buller. Now you're asking me to kill him myself."

"Correct," said Delaney. "Make no bones about this, Sebastian and I would like to see Buller dead. He's got away with murder, but that can be said for any number of people we've had the pleasure of meeting over the years. We don't just walk up to them and kill them. There is no justified reason. They haven't affected our lives. But on the other hand, you're different. He killed Lynn. He got away with it. You have good reason to want him dead. It may be justice, or revenge or to stop him killing others. Or it may be more to do with you than with Lynn. After all, she isn't around anymore. You may want him dead so that you can move on, live your life again. It's what Lynn would have wanted."

"Think about it," said Sebastian. "We don't want a decision now."

Sebastian made his way to the table and sat down. They were three friends again, head to head, talking over the ills of the world. Sebastian with his legs crossed, Delaney with his chin in his hands and Ben reflecting on what had just been suggested. But this was no usual discussion at a mate's house over a few pints.

In their hands, Ben realised, was the power to provide a solution. They could succeed where the system had failed. They could take matters into their own hands.

There were more questions than answers. It was impossible to give an immediate decision. Sebastian knew this, Delaney grudgingly accepted it.

Sebastian concluded. "You will not get caught, Ben. We will tell you everything you need to know. If you do exactly as we say, Buller will die and you will be free. You will never be associated with his death. There is just one thing we ask of you. You will need an alibi for the 24th December, the whole day. May I suggest that you discuss this with Lynn's father? Perhaps tomorrow?"

19ᵗʰ December

Since Lynn's death, the BMW Z4 had been one of the few thrills in Ben's life. It reminded him of her. He could still smell her perfume as he opened the door, which he closed quickly so it did not drift away. Her presence filled the car.

He sat for a while, enjoying her company. She made a play of putting her seat belt on, tightening it as much as she could and testing it a few times to ensure it was working. "Okay," she said, "I suppose I'm as safe as I'm going to be. Drive on Jeeves."

"Don't you want to drive?" Ben asked.

"Now why would I want to do that? I've got a perfectly good nine year old Ford Fiesta of my own, thank you. Anyway, I couldn't stand the abuse you'd give me if I did something wrong."

"Abuse? Me? Never."

"Always."

"Ah, but you like it."

With a smile on his face, he turned in her direction. The passenger seat was empty, but she was there. "Let's go then," he said.

Turning the ignition, he waited for the muted rumble as it sprang to life. It never failed him. It was the only time that idling, which wasn't in Ben's nature, could be so pleasurable. He listened. Perfect.

He lifted the gear stick and gently placed it into reverse. There was no objection. She glided out of the garage, coming to rest in the middle of the drive. He left her idling still, closed the garage door, stroked the front wing and returned to his seat.

Leaving his Satellite Navigation in the glove compartment, he set off on the twenty-three point seven mile journey to Lynn's parents. He knew the route. He'd travelled it so many times before.

He'd phoned earlier to check if they were going anywhere, which they weren't, and they'd said they'd be really pleased to see him. They were glad he'd kept in touch. It would have been so easy for him to forget them.

Ben had always liked Lynn's parents, especially her Dad. They liked the same things: football on the television, walks around the block, golf at the local course which was Dad's domain. Ben didn't mind buying the drinks after every round. He'd lose the game, but enjoy the company. They even voted for the same political party. And of course, they both loved Lynn, but in their different ways. They'd do anything for her, which was what Ben was relying on.

Ben's thoughts returned to the previous night. Sebastian had shown him to the door and out of the police station. There was nobody around. He'd been told to turn left at the end of the road, walk the hundred yards to the crossroads where there was a taxi rank. There'd be no trouble finding a taxi.

Ben used the taxi that was third in line. The engine was running. It pulled away from the others towards the front. Taxi drivers do not tolerate queue jumpers, it's their golden rule, but the driver of the first taxi never looked up from the paper he was reading for the second time that day and the driver behind him was memorising his A – Z, which he knew backwards already. They were otherwise engaged.

As he settled into the back seat, he leaned his head against the rests, legs spread, coat buttons undone, hands in pockets. The taxi pulled away from the kerb. He closed his eyes and he was home. He hadn't told the driver his address. He knew he didn't need to. Surprises were a thing of the past.

The key slid easily into the front door. He turned it and let himself in, something he could not have managed had the night worked out as he had intended. Who knows where he would have ended up or what time he would have arrived back home? Whatever the details, he knew the drink would have taken its toll and the vagueness in his brain and the lack of co-ordination would have rendered the 'key in the door' task impossible. His neighbour would have found him the next morning, asleep on the doorstep, and ushered him into his own house, using the key he had left with her. Before the rest of the neighbours saw him. It wouldn't have been the first time she'd had to do that. She understood. Knew he was a good boy. Knew he was going through a bad patch.

Knew he'd come out of it. Ben lacked the belief of the wonderful Mrs Robinson.

Until tonight. Now there was hope.

Sebastian had opened the side door and given him directions to the taxi rank. "Go home, get some rest, see Lynn's father tomorrow. Don't worry about our next contact. We'll be in touch," he'd said.

Ben believed him.

*

He loved this bend. He could drop her down a gear and accelerate through the length of it allowing the back wheels to drift a little as he came out. He had never told Lynn, would never have the chance to now, but when she wasn't with him in the car, he increased the pressure on the accelerator a touch, felt the drift a little earlier, straightened it up a little later. Just for the thrill of it.

He eased his foot off the pedal. She was with him in the passenger seat. He was grateful. He would need her help today. He would need her honesty.

A hundred yards after the bend was Lynn's house. It was another reason for liking the bend. She still lived at home. Whenever he visited, he knew, as he accelerated and drifted and straightened, he would soon be close to her. He had tried to persuade her to move in with him, but she thought it best if she left it until they were married. She had stayed overnight at his house on many occasions, normally at the weekends, but still enjoyed the company of her Mum and Dad. She saw marriage as the next step in her life, a separation, a parting of the ways, a new phase. Ben could not change her mind. He didn't want to. He admired her loyalty, the principle, the stubborn streak. It was refreshing in this ever-changing world.

And how Ben's world had changed.

He had slept well last night. He'd made his way up the stairs, undressed, gone to the toilet, cleaned his teeth, put on his sleep shorts, placed his head on the pillow and slept. On occasions, when the children in his class had important examinations or when he had an inspection, he found sleep impossible. He would make a cup of tea, watch the television, mark some books and return to bed. When his eyes closed, his brain remained awake and his body found no comfort within the comfort of his own bed. Sleep was impossible.

Last night, he had sanctioned the murder of another human being, before being asked to commit the murder himself, and he had slept. He placed his head on the pillow and he slept. He felt, somehow, at peace with himself. There was no reason for it. He knew he should have been soaked with guilt that he could consider such a proposition. That's what they'd called it. But he couldn't argue with his own feelings. He was calm. If Delaney had placed the gun in his hand last night and Buller had been standing in front of him, he would have pulled the trigger.

It was not acceptable, but he would have done it. He felt no different now. His feelings were so strong that he knew he would feel the same when he had to. Delaney had been correct when he talked of revenge and justice and saving other women from suffering at the hands of this animal. He had given Ben the excuse to excuse his thoughts. His future actions had taken on a moralistic direction. By killing this man, he would not only benefit his own life, but the lives of others too. He had been convinced, and with ease had convinced himself, that to kill Jimmy Buller was not only correct, it was moral.

Only one man could change his mind.

*

Tom stood in the front garden tending the roses. He heard the sound of the BMW and looked round. It looked similar to a car he had intended to buy in kit form and build from baseline up. Doris wasn't too keen. She preferred the comfort of the mass produced variety, the simplicity of the ordering and the driving away with the new registration plate that everyone could admire.

The reason Tom never bought his kit car was not because of Doris' opinions, but because of her pregnancy. Lynn came along and the mass produced car that he despised became the necessity. And that's how it had been until Lynn's death.

Tom realised the cliché was true. You do only live once. Okay, so it wasn't a kit car that took pride of place in his garage, but the orange TVR was about as close as he could get. It was a real beast. It shook every bone in his body, so close was he to the ground. The grunt of ruthless power when the key turned in the ignition was loud enough to wake the entire neighbourhood. Doris refused to go near it, which outweighed all the negatives. It was a man's car and only Ben and he would ride it. How long his body would be able to cope with the bombardment it threw at him, he did not know. Probably when Doris refused to be intimidated by it, when she accepted it. Then he would sell it and buy a BMW Z4, a much more suitable car for a man approaching his mid fifties. He had not yet told Doris of his plans.

Ben pulled his car alongside the front lawn, his usual parking place, the wide tyres dispersing any loose gravel in its path. Running his hand over the front wing of Ben's car, Tom made his way to the door and opened it. There was the softest of clicks.

"Sounds beautiful, Ben. Sounds beautiful. How are you, son?" He held out his hand. Ben shook it. Tom pulled him closer, hugging him. It was a habit he had fallen into since Lynn's death. Ben held him tightly. He enjoyed the intimacy.

"Fine, Dad. Just fine. And how's the beast?"

"Oh, she's fine. Just in the kitchen making lunch."

Ben laughed. It did him good to visit Tom. They were good company for each other. "I mean the beast in the garage," he said.

Tom's face took on a glaze of astonishment. "Ben, I would never stoop so low. There's no electricity in there. How would Doris be able to make me my cup of tea if she'd been confined to the garage?"

"Okay, I give up," said Ben. "How's the TVR going?"

"Still shaking every joint in my body. I'm sure it's determined to dislocate every bone that's in there. It's only my skin that's holding me together. Don't tell Doris though. Whenever she mentions the beast, I wax lyrically on the smoothness of its ride."

"Does she believe you?" asked Ben.

"I doubt it, but who knows what goes on in the minds of the female." Tom closed the door. There was a solid clunk as it closed. "Good week?" he asked Ben.

"As good as it could be."

"Aye, son. I know what you mean." He put a hand on Ben's shoulder and turned him towards the house. The gravel crunched beneath their feet, though their pace was slow. They liked this quiet moment after they met. They thought the same thoughts, though neither of them mentioned it.

It was Ben who broke the silence. "Roses are looking good."

Tom stopped at the door to the house. He surveyed his work. The lawn was well cut, though not too short to allow the winter frosts to damage it. The edgings were neatly trimmed and the soil nicely turned. Without turning towards Ben, he said, "Don't make small talk with me, Ben. There's no need. The roses are crap at this time of year and you know it. Never think of something to say just for the sake of it. I've been married to Doris for thirty-two years and I've known you for the best part of three and you know what? I know your thoughts better than hers. Be content in your quietness, Ben. Lynn was a special girl. Enjoy thinking of her. I do."

They both needed a few more minutes before entering the house. To face Doris with the slightest hint of gloom would be reciprocated. Doris had found Lynn's death difficult. She and Jo, her other daughter, were unable to hide the desperation of their sorrow. Their emotions were wrecked, as were their lives. Tears flowed easily.

"Isn't it amazing," Doris had said to Ben, "how many programmes there are on the television with funerals in them?" Ben didn't suppose there were more now than there ever were, but it probably just appeared that way. What was foremost in your mind stood out more. Ben didn't know whether to agree with her or not. He had watched little television since Lynn's death.

His companion had been the drink, not the television. It was difficult to decide which was the best choice.

"What you should have said," said Tom, "was, 'You've done a good job pruning the roses, Tom. Look crap when there's no flowers on them, don't they?' And I would have agreed. Ready to face the beast?"

"Your words, not mine, Dad," said Ben.

*

Doris was in her usual place by the kitchen sink. Ben often wondered if she had been born in a kitchen, so at home was she there. He had joked to Lynn the previous Christmas that Doris' ball and chain were wearing a bit thin and that such a gift would be welcomed by one and all.

Lynn had made it very clear in her response that if Ben thought it was going to be like that in their household, he had better find himself a new floozy. Anyway, he was far more creative in the kitchen than she was, a role reversed in the bedroom, so she said. Ben did not disagree.

Ben made his way towards Doris and kissed her on the cheek. She held her hands in the air, a habit she had perfected over the years, mainly because her hands were usually covered with flour.

"What's cooking?" asked Ben. He thought he'd throw her straight into her favourite topic. Avoid the tears.

"How does meat and potato pie sound?" she asked.

"You've not made it specially because I was coming, have you?"

"No. You know how Tom loves it too."

Ben did indeed know how much Tom loved it. About as much as he loved the dog dragging the lead towards him at nine o'clock on a windswept night in February. The thought of the same thing over again left him cold, but once he was doing it, Tom realised why he liked it so much. Meat and potato pie was comfortable. Taking the dog for a walk was pleasurable. It was all very homely. He just wished that, now and again, a red hot chilli would invade the pie or the dog would ravage an occasional February burglar. Just to break the monotony.

Ben would never have hurt her feelings by telling her the truth. "He loves everything about you, Doris," said Ben.

Doris cuddled Ben with her elbows. "Oh, Ben. I wish he'd tell me sometimes. He's getting worse you know. Sometimes I think he'd prune his pruned roses all over again or polish the car for the umpteenth time rather than spend a bit of time with me." She turned towards the sink and looked out of the window. The garden view was a picture. It reflected how much time he spent there. She continued. "He's been much worse since …. you know."

"We've all found it difficult," said Ben. "Tom, me, Jo, even you, the soul of the family. Give him a bit of leeway. He'll come round. He's no fool. He knows what's good for him. Where else could he get meat and potato pie like yours?"

She turned to face Ben. The tears in her eyes were accompanied by the smile on her face. She reached up and held her cheek to his. "Oh, Ben. You are the sweetest thing. Don't ever leave us, will you?"

"Never," said Ben.

Following at a distance, Tom came in and removed his Wellington boots. He flicked the mud onto the flower beds, now full with winter heathers that would soon throw a purple and white carpet across them. Nodding his garden a farewell, he closed the outside door and washed his hands. He had his own sink in the utility area. He had been banned from bringing his muddy hands anywhere near the sink where Doris cleaned her utensils.

He scrubbed hard, using an old nail brush that Doris had thrown out. He'd had a good few months out of it, but it was wearing a bit thin now. He'd have to replace it soon. He shot a glance across at Doris' sink to check on the one she cleaned the potatoes with. There was some life in that yet. Perhaps he'd better stick to the old one after all. Change wasn't always a good thing.

Rinsing his hands under the taps, he checked to see that all the mud had been removed from under the nails. They would have to be spotless before he was allowed at the table. They were. He was.

It was up to Ben to keep the conversation going over the meal. He talked about anything and everything. The car, for Tom's benefit, needed a service, so the in-built computer was telling him, but it could wait until after Christmas. He wasn't planning to use it much over the holidays. The house, for Doris' benefit, was being kept very tidy by Mrs Robinson who came in twice a week. Yes, her ironing was still as impeccable as ever and yes, he had bought new bags for the hoover.

Tom didn't speak to Doris and Doris didn't speak to Tom, but an outsider would never have noticed, so skilled was Ben in linking the various discussions, moving effortlessly from car to house to garden to cooking. He loved them both. He just wasn't sure if they loved each other.

During the occasional silences, old Jess, the night-walking dog, would come to the rescue and barge past, smashing his muscular tail against the leg of the table. Ben was certain he only did it to provoke a response, which it often did. They had a good understanding, Ben and Jess, working in cahoots to dispel any traces of an uncomfortable atmosphere.

After the meal, Doris insisted on doing all the womanly things as she called them, while the boys went into the lounge. There was a review of the Grand Prix season on the television. They didn't object.

Ben marvelled at how easily he had slotted into their family. His thoughts drifted back one whole year. A lot can happen in a year. Last year, Lynn had been the one who insisted the boys went to watch the Grand Prix review. She wanted a bit of time alone with her Mum. He remembered how she ushered him out of the room with her hand firmly on his back, closing the kitchen door behind him.

He knew why, of course. They had arranged this particular time, after the meal, to break the news that they were engaged. Lynn was to tell Doris and Ben was to tell Tom. For some reason it was Lynn who was the more nervous. Ben imagined himself dropping it into the friendly chitchat he was having with Tom. Derek Brundle had just mentioned the dominance of Fernando Alonso when Ben dropped the news.

"About bloody time," was Tom's response. He also commented how much improved Jensen Button was and how he would be a future world champion given the right machine. At that moment of prediction, the lounge door burst open and Doris screamed, "You'll never guess what, Tom!"

"They've got engaged," said Tom.

"And Jensen Button will be a future world champion," said Ben.

"Where's the champagne?" asked Doris.

"There's a bottle in the fridge," said Lynn.

"How do you know that?" asked Ben.

"I put it there," said Lynn.

That was then and this was now. This year there was a different kind of news to tell Tom. Now he was the nervous one, unsure of what Tom's reaction would be when he told him that he was thinking of killing someone.

*

Ben was determined to keep his date at Brands Hatch. Although Silverstone was the home of British racing, Brands Hatch still held affection deep at the heart of racing enthusiasts. Ben wouldn't dream of putting himself in that category. He'd only once been to a Grand Prix. That was at Silverstone and the day had been ruined by the rain and the mud in the car park.

This was before he owned his BMW and before he knew Lynn. His friend's Subaru, tuned to perfection for the day, was too low to escape from the clinging mud and there it remained.

The experience had affected Ben's approach to motor racing. Watching from the comfort of his armchair with a beer in his hand after Sunday dinner was now the preferred way, but if there was a chance he could experience the driving, then he would take it.

So Lynn had already purchased his birthday present for the following year: a day at Brands Hatch. The opportunity to drive a racing saloon car and then a single seater, if they thought he could handle it.

Lynn was always well organised, but a birthday present purchased seven months before his birthday was unusual even by Lynn's high standards. Perhaps she knew something Ben didn't. Perhaps she knew she wouldn't be alive.

Ben recalled his Dad buying a new car. He took the family for a drive along the M62 and insisted that Ben's mother drive back.

Motorway driving was not her forte, but he had been unusually insistent. "You'll be driving this car more than me," he'd said. Ben's Dad was dead a week later. Heart attacks were the simplest, most cruel way of destroying a family. His Mum kept the car for a while, out of loyalty, but it was too big and she sold it after a year. Her life moved on.

Before last night, Ben could never envisage his life moving on, but now there was hope. The chequered flag fell on another year's racing, the crowd invaded the circuit and Tom praised the efforts of Jensen Button, despite having an inferior machine. Ben took a sip of water from his glass.

"Need to say something?" asked Tom.

"Fancy taking the beast out for a spin?" he replied, rhetorically.

*

It was Tom's suggestion that they put the hood down. Hatless, yet clothed like Antarctic explorers, the boys rumbled down the country lanes. Bones rattling and joints stretched, Ben realised that the beast did this to everyone, not just people in their mid fifties.

It was exhilarating. He could feel the freezing cold on his nose, even though the temperature was mild for this time of year. Whatever cobwebs remained within him were dispatched by the ride.

As Tom pulled into the car park by the forest, the car bottomed out on the floor, hitting a couple of small potholes. "Not to worry," said Tom. "The exhaust system has to be robust on a machine like this."

He was making excuses. On any normal day he would never park on such an unmade surface. But Tom knew there was something on Ben's mind and he was impatient to hear it. He'd watched the entire Grand Prix review alongside Ben, had offered opinions and comments throughout the hour long programme and Ben had not responded. Not once.

They slammed the doors shut, it was the only way with the beast, and made their way along the path into the forest.

"I'm sorry I've not been much company," said Ben.

"That's okay. I'm sure there's a reason."

"Oh, yes. There's a reason." Ben had arranged to visit Doris and Tom. He had asked Tom to launch the beast. And now, they had arrived at the forest. Ben had rehearsed this moment, in his house, in the car and while he mindlessly watched the television, and now he began his pitch. The first few lines were easy. Then he'd let it flow and hope for the best. "You'll be tempted to interrupt, but let me talk, Tom. Please, hear me out."

"How long have I been married, son?" replied Tom in his usual relaxed way. He was making it easy for Ben. Ben wouldn't have expected anything else. It was Tom's way. "I'm a good listener. I have to be."

Ben talked and walked. Tom just walked. Neither of them noticed the robins on the holly bushes, the squirrels climbing the trunks of the beech trees, the lichen on the side of the branches. All that nature had to offer. Things they would normally point out to each other as Lynn and Doris chattered behind.

As the trees drifted by and the leaves rustled beneath their feet, Tom heard of Ben's struggle since Lynn's death. Days of drifting through lessons at work and nights of drink and more drink. Of warnings from his boss. Of despairing of the future. Of thoughts of taking his own life. He had no wish to live in a life without hope.

Last night had changed that. He introduced Tom to hippies and gyrating girls and police stations and finally to Sebastian and Delaney. He told how he was inspired by their confidence and how he became more hopeful as they spoke. When he thought he had laid the foundations, as Sebastian and Delaney had done so perfectly the night before, when he thought he had prepared Tom for long enough, he told of their ability to organise the death of Jimmy Buller.

Ben, stopping, waited for a reaction. He was disappointed. Tom kept on walking. Ben quickened his step to catch up with him. "Tom, did you hear what I said? Last night, I met two people who can organise the death of the man who killed your daughter."

"I heard what you said. I took it all in," said Tom and then with a rueful smile on his face, "I'm not incapacitated despite my age." There was no anger in his voice, no enthusiasm either. Ben's tale, all twenty minutes of it, appeared to have been wasted, an inconsequence. It had not altered Tom's manner or demeanour. The tone of his voice was the same as it was when he was talking of Jensen Button.

"Well, what do you think?" asked Ben.

Tom pointed to a seat at the edge of the forest. They often sat there and waited for the ladies to catch up with them, but there was nobody following, nobody to wait for. Ben bided his time. He tried to hide his anxiety, but he found it difficult to relax and stared at Tom, willing him to make some sort of comment.

Although Ben had tried hard to disguise his favour for murder, he was not sure he had succeeded. What thoughts did Tom now harbour about the man who would have been his son-in-law? He was probably thinking how fortunate his daughter had been after all. A life with this psychopath would have been worse than the fate that befell her.

Ben regretted the ride in the beast, the walk through the forest, the confession of his alcoholic life without Lynn and the hope that Sebastian and Delaney had brought. He decided that when he returned to the house, he would punch the BMW into life and leave Tom and Doris to their own confused existence. He would never reach his own house. He would do his very best to end his life before that. The bend would be ideal. Too much acceleration, too much drift, too much speed.

"Have you told anyone else about this?" asked Tom eventually.

Ben shook his head. He hoped Tom had seen, even though his eyes didn't look up from the ground. He could have answered him, but Ben thought that, just as he had previously requested quietness from Tom, the opposite was required now.

Tom continued. "I feel honoured, Ben. Humbled that it was me you came to. It's the final piece in our friendship, Ben, and true friends, good friends, will do anything for each other, even if they don't have the same opinions." Ben felt the blood drain from his face. He was relying on Tom for support, not to mention an alibi. And now it seemed that he had misread Tom's reaction to Lynn's death. Had he come to accept that everything that could be done had been done, that it was over, that Buller had been exonerated and that was the end of the matter? He would feel guilty if Tom's support was borne out of friendship alone.

After all, this gentle man would be an accessory if things did not go according to the well laid plans of Sebastian and Delaney. An accessory to murder.

"So," Tom said, calm as ever, "it's a good job I want the bastard dead as well. It makes things much easier."

"You bugger," said Ben, slapping Tom on the back as he did so. "I thought you were against me for a minute."

They remained on the bench for a few moments, reacting in the silence to the enormity of what they had just agreed. Tom laughed. "There's a real chance, then?"

"I think so."

"That's good enough for me."

Ben was struggling with what he next had to say and wrestled with leaving it for another date, but if Tom was to support him, get involved by giving him an alibi, then he had to know everything. "There is one other thing," he said.

Tom rose from the bench. He shivered, involuntarily. "I think we'd better walk. The cold is getting to me. I need to warm up the old joints before the beast does its duty."

Ben felt the tension within him build again. "Sebastian and Delaney will organise everything, but they won't actually do the deed. They say that, to them, Buller isn't personal. He's just another example of the guilty walking free." Ben hesitated. "They say that if ...." He stumbled over his words.

Tom helped him out. "If you do the killing, then not only will justice be done, revenge will be sweet. Two birds will be killed with the proverbial stone."

"They threw in a third bird as well. Buller cannot kill again if he's dead."

"Oh, yes, the saving of humanity angle. Their argument sounds all consuming. Justice, revenge and saving the world. How do you feel about that? Taking the life of a fellow human being?"

Ben took a deep breath. "There's no explanation for it, no rationale. Murder isn't in my psyche. In this case, though, the thought does not offend me. If you asked me to kill anyone else at any time, I would be repulsed by your suggestion, but this man, this case, is different. Sebastian and Delaney are right. When it's personal, anything is possible."

They continued to walk. Tom pointed to a robin, its breast resplendent red against the green of the holly. They watched as it lifted elegantly from the branch and settled further away from them, out of reach, out of earshot. Nature has a way of not intruding, unless it needs to.

Ben continued. "Can I ask you the same question? How do you feel about it all? Can you accept that your friend, the fiancé of your daughter, could be thinking of killing someone? Would you ever forgive me, Tom?"

"Nothing to forgive, Ben," he replied quickly. The speed of the response pleased Ben even more than his words. "I have such hatred inside me, Ben. I, like you, can't explain it, but its there, digging away, deeper until it breaks down my soul. I can relate to your feelings, Ben. You knew how your life was at an end. So did I. I have neglected, scorned, derided like you would never believe, the most precious thing in the world. I have become the most evil husband, changing beyond recognition in a matter of months. I know it, yet I can do nothing about it. And then you take me for a walk in a forest and offer me a chance to live, before it's too late." He stopped, placed a hand on Ben's arm and looked into his eyes. "There's nothing to forgive." Ben felt Tom's fingers tighten around him. "And now you need to tell me. How can I help?"

*

The beast's engine could not simply tick over. It was impossible. There was a resounding throb about it even when it was idling, a caged animal, waiting for an excuse to announce itself to the whole world. Its heater was not the best that had ever been inserted into a car, but it served a purpose and Tom and Ben were beginning to feel the benefits.

"Twenty-fourth of December," said Ben. "I need an alibi."

"Consider it done," said Tom. "Doris and Jo are going to visit the sister and aunty from hell. It's the Christmas ritual when all families become friendly by law, as long as you don't have to spend too much time with each other."

"So, they won't be around?"

"They leave me in peace on the twenty-third, are away overnight, spend all day there on the twenty-fourth and return for supper. I am tasked with the vegetables for Christmas dinner, which is small price to pay for the enjoyment peace brings."

"Sounds perfect."

The beast roared into life, the bones began to rattle, the exhaust scraped along the ground, more gently this time, and the boys began their journey home. The hood was up now. There were no cobwebs to be blown away, no secrets between them. There was no need for words, even if they had been possible over the noise of the engine. They were deep in their own thoughts.

It was the first time in months that Tom had had life breathed back into his ageing body without the aid of the beast. The smile on his face was fixed, and not by the cold this time.

Ben thought of what might happen next. Could he trust Sebastian and Delaney? Were they prepared to be as involved as they said they would be?

As the warmth from the heater reached his toes and the tingling began in his feet, Ben realised they were already involved. It was Sebastian who had recommended the trip to Lynn's parents. Their plan was unfolding. They were pulling the strings and Ben was dancing a willing dance to their tune. More would be revealed when it was necessary, bit by bit. He was in their hands and comfortable with it.

For a brief moment, Ben wondered if Sebastian and Delaney knew about Christmas rituals and sisters and aunties from hell. He wondered if they realised how easy it had been to forge the alibi. Of course they did.

Tom and Ben sat shoulder to shoulder in the cramped confines of the two-seater. Ben looked across the small space that lay between them.

He saw Tom's smile and smiled back. Tom was the consummate replacement for his own Dad.

They'd have got on well with each other, the two Dads.

20th December

"Grandma, what big teeth you've got," said Melinda.

"All the better to eat you with, my dear," replied Kyle.

Kyle chased Melinda round the room, throwing the cape from his head, revealing himself as the big, bad wolf. Melinda screamed loudly, so loudly that a young child began to cry on the front row. For a moment Melinda and Kyle stopped their chase but, urged on by prompts from the side, they continued with renewed vigour.

Kyle, following much rehearsal, tripped over himself perfectly, falling flat on his face by the table, whilst Melinda exited stage left. Ben put a hand out to stop her falling and said, "Fantastic. Well done." It never ceased to amaze him that children could learn so many lines and produce performances that had parents laughing and crying with pride at their angelic cherubs.

Ben had little time for parents. The joy was in the innocence of children.

Melinda whispered, "Was that okay, Mr Price?"

"Okay?" asked Ben. "You should get an Oscar for that. Now get out there, Red Riding Hood, and finish the big, bad wolf off." The joy on Melinda's face reminded him of why he loved this job. She waited for her cue, looked up towards Ben with those wide, brown eyes and leapt back on stage.

Melinda and Kyle finished their performance, took their bows, the wild applause and left, bringing tables and chairs and stools and tablecloths off the stage with them. The curtain closed and children in silver costumes ran on with rockets and breathing apparatus. Suzanna, drama-trained and enthusiastic, led her class to their places and issued final words of encouragement. The next performance was ready.

Ben strolled down the stairs to the classrooms where the children had changed. Melinda and Kyle were tucking into orange juice and sandwiches. Star performers had become children again. "You were great, kids," shouted Ben to everyone in his class.

"Thanks, Mr Price," said thirty children through food-filled mouths.

A tall, bespectacled man appeared at his side. "Well done, Ben," he said. Ben shook the hand that was offered to him. "Nice to have you back," he continued.

Edward Holton, headteacher, touched him gently, affectionately, on the arm as he turned and left. It was praise indeed from a man who found praise difficult to give. But there it was, recognition that Ben Price, advanced skills teacher, was on his way to being accepted back into the fold.

There had been signs throughout the day. Mrs Holliday, nobody knew her first name, school secretary extraordinaire, feared by everyone from headteacher to caretaker, had thrown a second look in Ben's direction as he passed her fortress of an office that morning. "Nice tie, Mr Price," she said. "And straight, too, for a change."

In the classroom, Ben checked his watch as the bell rang for playtime. It was as unreliable as ever. According to its Swiss efficiency, the bell should have rung ten minutes ago. He had not even noticed the time, which was remarkably different from previous weeks when time had dragged him into a pit of apathy. The more he had looked at his watch, the slower the world revolved.

Children say the most revealing things. "Ohhh," said Steven, laying great emphasis on the last letter as only children can. "Is that the time already? Can I stay in and finish?"

Steven was not the most enthusiastic of children when it came to work. For him to complain about the arrival of playtime, brought a smile to Ben's face. "Finish off after break," said Ben, smiling. "Take the football and go. Get rid of some of that energy."

Steven reluctantly left his work and took the ball from Ben's hand, scowling as he did so. As he closed Steven's book, Ben heard him running down the corridor shouting, "We're going to stuff you lot." Things felt like normal again.

The afternoon Christmas play for parents had rounded off a very satisfying day. The children had really enjoyed themselves, as had their parents. As had Ben. He felt that certain kind of pride when a job had been well done, a quiet feeling of satisfaction. Pride and satisfaction, feelings that had deserted him. Perhaps Edward Holton was right. Perhaps he was back. Only time would tell.

Ben wondered, as he made his way to the staffroom for après performance drinks, if thoughts of revenge and murder were meant to make you feel so good.

*

Ben was the last to leave the school. He was busy organising balloons and hats for the Christmas party the following day, putting one on each desk and the rest in the storeroom in case he needed them. He enjoyed being organised, didn't understand those who weren't.

The children expected something special. His parties were the envy of the school. Games, food, a short DVD for a bit of quiet and then home, exhausted, happy and grateful. Ben enjoyed it as much as the children. He got a buzz from seeing their smiles, hearing their laughter. He was confident it would go according to plan. It always did.

The BMW pulled away from the car park. He drove past McDonald's this time, although he did sometimes stop, much to Lynn's disappointment. She was a very healthy eater and had persuaded Ben that he should take more care of what he put into his stomach.

She'd also persuaded him that food on the go was not good for his indigestion. A little birdy had told her that he never sat down for lunch. He was always doing something with the children. Ben could guess who the little birdy was.

He'd accommodated Lynn's little whim by agreeing to a daily phone call on the mobile to ensure he was sitting down whilst eating. There was nothing serious in it, just a little joke. Anyway, it was nice to speak to her. Lynn always insisted on Suzanna coming to the phone and confirming that he was in fact sitting while he ate. Ben thought it was, in reality, an excuse to speak to Suzanna. She was on the phone longer to her than she was to him.

Lynn had become good friends with Suzanna. When Ben was involved in Saturday morning football with the school, the two girls would often 'hit the shops,' as they called it. They'd arrive at Ben's house later than he would and would often find him asleep on the settee, the television performing to an audience of zero. He would awake to the aroma of a plate full of healthy food wafting in his direction.

Before Lynn's death, Ben had asked Suzanna why she wasn't going with the other girls on their night out. Her reply had stayed with him. "I'm not as close to Emma as Lynn has to be. They've been kind of forced together with the job. Anyway, I just don't trust her," she had said.

"Who? Lynn?" Ben asked.

"No, you fool. Emma. I don't trust Emma."

"Why not?"

"Not sure. Just can't put my finger on it. You know what I mean. You must have felt the same way about someone."

Ben knew what she meant and nodded an acceptance. He'd felt the same the previous year when a newly qualified teacher had come to the school. Ben mentored him, but felt uncomfortable. He didn't know why until they went back to his place for a look at his files and he practically attacked Ben with a sexual gusto that had Ben running for his BMW. He felt it best that a female was assigned to the mentoring role from then on. It was not that Ben had anything against gay people, it was just that the relationship had 'tension,' the word he used when discussing the problem with the Edward Holton.

"There's just something about her," said Suzanna. "Lynn feels it too."

As he pulled into his driveway, he relived his conversation with Suzanna. She had remained a good friend. She would often call round and cook him a meal, bursting with goodness and vitamins of course. She'd even given Mrs Robinson her phone number, just in case.

As he placed the key into the door, he glanced round to see the curtains twitch next door. He didn't mind. It was good to know Mrs Robinson was monitoring his progress. He imagined her with her little book, recording everything, leaving nothing to chance. Maybe she would present it to him when he had fully and finally emerged from the gloom. They could have a small celebration. Just a select group of people who had seen him disappear from existence and reappear triumphantly.

He closed the door behind him. He flicked the light switch. Nothing. He tried again. Same problem. Again. Still no joy.

"It might be appropriate to close the curtains first. Don't want the whole world to know you have a couple of visitors." The voice was familiar. It came as no surprise to find Sebastian in his house without his knowledge. Delaney must have been there too, although he had not yet revealed his presence. There was no inkling that they might be there, no clues, but at the same time, he felt no anxiety. He'd been expecting them at some time. They'd said they'd make contact.

Meticulous, some might say nosey, though Mrs Robinson was, he was equally certain that she had no knowledge of his guests. Sebastian had commented, without arrogance, that the pair of them were perfect and Ben did not doubt it.

He pulled the curtains across the front bay window and ensured that the lining was also in place. No darkness entered the room and no light escaped. Ben heard the thud of heavy switches forced into place followed by the thin crackling of filaments springing to life. The room was bathed in brightness.

Ben noticed Delaney in the hallway, crouched down under the stairs, hand emerging from the fuse box. Panic must have engulfed Ben's face.

"Don't worry, laddie," said Delaney. "All curtains and blinds downstairs are closed, even the one across the front door. Nobody can see inside."

Ben knew how much the curtain squeaked as it was pulled across the front door, but he had not heard a sound. Delaney must have done it as he entered the front room.

Delaney continued. "I suggest the next thing you do is follow your normal routine. Go upstairs and close all the curtains there. Mrs Robinson will be expecting it. She knows how much you like to save on the heating bills. You've told her often enough."

Ben followed orders. It was not that he had to. He was, as Delaney so eloquently put it, simply following his normal routine. He pulled on the sash that allowed the blind to fall on the bathroom window. The curtains in the three bedrooms were closed, two of them easily, but the heavier one in his room battling over the small indentation in the curtain rail. It always clicked loudly as he yanked that little bit harder. It was how Mrs Robinson knew he was tucked in for the night. She could relax now and watch the soaps without interruption or worry.

When Ben returned downstairs, Sebastian was sitting in the armchair donated to him by Lynn's parents. It was close to a Queen Anne in design, but the buckled legs needed attention. He'd get round to it sometime, when there were less pressing matters to attend to.

"It's nice to sit in a decent chair at last," said Sebastian. "Back supported, legs at the right angle, feet flat on the floor. When you've had enough of it, give me a call. I'll buy it off you."

Ben laughed. "You'll have to hurry," he said. "According to you, I won't see you again after the deed is done."

"Quite right, Ben," said Sebastian. "But you never know, you may come in from school one day and realise that it's disappeared. Doors are no obstacle for us."

Ben moved over towards him, shook him by the hand and rested his frame on the settee. Delaney came towards the room, but waited in the doorway with one shoulder leaning against the frame. Ben thought that he only sat when he talked and when Sebastian stood guard. He was happier upright and alert, but not obviously so.

Sebastian resumed the conversation. "Nice play, by the way. You've got a couple of real characters there."

Ben sat up in astonishment. They had invaded his workplace and he had not known. Schools prided themselves on their security nowadays and he found it abhorrent that strangers had managed to bypass the system so easily and on such a joyful occasion. He made a mental note to ask Edward Holton to review procedures during children's performances. They were at their most vulnerable when their guard was down.

He suddenly felt fearful for the children's safety with those two around. They were self confessed organisers of death and they had been amongst his children. It was a reminder that Sebastian and Delaney were never to be fully trusted despite their apparent charm.

"They were a credit to you. Performance was great, behaviour was perfect. It seems you've cracked the ultimate parenting question. How do you get children to behave?" asked Sebastian.

And it suddenly dawned on Ben that Sebastian and Delaney might have children of their own. He could never imagine them as fathers. Cuddling children and putting them to bed just didn't sit right in their portfolio. Delaney – married to the same woman for fifteen years, loving father of two, killer of IRA members and God knows who else. Organiser of murder worldwide. Distance no barrier. Ben just couldn't imagine it.

"I never saw you," said Ben.

"We'd have been disappointed if you had," said Sebastian with a grin on his face.

"Lovely sandwiches," said Delaney from his perch by the door. "Took me back a few years."

"You shouldn't have been there. You had no right to be there. You didn't have a ticket." Ben realised the absurdity of what he had just said. If these guys could do half of what they said they could do, how would gaining entry to a school concert be an obstacle?

"Now don't go blaming the school or anyone in the school," said Delaney. "You didn't see the electricians checking the fire alarm, did you? Why would you? The mains electrics box is at the other end of the school. By the way, there were no problems with the fire alarm. It was fully operational."

"Relax, Ben," said Sebastian. "No harm done. No children kidnapped, no parents held hostage. This isn't Chechnya, you know. We're just two admirers of a man who excels at his job." He paused before commenting, with more than a little humour in his voice. "Takes one to know one."

Ben attempted to see the funny side, but found it impossible. On the other hand, he would be naïve if he thought he could split his life in two, personal and professional, and ne'er the twain would meet. After all, they had merged on too regular a basis over the last few months.

Eventually Ben replied. "Horses for courses, I suppose. You couldn't teach thirty children could you?"

"Good God, no. And you couldn't organise the death of Jimmy Buller could you?" said Sebastian. "Which brings me to the reason for our visit. Made a decision yet?"

*

Tom shifted the beast through its gears, letting it slow as it moved from fourth to third and then second. There was an expertise in his actions, a gentleness that the beast had grown accustomed to. Tom had the wretched thing in the palm of his hand.

When the situation required, he allowed it free rein and that was natural to the beast. It thrived on the freedom Tom gave it, powering its way along straights and over brows of hills, ignoring the road signs warning of danger. But he had trained it over time, reined it in, calmed it down, allowed the engine to recover from the excesses he demanded of it.

By the time he reached the gates to his house, the engine was subdued. The beast had perfected the art of stealth approach. There were times when Tom did not want Doris to know he was back home. Times when he needed more time to himself.

Tom didn't even have to calm the beast. It was under his command. He'd led it gently down the gears and now nudged it forward up the small rise from road to driveway. There was the occasional feeble snort from under the bonnet. It was simply a rebellious reaction from a young child, but it succumbed to the love Tom had for it.

Ben admired Tom's control. He never felt the same about the BMW. It gave in too easily, did exactly what he wanted every time. There was no challenge in taming a machine that was already tamed. It was broken in at the factory whereas the beast was let loose for the owner to break. Some owners succumbed under the challenge, but Tom had found the perfect balance, just as he had when Lynn was at home.

He allowed her freedom, gave her full rein, but required something back in exchange. She gave back in abundance. Theirs was a special relationship, borne out of undemanding, absolute love. Ben would often ask Lynn about it. She always had an easy answer, repeating something Tom had said many times. 'Give and take,' Tom would say. 'Never take more than you give and never give more than you can take.'

Lynn repeated other expressions of her father's, especially when Ben was finding a child difficult at school. 'Why make things difficult? Keep it simple.' Or 'Simplicity is an art which needs to be mastered.' Lynn often said it was like living with a philosopher, but not one who rammed it down your throat.

Ben believed one thing of Tom more than anything. He had the knack of finding the middle ground every time, especially when giving advice. Ben needed advice now, so he kept the question simple.

"Anything I need to know?" asked Ben.

"From whom?"

"From Sebastian and Delaney."

They sat side by side in the beast, listening to its engine cooling and preparing itself for sleep after the hard ride. Doris was unaware of their return. They had time. Tom's questions brought a clarity and a sense of reality back into the conversation. He made Ben fully aware of what he was about to do and even more strongly, what else he needed to know.

*

"There's just a few things I need to know," said Ben.

"Such as what?" Delaney asked, leaving the doorway and sitting on the settee next to Ben. The tone of the question was not aggressive, almost personable, but the fact that Delaney was sitting and talking was a little intimidating for Ben. He preferred the friendly approach that was Sebastian's trait, but that was probably because he knew more of Delaney's background and what he was capable of.

Apart from the pleasant voice and the impeccable dress sense and the charming manner, Ben knew nothing of Sebastian. Ben made a mental note to distrust Sebastian as much as he did Delaney, but that would be difficult.

"Such as," answered Ben. He hoped he could remember everything Tom had said the previous day. "Such as, who is this group of people who wish to right the wrongs of others? This mysterious group of people who fund killings at the drop of a hat."

"That's quite a loaded question, Ben. You must have been thinking about this quite a lot."

"I like to weigh everything up. It's not simply a question of killing Jimmy Buller, no matter what. How do I know it won't rebound on me? This group of people may have attacks of conscience and land me in it. They won't take the blame, will they?"

"Slow down, Ben," said Sebastian. "So many questions."

Ben knew he'd been rattling Tom's thoughts off, sounding like that annoying frog that had hopped its way onto morons' mobile phones, but he didn't want to forget anything. All the questions sounded perfectly logical when Tom asked them last night.

Sebastian continued. "First, the group of people, let's call them the Donors for simplicity, the Donors do not fund killings at 'the drop of a hat' as you say. They are extremely selective in their choices. You would not believe how many cases come to their attention and how few they act upon. Great discussions take place about which cases they pursue. It's a time consuming process because of the many factors involved."

"Such as?" asked Ben.

"Is the guilty person really guilty? It may be that the Criminal Prosecution Service got it right and there was no charge to answer. Or the jurors got it right. Or the judges." Sebastian rose from his favourite chair and strolled the room, stretching his back as he went. "Then there is the matter of organisation. Is the killing possible?"

"That's our business," said Delaney matter-of-factly, resting his hand on his chin and his elbow against the arm of the settee. "That's the bit we decide."

"And finally, there is the not so small matter of whether the client, that's you in this case, is capable of killing."

"And you obviously thought I was," said Ben.

"Oh, yes, there was no doubt about that. You were eating up inside and you needed to address the problem. The Donors gave you the chance. We knew you would take it."

"I haven't accepted yet," said Ben.

"You will," said Delaney.

"Do all your clients take it on?"

"Most of them. And all that did were successful and are living normal lives again. You could be walking past them in the street and you wouldn't know."

"Doesn't bear thinking about," said Ben. "Killers in our midst."

"Don't knock them Ben. You'll join their ranks soon," said Delaney.

"And then there was your Territorial Army link," said Sebastian completely out of the blue.

Ben looked across the room. "That was years ago," he said. "I only lasted a few weeks and left."

"You did twenty sessions, Ben," said Sebastian. "Your 9mm pistol results were quite something, the best in the group, which may come in useful."

Delaney, out of character, put an arm around Ben. He didn't actually touch Ben, rather he rested it on the back of the settee, but Ben could feel its presence and its proximity to his neck, which began to feel vulnerable. In a deliberate voice, slow and assured, Delaney asked, "Did you ask about the Donors having an attack of conscience?" Ben nodded. "I can assure you that, in respect of the intended victim, everyone in this operation is devoid of one thing. A conscience. It's a prerequisite to joining the club."

"Another prerequisite, excellent word by the way, Mr Delaney," said Sebastian, "is loyalty. They will all abide by any promise made. Any individual from within the Donors who defies that trust will be killed. They all know that. Mr Delaney and I will be the executioners. Have no worries, Ben. You are safe."

Questions were being answered, his mind slowly assured. Sebastian and Delaney were eradicating doubts that Ben and Tom had talked about. Ben had tick boxes in his mind and there were very few remaining blank. Better still, he was beginning to think on his feet, react to points Sebastian and Delaney had raised. It felt like an interview.

Ben, unlike most people, thrived on interviews. He looked on it as a battle of wits, a game to be won. He had never failed at interview.

"You mentioned my 9mm pistol results," he said. "Is that important?"

"It may be," Sebastian replied.

It was another point Tom had raised. Ben had not even thought about it, swept along as he was on a sea of euphoria. As the light faded and the darkness crept over them, they sat shoulder to shoulder in the garage throwing ideas at each other. Tom, acting as the devil's friendly advocate, had thoughts of practicalities rather than emotion. He had gently pulled Ben along, rationalising each emotion and breaking it down so that it lay exposed in reality. "I believe," Tom had said, "that choose your weapons and duels at ten paces at dawn have gone a little out of fashion nowadays, but you do need to know how you are expected to commit the final act." He avoided such emotive words as killing or murder.

"Will I have a choice?" Ben asked Sebastian.

"There is always a choice, Ben. In everything," said Sebastian. He flicked his hair back and straightened his tie. "In exactly which part of the operation would you like a choice?"

"In the final act. How exactly am I supposed to kill Jimmy Buller?"

Delaney spoke with enthusiasm. "As Sebastian said, there is always a choice. It depends if you want to look him in the eye when you kill him, see his face as he falls, maybe even tell him why he's dying. How he killed your fiancée and now justice is being done, revenge is being satisfied. That method, face to face, is, without doubt, the most dangerous and yet the most rewarding. Whether you do it with a gun or with a knife is up to you, but I will tell you this Ben, never in your life will you have experienced anything higher, not even those class A drugs they throw around universities."

"But there is a second method," said Sebastian, calming the waters, drawing Ben away from the bluntness of Delaney's violent approach. "We can supply you with a drug that can be administered easily. The effects will not show for at least six hours. This is the safer method for you. When he dies, you will be away from the scene and beyond suspicion."

"Is that possible?" asked Ben.

"It is proven. It will work. Every time."

Delaney shook his head and let out a sigh. "But you won't feel the buzz, Ben."

Ben turned towards Delaney on the settee. "I don't want to feel the buzz. I just want him dead. I don't care if I'm there or not when he breathes his last breath, I just want him dead."

Delaney pulled his arm from the back of the settee, stood and walked to the doorway. He leaned against the frame. He still looked awkward in the clothes he was wearing. "Okay, laddie," he said. "Drug it is then."

"So," said Sebastian. "It's decision time."

"Just one more thing."

"For fuck's sake, laddie," exploded Delaney. "How many questions have you got? It's simple. You say yes, we sort it out, you kill him. That's all there is to it."

"What Mr Delaney is trying to say, Ben, is that we have never had a client who asks so many questions, needs so much reassurance. Of course, doubts need to be allayed, fears conquered, but it's becoming apparent that this may not be a good idea after all. If you want out, then out you shall be. Mr Delaney and I will walk from this room and you will never see us again. But this is your chance. There won't be another."

Tom had warned him that this might happen. It was an effective tactic, used to great effect by Trade Unions in their heyday. Sebastian and Delaney were threatening to withdraw their labour. "Don't be intimidated," Tom had said. "Remember, Margaret Thatcher called the Unions' bluff and so must you."

Externally, Ben remained calm. He knew he always gave that impression. He had been told many times. Internally, his stomach and intestines were doing their very best to vomit everything he had eaten in the last twenty-four hours over Sebastian's chair.

"Humour me," he said. "Just one more thing. The Donors. Who are they?" At the dusk of the day, with the beast calm and asleep for the night, they had agreed that this was the most imperative question. If there were hidden motives, then Ben's answer would be no. Terrorist groups sprang to mind. Financial gain might be another, although why either would want to intrude on Ben's life, he did not know. But neither of these was the true reason for Ben's persistence. It was more simple than that.

He was curious.

Curiosity was borne out of unanswered questions. Who were these shady people? Which one of them had the inclination to create the Donors or was it a joint decision taken on a dark night midst a haze of alcohol? Had it been personal for them in the beginning, as personal as it was for Ben now? They were not glory seekers, but was it self preservation that kept them in the background? Who would be prepared to fund this kind of operation? Delaney and Sebastian would not come cheap for a start.

As Sebastian had said. So many questions.

Sebastian shook his head. "Ben, you're asking too much. Who the Donors are is irrelevant. They provide the resources. That's all you need to know. They are invisible, nameless and need to remain so. That way, the job gets done. You are happy and they are happy."

"So you won't tell me," said Ben.

"I *can't* tell you."

Sebastian stood away from Ben, hands in pockets, throwing his hair off his brow with a backward thrust of his head. There was an exasperated shuffling from the doorway, an impatient movement of one foot and then the next.

Ben rose from the settee. He looked first at Delaney, who refused to return the compliment. Instead, smothered in obvious frustration, he stared at the shuffling of his own feet. And then to Sebastian, who, in contrast, held his head high, almost aloof. He looked directly at his client.

Ben felt the need to swallow, but hoped the dryness in his throat would not reveal itself when he spoke. Slowly, he breathed in, disguising it as best he could. He felt his body relax, more controlled.

"Then the answer is no," said Ben. He reached out his right hand towards Sebastian. "I would like to thank you both for the offer you have made, but I'm sorry, the answer is no."

Ben's hand remained unshaken, hovering in mid-air between himself and Sebastian. Their eyes locked together, but Ben forced a smile. He did not wish to enter a staring match with Sebastian, weakest man first to blink. He knew he would lose. Immediately, he broke the silence.

"I'm really sorry you've gone to so much trouble for me, but I feel extremely uncomfortable receiving things without full knowledge of who it's from. Could never accept freebies, things that weren't justified. One of my drawbacks, Lynn used to say. Always wanted everything up front and out in the open. No secret Valentine's Day card for me. It had to be signed. If it wasn't, I wouldn't rest until I found out who my secret admirer was."

"Now aren't you the bloody romantic," murmured Delaney.

Ben continued. "I know there's only one way to find out who the Donors are. From you. As neither of you will tell me, then that's it."

"And Lynn's murderer goes unpunished?" asked Delaney.

"I'll have to live with that. Lynn will understand. She knows what I'm like."

"You're a bloody fool, laddie."

Ben's hand was still outstretched, still open, still unreceived. He nodded his head and opened his hand of friendship a little wider, repeating the offer. Sebastian's hands remained firmly in his pockets. He made a move towards Ben, but ignored the hand and sat down where Delaney had sat before.

There were no words spoken.

Ben lowered his hand. Tension gripped his body. He hoped it wasn't obvious. Normally, he could cover it, but this was no normal situation. He could not be sure what their response would be to his rejection. Hadn't they repeated on many occasions that they would disappear, never to be seen again? No grudges held?

Arguments of the mind can sometimes be destructive, yet necessary. The other side of the argument playing in Ben's mind was that he knew little about them, other than that Delaney could kill, and had done so, when the need arose. Was Ben to be killed to hide their secret?

Delaney stopped shuffling his feet and rested his dishevelled frame in Sebastian's chair. He encircled the ends of the arms with his hands, which would, Ben thought, give him more leverage should he need it. A sudden pull on his arms and he could be astride Ben, thrusting a knife, or anything else, into him.

Ben swallowed. It was deafening.

"Please. Take a seat, Ben," Sebastian said.

Ben did not wish to. The only seat available was between the two of them, a position he would sooner not find himself in. In truth, at this moment, he preferred to be some distance away from them, the greater the better. He took another deep breath, unnoticed he hoped, and glanced around the room.

Ben plotted a rapid, impossible departure. The doorway was empty, now that Delaney had moved to Sebastian's chair. He could be almost willing Ben to make a break for it, but Ben knew this would only delay the inevitable. If he wasn't stopped in his tracks by the pouncing Delaney, he would be followed, and found, and dealt with.

In reality, he knew there was no escaping the situation, brought on entirely by his own curiosity. He had returned from work and closed the door on everyone. The curtains had been shut. No light from the room penetrated the outside. The day was over and Mrs Robinson had seen him to bed, not literally of course.

Who cared what happened in the privacy of one's own home? They were alone, detached from the outside world. Nobody knew he had visitors in his own house. Nobody knew the danger he believed himself to be in.

"I told you he'd be a tough one." It was Delaney who broke the silence.

"You certainly did, Mr Delaney," said Sebastian. His teeth showed through his broad smile. "Sit down, Ben. We're not going to kill you or anything like that. It's been years since Mr Delaney here was involved in torture, so that's out of the question also. Our agreement stands. You decline the offer, we walk away."

"Why, then, have you asked me to sit down? Why aren't you walking away, out of my life, as promised?" asked Ben.

"Because Mr Delaney here persuaded me that we would somehow have to justify ourselves more to you than to any other client. He may look like someone who has been dragged through a hedge backwards, but Mr Delaney is impeccably perceptive when it comes to judging character. It's of no surprise to me that his judgment of you has been correct."

"And what was his judgment?" asked Ben.

"That you have morals."

"And what difference does that make?"

"It sets you apart from any previous client with whom we have dealt. When the offer is made, the usual response is one of revenge, less frequently of justice. But with you, we had to take it further, culminating in the 'stopping him from killing others' routine. Your decision was always going to be based on more than one reason, so we gave you many. And now you ask for more. We just hope that this little conversation we are about to have will satisfy you, Ben. Put simply, after this, we have nothing else to give."

Ben turned towards the Victorian fireplace which was the focal point of the room. A holiday picture of Lynn and Ben, relaxed and smiling, rested with its base on the mantelpiece. The frame was made from light pine. Darker smudges stretched along its right-hand side. They were from the thumb marks where Ben had lifted her and held her. It was where he had held her tight, gripped her, as the tears ran down his face.

He lifted her again and held her tight.

There were no tears. He had no more left.

Slowly, he bent his knees and reached down, allowing his body to descend to the rug before the fireplace. It was where Lynn and he had last made love the afternoon before she died. In front of the fire where the ashes remained in the grate.

He knew that there would be no return from this point. Sebastian was about to offer Ben the final piece of the jigsaw. Once it was complete, and if the last piece fitted perfectly, then he knew he would accept their offer. He wanted Lynn to be with him, so that the decision would be a joint one as everything was between them.

"I'll sit here if you don't mind," said Ben.

"It's your home, Ben. Sit where you like," said Sebastian. He continued. "Have you heard of Oscar Baker?"

"What, *the* Oscar Baker?"

"I suppose there is more than one of the same name, but only one who is so well known that his name beckons the response, '*the* Oscar Baker.'"

"Oscar Baker? The Member of Parliament?"

"Ex-Member of Parliament. The very same," said Sebastian. "A quick history to remind you. Oscar Baker was the most respected MP in the whole of Westminster. By far. By all parties. Married for over thirty years to the same lady, not a sniff of an affair because there never was one. Two daughters, both with first class honours from Cambridge, both declining offers of work with vast salaries, both working for Amnesty International on a pittance. Baker spoke calmly and eloquently for the victimized in society. Law was his big thing. He believed there should be justice for the victims above all else, even if this meant heavier prison sentences for the guilty. In private, he was in favour of the re-introduction of the death penalty in absolute cases, although this opinion never found its way into the public domain. His public message was popular amongst MPs and the public. He could say things that others could not, simply because of the admiration in which he was held. He had only one problem."

"And what was that?" asked Ben.

"He had the misfortune to be in the Liberal Democrat party. No matter what he said, or how he said it, he had little clout. He was in the wrong party at the wrong time. Being third every time wore him down. Perhaps the most gifted politician of a generation, he left parliament disillusioned and dismayed. His party and the public tried to persuade him to return, but once he had made up his mind, there was no turning back. Everyone soon got used to him being out in the wilderness, or making the occasional appearance on the television when light sentences were handed out to terrorists or child murderers."

Delaney interrupted. "God help the dumb British public. If only they knew. Would they still be hailing him the greatest Prime Minister Britain never had?"

"So, the Donor is Oscar Baker," said Ben, half statement, half question.

"Don't get ahead of yourself," said Sebastian. "You're getting the whole story, not just part of it."

"Aye and remember, you'll be laughed out of the country if you ever reveal this to anyone. Don't go abusing our trust now, will you?" said Delaney, with more than a hint of sarcasm. All three people in that room knew that if there was any revelation on Ben's part, laughing would be the last thing to worry about. Ben knew he would be dead, killed by his new found friends.

"You forget, Mr Delaney," said Ben. "I have morals. A wise old man once told me."

"Search your memory of the papers and the journals and the television news, Ben," said Sebastian. "What did Oscar Baker, workaholic, supporter of the victim, do with his time after he left parliament?"

Ben sighed. It was difficult to focus on any other answer, now that his name had been associated with the Donors. "I remember something about a farm," he said. "That's right. He found a new cause. Organic farming."

"Good memory, but incorrect. Organic farming was his wife's passion. It's just that everyone knew Mr Baker, not Mrs Baker, and so the newspeople as usual got it wrong and labelled Oscar as the farmer. He was happy to go along with it."

"As a cover for his more radical ideas?" asked Ben.

"Correct," said Sebastian. "The truth of the matter is that the day he left parliament, he was whisked away and asked to assess the possibilities for the creation of a small, secret organisation capable of providing justice where the courts could not."

"And the Donors were formed," said Ben.

"In its infancy, yes, but with the advent of time, it has grown, not unduly, and become the professional organisation it now is. It is highly successful, if a little controversial should its purpose become public."

"It's been even more successful since we joined," Delaney threw in modestly.

"Correct, Mr Delaney," Sebastian replied.

"And the money, the funding, where does that come from?" asked Ben.

"I told you, Sebastian," exploded Delaney. "I bloody told you that would not be enough for the laddie."

"You did indeed, Mr Delaney. And you also told me that if he pressed for more information, it would be you who would provide it. Your turn."

Delaney took over with relish, excitement covering every line in his furrowed brow, eyes alive, sparkling. Ben thought this might be the juicy part. Delaney would enjoy the telling. "Ever heard of the Black Hole?" he asked.

"Space? The final frontier? No-one knows what's in them, where they lead?"

"A different Black Hole. Think of economics."

"Oh, I see," Ben replied. "It's the difference between what's spent and what's in the bank."

"Well done. You're a clever lad, so answer this. Where is the biggest Black Hole in the whole of Britain?"

"Well, the opposition party is always saying it's the Treasury."

"And for once, they'd be right."

Realisation was beginning to dawn on Ben, although he found his own thoughts incredible, too incredible to be true. "Are you saying that the Treasury is funding all of this?"

Delaney's eyes were dancing. He nodded. "Taxpayers' money. And why not? Justice for all is the foundation of a democratic society. It's just that some money is out in the open and some isn't."

Sebastian interrupted. "Let me talk while you take all this in, Ben. Perhaps I can make it clearer." He allowed Ben more time and then continued. "The original idea came from within Government, as an almost off the cuff comment. It was such an outrageous idea that it was not only sidelined, but kicked well and truly into touch. But the seed had been sown. Hence the meeting with Oscar Baker the day he left parliament. Since that day, many Chancellors of the Exchequer have come and gone and the funding for this project has been lost in the enormous Black Hole of the Treasury. It is, in the context of the nation's wealth, such an insignificant amount that it wouldn't pay for the refitting of the Queen's bathroom. Put bluntly, no-one knows of the Donors' existence, no-one knows about its funding and no-one will ever find out."

Ben was now sitting up, more alert, still holding the photograph of Lynn. He was leaning on his left hand, eyes flitting from Sebastian to Delaney and back again, but staring beyond them into oblivion. Their faces were a blur, but he heard their words and attempted to assimilate them. There were more questions, but he hesitated to ask them in case the answers were too heavy to bear.

Of all the fallacies that the world has created, curiosity killing a cat has remained unproven. Rather, Ben regarded curiosity as a stimulant and he just could not resist. "Who was it that whisked Oscar Baker away? Who sowed the seeds?" he asked.

Sebastian's response was immediate. He knew that Ben could not resist the question. The answer was already on his lips. "Only two people were privy to the Donors' conception. One was Oscar Baker. The other was the Prime Minister."

"Holy shit," said Ben.

"Holy shit indeed," confirmed Delaney.

"That means that the Prime Minister has involved himself in illegal acts," said Ben.

Delaney guffawed with laughter. "All the time, laddie. All the time. If I may say so, you are naïve to the workings of the real world."

"As are ninety-nine point nine percent of the population, Mr Delaney," said Sebastian. "Ben is not alone in that. However in this case, Ben, you would be wrong. The Prime Minister was never involved illegally regarding the Donors. The only thing he is guilty of, if guilty be the correct word, is having a conversation with an ex MP about law and order in this country. Nothing was minuted, no proof can be attached. He would, if asked, deny emphatically that any such discussion took place at all, as would Oscar Baker. Since that initial meeting, the Prime Minister has never voiced the concept again with anyone. He is unaware that the Donors exist."

"Hear no evil, see no evil," said Delaney. "The unwritten law of all politicians."

Ben attempted to clarify the short sequence of events in his mind. "The Prime Minister talks to Oscar Baker. Oscar Baker goes away and forms the Donors."

"Sorry Ben," said Delaney. "The real world just isn't that simple. Although Oscar Baker was no longer a politician, old habits die hard. Hear no evil, see no evil."

"And this is the point where the mist descends and the issues become cloudy," said Sebastian. "Oscar Baker talked to someone else, who talked to someone else and the concept was subsumed into the underground corridors where the nation's real power lurks: the unknown civil servants. The people who return to their semi-detached homes after a hard day plotting the downfalls of leaders. There is a cup of tea waiting for them and dinner will be ready in half an hour, dear. Just enough time to complete the Times crossword that has been revisited on various occasions throughout the day. In other words the concept was lost, but never drowned. Who knows who the Donors are? Mr Delaney doesn't. I don't. Instructions rise from the bowels, they are acted upon, justice is done. And that, Ben, really is the whole story. You can ask more questions if you wish, but we won't be able to answer."

Ben pushed himself from the floor and placed the photograph back in its rightful position. Gently, he placed a finger on Lynn's lips, held it there for a few seconds and then let it fall. Crouching down, he removed the poker from its stand and raked the ashes until they had fallen into the tray below. He meticulously brushed the grate, the dust falling through to join the ashes below. Now everything was as clear as it could possibly be.

Standing tall, he looked down at Sebastian and Delaney. He and Tom had taken them to their very limit and they had responded. They had not shirked and hopefully they had not lied. Hope was all that Ben could hope for.

Ben smiled. "The decision is yes," he said.

21st December

Ben opened his eyes.

Apart from one outstretched leg, his body was in the perfect foetal position. He often woke like this. Before the alarm clock sounded. He would lie on his side thinking of the day ahead, running through the planning and preparation he had done the previous night.

He would follow his normal routine: shower, dress, breakfast, toilet and the habitual check in his bags to ensure he had everything he needed. By the time he closed his front door and waved goodbye to Mrs Robinson, he was confident that he had organised as best he could and that the day would run smoothly.

Of course, there was always the odd blip which threatened all his best laid plans. It could be something very simple like Joe's nose bleeding for no reason. It had happened enough for Ben to deal with it efficiently and calmly, but it always set the lesson back a few minutes and disturbed the other children's concentration. Any excuse.

It could work the other way. Disturbance could give impetus to the lesson, could wake the children from their slumber. After all, most of them had watched the television into the early hours while their parents slept. Some bedrooms were packed floor to ceiling with technology. Videos, DVDs, televisions and the inevitable headphones which allowed the children to watch and listen without disturbing their parents. Watershed times just weren't relevant anymore in most households. No wonder children were adults way before their time.

Sometimes, Ben despaired.

In his direct line of vision were red numbers staring back at him. Four twenty-six with the two vertical dots flashing as the seconds went by. If, like his headteacher believed, he was back to normal, he had woken early. Far too early. The red numbers usually showed between six thirty and six forty-five and he rose at six fifty.

The last few months had been different. Lynn's death had had a remarkable effect on time. It ceased to exist. He got up, he went to work, he came home, he drank, he went to bed, he slept. No clock, no time, interfered with this routine.

He did receive numerous early morning calls. Mrs Robinson's voice was reminiscent of the speaking clock, nudging him into life with gentle tones. 'Ben, I thought you'd like to know it's quarter past eight and I was wondering how you were this morning.' On a handful of occasions, she would sound closer. 'Ben, I've phoned twice this morning and you haven't answered,' and she would be standing, a little embarrassed, by his bed with a mug of tea in her hand. Long after the bell had heralded the beginning of the school day, he'd rushed in late one day, clothes awry, tie flapping around his neck, to be greeted by Mrs Holliday saying, "How was the dentist, Ben? Chipped teeth can be really nasty." And after the surprise revelation of his fictitious dental visit, Ben had replied, "Fine now, thank you."

Ah, Mrs Robinson. Provider of early morning wake-up calls, liquid refreshment and parental excuses.

Four twenty- seven. He was wide awake.

He got out of bed and tiptoed across the floor, taking extra care not to tread on the floorboard at the top of the landing. Ben knew it squeaked loudly, so loudly that Mrs Robinson had mentioned it to him one morning as Lynn and he were leaving the house, somewhat embarrassed that they had been caught. The floorboard had woken her husband the previous night and 'he just could not get back to sleep again and he needs his sleep at his age, you know. Oh and by the way, the flushing of the toilet disturbs him sometimes as well.'

Ben took careful aim in the toilet, making sure that he hit the sides of the pan and not the water in the bottom of it, but in that short moment he had been in there, his mind drifted away from Mrs Robinson's acute hearing and onto Sebastian and Delaney and he almost forgot the disturbing toilet. His hand was on the handle and was beginning to descend when Mrs Robinson's words came back to him. He stopped, there was a small gush of water into the pan and then silence.

Ben remained in the toilet, perched on its seat, for a few minutes until he was sure that his neighbours had not been disturbed. It was not that he was so conscious of waking them, it was just that he didn't want to answer awkward questions later on that morning, like was there a reason for him being awake at four twenty-seven in the morning? He wanted Mrs Robinson to believe that everything was getting back to normal and normality was a full night's sleep after a hard day's work.

He stepped over the third stair down. He knew that squeaked too. The kitchen was at the back of the house and was not overlooked. The curtains were closed, as was the blind behind them. Delaney had made sure of that. He was safe from prying, well meaning eyes.

He was glad he had filled the kettle with water after his guests had left. At least he didn't have to run the water from the tap, creating unnecessary noise. As he sat at the table drinking a hot cup of tea, events of the previous evening replayed in his head. He remembered every detail. The outcome was that Ben had agreed to kill Jimmy Buller. It was the correct decision. It was made and it was final. Now he just wanted to get on with it.

There was no discussion of the plan. Sebastian and Delaney had said that would come later. They would contact him. "And finally," Sebastian had said, "we know you like to be organised, so here's a few anecdotes you will relate to."

Delaney began. "What did you think of our dreadlocked, Glastonbury-loving, pissed-on hippie in the bar?"

"One of yours?" asked Ben.

"Of course. We knew you wouldn't relate to him," Delaney continued. "He was a bit of a smokescreen, a tester. We thought you might have gone for the girl sitting in your lap, offering herself on a plate to you. Well resisted."

"Actually we were quite proud of you. It confirmed a few things," interrupted Sebastian. "It proved to us how much you still love Lynn. How much you still hurt. How much you want Jimmy Buller dead. Most men would have found it extremely difficult to turn down such a good-looking girl."

"She could have been Cameron Diaz. I never noticed," Ben said, honestly.

"And then there was the drunken mob," said Delaney.

"All yours?"

Delaney nodded. "Everyone of them. All good operatives who were never told why you had to be arrested, just that you had to be." Delaney paused for effect before announcing, "And then there were the contingencies you never saw."

"Such as?"

Sebastian carried on. "If you had walked into the pub, sensed the atmosphere in the crowd and walked straight out again, you'd have been allowed a few seconds only before being questioned by the police for alleged possession of a knife. You'd have been searched and depending on your response, aggressive or passive, you'd have been arrested or allowed to go. The last thing we wanted was to draw attention to you, so timing was all important."

"We wouldn't have expected you to be aggressive," said Delaney, "so we presumed you would move on."

"Where you would have, quite literally, bumped into a well-dressed man about your age. His name is Carl. He would have picked your pocket and taken your wallet. He would have followed you into the next pub you decided to frequent, at a distance of course, and offered your wallet back to you. He had seen it fall following your collision, he'd have said. You'd have bought him a drink, it's in your nature, and you'd have struck up a conversation. You'd had a few pints by then, remember, so he would have worked it that you would have somehow been taken in by the police. Our police, of course. Carl's an expert. He'd have found a way. You would never have suspected a thing."

Delaney interrupted. "And if all that failed, you'd have definitely been arrested for being drunk and disorderly, having pulled down Amy's top, a well respected girl who was a friend of Carl and had joined the two of you for a quick drink. Amy's an expert as well. Of course, you wouldn't have touched her top, but a quick brush against her, a sleight of hand on Amy's part and all of a sudden her breasts are on show and you're in trouble."

Ben felt the smile cross his face. "Very clever," he said.

Sebastian was satisfied. "We suspect that the only niggling doubt that you harbour, and it is the smallest of niggles, is about the organisation. After all, that is your speciality. You like to be organised. You've built your reputation on it. Are you now convinced that our level of organisation is detailed enough for your very high standards?"

And Ben had no other option but to concur.

They left while Ben was in the kitchen filling the kettle. He didn't hear a sound.

*

"Couldn't you sleep last night?" asked Mrs Robinson. Ben had kept the morning noise to a minimum, but hygiene and habits required him to take a shower and flush the toilet and neither of those could be done in silence.

Ben continued towards his car, but out of politeness, responded to her question. He also wished to know what she had heard. "What do you mean?"

"I heard you in the kitchen," she replied. "Filling the kettle, I think."

"What time was that?"

"Oh, about an hour after you went to bed. I couldn't sleep either. Hope I didn't disturb you."

"No, not at all, Mrs Robinson." He was relieved to know that she had not heard him at four twenty-seven, a time which would have prompted more questions. As it was, Ben responded with, "I had things on my mind. It's a busy time at school. Plays, parties, presents, cards, decorations. So much sticking and glueing. By the time Christmas arrives, I'll be sick of it." He laughed, just to make sure that Mrs Robinson knew he was joking.

Mrs Robinson laughed with him. "Have a good day," she shouted after him as he pulled away from the drive. And then quietly to herself. "You're getting better, Ben. I told you it would just take time."

*

81

The Christmas party went particularly well, even better than last year's, Ben thought. The children had dressed accordingly, eaten their nibbles, danced till they dropped and burst their balloons. They went home exhausted, but happy.

In the aftermath, Ben was sitting in the staffroom, enjoying a relaxing mug of tea. He had one leg over the arm of an already comfortable armchair, to make himself more comfortable. The rest of the staff had gone home to their families and husbands. Beside Edward Holton, he was the only male on the staff, an all too common occurrence in primary schools, and apart from Suzanna, he was the only single teacher on the staff.

She had escaped the premises also. She had more shopping to do for presents. Lynn would have joined her if she'd been around.

Ben realised that he had not given a second thought to Sebastian and Delaney during the day. He was too occupied.

Doris had advised him after Lynn's death. "Keep yourself occupied," she'd said. "You love your job. It will help to take your mind off things." They were common words after the death of a loved one, keeping yourself occupied, words that Doris herself had struggled to adhere to.

But work didn't help. It had been impossible for Ben to take his mind off Lynn's death. Very occasionally, something would happen in the classroom, like Sharon remembering to learn her spellings and remembering to remember them during the test and getting the maximum ten marks, and he would feel the buzz that only teaching children could bring, but the moment would soon pass and he would drift back to his melancholic state.

But not today. Today, he had been at the top of his game once more. He felt good about himself. Not once had he thought of what the next few days would bring. Sebastian and Delaney, he imagined, would be adding the finishing touches to the planning and he was confident that everything would be perfect. So he had no reason to think about it. Everything was being prepared for him. All he had to do was deliver. He had no doubts that he would fulfil his part of the bargain.

As he sipped his tea and reflected in the quietness, the door opened and his boss walked in. "Tea in the pot?" he asked.

"Made a few minutes ago," Ben replied.

"Great party again, Ben," he said sitting down beside him. Ben hoped this would not be an inquisition into what had gone wrong over the last few months. He sensed it might be the opportunity the boss had been waiting for. He did not feel in the mood for reminiscing. Neither was he ready to be congratulated for his recent recovery nor praised for past glories. He wanted to be ignored, that was all, so he could do his job, in school and outside. No questions asked.

"Doing anything special over the holidays?" he asked.

Ben smiled at the absurdity of the possible answers. How about, 'Involving myself in an elaborate plan to seek out justice'? How about, 'Seeking revenge on the guy who killed Lynn'? How about, 'Just popping out to murder someone'? And then after all is done, 'I'll come back at the start of the term and teach the kids as if nothing had happened. No-one will know. Sebastian and Delaney assured me of that.'

His answer was less truthful, but less provocative also. "Sticking to the routine. Going down to Lynn's parents on the twenty-third. Staying a couple of nights and having Christmas Day with them. Then it's back home to watch a bit of television and get planning for next term. Usual stuff."

"Sounds good, Ben. Nice to be around family at this time of year. It will do you all good." Of course, he didn't know if it would do any of them any good at all, but it was the right thing to say. Ben appreciated that.

Ben only realised as he was driving home that he had never asked his boss what he was doing for Christmas. Thoughts about being around family struck a chord. He hadn't been able to see his own children the previous year. His ex-wife had taken them off to Barbados with her new boyfriend for a holiday. He'd spent the entire Christmas holidays at school, working, the only other place he could go. It was a stark reminder to Ben that he wasn't the only one who had problems.

*

On the whole, the twenty first of December was a quiet day for Ben Price. It was the last one he would have for a while.

22nd December

The usual stuff.

Handkerchiefs, elegantly presented in a box of three. One pair of socks complete with curious logo. The tie, highly coloured and eye catching. Previous year's aftershave with potent smell, made even more irrelevant by the fact that Ben didn't wear aftershave of any variety. All gifts were gratefully received with extreme enthusiasm. One gift was just as special as the next.

Some gifts were more useful than others. The golf balls were not his usual brand, but still designed for more touch and feel around the greens. It would be interesting to see if the maker's claims were correct.

Children who had not bought a gift were not ignored, Ben emphasising, in a quiet moment, that the greatest gift they had given him was their attitude, their behaviour and their work throughout the term. Every child in the class had given him that gift.

It was the normal end of term speech, delivered with feeling. Ben was not one to shirk when children misbehaved or when their work needed improvement. He would tell them straight. But he was fair, the children knew that. He would do anything for them as long as they responded. Praising their achievements came as second nature to him.

The bell sounded to mark the end of the school day, he gave his usual rendition of 'I wish you a Merry Christmas,' delivered at full belt with as little tune as possible, and the children were away and out of the classroom shouting, 'Have a good Christmas, Mr Price' as they left.

The children had stripped his classroom of all Christmas items and he had placed them as delicately as possible into the boxes which would be stored away until the following December. He took a few minutes to tidy his desk, ready for the new term. The spring term boxes were pulled to the front of the storeroom and the Christmas boxes took their place at the back. He wanted to be as prepared as possible for the new term in January.

A lot was happening in between times.

He was the last teacher to leave the school, throwing a "Don't get too drunk" to the caretaker as he left. Opening his car door, he noticed another car in the car park, one he had not noticed before. Sebastian and Delaney. He closed his door and made his way over.

It was a brand new car, latest registration plates. Modern, but easily concealed in a crowd. Not like his BMW which stood out from the rest. He thought that he might have to mothball his car for the next couple of weeks. He'd miss it, but needs must.

He approached from the rear passenger side, but was unable to see any figure in the passenger seat. Perhaps Delaney had final preparations to make and Sebastian had come alone. He hoped it was Sebastian. Of the two, he trusted him the most.

He would be expected, so he opened the passenger door and immediately heard an exclamation from the driver's seat. Staying outside the car, he leaned over and looked across. Edward Holton looked back at him, fear etched across his brow and in his eyes. He held a handkerchief in his hand, which he lifted quickly to his face. He looked away from Ben, enshrouded in embarrassment.

Ben had already seen the tears. "Are you okay, Edward?" Ben asked. The man was sitting alone in his car in an almost empty car park, tears on his cheeks and Ben had asked if he was okay. It was as tactless as asking someone the same question after they had been diagnosed with cancer. He felt stupid.

"I thought everyone had gone home," Holton said.

Ben looked around and pointed towards his car. Perhaps it wasn't so noticeable after all. "No. Still here," he said.

"I thought everyone had gone home," repeated Holton slowly.

Ben slowly lowered himself into the passenger seat. The interior was cold and Ben wondered how long he had been sitting there. Enormous pressure was placed on headteachers. Coupled with the problems he faced in his private life, Ben was sympathetic towards his plight. "Edward, what about you? Are *you* going home?" he asked.

Holton turned towards him. The fear had been replaced by anxiety. "Don't tell anyone, will you Ben?" pleaded Holton.

"Tell anyone what, Edward?" Ben's tone was light-hearted. "There's nothing to tell. We're just sitting here in your car, mulling over a few school matters. Everyone knows we're addicted to the job. Nothing to tell. Now, I think it's about time we both went home." Ben understood why Holton was concerned. A headteacher who showed weakness was deemed a liability, especially if the headteacher was a man. It was the macho thing. Ben saw it as a sign of humanity rather than weakness, but he realised his opinion was not held by the majority.

A man in a position of responsibility sitting alone in a car, tears streaming down his face, pleading for understanding would be ridiculed. It was a good job that it was Ben who found him. Anyone else might have taken advantage.

"The bastard has applied to adopt my children. Make them legally his. First he takes my wife, then he's after my children. What kind of man is he, Ben?" Holton had dropped his guard, allowing Ben a glimpse of the complexities of his private life. It had happened before on rare occasions, but this time Ben sensed that he was approaching the point of desperation. He needed advice and was reaching out to Ben for it. If the circumstances could be ignored, it was a pleasant surprise to see his emotional side. Ben would have to mention this in happier times. It suited him.

Ben acted on impulse, saying it how he felt, hoping he wouldn't make things worse. "Well, he's the kind of man that won't get your kids, that's for sure."

"You don't think so?" Holton asked with a little more hope.

"Not a cat in hell's chance. Look at it logically." Lynn would have been proud of him. "You love your kids, they love you. You've never harmed them, always conformed to access requirements, never missed a payment. And besides that, if you don't mind me saying so, you're only separated from your wife because the bitch ran off with someone else."

Holton was taken aback, but laughed, giggling at first, and then more openly, loudly. "I can always rely on you, Ben," he said.

Ben looked at the curved lines of the dashboard in front of him. The instruments were well laid out, easy to see. The gear stick was within distance, easily reached. He glanced behind. The rear window was clear and large enough to make parking easy. The car was functional. Perfectly functional.

It was the kind of car that would appeal to Doris, much to the chagrin of Tom. The addiction to plastic would disturb him. "Nice car," said Ben. "When did you get it?"

"Last night. Exactly one hour after I opened the letter from the bastard's solicitor. It was a jerk reaction. I thought, he's got my wife, getting my kids. I'll make sure I've got no money in the bank, so he can't get that as well."

"Good thinking," said Ben.

"Crap thinking. It's a heap of plastic. I should have gone for something like yours. Smooth, sleek, impressive. A bit like you, Ben."

"It would have suited you."

"Do you think so?"

Ben was doing his best to normalise the situation. He wanted Holton to think more clearly, be more positive, so that he would go home and Ben wouldn't have to worry about him. Then Ben could get on with what he had to do. Ben wanted this dealt with quickly and effectively, as much for himself as for Holton. He continued. "Well-heeled, well-dressed, single man like yourself? The world's your oyster, Edward. Don't get a BMW like mine though. Only two seats. You'll need room for the kids. A nice four-seater convertible. Just think how they'd look forward to having the roof down on a hot summer's day." And then as a devious afterthought, "Just think how the bastard would feel when you rolled up outside his house to pick the kids up."

Holton smiled. "I can see his face now."

"Look, Edward, we can talk about this after the holidays if you like. Just you and me. No-one else needs to know."

"I'd appreciate that, Ben."

Ben opened the door. "Home?" he asked.

"Home," Holton replied. "Anyway, I've got to get the turkey in. Kids are coming to me for Christmas. It will give the two lovebirds a chance to have time on their own."

"That's great news," said Ben. He placed one foot outside the car, but leaned back and stroked the palm of his hand tenderly across the panel in front of him. "Nice plastic," he said.

"Piss off," Holton replied.

Ben jumped out of the car and walked across to the BMW. Behind him, he heard the engine turn and the gears engage, first reverse and then first. He reached down to open his own car as Holton drove past. Ben saw his hand waving by the window and returned in kind.

He thought of his grandfather who had once told him that the only time he felt the whole country was united was during times of conflict. Adversity had the strangest way of drawing people together. It was true. Perhaps this was the beginning of a warmer relationship for Holton and Ben, but Grandad also told him that once the moment of adversity had passed, the united became disunited again. Ben would have to wait and see.

Ben was not aware that he was following him until he drifted round the corner into Holton's street. It was not a massive detour from his own route home, but he had made it without thinking, seeing his charge safely home.

As Ben took a left turn before he got to Holton's house, he glanced down the road. Holton was already out of his car and heading for the door. Ben was satisfied that he would be okay. Now he could get on with his own business.

*

Ben placed the key in the latch, opened the door and closed it behind him. "Hello, you two," he shouted.

There was no reply.

He was disappointed. He had felt sure Sebastian and Delaney would be there waiting for him. He flicked the light switch and took a quick recce of the downstairs. He was alone. Moving to the front window, he noticed Mrs Robinson at hers. He could never imagine her living in a house without a bay window. Some would say she was nosey,

Tom had commented, but Ben could not forget her kindness. It was a compromise he could put up with.

He waved and received one in return, along with a smile. He smiled back and they both laughed at their little ritual. The curtains were drawn in perfect harmony.

Ben turned into the loneliness. Lynn's photograph looked at him from its place on the mantelpiece. He took it in his hand and stroked it. She had the most beautiful smile, warm and friendly. It would stay with him forever, in the photographs and in his memory. Years after his father's death, his mother had once told him that she was beginning to forget the details in his face. She would look at the photographs, but the lines were fading like her memory. Ben thought he could never forget the details in Lynn's face. The way her nose crinkled in her embarrassed moments. The laughter which spread from her dancing eyes to her mouth. The small brown beauty spot that rested just below her left eye that she hated and he loved. He would never forget.

He could feel the tears welling up, but forced them back and replaced her photograph. A final look, a throw of a kiss and he made his way to the kitchen.

He wondered what was in the fridge. He couldn't remember the last time he had visited the shops, but there always seemed to be something in there. Perhaps he was shopping on auto pilot, but he rather suspected it was Mrs Robinson, treating him as the son she never had. He'd have to mention it to her at some point, but not yet.

Bacon, sausage, eggs and tomatoes. After a tiring day at school, with the odd bite between storing and tidying, it seemed like the perfect feast. He wasn't sure that Lynn would approve, but he'd make sure he grilled the bacon, sausage and tomatoes and poach the egg rather than frying. Not the perfect ingredients, but Lynn's legacy lived on.

"Wouldn't mind a bacon sandwich myself," said Delaney. "Fried if you don't mind."

Ben never flinched. If they had tried to catch him out, then they had failed. He knew they'd make contact. They'd said they would. They'd never let him down yet. He had learned to be flexible, to expect the unexpected.

"You'll get grilled or none at all," Ben replied, without turning. He presumed Sebastian was there also, so he coolly asked, "And what would Sir Sebastian require?"

"It all looks wonderful," he said. "I'll have the full monty, if you please."

Ben lifted the food from the fridge and placed it on the worktop. It was only when he had closed the fridge door that he turned to face them. They were leaning against the cupboard, side by side, arms folded, feet crossed like a couple of swells in a Fred Astaire dance sequence. Delaney broke away and opened a unit. "Any bread, Ben? I'm starving."

"Don't think so. It all depends if Mrs Robinson remembered."

"She did," said Delaney, rising triumphantly with a loaf of Nimble in his hand. "Not the most filling, but it will do nicely. What a fine woman she is. Is she married?"

"She is, happily," said Ben. "And you know it." He'd come to the conclusion that they knew everything about anyone associated with him. If he stopped to think about it, he would be appalled by their intrusion into his life, and those around him, so he refused to stop and think. There would be time for that when all this was over.

While Ben cooked, they chatted. It wasn't deep and meaningful. It was more matter of fact. That's what Delaney and Sebastian dealt in. Flights of fancy were not in their nature. Nothing they said was a surprise to Ben. Sebastian spoke of early morning tea and presents from children and Edward Holton who sat in his car and cried, passing comments and moving on.

Delaney sniffed the air and talked of stomachs thinking that their throats had been cut. He hadn't had a bacon sandwich for months. Sebastian reminded him he'd had one that morning in the transport café down the road. When did they sleep, thought Ben?

It all appeared so perfectly normal that Ben almost expected Delaney to crack open the beers and for them to ensconce themselves in front of the television to watch the football. Ben could imagine them in heated dispute over that penalty decision and that disallowed goal. And further beers would be opened and they'd laugh about the referee being a wanker and everyone would agree on that.

Then things got serious.

The dirty dishes lay in the sink, Ben saying he'd wash them later. Sebastian claimed his chair, leaving Delaney to sit with Ben on the settee. The mood changed. The plan was unfurled.

"We don't deal in paper, Ben," said Sebastian. "It's too dangerous. We don't want anything to come back and haunt you. Or us."

"So I hope you've got your memory hat on," said Delaney.

"I'm all ears," said Ben.

Sebastian began. "We like to keep things simple. One thing flows into the next. Once you've got one bit, the rest will follow. You've arranged to go to Tom's house tomorrow?"

"That's right. I'm staying overnight."

"No, you're not," said Delaney. "You're driving down there tomorrow and your car is staying overnight. It will sit in its position on the drive and won't move until you're back, job done. If necessary, neighbours will be witness to you not having moved from the house. They suspect you're spending quality time with your ex future father-in-law."

Sebastian took over. "By ten thirty, Tom will have gone to bed. He's normally asleep by eleven, so that gives him plenty of time. All you have to tell him is that when he wakes the following morning, you won't be there. He need not worry. You'll be back by midnight. Just to reassure us, Ben. Tom can be trusted, can't he?"

"Completely," Ben replied. "If he had the opportunity, he'd take my place. Willingly."

Sebastian nodded his head a few times and threw his hair back from his face. "Just after midnight, take a rucksack complete with the usual snack and water, leave the house and walk to the end of the road. A car will pull alongside and you will get into the back seat. It will be a long journey, so sleep. There will be a blanket on the seat next to you. You will arrive at Luton Airport between six o'clock and six thirty."

"Luton Airport?" asked Ben.

"Where you will catch the eight o'clock Easyjet flight to Dortmund, Germany."

"Germany?"

Delaney spat the words. "That's where Jimmy Buller now resides. He was shunted over there to keep him away from his estranged wife and children. For their protection. The army is deciding what to do with him. They won't need to. You'll get to him first."

Ben had not wanted to say anything banal, but he couldn't help it. "I've never been to Germany."

"Always a first time," said Delaney.

"But I can't speak German."

"You won't have to say a word," Sebastian assured him. "With the blanket on the back seat of the car will be your passport, your driving licence, your ticket and a pen. Sign illegibly the licence and passport. Anything passes for a signature nowadays. From that moment, you will be John Cooper. That's what your passport will say. When you arrive at Dortmund, the German customs will be a bit methodical. They'll check everybody's passport, not just yours. There'll be a queue, so it may take you a bit of time to get through. It's the Germans being German, nothing else. They won't suspect anything and they won't ask you why you're going to their wonderful country. They're used to English people arriving and departing on the same day. That's what Easyjet is for. Okay so far?"

"Yes," said Ben.

"When you're through customs, go to the Europcar desk. Simply say your name, show your driving licence, sign the forms in the same illegible way you've signed your passport and you'll be handed a key for a hire car. It's already paid for. No credit card required. On the front seat of the car will be a map and directions to take you to Hampshire Barracks near Dusseldorf. You're a good driver and you've driven left hand drive before, so there won't be any problems."

Ben was confident before this conversation, but now his confidence was as high as it could go. Sebastian and Delaney were telling him he *would* do these things, not *could* do them. They were saying there *won't* be problems, not there *shouldn't* be problems. They had confidence in him, so why shouldn't he have it in himself. He'd used the same techniques with children. It worked.

"There won't be," Ben heard himself saying.

"Good. On the map, close to Hampshire Barracks, you will find a Lidl supermarket marked lightly in pencil. Park in the car park, in the middle of other cars if you can. In the boot of the car, you will find some running gear, complete with woolly hat and training shoes, your size. There's a McDonald's next to Lidls. The toilet is in the entrance hall. Go in, change into the running gear and leave your other clothes in the boot of the car."

It was Delaney's turn. "Now you're going for a run, laddie."

"How far? I've not been doing much lately."

"About two miles. Enough to get a sweat on. Enough for the guards on the gate to think you're coming back into barracks following a run. As you're going through the gates, choose the left hand side. The guards are on the right. It's more than likely they'll just let you in, especially if you time it for when a car is being checked. If he takes a longer look, look natural. Smile, say you're too old for this sort of thing and reach down to your pocket for your ID card. There will be one in the right hand pocket under the name of John Cooper and it will pass scrutiny, but it will be best if your false name is used as little as possible. It's ninety-nine percent certain that if you're wearing a hat, looking knackered and sweaty, he won't even check it. He'll just take you as one of the hundred or so that run in and out of the barracks every day."

"Will it be that simple?" queried Ben.

"Easy. I've done it myself a thousand times, some legitimate and some not. Security's a joke at these places. Use it to your advantage. Once you're in, take a left as you enter the barracks. The Sergeants' Mess is eighty yards down that road on the left. There's a security code to get in. It's 6645. Easy to remember. 66 for the year we beat the Germans in the World Cup Final and 45 for when the Second World War came to an end. Sergeants living in a fellow NATO country have the most sensitive sense of humour."

Sebastian carried on. "There will be few people around, if any. Most sergeants are married men and live in married quarters off camp. Most singlies staying in the Mess are allowed home for the Christmas holidays. If you do see anyone, say, "Morning" and keep walking. They won't bother you. They'll probably be hung over from the night before.

Strange faces are common place in Messes. That's what they're mostly used for: visitors on courses or short term, unaccompanied detachments. If you feel the pressure rising and need a place of sanctuary, there's a toilet at the end of the corridor. You can see it from the entrance."

"Do you think I'll need a place of sanctuary?" asked Ben.

"We're covering every possibility, just in case," Sebastian replied. "I can guarantee that you'll run through the gates, walk into the Mess, do your deed and leave. There will be no hitch, I promise you."

"Ah, yes. The deed," said Delaney with relish. "By the toilet is a communal kitchen. Fully open the cutlery drawer. Behind the tray that's inside it, you will find a key and a very small brown bottle, unlabelled. Buller's room number is twenty-six, which, coincidentally, is your birth date. Easy to remember. Let yourself in with the key. There will be a glass of water on the bedside table. Empty the contents of the bottle into the glass. It will mix immediately, leaving no trace, no discolouration. No stirring will be required. There is no need to touch anything else. You will leave the room, lock it and exit the Mess."

"And where is Buller when all this is taking place?" Ben asked. "Is he lying in bed and saying, 'Sure, Ben, help yourself to the water, pour the contents of the bottle in it and I won't mind one little bit'?"

Sebastian, ignoring the hint of sarcasm in Ben's voice, said, "Buller is a creature of habit. When he is off duty, as he will be on the twenty-fourth of December, he always sleeps late and then goes for a run at one thirty. He takes exactly one hour. Anything less would be unmanly. When he returns, he drinks the water he has left, has a quick shower, dresses and goes to the bar. Every time."

"Which means, laddie, that you will have to be running through those gates between one forty and ten past two. Too early and you run the risk of meeting Buller on his way out. Too late and he will catch you red-handed. Buller, the creature of habit, will play his part. You make sure you play yours."

"We're confident you will, Ben. You have plenty of time, there's no need to rush."

"What do I do with the key and bottle?" asked Ben.

"Bring both of them out with you. They're so small they won't be noticed in your pocket. The guard will have changed by then, so the new guard will presume you're just starting your run. IDs are never checked when leaving a military establishment. Go back to McDonald's, change your clothes in the toilet and place the key and the bottle in the bin. They will be removed within seconds of your car leaving McDonald's car park. Drive straight back to Dortmund Airport."

Delaney threw out a warning. "Nice and steady in built-up areas. That's where the police are at their keenest. In Germany, a yellow sign with the town name on it denotes you are entering a fifty kilometres an hour area. You won't see the number fifty anywhere, so remember. We don't want Europcar chasing up John Cooper for speeding. We want John Cooper as anonymous as possible. By the way, if you're feeling hungry by this time, there's a McDonald's about three hundred metres from Dortmund Airport. Big Mac is the same in any language."

"Your return flight is at five minutes to seven," said Sebastian. "Be there for half past five. Leave the keys, the map and the directions in the car. They will be dealt with. Inside the airport, security will be tight. It's probable, not possible, that they will stop you and frisk you. Don't worry, they do this with forty percent of passengers. You've got nothing to hide, so there's no problem. As I said before, they have a lot of passengers travelling out and back on the same day, so it's not unusual for them. When you arrive back in Luton, you will be met by a man with a board bearing your name. Remember, it's Cooper you're looking for, not Price. He will drive you back to Tom's road. Leave the passport, remnants of your ticket and the driving licence with the blanket on the back seat. That's it. The job's done. Go back to Tom and Doris and enjoy your Christmas Day."

Ben stood and strolled around the room, head down, forefinger gently moving horizontally along his lips. This was what he did when he was deep in thought, when he was preparing himself. Some people screw their face into various contortions when they are concentrating, but Ben applied the opposite technique. Relaxed muscles are working muscles. Tense muscles are not. He'd read this in a golf book written by a sports psychologist. Ben found that the ball went further and more accurately when he was relaxed.

When he was a student, he was dragged along by his roommate to a visiting hypnotist. As luck would have it, he was picked as a subject and sat, along with nine other people, at the front of the room. Just for the hell of it, to be bloody-minded, he decided to test the theory. He relaxed his muscles and thought only of his dream of one day owning a sports car. He never listened to a word the hypnotist said. That evening, he was the only subject who did not take his pants down.

Listening to Sebastian and Delaney, he had listed important words in his mind. Now he recalled them. Passport, John Cooper, queue, Europcar, McDonald's, woolly hat, 13.40, smile, 6645, kitchen, 26, water, 14.10, bin, frisk, Cooper, passport. He went through them again and again. When he was satisfied, he stopped and leaned against the mantelpiece. He looked at Sebastian and Delaney.

"Do you want to hear my list?" he asked.

"Go ahead," said Sebastian.

Ben began with passport and finished with passport. And when he had finished, he went through them again. And again. And again. There was no arrogance in the repetition, no seeking of approval. It was his way of ingraining every detail into his mind, so that he would never forget. Like the beauty spot below Lynn's left eye.

It was Delaney who broke the sequence. "Aye, but laddie, can you do it backwards?" he asked, intimating, in his own way, that Ben might be ready.

"Learning it backwards won't help me kill Jimmy Buller," said Ben.

*

Ben allowed the water to flow into the sink. Placing his hand over the mixer tap, he waited for the coldness to affect the palm of his hand. The habit was a throwback to his student days when it could take a few minutes before the water was cold enough and clear enough to drink. Now, it took just a few seconds.

Filling all three glasses, he placed them together triangularly, another student practice perfected in the student bar midst crowds of beer swilling rugby players, and lifted them between both hands.

"Want a hand?" asked Delaney who had followed him into the kitchen.

"No, it's okay. I've got them," replied Ben. They made their way back to the front of the house, Delaney talking as they went.

"Everything clear, Ben?" he asked.

Ben placed the glasses, without a drop being spilt, on the table that housed the place mats. "So many questions, Mr Delaney. I thought I was the inquisitive one."

"Touché," said Delaney. He lifted one of the glasses and took a sip. "Best drink in the world. Full of all the goodness nature has to offer. Cleanses the mind as well as the body."

"I never really took you for a water drinker. More of a beer man I would think," said Ben.

"Not when I'm working." Delaney drank again, half the glass this time in equal swallows. He lifted the glass and looked at Ben through the distorted water. "Of course, in my line of work, you learn by experience. The one requirement is that the mind has to be crystal clear. Otherwise, you're dead. It has to be alert, active to the point of hyper, but not quite. Situations arise, some unplanned for, and they have to be dealt with. A clear mind gives you that micro second which can mean the difference between seeing your loved ones again and breathing your last breath on earth. Make no bones about it, Ben, I've been one breath away from death on many occasions and survived. Why? Because I was alert to the dangers, but not frightened by them." Delaney took another sip and returned to gaze at Ben through the distortion. "Luck plays its part. I lost three good friends doing the same job as me. Two were careless and the other one could have been me. So I rode my luck and got even luckier, but never foolhardy. After a while, it became a way of life. Some would say my life was dangerous. I would call it normal."

It was unusual for Delaney to talk about himself, out of character. He would drift into the background when Sebastian recalled his achievements, as if embarrassed. But now he had followed Ben purposefully and opened himself up. There was reason to everything they did, but as yet, the reason for this was unclear. One thing was for sure. This was the first time Sebastian and Delaney had been apart and Delaney had grabbed the chance to speak to him alone.

Ben had also noticed that, when he returned to the front room, Sebastian was not there. He wondered where he was, but he was not that curious that he felt the need to ask. He was beginning to challenge his own curiosity, separate it from that which he was required to know. Delaney continued to view him through the glass.

They remained alone. Ben took the positive approach. "Nice speech, Delaney," he said. "But why shroud your doubts in mystery? Let's be up front. What you really meant to say was that you don't think I'm ready for this. It took you years to master this killing lark and you don't think I can just go across to Germany and do it."

He took a step closer to Delaney and slowly moved the glass to one side with the back of his hand. Ignoring the intensity in Delaney's eyes, he looked back at him. "Let me tell you this, unequivocally. I'm going to pour the contents of the brown bottle into Buller's glass and he is going to die. I'm going to kill another human being for the first time in my life. The reason? It's personal to me. That's what you told me, Delaney, and you are right. And there lies the difference. It took you years to get used to killing. And the reason? Nothing was ever personal to you. Never."

Delaney looked away from Ben towards the empty fire in the grate. His eyes lifted to look at the smiling faces of two lovers on holiday. "That's where you're wrong, laddie," he mumbled.

"Unequivocally, Ben," shouted Sebastian as he made his way into the room. "Excellent choice of words." Ben was unaware how long he had been standing there, how much he had heard, but nothing seemed to be spontaneous with these two. They organised meticulously and left nothing to chance. Maybe Sebastian thought that Delaney had overstepped the boundary. Maybe his interruption was necessary. Maybe they were introducing Ben to the human side of Delaney's character. Or maybe it was part of the plan.

For a brief moment, when Sebastian had disturbed them, Ben had looked away from Delaney, but now he returned directly to his eyes. Delaney had allowed Ben a glimpse of his deepest thoughts, those so deeply hidden that they rarely emerged from their miserable tomb. As the tension between them began to subside, Ben recognised that something had passed between them that he had not seen before. Ben had always respected Delaney, but sensed the feeling was not mutual. Until now.

*

Over three glasses of water, they sought more possible hitches and solved them.

Now that Ben had heard the plan, he realised that Doris and Jo would be back from their Christmas visit before he returned from Luton. "Lynn had a friend who lived in the next village. Tom could say I was visiting her," said Ben.

"And does Doris ever bump into this friend of Lynn's?" asked Sebastian.

"Rarely. I suppose she may see her in the shops from time to time, but it's unlikely."

"Rarely and unlikely were not the words we wanted to hear Ben," said Delaney. "Never and impossible would have been far better."

Sebastian concurred. "The fewer people who know about this, the more chance of success. We need to eliminate anyone who is not essential." He quickly retracted his misuse of the word. "When I say eliminate, I really mean exclude."

The conversation was more relaxed now. Humour wavered below the surface and emerged from time to time. They were smiling at the same things, laughing even. It was something that could not have happened before this day. There was always a nervousness about trusting each other, but now that the plan had emerged, they were aware of their roles and capabilities. If they each performed them well, then Mrs Buller would no longer have anything to fear from her husband.

Ben understood the point Sebastian was making. "You need something very simple Ben," he said. "Your alibi needs to put you on your own with no witnesses. No-one who can discredit your story."

"Okay," Ben answered. "How does this sound? Since Lynn's death, I've got into the habit of taking a walk down to the village and round the block back to the house. All footpaths, no roads. Just to be alone for a while."

"Perfect. Your first Christmas without Lynn. You need to be alone for a while. If Doris gets back before you, then that's what you're doing. She would understand."

"Will Tom cover for you?" asked Delaney.

"No problem," Ben replied.

*

"How long does Buller have after he has taken his medicine?" Ben asked. It was the one question left. All the others had been answered.

Sebastian clapped his hands, almost childlike. "At last. You have been remarkably patient, Ben. We were expecting you to ask about the compound before this time. We even thought it might have been one of the sticking points."

"There are no sticking points," Ben interrupted.

"Not anymore," said Delaney, somewhat annoyed, but not at Ben. "But there have been on the way." He held out his hand towards Sebastian. It contained a five pound note. Sebastian took it, straightened it, folded it neatly and placed it in the top pocket of his jacket, hiding it from view. Delaney continued, looking at Ben. "And by the way, why did you have to ask about the bloody compound? There was no need. I could have told you when he was out of the room. You've just lost me a fiver."

"I didn't really ask about the compound, as you call it. I asked how long Buller had got."

Delaney's eyes lit up. He was a child again and all his Christmases had come at once. He looked towards Sebastian, but didn't

101

have to say anything. The five pound note was already on its way back to its previous owner.

"When you've finished your childish little game, I wouldn't mind an answer," said Ben. For a moment, he believed he was the only professional there. Things soon got back to normal.

"After the compound has been absorbed into the body," said Sebastian, "there will be no reaction for around six hours. It will then begin to take effect. This will give you ample time to leave the area and leave the country. You will probably be in the air when Buller feels the first symptoms."

"And what will those symptoms be?" asked Ben.

"Why do you want to know that?" asked Delaney. "All you need to know is that it will work and Buller will die."

"I just want to know how I'm killing him."

With a shrug of the shoulders, Delaney responded, holding nothing back. "The compound stimulates a heart attack. When everything kicks off, the end will be rapid. He'll feel dizziness, then pressure around the chest, a squeezing sensation that will spread to his shoulder and probably his jaw. At first, he won't realise what's happening to him and when he does, it will be too late. You see, severe pain is not always a symptom of a heart attack, a quarter of them are referred to as being silent attacks. They creep up, disguised as heavy indigestion, and that's what Buller will feel at first. He'll be dead within an hour. If it's any consolation to you, Ben, if it makes you feel better, he won't suffer too much. He'll die thinking he's got bad indigestion."

For some reason, Ben had imagined poisoning him, convinced himself of it. The stimulation of a heart attack had come as a surprise to him. It had knocked him off balance. He remembered his father's heart attack and the pain he suffered, an intense pain that gripped his entire body, a memory Ben would keep with him always. There was a brief moment of guilt, but it was so brief it failed to surface, replaced as it was by anger that this man was going to die in the same way, but not suffer as his father had. It was a further reminder that life was not fair, but there again Ben had known this for some time.

Sebastian leaned forward on the chair that he had claimed as his own. He held his position until Ben noticed him waiting. "You have that inquisitive look on your face again," said Sebastian. "Ask your questions. There must be no secrets, no doubts."

"It's nothing to do with the plan and its implementation. All that will work out okay. It's just that I'm naturally ...."

"Curious," interrupted Delaney.

"That's right."

Sebastian repeated, "Ask your questions."

"Okay. Will this drug, this compound, be traceable after death?" asked Ben.

Delaney shook his head. "Impossible. It has been well tested, both in trials on animals and on humans. It has a one hundred percent success rate. We told you, we don't deal in failure. If we were not completely certain that this drug would work, we would not use it. And before you become all moralistic on us, you heard me right. It has been used to kill certain individuals the world is better off without. You're not testing a product here, Ben; you're using a certified death drug."

Ben shook his head. A few days earlier he had been drifting through his desperate life until it ended, the sooner the better. He was on a course of self-destruction. His mind was shattered into a million pieces and his liver was deteriorating rapidly. He could never have foreseen that he would be learning of compounds that effectively stimulate heart attacks and kill people undetected.

"It just seems so outrageous that this could be developed without public knowledge. How did the media not hear about this?"

Delaney laughed. "The media think they're so smart. Smart arses more like."

Sebastian explained. "Picture an iceberg containing every British secret. About one third of the total mass of ice is visible. The great British press only know the tip of what they can see. And they only know that much because they're allowed to know it. The iceberg never relinquishes its secrets unless it wants to."

"And that's a bit more you've learnt about the real world, laddie," said Delaney.

Sebastian stretched his legs. "Have you ever noticed that when the British go to war, they always hold back a little at the start of the campaign. Why? They've done the training, they've got the planning sorted. What they haven't got is all the equipment. Sure, they've got what they've been training with, but when the crunch comes, out come the secret gizmos and gadgets they have never seen before. They need time to get to know them. Hence the delay."

"Which is different from the Yanks," interrupted Delaney. "The new stuff comes out and then it's gung ho, let's kill them all. It's like a fucking games console to them. Trouble is they haven't got used to the new equipment and kill a few of ours and theirs along the way."

Sebastian pulled Ben back to the present. "This particular compound hasn't been used during conflict. It's specifically designed to use on individuals. If you like, it's a peacetime solution for sentencing certain people who will, in the future, be a danger to life and interests. It's preventative as well as cure."

"But who would invent such a thing?" Ben asked.

"It was a collaboration between Britain and the United States."

Delaney wiped imaginary sweat from his brow. "Thank God, at the moment it's in the hands of the military. If the politicians ever got to know of its existence, they'd be dishing it out like candy from a sweet store."

"Doesn't Oscar Baker know about it?" asked Ben.

"He doesn't even know about us. Remember, hear no evil, speak no evil," Sebastian replied.

Ben accepted what they said, rose from the settee, lifted the glasses and like the good host that he was, asked, "Refills?"

They nodded their acceptance. Ben turned his back on them, but continued to question. "Won't the doctor be suspicious? After all, Buller is a superfit soldier who regularly exercises."

Sebastian answered. "All the symptoms will be clear cut. There will be no other explanation for his death. Okay, there are bound to be questions asked, but easily answered. For example, there are two facts about heart attacks that are widely known in the medical profession, but not amongst the general public. In northern regions of the world, heart attacks occur more regularly in the winter months. The reason is still unclear. It may be the diet, more fat to keep warm, or it may be the cold, but for whatever reason, north European doctors expect more heart attacks in the winter months. The second fact is that, although keeping fit is generally regarded as being good for you, there are some people for whom extensive fitness regimes are in the long run, bad for you. The symptoms won't show until it's too late. That is, the patient will already be dead. On the surface, Buller seems okay, but he's had a tough time recently. Separated from his wife, Christmas away from the kids, accused of something he says he didn't do. All this increases stress levels, sometimes to an unsustainable high. Something's got to give. His heart. Remember the drug is undetectable. Put all that lot together and a verdict of death by natural causes will be accepted."

Delaney cast his four pennyworths. "And remember one other thing. Buller has outlived his usefulness with the British Army. He's now a liability. His death will mean there's one less problem to deal with. They won't probe too hard. No-one will want them to."

Ben returned with full glasses. He assumed they both wanted water again. "What's the secret of good comedy, Ben?" asked Sebastian.

"Good comedy?"

"Yes."

"Well, I suppose ..."

"Timing, Ben. Timing. And it's the same with this operation. On which date will Buller die?"

"Twenty-fourth of December," Ben replied.

"Correct. The most important date in the whole year for Germans. It's their Christmas Day, the evening when presents are opened and the family gets together. The one day when Germans like to be at home with the log fire burning and the whole family around. The day when the visiting doctor is less likely to linger, to discover problems. Especially when the causes are so clear cut. Timing, Ben. Perfect timing."

Ben wondered how they had made the leap from Jimmy Buller's death to the secret of good comedy, but somehow it made sense. He glanced across to Delaney, hoping for some kind of reaction. His eyes were closed. He had become disinterested in the conversation, more so with the constant questions. He had decided to exempt himself from the proceedings.

"No stone has been left unturned," continued Sebastian with a confident air. "BMWs left in driveways, false passports, false names, long walks late at night. None of it will be necessary. Backups are only required when things go wrong," he commented as way of an explanation. And that was all that needed to be said. They all knew that the plan and execution of it would succeed.

Jimmy Buller would be dead in two day's time.

23rd December

Ben slept in, but this time the drink had nothing to do with it. Mrs Robinson did not come calling. When he woke, he did not find her at the side of his bed with a mug of tea in her hand, apologising for being there. She had grown accustomed to his routine, even during the holidays.

He had told her the previous day that it was the last day of the school term and didn't have to mention that the best thing about the first day of the school holidays was that he could lie in. This was especially true at the end of the winter term, which was usually accompanied by cold weather. There was truly nothing to get up for, especially this particular year. The beginning of the day could be postponed until later. He preferred it that way.

After Sebastian and Delaney had left, he had made a chronological list of what he had to do, in his head of course. Nothing written down. He had worked backwards from leaving Tom and Doris' house around midnight, giving himself a few hours to watch the television with Tom in the evening following tea which Doris would undoubtedly have prepared and previous to that, an hour to travel to their house. He promised himself he would continue Lynn's tradition of having a tidy house for Christmas Day, even if they were elsewhere, so he allowed himself a couple of hours for the cleaning and dusting and hoovering. He would have a light lunch before that. All this meant that he would not have to move from his bed until eleven o'clock.

From within the duvet that curled around his head, his eyes searched for the red numbers on the alarm clock. He first saw the ten and then the forty-three. The red dots dragged the seconds along. By the time forty-four appeared, and Ben had counted every one of the sixty flashes of the red dots, he was awake and bored. Although he had planned eleven o'clock, he welcomed the flexibility that holidays brought, so he rose and made his way to the shower. Plans had to be changed if the necessity arose and he feared that if he stayed within his duvet tomb, he would think too much of the day ahead.

Too much thought could be bad for your health, he decided, as the water pounded onto his head. He intended to keep himself occupied in whatever way he could find. Robbie Williams entertained him from the radio, James Blunt told him he was beautiful and Madonna hinted that he might be a virgin touched for the very first time. He sang along with all of them.

He dried himself, mournfully, to Johnny Mathis seasonally singing of rays of hope when a child is born and shaved to Louis Armstrong attempting to convince him that this was a wonderful world. He almost succeeded. Try again in a couple of days, thought Ben.

When the presenter announced that they were about to play the best selling Christmas record of all time, Ben envisaged either 'White Christmas' or 'Do they know it's Christmas?' but couldn't bring himself to listen to either. He flicked the off button, entered Dire Straits Greatest Hits CD into the machine, heard Mark Knopfler hit the first few notes of 'Sultans of Swing' and his spirits were lifted again. He went to the bedroom to dress.

Opening the wardrobe door, he wondered what the best dressed murderer would be wearing nowadays and found himself discussing, with himself, whether anything black was suitable or would it make him look more guilty. He would look uncomfortable, too formal, in a shirt and tie, so he settled for the incongruous invisibility of blue jeans, black tee shirt, v-necked pullover and black shoes. The dark, winter coat, bought by Lynn on his last birthday, would complete the outfit. He would not win any fashion contests, but neither would he stand out in a crowd, no matter how big or small.

Scooping out six spoonfuls of his usual muesli breakfast and covering them with a fair portion of milk, he went into the lounge where he flicked on the television before sitting in Sebastian's chair. Assuming that everything went well, he could now reclaim it for himself. Sebastian and Delaney had left the room the previous night confirming that he would not see them again, although they would be with him every step of the way. Ben could not see how this was possible, but believed them anyway.

They had shaken hands, he had thanked them for everything they had done and they had asked him to take his seat again and stay there for five minutes while they left. He agreed. Delaney turned his back without a word and waited in the hallway. Sebastian took hold of the door handle, smiled a final smile full of teeth, left the room and closed the lounge door.

Ben, staring at his unreliable watch, watched the hands turn for five minutes exactly and realised he was now on his own, but not quite. He had wondered, on more than one occasion during the evening, if one of them, Delaney he would think, had remained in his house. He even listened out for him, but then decided that if he was there, it should be a comfort rather than an invasion. So he accepted it, whether he was there or not.

The television burst into life. The news was as depressing as ever. Warnings of pensioners dying from the forthcoming freezing temperatures, dogs that were not just for Christmas, wars all over the world and the annual natural disaster that had experts warning of everything from global warming to the end of the world. He finished his cereal in a daze, fearing the worst for the entire planet.

The planet could wait.

Everything he had listed chronologically was completed, chronologically. The timescale had been kept and he took a last look around the house before closing and locking the front door. Automatically, he looked across to the bay window and saw Mrs Robinson with her cheery smile and her mimed, 'Have a good Christmas.'

He waved, mimed in return and made his way to his BMW. Throwing the rucksack onto the passenger's seat and placing the carrier bag on the floor, he pulled himself into the driver's seat and turned the key. He had enough clothes for four days; in case Doris persuaded him to stay for longer, but thought they would not all be needed. Better to be safe than sorry though.

Casting a final wave in Mrs Robinson's direction, he pulled away down the road and visualised what lay ahead. He applied the pressure on the accelerator pedal and ran through his list from passport to passport.

The correct sequence was now second nature. All he had to do was put it into action.

*

It was a beautiful spot, peaceful and atmospheric. There was a calm that shrouded every blade of grass, every stone. A robin dashed from ground to holly bush and rested on the soft prickles at the end of the leaf, a perfect Christmas scene. Yew trees motioned slowly, protecting against evil, bowing the smallest of their branches in time to the distant music that drifted by on the changing wind.

Wearing his coat to combat the coolness of the wind, Ben stood, alone and silent. Although the buttons on his coat remained undone, his hands were in the pockets of his jeans, retaining their warmth. He failed to notice the robin or the nodding of the branches or the distant music.

He had remained motionless for ten minutes, but if he had been told that, he would not have known. He was immune to the passing of time. Staring endlessly at the ground, his feet firmly fixed, he was in a different place, removed from the present, recalling the past, anticipating the future. It was a place that did not yet exist for Ben, though he recognised the people there. His father and Lynn, standing alongside, like old friends, yet unknown to each other during their lifetime. Lynn placed her hand through the space between his father's ribcage and upper arm. She held him and pulled him closer. Their faces showed no signs of concern, yet they must have known of the journey on which he was about to embark. His father raised his free hand and waved towards him, raising his thumb in a gesture resembling approval. In the same moment, Lynn touched her lips with her fingers, then blew across them as she did when they parted. Ben felt the gentle breeze across his face. They became less distinct, more transparent, until they eventually drifted away from view.

They had brought him comfort when he had most needed it, visiting him and encouraging him in what lay ahead. Had he imagined these things? They were as clear as the headstone that bore Lynn's name and told of the date she died. The weather had already affected the gold

110

lettering that was her name, the cutting edge of a solitary stone scarring its perfection.

Ben crouched down. Delicately, he brushed his fingers across her name and cleansed it, before tracing the letters, each at a time, and flicking the dirt away. He rested the palm of his hand on the granite headstone and leaned against it. Closing his eyes, he silently asked for the strength he would need over the next day and for the forgiveness he would require for the remainder of his life.

The temperature was falling, the cold wind slicing the air like a knife. Suddenly, Ben shivered uncontrollably.

It was not the cold that forced him to shiver.

Looking up, he saw the tall spire of the church, immaculately carved in curves and crosses, pointing heavenwards. Perfectly symmetrical, it reached upwards from the heavy doors below. Turning the heavy iron ring on the doors, he entered. The organ played its melancholy tune. He rested at the head of the aisle, gazing at the light beaming through the stained glass windows, highlighting the slight, pained figure hanging by nails from the cross. Blood trickled from the thorns surrounding his head and hung there for eternity on the creased, weary lines of his forehead. He died an exhausted man, exhausted from failure, failure to change centuries-old thinking, thinking that remained, embedded in Man, centuries after his death. He was God's son, on earth to challenge the established teaching of the old Judaism. Ben found himself apologising to the man in the window. Tomorrow, thought Ben, I will not 'turn the other cheek.' I will have my 'eye for an eye,' my vengeance, my revenge.

Turning away from the wooden pews, he left the church and closed the doors behind him. Despairing notes from the organ followed him along the path between the headstones until he reached the lychgate, where they drifted away on the breeze. One last look towards Lynn. One last apology. One last thank you.

*

Conversation was limited.

Ben did not speak of planes or Germany. He spoke only of time and absence.

Tom rose from his seat at ten thirty, pausing briefly at the door. "Be safe," he said, without turning, and went to bed.

24th December

Ben closed the door silently, chose the lawn rather than the gravelled driveway and stepped over the small wall onto the road. He knew the road well, even in the dark, straight for a hundred yards or so and then a slight bend to the left before reaching the junction.

There was no delay. The car drifted into position as he reached the end of the road. He opened the back door, received no welcome from the driver, threw his rucksack to the other side and sat next to the blanket.

He opened the blanket and found the passport, driving licence, ticket and pen. He opened the passport and saw a recent photograph of himself staring back at him. John Cooper. He signed, illegibly, and placed the items in his rucksack. The car pulled away.

Remembering it would be a long journey, he wrapped the blanket around his front, closed his eyes and attempted his first sleep of the night. He slept fitfully, which was no surprise, but he still had to be wakened with a tap on his knee from the driver as the car pulled in front of the airport terminal.

He folded the blanket and lifted his rucksack. Leaving the car, he checked he had everything and issued his thanks. There was no reply. The car pulled away.

There was plenty of time to spare, but he decided to book in early, but not too early, and go through to departures, where he would become as insignificant as possible. The passport passed inspection. Ben thought that a newspaper would offer a modicum of cover, so he bought one and turned to the sports pages. Before long, he heard his flight being announced. He joined the queue, tickets thirty one to sixty, in the middle, no communication, no eye contact.

Boarding the plane, he made his way to the back row and sank into the window seat. He prayed that no children would descend upon him. For a couple of reasons. He needed a break from them and they seemed to attract attention to themselves. Which was the opposite to what he wanted.

A pretty, blonde haired German girl placed her very neat backside on the seat next to him. Fortunately, she was recovering from what had obviously been a very entertaining evening and she needed the rest. She closed her eyes and was asleep before the plane left the runway.

Ben wondered if she was part of the plan, planted in that seat by Sebastian and Delaney. He tried not to stare in case she woke to find this Englishman ogling her, but he was able to look without suspicion and concluded that he did not recognise her. That didn't mean a thing. He left the plane none the wiser.

Joining the queue at the customs desk, he waited to have his passport checked. The blonde haired girl was in front of him. She looked more awake for the sleep, but the alcohol was still in her bloodstream and she swayed slightly from side to side. He thought about switching queues in case she collapsed, which would result in Ben breaking her fall, which would result in heads being turned in his direction. In the ensuing commotion, John Cooper would be easily identified. But he doubted whether the Germans would appreciate a queue dodger, and that might create a reaction, so he chose the lesser of two evils and stayed where he was.

The officials were very thorough, viewing each passport with equal suspicion, occasionally pushing a few keys on the keypad and checking something on the monitor. This did not concern Ben. Sebastian and Delaney would have thought of that.

The blonde-haired girl handed over her passport. She rested her hand on the glass of the booth, but swayed a little still. She was given a closer inspection, checked against her photograph. Keys were punched, passport handed back and she moved on. There was no change in expression on the official's face.

Ben stepped forward. A quick glance at the photograph and the passport was returned. Ben moved through, without suspicion, without delay. Surely, the official wasn't one of theirs as well.

At that moment, Ben didn't care. He thought this might have been one of the more difficult moments, but he had been ushered on with the minimum of fuss. On the other hand, Ben warned himself against complacency. Sebastian and Delaney couldn't organise everything. He mustn't presume everything would simply slot into place, that everyone he saw was on the payroll. That would be impossible. Wouldn't it?

He walked by the girl, who was now leaning against the wall and looking seriously ill. Of course, an English gentleman would have stopped and asked if she needed help, but John Cooper was no gentleman. He couldn't be.

The Europcar desk was easily found, its stark green lights beckoning him. "John Cooper," he said.

"Welcome to Germany, Herr Cooper," said the man behind the desk.

Ben grunted something he hoped was completely indistinguishable as he handed over his driving licence. The man smiled. A form appeared from nowhere with squiggles for initials and signatures. Ben duly obliged. Hiring a car was the same the world over. The local language was not necessary. Just sign and initial and the car was yours.

The car was a Mercedes, which Ben thought was overgrand until he realized that almost every other car on the road was a Mercedes and almost every other one was a BMW. He blended in perfectly.

The map was on the front seat of the car, along with directions to Hampshire Barracks. He compared the two, running his finger along the roads on the map as he followed the directions. There was a thin pencil circle close to the barracks, Ben presuming this was the Lidl supermarket where he would park the car. He checked his watch. He had plenty of time.

German autobahns are fast and easy. One runs into the next with perfect efficiency. Ease the foot off the accelerator as you drive on the slip road, spot a gap in the traffic and power on. Ben found himself cruising at one hundred and forty kilometres an hour, ninety miles an hour he calculated, and being overtaken on a regular basis.

Grannies in old Mercedes were passing him by, their heads appearing over the steering wheel, so that only their grey hair was visible. He imagined them being propped up by three or four cushions on the seat and their feet reaching down to elongated pedals.

Ben was a natural driver. He soon understood the difference between the M6 near Manchester and the A2 near Dortmund. Here, you could go as fast as you liked, nipping in and out of the usual two lanes of carriageway, with hardly a signal. Drivers drove as they lived their lives: push, push, I am always right – until you stood up to them, until you nipped out in front of them, then they would relent and drop back allowing you through. There was an expected courtesy within this motorway madness. Drive hard, allow others to do the same. Ben enjoyed himself.

Before long, he had left the racetrack and entered normal roads with yellow signs denoting town entry. Fifty kilometres an hour, thought Ben, and he dropped speed accordingly. John Cooper was being the perfect driver, even though he hadn't seen a solitary police car.

Lidl supermarkets were becoming an increasing sight on England's streets, so when he saw the blue and yellow sign in the distance, he recognised it immediately. He pulled into the car park, finding a gap between the mass of cars.

Turning off the engine, he suddenly felt a quickening in his heart beat. He lifted his hand to his forehead and wiped a couple of beads of sweat away. He had gone through the routine of this day, first in his head and now in reality, and at last, the enormity of what he was about to do appeared to be affecting him.

There was no conscious reaction, no expectation that when he pulled into the Lidl car park, he would begin to sweat a little and his heart would race. It simply happened. Ben analysed why and he was satisfied. He had no fear of what he was about to do. He remained intent on killing Jimmy Buller. There was no turning back from that. It was why he was near Dusseldorf for the first time in his life, for that one purpose, and it would happen.

So, why the sweat and racing heart? Simple, he decided. It was an awakening of adrenalin. He had the rush, the buzz. It occurred at the most crucial times when extraordinary feats were required. It was his body feeding him with that extra element that might only be needed once in a lifetime. The body was capable of doing that.

He had once read of a man driving home, following his wife's car, when another car raced by, driven manically by a drug-fuelled teenager. He rammed into her car, forcing her down an embankment. The man saw his wife's car roll over, again and again and by the time it came to rest on its roof, the fire had already caught hold. He raced down the hillside and saw that his wife was motionless, yet breathing. She was wedged between the seat and the roof and could not be rescued. So where did he get the energy, the strength required to roll the car back onto its wheels? How was he able to pull the door from its hinges, release the suffocating seat belt and drag her to safety? The husband could not give an answer. He'd never been to the gym in his life. He was a banker, for God's sake, stuck behind a desk all day. Yet he had saved his wife's life. "Just as long as she doesn't expect the same vigour in the bedroom," he had quipped, making light of the adrenalin rush he had.

Ben checked his watch. Twelve thirty-five. Plenty of time. He ran through his list from passport to passport. And again. To pass the time. To keep his racing heart under some measure of control. Regulating his breathing, he felt his muscles beginning to relax and his heartbeat slowing. Closing his eyes, he repeated his list as if it was the shopping that Lynn had asked him to pick up. Thinking of Lynn helped. He relaxed and drifted. Relaxed muscles are working muscles, he told himself.

One o'clock. He flicked the catch to open the boot. He realised that he had not checked to see if the running gear was there. He presumed it would be. It was.

Sebastian and Delaney had not spent a fortune on him, not even washed the bottoms and the training jacket that he would wear. He was pleased to see that the running shoes were Adidas, but less pleased to see that they were splattered with mud. But, on reflection, all this was perfect. He would look particularly odd, draw particular attention to himself, if he ran through the gates wearing pristine running gear, shoes shining like a new pin. He remembered the ribbing team mates received if they entered the changing room and proceeded to draw new gear out of their bag. The guard on the gate would react in a similar way. New gear, clean gear, would draw attention. John Cooper didn't want that.

He changed in the McDonald's toilets and returned the rucksack, now containing his day clothes, to the boot of the Mercedes. Running had been replaced by drinking in his latest training regime, so he thought it best if he stretched his muscles into some semblance of action, reminding them of the concept of exercise. Gently, though, he told himself. It was as easy to twist or pull something in the warm-up as in the run itself.

Normal walking pace was around four miles an hour. That would be fifteen minutes for each mile. Delaney had said it was two miles to the barracks, so that would be about a twenty five minute run. At one fifteen he had stretched enough and began the run to the barracks.

The street names were easy to remember. Composers. Turning left out of the car park, he made his way along Mozart Strasse. At the end of the road, he turned left into Beethoven Strasse and headed away from the built up area into a more rural location. He knew he would be on this road for about ten minutes, so he relaxed and dropped into an easy rhythm.

The first bicycle was a bit of a surprise. The ringing of the bell made him jump. He turned and saw it approaching directly behind him. He moved to one side and let it pass. It was closely followed by a second and a third. All three of them disappeared into the distance, one behind the other on the red section of the pavement. For the first time, he noticed that there were grey and red sections running parallel along the entire length of the pavement. Glancing behind, he saw more bicycles, some of them overtaking, but immediately after they had done so, they once more returned to follow the red path. It was a variation on the Wizard of Oz. It didn't take a genius to work out that red was for bicycles, grey was for pedestrians. Ben stuck to the grey.

Turning right into Handel Strasse, he caught a glimpse of green fencing. As he approached, he noted the barbed wire entangled along the metal struts at the top of the fence. Green heavy plastic was attached to the fence, making it impossible to see through. Signs in German and

English noted that this was a military installation and entry was forbidden.

He ran on, increasing his pace now. Sweat ran down his face from under his woolly hat. His breathing became more rapid, his lungs gasping for more air. He knew that at the end of this long run of fencing was the camp gate. The guards would be waiting.

He ran the instructions through his mind. Delaney had insisted that security was a joke and that entry would be easy. Just look the part, Ben told himself. Look like a guy coming back from a long run in need of a shower and a drink.

He caught a glimpse of a gap in the greenness. Another hundred yards. Timing. The secret of everything was timing, Sebastian had said. He looked for the approach of a car. He slowed his pace, but he couldn't stop and wait. It would draw attention to himself. If no car appeared, then there would be no distractions for the guard and he would have to bluff it all the way.

Although his pace had slackened, his breathing had become more laboured and his heartbeat had increased. His throat was dry and he ran his tongue around the inside of his mouth to create more saliva. It made no difference. He could wait no longer. He had to go in.

And then salvation appeared in the form of a lorry, proudly declaring that Eddie Stobart was 'Delivering for Naafi.' It began its turn into the entrance. Timing. He pulled alongside the rear of the lorry and kept pace with it. Not too quick, not too slow. The guards would be on the right, Delaney had said, so he was in perfect position.

About fifty yards away, he could see the red and white barrier stretching across the width of the entrance, but there was a small gap for pedestrians on the left. He headed for it. The lorry slowed as it reached the barrier, trailer jerking as the breaking began. Ben retained his own pace. He was now closer to the front of the cab and there was no turning back. Look confident, as if you did this every day, he thought.

Without warning, the guard appeared around the front of the lorry. Dressed menacingly in black, handgun in his belt, he glanced in Ben's direction and raised an arm in his direction. Ben was already reaching for his pocket where he hoped John Cooper's ID would be. He hadn't checked. There was no need to. With a flick of his wrist, the guard waved his fingers back towards him, indicating Ben should proceed. Ben raised his hand in acknowledgment and continued his run beyond the barrier.

'Holy shit,' Ben thought. 'It's working. I'm in a military establishment with a false ID card. Now what the hell is next? At the junction, turn left. The Sergeant's Mess is eighty yards down that road on the left.'

Ben kept going. Sebastian and Delaney had good reason to have confidence in what they did. Sebastian had said that they were perfect. Ben had no reason to doubt it. The only untoward thing that had happened had been running on the red cycle path, hardly a reason for panic.

He slowed as he reached a nondescript, single-storey building with a double fronted glass door at the entrance. Now he walked in small circles, regulating his breathing and glancing at his watch as all runners do after a run. One forty-five. If Delaney was correct, Buller would be out of his room and on his own run by now. What was he thinking? *If* Delaney was correct. Of course Delaney was correct.

The security panel was by the door. Ben punched in 6645, heard the opening click and pushed on the bar that reached across the glass. He ran through his list.

At the end of the corridor, he could see the toilet door. Walking slowly, treading softly, he made his way towards it. The kitchen was alongside. He went in and headed directly for the sink, which was surprisingly clean. Maybe no-one had used it, maybe no-one was around. He pulled open the drawer, fully. The cutlery tray was a perfect fit, crammed against the side, with no room for anything else. He managed to stretch his fingers around the back and fumbled for the key and bottle. He found both. The size of the bottle surprised him, no bigger than his thumb nail. He eased both of them away from their hiding place and placed them in his pocket.

Turning back down the corridor, he sought number twenty-six. He placed the key in the lock, turned it gently and entered the room of Sergeant Jimmy Buller.

Ben was surprised. The room was in worse condition than the flat he had shared with three other boys during his student days. The walls were light green in colour, but there was evidence of many shades peering through. In one corner was a brown wardrobe and in the opposite corner was a set of drawers, brown of course. They were old, parts of the handles hanging loosely. Under them ran perfectly formed semicircles where the varnish had worn away with the constant scraping from the metal edges of the broken handles. They must have been hanging like that for years. The handles had never been replaced, the patches never re-varnished.

Between the two pieces of furniture was the metal bed. The last time Ben had seen something similar was a television reproduction of the dormitory beds in Tom Brown's Schooldays. A brown blanket could be seen through the holes in the green flowered bedspread.

There were no pictures on the cold walls, but then Ben thought the walls might not take a picture hook because of the damp within them. Apart from the larger dark patches on either side of the radiator, lighter coloured splashes littered the whole room. Ben tapped one of them with his knuckle, out of curiosity. He wiped the wet away from his finger with the palm of his hand.

He was reminded of the police station in Manchester with its peeling paint. Work for public services and this was what you were entitled to. Fight for Queen and country, put your neck on the line and this is what you come home to.

Cuttings from British newspapers flashed through his mind, stories he thought were exaggerated at the time. Soldiers in England had been removed from barrack blocks so that refugees could be housed. They lasted a month and then refused to live there because of the conditions. They were moved to hotel accommodation. The soldiers were re-instated. Not good enough for refugees, good enough for troops of the British Army.

One redeeming feature was the tidiness, with shoes beautifully polished and lined neatly under the bed, but this was due to the occupant, not the landlord. The bedspread with its holes was neatly laid on top of the bed, corners folded in perfect symmetry. Jimmy Buller had left the room to go for his run and he had left it immaculate. It was a credit to him.

To Ben, it didn't matter if his room was tidy or not.

He had killed Lynn and he would have to die.

Attached to the fixed wooden bedhead, matching the colour and condition of the rest of the furniture, was a shelf. The glass of water waited for Buller's return. Taking the brown bottle from his pocket, Ben unscrewed the top and emptied the contents into the water, ensuring the last drop fell by shaking it gently. The level rose slightly, but that was the only difference Ben could see. The colour of the water remained the same.

He pocketed the bottle and turned to leave, but something caught his eye.

Next to the glass on the shelf was a photograph. He recognised Jimmy Buller, sitting on a rock with his arm around a pretty brunette. His other hand was reaching down to rest on the shoulder of a young girl, perhaps five years of age. By her side was an older boy about nine years old holding on to the brunette's arm, which was draped across his chest. Ben presumed it was Buller's wife and children. All four of them were smiling. It was a photograph of a loving family unit, but on closer inspection, there were flaws. The brunette was leaning away from Buller, turning her shoulder in protection. The girl's hands were hanging low, as far away from Buller's hand as possible, and the boy was clinging tightly onto his mother's arm. There were smiles, but there was no laughter. This was a stage managed photograph and Buller was in control.

Ben was tempted to lift it from the shelf for a closer look, but remembered Delaney's warning, 'There is no need to touch anything.' So he didn't. He had been studying the photograph for some time and this had delayed his exit. He glanced down. There was still time. His watch showed five past two. He left the room, turned the key in the lock and made his way towards the glass door.

For a brief moment, he was stunned.

This wasn't supposed to happen.

Looking through the glass, he saw Buller, not ten yards away. He was leaning forward with extended arms, legs apart, stretching the hamstrings. His run was completed and he was warming down. Sweat showed through his green army tee shirt, the result of a vigorous work out, and his shorts rose high on his legs.

His head was low, the back of it towards Ben, but when he rose from his stretching, they would be in direct line with each other. Buller would see him and wonder why he was there, wonder why he was hesitating by the door.

Ben thought of turning, but where was he to go? The sanctuary of the toilet was too far away. The only key he had was to Buller's room. He couldn't go there. What if Buller stopped him and searched his pockets, found the key and the bottle? Put two and two together, the bottle and the glass of water, dragged him to his room and battered him? He would force Ben to drink and he would be dead in six hours.

This wasn't supposed to happen.

Ben's brain was working overtime, predicting reactions and consequences in split seconds, and yet his legs wouldn't move. His feet remained planted on the ground. Buller's head began to rise. It was all happening so slowly. Everything around Ben had hit the slow motion button. Ben felt his shoulders turn, but his head and feet remained where they were. Parts of his body seemed to know how to react, but were having problems convincing the others.

Buller was almost upright now and Ben watched as his neck began to straighten and his chin began to lift. They would soon be eye to eye and that would be the end of Ben. Buller had murdered before, so why would he not kill again?

And then he turned. Away from Ben. To the right. The rest of his body followed and he became erect, proud. He brought his ankles together, raised his head that extra notch, pulled his shoulders back and thrust his chest out at the front. His right hand left his side, pointed fingers and thumb forward and lifted upwards until the tip of the forefinger rested against the side of his forehead, just above the temple.

"Off duty, sergeant," Ben heard. "Put it down."

Buller dropped his hand and relaxed, legs astride, hands behind his back. "Natural reaction, sir," he said.

"And get out of that 'at ease' stance. Not necessary. You're out of uniform, man. How was the run?"

"Good today," Buller replied. "A bit faster than normal, I think. Must be the thought of Christmas, sir. You know, eat more, train more."

"Know what you mean. Must follow your example, man. Are you not going home then?"

"This is home, sir."

From around the corner of the building appeared an officer, dressed in full uniform. He made his way towards Buller, continuing his polite chitchat, Buller responding with answers but asking no questions. He was like a child. Speak when you're spoken to. It was the army's way.

Their conversation became quieter as they faced each other, the words less distinct. Ben knew he had to act fast. This distraction would not last forever. He slowly opened the door, stepped outside and closed the door behind him.

Buller must have heard the click as the catch slotted into place. There was a turning of his shoulders, the head following. Slow motion. For a brief second, Ben froze, but heard Delaney's instructions, 'Act naturally.' Buller was not yet facing him, had probably not seen him, except as a blur out of the corner of his eye. Ben needed to do something, not just stand there like a rabbit caught in headlights.

Without warning, a hand gripped his arm. Another hand pushed the centre of his back, between the shoulder blades. His body was thrust forward, forcing him into a run. His natural reaction was to resist, but he couldn't. He was moving forward and the figure by his side was whispering, "I'm getting too fucking old for this, laddie."

They ran together, away from the doors, passing close to Buller and the officer who was still talking. Ben looked across. He couldn't resist. Their eyes never met, but he was not disappointed. The job was done.

Beyond Buller, the officer raised his head. He could only be an officer of the British Army, such was his standing and poise. The floppy hair was hidden beneath the peaked cap, but Ben recognised the features that he had first encountered across a desk in a police station. 'We'll be with you all the way,' they had said.

*

There were the occasional whispered words. 'Steady, not too fast,' and 'Keep your pace,' and 'You do this everyday.' Delaney forced Ben into the steady rhythm expected at the beginning of a long run. They waved acknowledgement towards the new guard at the gate. Ben smiled as the guard held up his hand in return.

Only when they had passed the barrier did Ben take a look at his running partner. He was suitably dressed in full gear, hat and all. Sweat had already begun to form on his face and his breathing was laboured.

"I'll be okay when I get my second wind," said Delaney.

Ben thought this might be a touch of bravado, but much to his surprise, Delaney's breathing soon eased and he was able to keep pace with Ben as they made their way alongside the green fencing.

"At the end of this road," said Delaney, "you'll take a left and I'll go right. We'll give each other a nonchalant wave and never look back. We'll never see each other again, Ben. As promised."

He never once looked in Ben's direction as he talked. There was no eye contact and this was how it had to be. Because Delaney wanted it that way. Ben wanted to stop him and thank him, shake his hand, show his appreciation, but knew this was not in the plan. And the plan was everything.

As they neared the junction at the end of the road, Delaney ended their friendship in the only way Ben would have expected. "Buller's run was no quicker. Arrogant bastard. When you get home, buy a new fucking watch."

They turned away from each other and went their separate ways. Ben knew Delaney's hand was in the air as he heard him say, "Good job, laddie."

Ben ran on, never looked back, satisfied with this seal of approval from the master.

*

Dortmund Airport is a typically clean German airport. Remnants of cardboard coffee cups are instinctively placed in litter bins by their users and the occasional china plates that are used are whisked away from tables when their use is over. Tables are cleaned, awaiting the arrival of the next occupant.

There is constant movement from the cleaners who wheel their trolleys loaded with every conceivable cleaning aid for every conceivable situation. The cleaners are foreign workers, welcomed into Germany to perform the more menial tasks, like the influx of West Indian workers brought to England in the 1950s for the same purpose. A dozen languages pass between the cleaning staff alone.

The airport, like so many, had sprung up from nowhere on the back of budget airlines that flew passengers all over Europe for less than the cost of rail travel. Some of these were in the back of beyond, away from any city of any note, but Dortmund was the exception. It was well constructed and had pretensions of turning itself into an international airport. A quick check of the departures board showed that it was well on the way, destinations stretching beyond the borders of its own continent.

Ben checked the flight time. There was no delay. Good news. He wanted to be home now, to spend Christmas Day with Tom and Doris. It would be difficult, their first without Lynn, but necessary and comforting to be together.

Tom would want to know what had happened, but for his own sake, Ben had decided to tell him that the job was done and that Buller had paid for his crime. No details. The matter was over and the future had begun.

Glancing mindlessly over photographs in a magazine he had purchased, he relived his day. The watch was a problem. Everything else had gone according to plan.

As he had pulled away from the car park at Lidls, he had checked in his mirror for those retrieving the bottle and key. He had seen nothing. He had lingered awhile at the rental car drop-off point, but had seen no-one. He didn't expect to. Why should he? He was an amateur dallying in the world of the professionals. It was a world he was glad to be out of.

He dozed briefly on the plane, but it was a short flight and if truth be told, the day's events denied him the comfort of real sleep. After all, he had just killed someone. Premeditated. For Ben Price, this was not an everyday occurrence.

The plane landed and taxied to its waiting gate. He glanced at his watch as the stewardess reminded passengers of the one hour time difference, announcing local time to be five minutes to seven. Buller could be dead by now. If not, his demise would not be long away.

*

John Cooper showed his passport for the final time and moved through customs, such as it was. Passing through the sliding doors, there was the usual mass of relatives and friends collecting from the airport. Midst them all, Ben noticed the name Cooper, written in black on a white board and held at chest level.

He followed his man out of the terminal and towards the car park. There was no telling if he was the same driver who had brought him here through the night. Nondescript, emotionless. He had spent six hours with him in the confines of a car and only left him thirteen hours ago, but could not tell if he was the same man.

They reached the car. The rear door was opened for him and he slipped inside. Now he was back at Luton, in England amongst familiarity, he was more comfortable. He was safe. Surprisingly, Ben had felt little tension throughout the day, but it was present, because now it drained from him. He slumped into the seat and let go a deep sigh. His entire body relaxed. He vowed he would sleep on the journey home.

He heard the driver's door click open and clunk shut, but his eyes were already closing and his brain was already shutting down. Behind his eyelids, he saw Mrs Robinson waving to him from her bay window before announcing closure on another day. Pulling his own curtains, he listened for the increasing volume of the television next door, and then he knew it was time to be alone and to rest and to open another bottle and to drink the contents until the bottle fell from his fingers and his body descended into oblivion. It was mid-week and that was what he did in mid-week.

This sleep was different. Peaceful.

No demons rose to invade. There were no panic attacks, no images of Jimmy Buller in the identity parade, no ghastly imaginary re-creations of Lynn's final minutes and no feelings of guilt for not being there when she needed him. He could not see the rape of Emma Parker nor hear the laughter of the men who stood around her. And when he woke, eyes staring forward, he did not jerk upright, clawing at the sweat that drenched his body. There was a calmness in his sleep and in his waking.

Opening his eyes, he could make out the silhouette of his driver, sitting upright with both hands on the steering wheel. There was no acknowledgement of Ben's presence, no glances in the mirror, no communication. Ben did not exist to him. He was simply following orders. Meet John Cooper at Luton airport and drive the car. Leave him at the end of a country road and return to base. He'd be paid for his troubles, just like everyone else. He would go home to his family, buy food and toys for the kids and they'd never know that he'd driven a man who'd become a murderer and felt better for it.

But there was something out of place. No sound came from the engine.

Ben saw groups of people dragging heavy suitcases, individual figures distinct against the lights from the airport terminal in the background. The car, Ben realised, had not moved since he had slumped into the rear seat.

The opposite rear door clicked open, distracting Ben away from the driver. A second figure entered the car, slipping his frame next to Ben. Instinctively, Ben reached for his own door handle, but the lock shut down with an uncompromising thud. He felt his arm being gripped by the figure who had joined him. He was being pulled back to his sleeping, slouched position. There was hardly a struggle. He was too tired to resist.

Ben lay against the seat and looked back at the mirror, ignoring the tightness of the hand around his wrist. The eyes were familiar. There was a sadness reaching out from them towards Ben, apologetically. But he found comfort in seeing them again. He was in no danger. This was no mugging, no everyday drug related attack.

The voice from his side did not come as a surprise.

"I just thought you would like to know that Sergeant Jimmy Buller has breathed his last breath," said Sebastian.

*

"I'm sorry about the watch," said Ben.

"No problem at all," Sebastian replied. "One of the smoothest operations we've ever run and most of that was down to you, Ben. Don't you think so, Mr Delaney?"

Delaney offered a drop of the chin as a sign of agreement. "Well done," continued Sebastian.

"I only did what you told me to do," said Ben.

"It still had to be done, Ben," he replied. "So, well done."

"I never thought I'd see you again to thank you for everything."

"Ben, no problems at all. No drama."

The scene was awash with embarrassment. What should have been a joyful reunion, a cracking open of the champagne, an outpouring of gratitude and back slapping was exactly the opposite. Ben was natural and sincere, but the response from Sebastian was all too stilted.

Different scenario, different person. Sebastian found it awkward when emotions had to be shown, like Ben's boss, Edward Holton. Give him an operation to plan where humans were bit players in Sebastian's Game and he would be clinical in his delivery. Perfect.

He could not relate to his own kind, except when he had meticulously covered every possible outcome. Sebastian had not had time to plan this conversation, to work out the variables on how the conversation would go. He was playing it off the cuff and he was a sorry man.

In the embarrassing silence, other thoughts were on Ben's mind. Thoughts of self-preservation.

Hadn't Delaney said, as he ran away from Ben, "We'll never see each other again. As promised." So why were they here? Ben was thinking hard. Sebastian had said Buller was dead, but could he believe him? Perhaps he had a preference for beer instead of water that afternoon, became less the creature of habit. Buller had been suspicious of the stranger coming from the Mess. The water had been tested and the drug found. An investigation was already underway.

Or perhaps, he had died, but there was a mistake in their organisation. Ben knew his part had gone okay, so was that why Sebastian felt so awkward? He was searching for the right time to tell Ben that they, the professionals, had failed where he had succeeded and there was nothing they could do about it now. An investigation was underway. Ben was in the frame.

But then why would they bother telling him? Why not just let him get arrested, tell his side of the story? No-one would believe tales of Donors and IRA undercover operatives. It just didn't sit with Ben's boring background. The investigation would be intense. Traces of DNA would be found. Ben Price could be put at the scene of the crime.

Ben was beginning to get tetchy.

"I think it's time we went for a drive, Mr Delaney," said Sebastian.

*

Delaney drove. Sebastian talked. Ben listened.

Sebastian began. "What was it the Musketeers used to say, 'All for one and one for all'? There were three of them too. Not counting d'Artagnan of course. Porthos, Aramis and Athos fighting the cause of justice and protecting the young upstart as they went. Something we didn't have to do for you, Ben. You took care of yourself. You knew the plan and executed it. Efficiently."

Ben thought of Sebastian talking to Buller outside the Mess and knew he hadn't done as well as Sebastian was making out. Buller had been three minutes away from finding Ben in his room with the key and bottle in his possession. It hadn't been perfect, but the job was done. It was all Ben cared about.

He was wondering where this conversation was taking them, but had learnt during these last few days not to let his curiosity get the better of him. He was prepared to wait. Sebastian would tell him eventually, when he had fought through the muddle in his own mind.

The pauses were long, cutting the air like a knife. Ben neither looked across at Sebastian nor at Delaney in the mirror. Sebastian was ill at ease. Ben's interruptions might only help him out. Help him relax. Ben didn't want that. Up to this moment, he had been Mr Perfect. It was good to know that Sebastian could feel uncomfortable as well.

Sebastian talked more of the day and its success, going round in circles, repeating expressions. Ben began counting, but stopped when Sebastian mentioned for the tenth time that Buller was dead. No assistance came from the front of the car. No double act like in the police station or at his home. Sebastian was on his own.

Delaney kept driving.

And then, quite suddenly, Sebastian took control. While half of him had been talking and Delaney had been driving and Ben had been listening, Sebastian's other half had been planning the remainder of this conversation.

And when Sebastian said, "Let's not beat about the bush anymore," Ben felt relief that he was going to know at last why he was driving round endlessly in a car with two strangers who became partners who said they'd never see him again.

"There's another job that needs to be done," said Sebastian.

"And what has that to do with me?" asked Ben.

"We need someone who is efficient and trustworthy. That's you, Ben."

"Thank you for the compliment, but no thanks for the job," said Ben.

"No new things to learn, Ben. Same job as the other one. Same drug. In and out, drug in the water. Job done. Easy for you Ben. You're practically a master at it."

"No thanks."

"But we need you, Ben."

"Why don't you do it?"

"We're backup, Ben. I thought you would have understood the importance of that in Germany. We were there for you when you needed us, Ben. Let's just say that two have become three. You're one of us."

He had touched a nerve. Ben knew he was right. Without their intervention outside the Mess, he would have been caught. God knows what might have happened to him.

"What you say is true," replied Ben. "But that was Germany and this is England and while you've been talking, I've been racking my brains for someone else I want murdered and there isn't anyone. Now that Buller has been dealt with, I can't think of a single human being who I would like to see dead. There is nothing personal in what you are asking of me and for that sole reason, you gave me the opportunity to kill Buller. So, unless I have some interest in the intended victim, the answer's no."

Sebastian wriggled in his seat and sat more upright, placing an arm across the top of the seat. "Look, Ben. I admit you have nothing against the intended victim, but there are times when you have to put personal interest to one side. Sometimes there is a greater need. This killing is not for you, Ben, not even for us. It is for the good of the country."

Ben turned to face Sebastian. In the greyness of the evening, momentarily interrupted by the headlights of oncoming traffic, he could see the intensity in his face. Gone was the bumbling oaf struggling for his words. He was now in complete control of the situation and of Ben.

Ben knew that if he refused again, there would be another reason, another onslaught, and then another, until he relented. Sebastian's eyes said it all. There was no possible refusal of Sebastian's request.

But that did not mean that Ben was willing to give in just yet.

"If it's for the good of the country," said Ben, "then there are a thousand men and women more expert than me. Special Branch. MI5, MI6. Trained personnel to do this kind of job. Get one of them."

"Impossible, Ben. Then there would have to be requests and authorisation and meetings, not to mention enough paperwork to destroy a rainforest. Each department would vie to do the job, argue endlessly until the moment had been lost and the chance gone. This needs to be done on the quiet as quickly as possible. Boxing Day."

"It's already planned?" asked Ben.

"Of course. You know us, Ben."

Ben looked towards the mirror. Delaney's glare was fixed on the road ahead without a glance in the rear view mirror. He was leaving this to Sebastian.

"I need to know more," said Ben.

"Sorry, no can do. This is a simple job with no possibility of failure. Just get in and do it, Ben."

"I need to know more," repeated Ben.

"The more information you have, the increased danger. We've grown fond of you. We don't want any harm to come to you. Just trust us, like you always have."

"What's this word 'us'? Seems like you're asking me to trust just you, Sebastian, not Mr Delaney. He seems as if he doesn't want to have a say in this matter."

"He's concentrating on the driving," Sebastian replied and then a little impatiently, "Are you in?"

"No, I'm not," Ben said in defiance.

"A pity." Silence exploded within the car, clinging to every corner, swirling its way around its inhabitants. It was a restless silence that would, at some point, be shattered, the calm before the storm.

133

Somehow, Ben knew that once the storm broke, the silence would crumble before it and there would be no turning back. Had he been foolhardy to push it so far?

In for a penny, in for a pound. He took the initiative.

"Have you set me up for this?" he asked.

"I don't understand," Sebastian replied.

"Was this job planned all along? Did you entrap me into killing Buller, see how I performed in Germany with this job in mind all along?"

"I can promise you that that is not the case."

"How do I know?"

"You don't. Trust us, Ben."

"I think that trust went out of the window when you slithered into the back seat of this car."

Sebastian lost his cool. Voice rising in pitch, patience confined to the past, he attacked Ben with a verbal savagery that could have only one outcome. "Okay, Ben. Listen to me and listen very well. You murdered someone tonight, a soldier whose military service was steeped in glory, highly respected for his gallantry and leadership. You killed through revenge alone. Enquiries had confirmed that Jimmy Buller was not responsible for the death of Lynn Thomas. You could not accept that. You became all consumed in your hatred of this man. It affected your job and your life. There's proof of both. The nights out, the increased drinking, the lack of punctuality and the reliance on your elderly neighbour to wake you from your drunken stupor. Is this enough evidence to turn you into a suspect? Definitely not, especially when Buller died of a heart attack. But when the authorities receive a passport under the name of John Cooper, bearing a photograph of Ben Price, when John Cooper can be placed in Germany at the time of Buller's death, when John Cooper's name is on car hire documents, when the car mileage records correspond to the distance between Dortmund and Dusseldorf, when a German girl suffering from the effects of mild epilepsy identifies the Englishman who offered no help on the plane and at the airport, then you will see that things get a little more complicated. Of course, when the police arrive at your house brandishing a search warrant, the discovery of a key and small bottle will make things impossible for the law-abiding teacher driven to murder by his own irrational mind. Oh, Ben, it is easy to frame the innocent, but even easier to frame the guilty."

"And what about my alibi?" asked Ben.

Sebastian shook his head and sighed. "Ben, do you really want to drag Tom into this? Accessory to murder is the official term, I think. What would happen to Doris? First she loses her daughter, then her husband ends up in jail. Is that what you really want?"

Ben knew that Sebastian had him in his grasp.

He had attempted to delay the inevitable in the hope that there would be some kind of escape. He had failed. "What's the job?" Ben asked.

"We pick you up from the end of your road at seven thirty Boxing Day morning. You need nothing with you. There will be no trips abroad, no need for passports. As I said, it's a simple in and out. No problems, no drama."

"No clues?" asked Ben.

Sebastian shook his head. "Have an enjoyable Christmas Day with Tom and Doris. They've invited you. It would be a shame to let them down. Go home in the evening as planned. We'll see you bright and breezy at seven thirty."

"And what happens if I decide to be ill and not go to see Tom and Doris. What happens if I race off to Scotland for a few days instead and miss your Boxing Day plans? Then maybe you'll have to find an alternative."

"There will be no alternative, Ben. You should know us by now. We don't do Christmas. We'll know where you are. From the time we take our leave."

The car pulled to a halt in the car park at Luton Airport. Passengers were arriving and departing, just like any other day of the year. Two shadowy figures left the car to be replaced by one driver who calmly pulled his seat belt into place and began the journey that would take Ben to the end of a country lane.

And then the driver would go home to spend a peaceful Christmas with his wife and children.

25th December

Ben arrived at the house a few minutes after midnight.

The driver had made good time, despite the unscheduled appearance of Sebastian and Delaney. There had been few vehicles on the road and maybe the odd speed limit had been broken, but the journey had been without incident.

Perhaps he had wanted to get home quickly, to spend more time with his family, maybe to wrap the presents he hadn't had time to wrap. More likely it was that Sebastian had decreed a little indiscretion so that Ben would be home on time. No suspicion aroused.

A solitary light shone above the front door.

Ben placed Lynn's key in the lock and quietly entered the hallway. Glancing left, he saw Tom's silhouetted profile in his usual chair. Walking through, Ben sat on the settee. Tom looked ahead.

Before him, the smallest of the nest of tables had been placed in preparation. Eyes growing accustomed to the dark, Ben noticed two small glasses. About a centimetre of darkness lined their base, whilst the clarity of the remainder of the glass revealed the expensive crystal pattern reaching to its rim.

"Whiskey?" Tom asked, still looking forward.

Ben was unsure. He didn't need it, but this was a social drink with a friend in his house, not a drunken crawl from pub to pub. It would be impolite to refuse.

"Thanks," said Ben, lifting the glass aloft, waiting for Tom to reciprocate and then both of them taking a sip, together, running it round their mouths, allowing the burn to hit their tongues before the fire slid down their throats.

"Success?" asked Tom.

Ben simply lifted the corners of his mouth and lowered his head, nodding it a few times in confirmation. Clinking the crystal together, tilting their heads in unison, throwing the remainder of whiskey into their waiting mouths, they gasped and placed the glasses delicately onto the table.

Tom rose from his chair and made his way to the door. "Merry Christmas," he said as he placed his foot on the first stair.

"Merry Christmas," Ben replied.

*

A dull, grey dawn attempted to bring light to the room. Spasmodically, it succeeded.

Ben could hear Doris in the kitchen below, opening and closing cupboards as quietly as she could, delicately placing pans on the rings of the oven, offering the men the chance of rest, but failing. How noisy we are when we attempt quietness.

He thought of Lynn sliding out of their bed, gently disturbing the duvet, thinking she had left him to sleep until she woke him with breakfast on a tray, full of healthy food. He always played along with her. Did she ever know he was always awake before her? Did she know that he would watch her in her sleep, lying on her back, her breasts gently rising and falling with each breath, her hand raised and resting against the side of her head, strands of hair lying across her face, until she opened her eyes and he closed his?

He would never know if she knew.

Ben reached across to the curtain and pulled it open, letting it hang, the bottom hem weaving around itself like a hanging rope. It made no difference to the room and no difference to his mood.

He had lain awake in the night, catching only a few moments of sleep when exhaustion attempted to push aside the task that lay ahead. The respite was brief. Thoughts of Boxing Day sped back to invade his mind and wake him back to reality.

Sebastian was asking too much. The proposition that had first been placed before him, and that he had agreed to, made no reference to a second killing. Now Sebastian had reneged on the agreement, expected more from him. Ben would tell him he could not go through with it. He would remind him that he had morals, their assertion not his, and someone with morals didn't go around killing strangers indiscriminately.

After listening to his explanation, they would relent and move on to the alternative plan.

But they wouldn't. Ben knew that. They would respond with talk of trust and friendship, regale their success as the gang of three, play the loyalty card and if all this failed they would mention, casually, the names of Tom and Doris. The consequences of his actions, or more appropriately, inactions, would be great. Above all else, Ben knew Sebastian and Delaney would carry out any threats they made. It was second nature to them.

Ben had spent the whole night running scenarios and options through his mind. When he slept, they were in his dreams. When he lay awake, they danced around the patterns in the curtains. When he closed his eyes, they flickered beneath his eyelids. Wherever he turned, they would not go away.

He could not escape from the bed, could not prowl the rooms of the house as if it were his own, did not dare wake his hosts for that would mean questions and he was in no mood for questions because he did not have answers. The bed had been his prison.

Now he could hear Doris. He was not alone in his waking. He imagined her preparing the turkey and placing the crackers on the table. It was what Doris liked to do. The command was hers. It was her day as it had been the previous year when there had been five. Ben wondered if, tuned to automatic, she would set a place for Lynn, but time had begun its healing process and Ben thought not.

He could have risen, descended the stairs, kept her company, drunk tea with her, chatted about everything but Lynn, but he did not. He lay there, listening to her quietly making noise. He was not alone.

He only stirred when he heard Tom's singing in the bathroom. He indulged himself in the Louis Armstrong classic, 'What a Wonderful World.' There was cause for celebration, but then Tom only knew half the story and that was all he would ever know. Ben decided to embrace Tom's uplifted mood. He would pull the curtains wide apart, enter stage left, put on a show until the final act was played and he would kiss the cheeks of Doris and Jo, shake the hand of Tom, wave his goodbyes and sit alone in his BMW and contemplate living with himself.

Showering, shaving and dressing, he looked in the mirror for the final time, was pleased with what he saw, lifted the carrier bag from the side of his rucksack and made his way to the kitchen.

He was surprised to see Tom with his arms around Doris. It was the first sign of affection between the two since their daughter's death. Doris had tried, but had been met by a stone wall. Tom had tried, but once you are within your wall, it is impossible to break free from the stones that surround you. Unless someone smashes the wall down. If Ben needed justification for his Christmas Eve actions, then seeing them like this was it. Ben had smashed the wall, scattering the stones in several directions.

"Morning, Ben," said Doris, cheeks a little flushed. She gently pushed Tom away, re-arranged her hair and smiled with embarrassment. But there was no denying that she enjoyed being caught in a clinch with her husband, throwing Ben a coy smile that said there was life in the old dogs yet.

Four places were set, Lynn's name never mentioned, crackers pulled and stomachs filled. Doris retired to the kitchen, Tom promised to buy her a dishwasher for the following year and the men collapsed in their seats in front of the television.

With Doris immediately falling asleep after joining them, Ben made his excuses and announced he was off for a walk. Tom nodded his approval and knew exactly where Ben was heading.

He was not alone in the graveyard, just a few groups assembled, each standing around their life, but there could have been a thousand others there for all he cared. He spoke to Lynn and she spoke back. His father drifted in and out of the conversation and neither of them had a bad word to say about him. He'd come to ask what they thought of the new development. 'Do what you think is right,' were his father's words. 'You'll know what to do,' were Lynn's. They had confidence in his ability to make the right decision.

And when they had finished talking and he had finished listening, he lifted his body from its crouched position and looked at Lynn's name on the headstone. Putting his fingers to his lips, he leaned forward and placed them on each letter.

"Do you find it good to talk to her?" asked a voice from beyond the headstone. Ben recognised it immediately, but did not lift his eyes from the letters of her name.

"Yes, I do," Ben replied. "She always listens, you know. Does she listen to you?"

"Only when I have a problem. She always was a good listener."

"And she still is," said Ben. "Don't ever forget that. She'll be your agony aunt for all of your life."

"What was her advice to you, Ben?"

"To me?"

"Yes. I know you've asked her about something. I've been sitting over by the church since before you arrived. Saw you come, saw you talk, saw you listen. Now you look less worried, more content."

"She told me to trust my instincts." He raised his head. He held out his hand and she took it. "Are you ready to go back?" he asked. She gave one glance towards Lynn's name and turned away, taking Ben with her. They walked along the path, not saying a word until they had passed through the lychgate and back along the lane to the house.

It was Jo who broke the silence. "What was your problem?" she asked.

Shaking his head, he replied, "My problem is not your problem. I wouldn't want to burden you."

"I'm not a kid anymore," she said with a hint of aggression in her voice.

"I know, Jo. You're an adult who should know when to butt out."

"Or when not to," she insisted.

"Okay, I'll tell you this and then that's the end of it. Deal?"

"Deal."

"Have you ever been asked to do something you don't think you should do? And yet, there is no way to get out of it. You have to follow it through."

"Yeah," she said, still holding his hand in hers.

"Well, that's my problem. At the moment I can't see a way out, but one might come along."

"And if one doesn't, what will you do?"

"Trust my instincts," he replied. "End of conversation."

They walked hand in hand to the driveway of the house. He patted the back of her hand with his free hand, leaned forward and kissed her cheek. "Thanks for the chat," he said. "Now let's get back in. I think it's about time for presents."

*

Ben had chosen well. Each present was greeted with exalted surprise. A turquoise pashmina for Doris – it matched her coat perfectly, she said. 'Men Who Defied Death,' a pictorial book of earlier Grand Prix drivers, for Tom who immediately turned to the index and searched for Stirling Moss, his all time favourite. Quickly found. A necklace for Jo, which he would never have chosen himself, but which she was delighted with. The rather large pendant hung low across her chest for the rest of the day.

Thank goodness Suzanna had asked what he was doing for Christmas. She was pleased that he had made arrangements, but astonished, even in his morose state of mind, that he had not given a thought to presents.

She had dragged him out late night shopping after work, had talked presents all evening and, if truth be told, eventually did most of the choosing. She was more in touch with pashminas and large pendants than he was. Tom's book was different. It just jumped off the shelf at him. There was even a rather ornamental ornament waiting for Mrs Robinson back home. Suzanna had commented that it would look particularly nice in her bay window.

To put it mildly, he had not enjoyed the shopping experience, but to see the pleasure on their faces made the hell of that evening all worthwhile.

After cold turkey sandwiches, accompanied by the traditional salad, they made their way to the front door. Doris hugged him and held him tight around the neck for longer than usual, kissed him on the cheek and wiped the lipstick away. Jo held both his hands in front of her and reached up to kiss the other cheek. Tom shook his hand, smiled and led him to the BMW.

He held the door open and watched as Ben slid into the seat. He turned the key and the engine came to life, classy, purring like the proudest of lions. He looked up at Tom from his seat. "Well done, Ben," said Tom. "Now we can live again."

Ben smiled and nodded. He pulled gently away, lowering the window and waving, hand held high until he was out of sight. Except for the scene in the churchyard, Lynn's name had not been mentioned all day and that was how they had coped.

The performance was ended and the audience could now relax in their home. The actor had another performance tomorrow, one he was dreading, for he did not know yet if he could follow the script or whether he would have to improvise.

When the time came, Lynn would tell him. He needed her now more than ever.

26th December

They were there as they said they would be.

They always were.

Ben opened the rear door and sat next to Sebastian and wondered if they always would be. There. In his life. Never letting him forget that he had killed Jimmy Buller. Never letting him forget that they knew.

And they could prove it.

Ben wondered if this was the beginning of the rest of his life. It all sounded a bit melodramatic in his head, but was he now one of them, their unpaid assassin? Was he to be called upon when he was required? At their beck and call?

It was all so unreal and yet there was Delaney staring straight ahead, eyes on the road. And there was Sebastian, all politeness and bonhomie. "Good morning, Ben," he said cheerily as if they were off for a day out at the seaside. "A beautiful day, don't you think?"

Ben could not think of an appropriate response, so looked away out of the side window. He was there because he had to be. He was not there to make polite conversation with those who had entrapped him, forced him into this. Still hoping there would be a way out, he had spent the whole night threshing around various options and had not got anywhere near finding an escape.

"You'll be home by ten o'clock, in time for the midday football," said Sebastian, which surprised Ben. He had imagined a long trip to London, for some reason, not a trip round the corner. He ran possible towns through his head. There and back, with a few minutes for a quick killing in between, in two and a half hours.

Liverpool was the obvious choice. Leeds another. But why would it have to be one of the large towns? Warrington, Blackburn, Bury. There was no point in guessing. It could be any one of fifty. Besides, it might not be a town at all. Perhaps a house in the middle of nowhere, up on the moors, isolated from everywhere and everyone.

And then a further possibility hit him with so much force he felt his whole body involuntarily shudder. It was something he had not yet considered. Perhaps he wasn't going to kill anyone at all. Perhaps he was about to be the victim himself. They would drive him to the top of the moors where no animal or human ventured at this time of year. They would stand him by a hole already prepared. Delaney would blast a hole in his head with the end of the gun resting against his temple. He would feel intense pain for a micro second and then nothing. He would not see the blood and bone splinters erupt from the side of his head, nor hear the thud of his own body hitting the ground, nor feel the soil thrown on top of him. Delaney would be professional. Quick and clean. The only positive.

He could feel the heat of his body within his clothes, temperature rising to produce pearls of sweat on his forehead. So he breathed long shallow silent breaths and he felt the calm return. Every thought he had had since he had been recruited for the second time had been hypothetical. There was no point in pre-supposing. Just accept the inevitable.

Driving along quiet roads with buildings leaning towards them from either side, there was no rush to head for any one of several motorways that would lead them out of the city. Delaney drove with purpose, knowing his destination, and heading via the quickest route.

Ben's knowledge of the area was extensive. He noticed that Delaney never backtracked or criss-crossed. After a long twenty minutes, Ben realised that there could only be one place he was heading.

Deansgate, trendy part of Manchester, crammed with its fashionable pubs and bars. Favourite haunt of celebrities and professionals where girls, dressed in their fineries, had every chance of hunting down the man of their dreams. Well, for one night anyway. If they could talk their way round the bouncers down at the Deansgate Locks who were employed to keep the riffraff away from the rich and famous.

Delaney slowed to a halt outside the spot where once stood the world famous Hacienda, the Manchester club that was at the very heart of the British club scene. A place where live bands gave way to DJs and Ecstasy gave way to drug battles between rival gangs, each vying for supremacy in the ruthless world of supply.

Ben looked through the window at the block of flats that replaced it after its demolition in the late nineties. Some were saddened, even distraught, over its demise, before moving on to newer establishments, where the same drugs were available to ruin different lives. Ben was glad to see the death of it. He'd visited once during his student days when you could show your student ID and be welcomed into a drug hazed, music thumping mass of humanity where naked girls would writhe their bodies before their gods of DJ. It was not for him. Perhaps he would have felt differently if he had been mixing the music.

Sebastian brought him back to the present. "Recognise this?" he asked. He was holding a small brown bottle between his forefinger and thumb. There was no response from Ben. "The same compound is inside. We will take you to an apartment block. The security code to enter is 2418. Easy to remember. 24 – the date you murdered for the first time and 18 – the age of Lynn's sister Jo, with whom you looked pretty cosy in the cemetery yesterday." Ben faced him, seething inside, wanting to wipe the grin from that posh boy face of his, but knew he wouldn't and knew he couldn't, even if he tried. "I told you. We don't do Christmas. You need this key" – he produced it from his jacket pocket and held it before Ben's eyes – "to enter apartment eight. The occupant is not at home. Pour the contents of the bottle into the milk container which is in the door of the refrigerator. It will be a nice surprise on the corn flakes in the morning."

In a trance, Ben took the bottle and the key from Sebastian and placed them in the pocket of his coat. "Have you got all that?" Sebastian asked. Ben refused to acknowledge him, looking out of the window and thinking that the Hacienda wasn't such a bad place after all. He'd trade a night in there any day of the week for what he was about to do. "I trust you do understand," Sebastian continued. "Touch nothing else, there's no reason to. We will part company outside the apartment block and will meet you at the same place exactly ten minutes later. Straight in, straight out. Job done. No dramas. Then we'll take you back to Mrs Robinson and everything will be as it was."

Delaney turned the key in the ignition, engaged first gear and began the final drive to the apartment block. No more than five minutes was all it took. The car slowed to a halt and Ben opened the door, thankful to be leaving their company. They had somehow acquired a stench of the sewer about them.

Standing outside 'The Kings,' Ben regarded the new development of apartments close to the Salford Royal Hospital and Salford University, and began to wonder who would live in such a place. He shook his head and cast those thoughts aside. This was a job, pure and simple, a job that had to be completed for the sake of all those around him. It could not be personalised in any way. That would make the task impossible.

He moved towards the door, remembering the combination of 2418, which he punched in. There was the faintest of clicks and the door eased off its lock. Pushing the door open, he noted the cleanliness of the entrance complete with a variety of pot plants with their green, well watered leaves. Someone was looking after the communal areas, not always the case in apartment blocks.

He studied the list of apartment numbers on the diagram immaculately backed and stapled onto the notice board. No names showed, just numbers. He liked that. He would be administering death to a number, rather than a person. Number eight was on the second floor.

Figuring that most people would be using the lift, he took the stairs and was soon outside the door, a number eight in brass showing clearly above the lock. He withdrew the key from his pocket, placed it into the lock and turned. The door opened without a sound.

Everything so far had suggested that this was a well organised, not inexpensive, block of apartments. The inside of number eight confirmed this. The lounge was furnished minimalistically, but expensively. Chic black sofas faced each other across a plush rug which covered, in part, the real wooden flooring. The integrated dining area and kitchen were tasteful, allowing a few modern accessories to appear amongst the more traditional units.

Whoever lived here was not on the edge of the poverty trap, that was for sure. But there he was again, personalising things. He shook his head and made his way into the kitchen area. Everything was fully fitted, each door the same. He began opening the doors, searching for the refrigerator.

Finding it at the third attempt, he lifted the milk container and placed it onto the worktop. He unscrewed the top, took the brown bottle from his coat and unscrewed that. As he held the bottle, tilted, over the milk, he caught sight of a photograph on top of the microwave facing away from the living area and towards the kitchen.

It was a photograph of unadulterated happiness. It featured two people facing each other, their eyes smiling towards each other, looks of utter contentment on their faces. In the background were the contents of this apartment, chic black back of the sofa behind them. Their noses were together, squashed a little as their lips met beneath. One arm was delicately placed around the shoulder of the other and one hand was gently caressing the cheek. It was a photograph of true love, similar to the naturalness of the photograph on his own mantelpiece at home.

The photograph was of two girls very much in love. Both were around twenty years of age. One had dark, shoulder length hair tucked behind her ear, revealing a dazzling ear ring which hung just the right amount from her lobe. The brown of her eyes sparkled with happiness as she gazed adoringly at her partner. Her high cheekbones and strong jawline complemented her regal look, imparting a quiet, shy elegance. She was an exceptionally attractive young lady.

The second girl had short, blonde hair, slightly cropped, which combined perfectly with her creamy white skin and blue eyes. An archetypal English Rose. The laughter lines reached out from the corners of her mouth and eyes as she stroked the cheek of the girl she loved. There was a tenderness in her touch, fingertips stroking across the skin delicately. Here was a girl exuding happiness and fun and humour and love.

Here was Emma Parker.

*

The photograph was a couple of years old, taken in a time when Emma was shrouded in innocence, before life had taken hold and drunken twenty-first parties got out of hand. He thought back to when he had taken her to her home, heard her pleas of apology and placed her on the settee. He had given her a final look as he left. He hoped he had been able to hide the sadness he felt for this pathetic creature who had, indirectly, caused the death of his fiancée. He could not hate her, though he wanted to. But she lay there with her creamy white skin pockmarked and blotched red, mascara smudged black on her cheeks and beautiful blonde hair matted with alcohol and vomit. He felt nothing but pity.

He compared the photograph in his mind with the one on the microwave and it was difficult to believe it was the same girl. What possible degree of hideousness had life thrown at her to effect such a devastating change? In such a short time.

He placed the bottle on the worktop, the compound still inside, while his eyes searched the room with growing intensity. There was little to see except for the furniture and accessories. No clothes, no books, no more photographs. Who lived here?

It could not possibly be Emma. She was a student nurse from a working background. Managing money was not one of her strong points. He knew she had borrowed from Lynn on a number of occasions. Small amounts, a few notes, nothing more. Nothing paid back. Ben heard Lynn's voice telling him Emma needed a little support and Ben heard his own voice saying money for alcohol was no support at all. Lynn had shrugged her shoulders, agreed with him and loaned Emma the money anyway. Ben often thought Lynn was on a crusade to save her. He also thought she was wasting her time.

So with no money and little acumen for money, Ben could not place Emma and this apartment together. Not with rent at, what, six hundred pounds a month? Impossible.

Which left the dark-haired girl in the photograph, or someone close to both of them.

If it was a third person, why were there no photographs of the three of them? And how could the apartment be so, what was the word, respectable if three girls, at least one of them being a student, shared this one apartment. Students just weren't neat and tidy. They did not clean their place before they left in a morning. They did not wash the pots and pans from the night before, let alone put them away out of sight in the cupboards. The only answer was that a cleaner was employed and cleaners cost money.

Was the third person a man who was involved with both of them and the apartment belonged to him? This was where they met. These were crazy thoughts. He realised he had to put a stop to all the conjecture and stick to solid facts. Sebastian had told him to touch nothing, but he couldn't just leave without further investigation. Somehow, Emma was involved and if Lynn was no longer here to look out for her, then Ben felt an obligation to.

After all, if she was a regular visitor here, he could have killed her with the stuff inside the brown bottle. Lynn would not have been pleased.

Ben lifted the photograph and concentrated on the dark-haired girl. He had never seen her before, of that he was sure. The earring, the stylish hair, the subdued make up. Hers was the look of understated wealth. He could place her in this apartment, living here. Everything complemented her. The minimalistic chicness of the place. He could also see the fascination she could have for Emma, the blonde-haired, creamy-skinned, fun-loving student from a different background. It was an attraction of opposites, a delightfully sincere and wicked combination.

The photograph had been placed specifically in the kitchen away from prying eyes, facing away from the living area, but instantly available for fingertip touches and coy smiles. It could also, Ben thought, be quickly hidden if the need arose.

Placing it back in position, he moved through the living area and opened the one internal door that led from it. The bedroom mimicked the rest of the apartment. Perfectly furnished with attention to the little details required.

He faltered as his hand reached for the door of the wardrobe. Surely this was a step too far, invading the privacy of a person's life with no permission and no valid reason. He knew how bad that felt. His life had held no privacy since the day Sebastian and Delaney had entered it. But something was pushing him on. Was the old curiosity making a welcome return? Was he actually thinking for himself rather than following instructions? He slid the door ajar.

Unless the occupant was a demure size ten transvestite who had a penchant for modern fashion, then all clues led towards the dark-haired girl. On the hangers were an assortment of trousers, blouses and skirts, all ironed with perfect creases. It was to the right of these that Ben's attention was drawn. Five ball gowns, various colours, were each given their own space, ready at the drop of a hat to be used when necessary. This was not a girl who waited until the night before the ball to go out searching for a new dress.

Ben took a closer look. He did not consider himself an expert on ladies' clothing, but neither was he a novice. He had spent enough time outside fitting and changing rooms to make a reasonable assessment. In this case, he was considering money. None of the dresses could be bought for less than three hundred pounds, thought Ben.

A quick look in the bathroom attached to the bedroom confirmed his thinking. Expensive conditioners and shampoos and plenty of them. The occupant of this one bedroom, quality apartment was the dark-haired girl in the photograph.

But who the hell was she?

*

Arranging the clothes neatly back into position and ensuring the bathroom and bedroom doors were closed, Ben moved quickly across the wooden floor of the living area. He leaned against the worktop, staring at the brown bottle before him.

He had done something he was determined not to do. Silently he ticked himself off. If he had not looked at the photograph, he would not have seen Emma. He would have simply emptied the contents into the container of milk and left the apartment. The dark-haired girl would have taken the mixture and been dead approximately six hours later. That's what he had done with Buller, that's what he should have done here.

But it was Emma.

151

And it was Lynn's relationship with Emma that had led him to all this conjecture and theory and led him to the bedroom and the bathroom and into the life of the dark-haired girl in the photograph. He had personalised the whole situation. He felt he knew her, briefly, but knew her all the same. And he liked her. She had that certain something that was indescribable, but when it happens, you know. He didn't love her. Nothing like that. He just didn't believe that she deserved to die by drinking a deadly mixture dreamed up in some secret laboratory by the scientists of Britain and their good friends the United States of America.

He had already considered his next move.

Placing the bottle, contents secure, into his coat pocket, he left the apartment and made his way down the stairs. As he left, he saw the car pull round the corner. Making his way towards it, he heard the door of the apartment block click back into place. Any possible escape route was closed. If he chose to turn and run, either one of the occupants of the car could be next to him before he had time to use the code. There was only one place to go.

He opened the door himself, placed himself next to Sebastian and the car eased away. No fuss, no attention. Glancing forward, he caught the eyes of Delaney watching him, but then turning away so there was only a short moment of acknowledgement.

They had been driving for a few minutes when Sebastian asked the question. "Everything okay?"

Ben nodded.

"Only you took a little longer than we had anticipated," he continued. "Poor old Mr Delaney here had to drive round the block a few times. Isn't that so, Mr Delaney?" There was an insignificant movement of the head from the front seat.

The silence returned. At first, Ben felt comfortable with it, but when he realised that Sebastian was staring at him, and probably had been since he began his one-sided conversation, he moved his neck to relax the tension.

The next moment, he felt both lapels of his coat being yanked forward and sidewards in Sebastian's direction. Ben tried not to look at him, but Sebastian released one of his hands from the lapel and took a firm hold on Ben's jaw, thumb gripping one side and fingers pulling on the other. In spite of the intense pressure, Ben refused to look at him, favouring the sight of the back of the seat instead.

Too quick for any response from Ben, Sebastian withdrew his hand from his jaw, slapped Ben across his cheek and resumed his grip, more forcefully if that was possible. "You didn't do it, did you, Ben?" asked Sebastian. He slapped Ben again. "You didn't fucking do it, did you?"

There was a hint of hysteria in his voice now. "All you had to do was take a piddling bottle into the place, pour the contents into the milk and get the fuck out. So what was the problem? No fucking milk?" Ben was still looking away, refusing the offer of eye contact. Sebastian took his hand away and Ben tensed his face in expectation of the incoming blow.

When it came, it was loaded with surprise. No slap this time. A full fisted blow under the rib cage, forcing the air from his lungs, up through the windpipe and out in an involuntary gasp of pain. Ben bent double in the back seat of the car, but felt his hair being wrenched backwards. *Now* there was eye contact.

Sebastian's hair had fallen forward over his forehead, but he let it lie there. It was of no importance. His eyes, glaring through the locks of hair, were eyes of hatred. He had organised the operation perfectly and now it had failed. All because some smart alec teacher had decided to think for himself. Conversely, his voice had returned to normality. Calmly, he continued. "That's only the start, Ben. Now, please, start talking. What went wrong?"

Everything happened so quickly. Over Sebastian's shoulder, Ben saw the red glare of what he assumed was a traffic light racing towards them. If Ben had seen it, surely Delaney had, but it was a few seconds later before he heard the brakes being applied and felt the rush of his body towards the front seats. Sebastian was at an angle in front of him and came into contact first, his shoulder slamming against the headrest in the front. Ben felt the grip on his lapel and his hair loosen, enough for him to slip away, reaching for the handle of the door.

He was almost out of the car when he felt himself being wrenched back in. His body was clear, his feet attempting to run, but his coat was being yanked in the opposite direction. He looked back to see that Sebastian had one hand on the bottom of the coat and the other pulling hard on his pocket. And then it gave way. The pocket tore and then ripped and then disengaged itself from the rest of the coat, the bottle that was inside falling to the ground.

For a moment, Sebastian was caught in two minds as he saw the bottle hit the ground and roll away along the side of the pavement. Sebastian released the grip on the coat and plucked the unbroken bottle from the gutter. He looked up to see Ben disappearing amongst the crowd heading for the interminable variety of shops that swamped the centre of Manchester.

*

Ben walked quickly past shops of all kinds boasting best ever post Christmas sale prices. The city was heaving with hungry shoppers desperate for bargains. They were determined to spend their money even if they didn't find anything they liked.

Glancing round, he searched the mass of people for any sign of Sebastian. Well dressed, erect Sebastian. By now, he would have pulled his hair back from his forehead and recovered his composure. He would have forced the bungled operation to the back of his mind, concentrating solely on finding Ben. Whatever the cost.

Delaney might have stayed with the car or he might also be looking. Searching for two people was infinitely more difficult. Delaney would be a problem. Not as tall as Sebastian, he would remain within the crowd. He would be there, by Ben's side, before Ben could spot him. Good God, he'd tracked IRA terrorists and assassinated them before they had a chance to utter a sound. This was hopeless. Ben didn't stand a chance.

He was looking for a tall, well dressed man and a medium-sized, medium-height, medium-featured man, scruffy but wearing a suit. And the penny dropped. That was it. The suits. That would be the giveaway.

It was Bank Holiday, a day when work wasn't mentioned and city centre suits were left hanging in the wardrobe. Except for Sebastian and Delaney. They were always at work.

Ben decided to stop awhile. While he was on the move, he was finding it impossible to pinpoint individuals amongst the bobbing, weaving mass, even those wearing suits. Standing on the second step by the statue of Richard Cobden in St Ann's Square, he scanned the crowds for any sighting. Still impossible. He was tempted to climb the remaining steps, closer to the statue, to gain more height, but he realised it would have been madness to do so. If he raised his head above the parapet, then he would be highly visible to them. They would sight him before he did them.

Perhaps they weren't even following him. Maybe his value was insignificant to them. They could find more tools for their trade and had done so before now. Ben was probably not their first weapon. But such thoughts were risky. They could make him careless. They could get him killed. He shook them from his mind. With one final look around the crowd, final reassurance that they were nowhere to be seen, he turned to descend the steps away from the radical reformer, independent thinker that was Richard Cobden. Apt, Ben thought, that his own independent thinking had landed himself here next to the statue that commemorated Mancunian rebelliousness.

Ben thought of bus routes and timetables. There were many that would take him away from the hubbub of the money-guzzling gluttons of Boxing Day revelry. He made his way past the statue and on towards the bus stop.

Feeling something snag under his foot, he looked down and noticed that his shoelace had come undone. He crouched down to retie it and was immediately aware that he was being watched. He didn't know how close they were, didn't know if it was both of them or just one. He couldn't see them, couldn't hear them. Lots of unknowns, but one certainty. He was not alone.

It was inevitable. He finished tying the bow in his laces and slowly rose. Sebastian was standing directly in front of him about five metres away, hands by his sides, smile of arrogance across his face. His hair, as predicted, was perfectly in place. Legs slightly apart, he was almost daring Ben to make the first move, an attempt to pursue his futile dash for freedom. But Ben waited. The reason for this was very simple. He just did not know what to do. He was out of ideas.

When things could not get any worse, they did. He sensed movement from behind. It appeared that Delaney was about to join the fun.

"Ben?" he heard, almost whispered, and there was a spontaneous quickening of his heart rate. He wanted to turn, but was unable to take his eyes off Sebastian. That was where the most potent danger lay.

"Ben?" he heard repeated and in the sound of his name was confirmation of what he had first thought. If he turned, would Sebastian be able to get to him quickly enough to lay hands on him, without causing a stir amongst the shoppers?

Ben's options were fairly limited at that particular moment. He had to take the chance, so he swung round quickly, almost colliding with Edward Holton in the process.

"Ben, I thought it was you." Holton stretched out his hand and Ben took it, more gratefully than Holton could ever imagine. "Merry Christmas," Holton said.

"And a Merry Christmas to you," Ben replied, hoping that the relief he felt did not show in his words. "Did you have a good one?"

"Excellent. Didn't we, kids?" For the first time, Ben noticed two young children resuming their grip on their father's hands, one on each side of him, wide smiles stretching endlessly across their faces.

"Fantastic," shouted the smaller one, jumping up and down, brimming with excitement.

"Oh, Amy, calm down," said the taller one. "Christmas Day is over."

"Yes, but we're getting new clothes today, aren't we, Daddy?" and she resumed her bouncing, causing her father's arm to bounce along with her.

"We are, we are," said Holton, jumping up and down himself, in time to her movements. Ben had never seen Edward Holton so relaxed, the exact opposite to the destroyed father he had sat with in his newly purchased car on the last day of term. Was that just four days ago? The four of them stood in St Ann's square surrounded by its pink sandstone buildings and laughed together, laughter brought on by a child's unbounded enthusiasm. And the odd promise of a present now and again.

"So, if you are Amy, then," he turned to the taller one of the two, "you must be Emily," said Ben.

"Pleased to meet you, Mr Price," and she held out her hand towards Ben, which he took and shook. Eight years old and all grown up.

"You're not in my class, Emily. My name's Ben. I don't respond to Mr Price outside school, so if you don't call me Ben, I'll never speak to you. Ever again." Emily giggled. "So, good morning, Emily."

"Morning, Ben," Emily replied. He had always had this way of communicating with children, could nearly always get them on his side. He was pleased to find that he had not lost the knack, despite being recently installed into the union of assassins and despite being watched, he presumed, by his accomplice who was patiently waiting for his moment of opportunity. This chance meeting had given Ben some hope.

He looked away from the girls and towards their father. "How are you, Edward?" asked Ben.

"Feel good," he replied. "Can't thank you enough, Ben."

"What for? Spending a few moments lying to you that the car you had just bought was a beauty, highlighted by the limitless grey plastic stretching across the dashboard?"

"You know what I mean," Holton said, more seriously.

"Buy me a drink then," said Ben. "Hot chocolate. There's a Starbucks in the Arndale Centre."

"It's a deal. Come on my beautiful daughters," he said, swinging their arms, Amy whooping uncontrollably, Emily attempting a more mature approach, but not quite managing it as she swung both legs off the ground.

Ben felt a reluctance to follow them, not wanting to involve them, but there was no other option. Taking hold of Emily's hand, he positioned himself further away from Sebastian with Holton and the two girls unwittingly protecting him. A moment of shame washed over him. Hiding behind two innocent children. Had it come to this? Ben knew that he would never place them in danger. If Sebastian, or the forgotten Delaney for that matter, made a move on him, their safety was paramount. He would give himself to them rather than inflict suffering on the two children.

At present, there was no danger. Sebastian was still there, grin on face, but he nonchalantly turned away, allowing the group of four to pass by. He would of course follow. This was just a respite, a time for Ben to assess the situation. He might, in the end, have to give in, hand himself to them, but for now he would use the time in pleasant conversation, whilst at the same time searching for options of how he would save his own life.

They entered the Arndale Centre via Market Street. Despite Amy's attempts to enter each and every one of the clothes shops, Holton dragged her on, offering in exchange the temptation of a Frappe in Starbucks. This seemed to do the trick. Bribery had its place in the modern world.

Ben was pleased by Holton's insistence. Much as he had fallen for the charms of young Amy, he did not wish to go shopping with her. There was always the chance that, having entered the shops, the girls would want to try something on and that would mean Holton's complete attention would be on the girls. Sebastian would not waste the opportunity. Coffee shops were more open. There was less likelihood of separation.

Ben was pleased that the girls took so long to finish their Frappe, even though Holton had ordered the smallest one for them to share, ironically entitled 'Tall.' They had talked about their presents and the programmes they had watched on the television. Emily revealed her surprise at the Christmas dinner with all the trimmings. "I didn't even know that Daddy could cook," she said, still apparently baffled by the thought of it. Crackers were pulled, paper hats worn, cracker jokes read out. "Amy tried really hard, but I had to help her," said Emily.

Soon, too soon in reality, it was time to go. If Ben could have convinced them to spread out the camp beds and sleeping bags in

Starbucks, he would have. But Amy had the shopping bug and Emily couldn't stand her whining anymore. "Sisters," she sighed.

"Where to then, kids?" asked Holton as he headed for the door.

"Next," Emily replied.

"Yeah, that's right, where to next?" asked Holton, prolonging the façade that Daddy was completely and utterly hopeless on the shopping front. Ben felt he was about to prove to the kids that he could shop as well as he could cook.

"Next. The shop," said Emily in total exasperation.

Holton stood with a bemused look on his face. "Lead the way," he said.

The girls did the leading, Holton still holding on to them. Ben walked alongside, scanning the area for Sebastian. There was no need to scan. He was there, ever present, openly on view. It was one of those situations where if you know something is happening, then you can't understand why people around you are completely ignorant of it. It was obvious from Holton's actions that he was oblivious to Ben's plight.

Ben's main aim was to get away. What to do after that would have to wait till later. While the hot chocolate warmed his inside and the children monopolised their Dad, greater clarity came to Ben.

The question that Ben had been wrestling with was, did he have any advantage over Sebastian and Delaney at all? They were the professionals, he was the amateur. They'd done this before, he hadn't. They had killed many times before, he was a novice. If he was a betting man, he couldn't have got odds on his escape. Nor on his survival. But there was one advantage he held. As he looked through the window towards the buildings that he had seen many times before, often here with Lynn at this very table, the answer dawned. Manchester. The city itself.

Although he could not claim to know the place like the back of his hand, he had seen its development over the years. He had walked the streets with Lynn, entered the myriad of shops, knew the aisles and the layout. He was on home ground and he had to use it. On Manchester, did he believe that Sebastian or Delaney had greater knowledge than him? No.

159

So, as Amy slopped the Frappe down her coat and Emily wiped it clean, he plotted his initial route. If he couldn't shake them off quickly, then he would have to improvise. In addition, he had noted Sebastian's habit of turning away when Ben looked in his direction, in case Holton noticed him, Ben assumed. The movement was immediate and lasted a few seconds.

As the opening to Next drew near, Ben explained that he would have to leave them as he needed to buy something for Lynn's mother and father. He'd forgotten their Christmas presents, he lied. He was really glad they'd bumped into each other, thanked them for the drinks, said he'd see his boss at the start of the new term, turned his head to note Sebastian turning his away and left suddenly via the exit into Corporation Street.

Running across the pedestrian zone, filling by the minute with more shoppers, he entered Marks and Spencer by the permanently open doors to the left and headed straight for the escalator. Jumping aboard, there was no slowing of his movement and he bounded up the metal steps as if he were on a staircase.

The last step was the trickiest, a human jam forming, but he was able to bypass an elderly lady with hovering walking stick ready to alight. As he walked quickly on to the men's section, he glanced round to see her give a slight shake of her stick in his direction, but she was on terra firma and looked in fine fettle. No permanent damage done.

Through the men's section, he jumped on the next escalator, taking him back down to the ground floor. He looked back, stretching his neck to gain the greatest possible access. There was Sebastian, emerging from behind a still startled elderly lady, avoiding the walking stick which by now had taken on a life of its own. Ben was certain he had not been spotted.

The plan was taking effect. All he needed now was a bit of luck. He hoped that his father's assertion that he could fall into a pile of shit and come out smelling of roses was about to transpire. Reaching the final step, he looked around for Delaney. He knew that, for now, Sebastian did not present a problem. There was no sign of either.

Heading for the food section, he was pleased to see a group of about ten people standing around, waiting for the lift, some in conversation with each other, others complete strangers, not conversing, unaware of the others in their group. All showed a lack of interest in Ben, standing as he now was, at the rear of them.

What was the art of good comedy again? Timing. And that was all that was now required. Things had to happen before Sebastian appeared. He began to get edgy, feel the pressure, but then he heard the operating system click into gear. He chanced a glance around. No sign of any suits.

The noise became louder, although not obviously so. There was a final solid clump, the doors opened with an almost silent hiss and the group, followed by Ben, entered the lift. Buttons were pressed, the doors slid shut and the ascent began.

Ben managed to move to the rear of the compartment. He was taller than most there, so slowly he lowered himself, low enough not to be seen, high enough not to attract attention from his fellow travellers. He already knew that the lift would stop on Level four, his choice of floors, a rather buxom middle aged lady having pressed the red light on her way in.

The doors opened on Level one, the most dangerous floor. It was where he had last spied Sebastian. Ben prayed that not all the customers were interested in menswear, that some of them would remain in the lift to provide him with the necessary cover. Buxom though she was, he didn't feel that the middle aged lady would be sufficient on her own.

Ben counted them off. Including the baby in the pram, five made their exit. Ample cover remained, but then his luck ran out. Seconds before, he had been smelling of roses, but now it looked as if the shit was fast approaching. At the last moment, as the doors were beginning to close, a couple of giggling teenage girls spotted something they fancied and made the greatest possible commotion about it. They pointed towards the hat section and decided that men's headwear was the fashion statement of the moment. One of them placed her leg across the decreasing space between the doors, causing them to spring open again. Her friend grabbed her arm and pulled her back, feigning alarm that the doors might trap her friend's leg and do permanent damage. Both held their hands to their mouths, shouting, "Oh my God" at the same time. They wore the same clothes, the same hairstyle with red streaks and they exclaimed the same words with equal faked alarm. They must have spent hours practising.

Ben wished they hadn't. Through the gap between the two people in front, Ben saw the girls tumble out of the lift, laughing loudly, drawing attention to themselves. As they held each other by the arms and then hugged each other as if they had escaped death by a fraction of a millimetre, Ben saw the calm figure of Sebastian a little ahead of them, staring in their direction.

Ben slowly moved his head until he was behind the man in front. There was a chance he hadn't been spotted. In their false excitement, the girls had remained mobile, as if worked by strings from above, some part of their body constantly on the move. From his observations in St Ann's Square, Ben knew how difficult it was to focus on something other than the focus of attention, but then Sebastian was a trained expert.

He waited in dread. He dared not look into the world outside the lift, could not risk leaning out from his hiding place, fearful of confronting Sebastian's smiling face with those hateful eyes staring back at him. No matter how slight the movement from the man in front, Ben moved with him.

What would be Sebastian's reaction if he had seen Ben? He certainly wouldn't stand there and wait for the numbers on the lift to tell him where Ben was going. He was too close to the lift for that. He would be positive. He would step forward and halt the doors again. He would enter and make his way to the back of the lift. 'Morning, Ben,' he would say, all charm and charisma and the buxom lady would look towards him and smile. Ben shuddered at the thought.

As the doors of the lift began to draw together, Ben closed his eyes and prayed. Not to God, not to anyone in particular. He just prayed. 'Please,' he prayed. 'Please. Please.' And the doors glided across the space, shutting out the light from menswear. He dared to open his eyes and glance around.

Sebastian had not made the trip. Was that because he couldn't or because he didn't want to? Surely if he had had the chance, he would have taken it. He needed to be close to Ben, to whisper to him, reminding him of the consequences of his actions for others, and encourage him to leave with him, with no fuss.

There was silence in the lift, now that the baby in the pram had left and the giggling teenage girls had taken their rehearsed conversation elsewhere. Level three was passed without stopping, and Level four shone bright red before the hiss came and the doors slid open. The strangers moved out en masse and then split in different directions.

Ben knew he had to move quickly. He had been here many times before, so knew the floor well. Baby and children's clothes to the right and ladies' lingerie to the left. He turned left.

Passing between the lines of panties and high cuts and thongs, he spotted the changing rooms in the corner. He made his way through push-ups and pull-downs and naturals and basques and God knows what else before waiting by the nighties and baby dolls.

An assistant was waiting, tape measure at the ready for the expected influx of returns. Men meant well, but they rarely got lingerie right. They'd seen the models in the magazines and they'd pictured their wives in the same attire. Imagination running wild, they'd ignored the airbrushing and the age difference and they'd bought in anticipation. Most women knew what would suit and what would fit and most didn't take them out of the box.

Hence the assistant with the tape measure. The ladies would return the well intentioned items, buy something more suitable, wait till the kids had gone to bed, wear it for him and he'd realise that she was far more sexy than anything that appeared in his magazines. He'd feel a right prat, she'd give him words of consolation and they'd make love because it was love that made women sexy, not pictures. Women, undoubtedly, knew best.

Ben hung around, but time was ebbing away. Sebastian could be here at any time. He had to force the situation, take a risk. He moved towards the assistant who smiled in his direction. "You see that lady over there, my aunt," said Ben, "I think she may require a bit of help."

Ben looked across at the unsuspecting middle aged buxom lady who had accompanied him in the lift.

"We'll see what we can do then," said the assistant. She repeated her smile, removed the tape measure from her neck and made her way across the floor. Ben searched the aisles, saw that no-one was looking in his direction and disappeared into the changing rooms.

He'd been there once before when Lynn had dragged him in to pass judgment on a little black and red number she was thinking of buying. Suzanna had kept the assistant occupied. He had commented to Lynn that M&S seemed a good place to work. They had everything they needed in there, staff toilet included. He remembered saying how he'd been waiting for her for so long that he needed to pee. 'Do you think they'd mind?' he'd said. She managed to persuade him to hang on.

At that moment, nowhere felt safer than the staff toilet in a soon to be very busy lingerie section in Marks and Spencer. He opened the toilet door and entered. He presumed that Sebastian would not think to look in this unlikeliest of places. By now, there should be no indication of what floor Ben was on or even if he was in the store at all. Sebastian had lost sight of him. He only hoped that Delaney had as well.

There was a chance he'd be discovered, more probably by the staff, but not for some time he hoped. And time was crucial. He leaned against the wall behind the door, his mind wandering.

Lynn had bought the little black and red number. It fitted perfectly. He had been tempted even in the confines of the changing rooms and he had felt himself becoming aroused, but she had managed to calm him and promise him that he'd see it again later. It was a good thing. He could never perform when he was so desperate for a pee. He smiled at the thought.

'Oh, Lynn what would you think of me now?' The situation had changed since her support in the graveyard. Now he was on the run from a pair of thugs who would stop at nothing to preserve their identity. Delaney, of course, didn't exist, but Sebastian had so much to lose. He himself had said that they were well paid for their services, and if the service was no longer foolproof, then what would the Donors think of him then?

He glanced at his watch. He doubted whether he would be back home for the midday football. What was he thinking: going home? He couldn't go home at all. It was the first place they would look for him, if they had to abort their search in the heart of Manchester. Returning home would be out of the question. He hoped Mrs Robinson would be safe, and then he remembered she always went with her husband to stay at her sister's house for a few days over Christmas, leaving on Boxing Day. Maybe she had gone already. He convinced himself she had.

Time went slowly, but he didn't mind that. He could put up with anything except the door opening and Sebastian making an entrance. The boredom was interspersed with bouts of humour and occasional embarrassment. "My tits won't go anywhere near that."

"Are you sure that bloody tape measure was the right way up?"

"If this doesn't get the old bastard rising to attention, then I don't know what will."

But the most difficult moment was when he heard "How many pairs have you got on?" to which someone replied, "Seven. If the alarm goes off, I'll be so weighed down I'll never be able to outrun them." At that point, Ben reached for the handle before having second thoughts. What was more important, seven pairs of stolen knickers or Emma Parker?

Another look at his watch. Two hours was long enough, he thought. He would have to chance a break for it at some stage, but finding the right moment was difficult with so many ladies returning so many bras, not to mention so many tokens being exchanged for gifts. Some men had learnt their lesson and were in for a treat.

He had grown accustomed to the sound of the assistant's voice, had even got used to her sales technique. It was a voice he could no longer hear. Taking a deep breath, he reached for the handle, opened the door, looked towards the floor and walked quickly through the changing rooms, issuing a "'scuse me ladies," on the way out. No-one said a word. He was beginning to smell of roses again. Making his way to the lift, he noticed a large crowd waiting, too many for the one lift. He couldn't afford to wait. He had to keep moving, even if it meant using the escalator.

Looking around him, he descended quickly from one floor to the next until he stood by the open doors through which he had entered two hours previously. There was no sign of either of his adversaries.

Heading away from the Arndale Centre, he made for the bus stop on Victoria Street. The Metroshuttle ran every five minutes and had gained a reputation as being as innovative as it was reliable. Orange and Green routes transported the hordes from one busy area to another, free of charge and without delay, all within the city boundaries.

Ben knew it well. This was his town. He was comfortable there. So, there was no panic when he arrived at the bus stop and had to wait in the queue. He knew there would be another one along soon. It gave him a chance for a good look round.

Not one suit could be seen. There was nobody skulking in doorways, nobody pointing a hand in his direction. The transport arrived and Ben got on, waiting until the last moment. Neither Sebastian nor Delaney was ahead of him and the only thing behind him was the sound of the doors closing.

He rode the Orange route which took him, via a few stops, to Piccadilly. Leaving the bus behind, he made his way directly to the Metrolink, another example of Manchester's modern transport links. This would take him away from the centre and towards the outlying areas. Trams ran every twelve minutes, a longer wait than at the Metroshuttle. He would have to keep on the move.

Although he hoped that Metroshuttle and Metrolink were unknown to Sebastian and Delaney, there was no certainty, so he bought a newspaper and looked over the top of it, surveying the crowd. He recognised no-one.

Hearing the unmistakable sound of the approaching tram, he slowly walked over to the doorway, which glided open. Making his way to the back seat, he flicked open his newspaper and resumed his search. No eyes looked in his direction. He was as anonymous as all the passengers. They all looked remarkably normal, but then again, so did he. But he was not normal. Not now. Dark thoughts swam around his head.

He wondered what great secrets his fellow passengers held? What revelations could they impart that would shock their fellow travellers? Perhaps if Ben told his story, he would open the flood gates and the journey would be more interesting. He smiled at his own crazy idea.

The tram continued on its journey, occasionally stopping, passengers disembarking, to be replaced by others. Within a short space of time, the shops gave way to houses and to flats, many flat-roofed and box-like, built in the 1960s to house the ever-increasing population. Each little box looking the same, each occupant presumed equal. Which they were not.

More seats became available. Fewer people were leaving town than entering. Ben saw queues of people waiting for the inward journey, laughing with friends, eager to spend the remainder of holiday cash that remained in their purses and wallets. He hoped his host at his intended destination was not one of them. Ben prayed again to his unknown god. 'Please, let her be at home.'

*

Old Trafford is known the world over. It is the home of Manchester United football club, the biggest football club in the world. Financially speaking that is. Real Madrid, AC Milan, Juventus were perhaps more successful on the pitch, but it was United that grabbed the media attention, born in part from a football disaster of overwhelming proportions.

Following a match in Europe in 1958, Manchester United were returning home from Munich when their aeroplane crashed during takeoff. Almost the entire team was killed on that fateful snow covered night, but over the years the club, supported by the whole football world, re-emerged in strength. The idea of shirt sales and souvenirs was initiated. It was a massive success, which they managed to keep quiet for a while before their rivals followed suit.

Whilst others were at their formative stage, United were staying way ahead, selling to such far flung places as Asia and Australasia, places around the world where football was being introduced. Manchester United became the premier name in the global game. Players became heroes and, just like the club they played for, made fortunes because of it.

One of the greatest names in Manchester United folklore is Sir Matt Busby. Manager at the time of the fateful aircrash, he rebuilt a team from the ashes, going on to win the European Cup, the first English team to do so. He was a legend in his own lifetime.

Ben was not a fan of Manchester United, preferring the lesser known Manchester City, but even he felt his heart skip a beat as he looked up at the sign marking the street name. Sir Matt Busby Way is so close to Old Trafford that you can almost touch it. He walked down the line of Victorian houses, looking for the distinctive white window frames and red window sills that Lynn had told him about.

He found it close to the junction at the end of the street. There was no hesitation. He rang the doorbell. "Just a minute," he heard from inside and he saw movement through the opaque window in the centre of the door. Two locks clicked out of place and the door opened as far as the safety chain would allow. Eyes looked at him from round the door, the chain unfastened and the door quickly opened. "Ben, are you okay? You look bloody awful." And she grabbed hold of him and yanked him into the sanctuary of her house.

*

Ben was pleased that most of the original fixtures had been preserved, even down to the tiling around the fireplace. The dado rail ran round the room, pictures hung from brass chains, while the door had been reclaimed from behind years of sloppy paintwork. Hanging from the circular rose design at the centre of the tall ceiling was an ornate light which would have looked out of place anywhere else. In this room in this house, it was perfect.

He had never been in the house before, although Lynn had enthused about it. She had also revealed the immense sadness that had preceded the purchase. Mother had died giving birth, father had died of grief. Child brought up by a loving aunt inherited money from the parents' estate at twenty-one years of age, enough to buy the house.

"It's one sugar, isn't it, Ben?" came the shout from the kitchen.

"Yes thanks."

"I'd best put three in then, the state you look."

Standing in front of the mirror above the fireplace, Ben understood what she meant. Lack of sleep, added to the strain of the morning's events, was taking its toll. He looked as bad as she said he did, worse even. Dark rims around the eyes were accompanied by untidy hair and drawn features.

"Not a pretty picture, eh?" asked Suzanna as she entered the room holding two mugs in her hands. Suzanna's tea was perfect. It was made with such precision. Heat the cups first, brew the tea in the pot for five minutes, sugar and then milk in the mug, and finally the tea, poured gently from the pot. A consistent stir, clockwise and anti-clockwise and the result was the perfect mug of tea. It had become a ritual at school following Lynn's insistence on Ben sitting for at least part of his dinner time. Suzanna had been Lynn's enforcer.

She placed the mugs on the coasters on the table. "Here," she said, "let's take your coat off you." Placing her hands on the collar, she lifted the coat from his back and lay it across the arm of a chair. She felt it best not to mention the ripped pocket, even though she'd seen it. Ben sat on the settee, watching the steam rise from the mugs. Momentarily, the pressure was off. He was safe. Surely Sebastian and Delaney could not trace him here.

"It's a beautiful house," Ben observed.

"It's a normal house in a beautiful street next to a beautiful football ground," Suzanna replied, wrapping her dressing gown closer round her neck and tying the cord tight.

Ben laughed and took a sip from his mug. "Lynn told me I couldn't miss it. White window frames and red window sills."

"The only colours it could have been."

Suzanna was addicted to Manchester United, the Red Devils, red shirts and white shorts. She was a season ticket holder and watched every match played at Old Trafford. It was almost impossible for her to watch her beloved team when they were playing away from the Theatre of Dreams, such was the demand for tickets. So she had slipped into a routine on alternate Saturdays of football and shopping. Hence the friendship with Lynn.

She continued. "So, what brings you here on a Saturday dinner time? You've not come all this way to watch the football preview."

Ben shuffled uncomfortably. He knew what he had to say, but was reluctant to involve another innocent in his problem. First Tom, then Edward Holton and his two children and now Suzanna. The circle was widening. And they could all get hurt.

"Ben, spit it out. You arrive on my doorstep looking like death warmed up, sit on my settee and drink my tea. And you say nothing, well nothing of importance. I like to think of us as friends, Ben. You've come here for a reason and if you can't talk to me, who can you talk to?"

She was wise beyond her years. And straight talking too. It's what Lynn and Ben liked about her, amongst other things.

"Emma Parker," said Ben. "You once told me that you didn't trust her. Any reason for that?"

"Just a feeling," she replied. "Can't put my finger on it, but there was something about her."

"Like what?"

"Like … why was she always out of it? You can never trust someone like that."

"What do you mean, out of it? Drunk?"

"Sometimes, but that was just the tip."

"Come on, straight talker. What do you mean?"

Watching her take a drink from her mug, Ben could tell she was in two minds. She had something to tell him, but wasn't sure if she should. He recognised the signs. Christ, he'd been in the same situation a thousand times over during the last few days. "Oh, what the hell," she said. "Can't do any harm now. Unless she's watching over me. It was Lynn. She asked me to keep quiet about it. Didn't want anyone else to know, not even you. Especially you."

"Suzanna, what the hell are you talking about?"

"Lynn knew you thought Emma was a lost soul. She also knew you didn't like her championing Emma's cause. So she didn't tell you the half of what she thought Emma was up to."

"Like what?" asked Ben, fearing the worst, hoping for better.

"Lynn met Emma when she was a bright young student nurse straight out of school. She was full of good intentions and enthusiasm. Lynn recognised how she was herself many years before, could identify with her. She'd also seen many Emmas enter the profession, but leave too soon because of the workload or the working conditions or the money. Lynn was determined not to let this happen to Emma. She was too good a talent to let go. Then there were a few slip-ups. Nothing serious, just the odd bedpan forgotten and a few mornings when she rolled in late. You know all this, don't you?"

"Yes. Nothing to worry too much about. But there's obviously more. What was it that was so bad that Lynn thought she ought to keep it from me?"

"She got a feeling that Emma had crossed the line and got into drugs. Worse than that, Lynn later suspected she might have been taking drugs from the hospital and if that was the case, then the only way Emma could cover herself was to withhold the required dosage from patients, putting their lives at risk."

"But Lynn wouldn't have stood for that. Patients always came first."

"Always, but she couldn't prove anything. She'd only suspected Emma the day before she died and Emma was not on duty till the following week. For the time being, no patients were at risk. She decided to confront her after her party. She told me the very same day."

"Why didn't she tell me?" asked Ben. "I could have helped."

"You know Lynn. Miss Independent. She wanted to deal with this herself and, by God, given time, she would have done. Better than you. Better than me."

"And she knew how I would have reacted at the first mention of Emma's name. That's why she didn't tell me."

"It wasn't that at all, Ben. She just wanted to deal with it. She knew Emma. You didn't. What help could you have given?"

Ben slumped back on the settee. "I let her down," he said.

"In that case, while you're wallowing in a sea of self-pity, get ready for this one. Lynn thought Emma was mixing alcohol and drugs, a deadly cocktail as you know. The main reason she went to the party that night was to look after Emma. She was worried what might happen to her."

Ben looked up at Suzanna. "I wonder," said Ben, "if that self-centred bitch ever worried about what might happen to Lynn."

"I very much doubt if she gave it a second thought. But that's not the point right now. Get it into your thick skull, Ben, that you couldn't have helped and Lynn wouldn't have wanted you to. Let's face it, you didn't burden Lynn with all the problems you had at school. Annie Fraser, poor kid. Abused by her father since the day she got out of nappies. Kept it to herself for all those years. Hateful and fearful of all men in equal doses. Until, Ben, she came into your class. You were the first bloke she felt she could talk to. I remember you holding her hand and walking her down to the staffroom, calling me in and telling her that it was alright, she could trust me. You cracked open a bottle of coke and sat with her while we listened and she off-loaded everything. Once the flood gates were open, you let her talk. She didn't want to stop. We were seething inside about what had happened to her, but didn't dare show it to little Annie. You even asked her if she would repeat it to the police and welfare. Do you remember what her reply was?" Ben remembered it clearly, as yesterday. "Only if you'll stay, Mr Price. That's how much trust she had in you. Annie Fraser has never left you, Ben. Every bruise you see on children, every melancholy face, every cry for no reason, you think of Annie and what happened to her. Now here's the question, Ben. Did you ever tell Lynn about Annie Fraser?"

Ben knew she was right. There were things about the job that you kept to yourself. You didn't want to burden anyone else with the problems. You could deal with them yourself. That's what he had done with Annie Fraser. That's what Lynn had done with Emma Parker. Lynn would have dealt with it better than anyone. She just wasn't given the time she needed.

A faint smile crossed his lips. He'd seen Elizabeth Fraser, Annie's mother, at the leisure centre one day, playing netball. She came over to talk to him, brought him up-to-date on Annie and about how life was great, since the father had gone. And as they shook hands, she looked at him and said quietly, 'Thanks, Mr Price. She'll never forget what you did,' and he replied, 'The name's Ben, Mrs Fraser. We're out of school.'

"Why is it," asked Ben, "that the female of the species is always right?"

She laughed that filthy laugh that brought a smile to anyone's lips. "Not sure. It's in the genes, I suppose." She lifted her mug to her lips and continued. "Why did you ask about Emma Parker?"

"Can that wait till later? First of all, I want to ask a favour," Ben said.

"Ask away."

"I need to write a quick note to Tom, you know, Lynn's Dad, and I want you to take it to him. You know where they live, don't you?" She nodded. "The note will ask him to get in your car, bring Doris and Jo with him, and come back here with you. This all needs to happen as quickly as possible." Ben waited for the reaction and when it came, it was what he expected. Straight and to the point.

"This is all very weird, Ben."

"I know. I can't tell you anything else for now, but I promise that when you are all back here, I will tell you everything."

"Okay. That's good enough for me." She turned and opened the cabinet in the corner of the room. Lifting a writing set from it, she placed it on the table. "You'll be needing this then," she said as she left the room and climbed the stairs. Ben could hear the opening and closing of doors and drawers. Getting dressed took her no more than five minutes. Ben heard the jangling of car keys as she came back. "And what are you going to be doing while I'm doing you favours? Staying here, lazing around?" she asked.

"No. I've somewhere else I need to go. If I'm not here when you return, wait for me. I won't be long." Ben handed her the note for Tom.

He had sealed it in an envelope, just in case Suzanna became inquisitive. It was more for her own protection than from lack of trust.

"See you later, then." She headed for the back door. He heard it open, but before she closed it behind her, she shouted, "Take the key off the washing machine. Oh, and one more thing. I'm not going to get killed doing this favour of yours, am I?"

Before Ben could reply, she was gone.

The note also warned Tom to be on the lookout for anyone following them. He thought it would be best if he kept that from Suzanna for now.

*

Ben never drove his BMW into the centre of Manchester. It was true that he wished to reduce the risk of damage to his pride and joy. It was also true that car parking was a nightmare, but these were not the ultimate reasons for his decision.

Public transport around the area was so good that he could get to places quicker without his car. Consequently, because he used it so frequently, he knew the transport system well. The journey to Castle Irwell, with its complex changes in bus routes, might have caused problems for visitors. Not so for Ben. He knew it would take him time. He was prepared for that.

It gave him a chance to review the day. Not quite the Boxing Day he had grown accustomed to. Early start, breaking and entering, preparations for murder, chase through the city, placing lives of children in danger, hiding in toilets in lingerie sections. The list went on and on.

His most recent venture of requesting Suzanna, without explanation, to bring Lynn's family to stay at her house was equally unusual, but it was for their own protection, assuming Sebastian had not followed him to Suzanna's.

He was certain he hadn't. If he had, he would not have allowed Ben freedom to leave, especially after Suzanna's exit, leaving Ben alone in the house. Ben had remained there for half an hour, waiting for Sebastian. He never came. Ben knew he was safe there. Moreover, Ben knew that if Sebastian was unaware of his whereabouts, then he would be unable to follow him. He left the house confident that he was travelling alone.

Sending Suzanna as chauffeur was a risk. Ben decided it was small enough to take. He was certain that the involvement of Suzanna was unknown to Sebastian, but he could not be so sure that Lynn's parents were not being watched. If they were, then all his friends who had so willingly put themselves on the line for him were in grave danger.

On the other hand, Ben hoped that Sebastian, in his arrogant way, believed that there would be no hitch in his plans concerning the second victim and, during this holiday period, he had not enrolled a large team to assist. It was, after all, a simple murder. One driver, one backup, one killer, no witnesses. It could not go wrong.

Ben couldn't see them, but he knew they would be working hard. He imagined that Sebastian had assigned Delaney to the city centre, whilst heading off himself to Ben's house. When human resources were reduced to two, they were the two logical places to survey. Sebastian knew that Ben lacked car mobility and so reaching Tom's house would be impossible in such a short space of time. Ben hoped that Suzanna could bring them home before Sebastian revised his plan.

Ben stepped from the bus. Looking across the playing fields that were part of the Castle Irwell complex, he saw lines of terraced houses. They were unlike the Victorian houses that he had not long since left. These were purpose built student accommodation within their own grounds. Each terrace housed twelve students, each in their single study bedrooms. It was a peaceful location, the River Irwell meandering its way onwards at the edge of the fields.

This was not Ben's first visit to Castle Irwell. He had been persuaded by Lynn to divert from their route north one spring day. While Lynn headed for Block Six, Ben retired to the Pavilion. It was where all students headed in their spare time. The beer was cheap and the sports channel was showing on the television.

There was no time for the Pavilion today. He made his way directly towards Block Six. The door was open. The coldness of the outside fought with the heat from the radiators, but as Ben climbed the stairs, the temperature rose. There was a communal kitchen in the centre of the third floor. As he approached, the waft of toast invaded his senses and he realised that he had not yet eaten.

A man in his early twenties was leaning against the sink looking through the window. His tousled hair and ghostly appearance matched his dishevelled clothes. His shirt hung loosely over his trousers, which in turn sat awkwardly half way down his backside. Ben recognised the symptoms. This was a very serious hangover.

Why anyone would think that eating burnt toast was a remedy, Ben could not think. But it was what students did. Go out, get drunk, come back, eat toast. It was a tradition from long ago and long may it continue.

"Bad night?" asked Ben.

The man fell to the floor. His hand slipped from its holding position on the sink, causing him to lose his balance. The remainder of his body was unable to react and he crashed in an untidy heap on the blue Marley floor tiles.

Ben reached forward, taking him by the arm and helping him to his feet. "Sorry," he said. "I didn't mean to startle you."

"No, that's okay," the man replied, brushing himself down. Not that it made any difference.

"No damage, I hope," said Ben.

"Not at all. All in one piece still." He checked his elbows for any grazing and his wrist for lack of movement, but everything seemed to be okay. "In a world of my own."

"It *was* a bad night then," Ben repeated.

"Not good," the man said. "Bad accident on the motorway, all hands on deck. Not a pretty sight." Ben felt guilty. A hangover was not the problem. This man was dead on his feet through sheer exhaustion.

Ben reached forward and pulled the toast from under the grill, replacing it with more bread, and placed it on a plate. "Sit yourself down," he said and the man obeyed, zombie-like. Ben boiled the water in the kettle, buttered the toast and sat down at the table eating and drinking with his new companion. They didn't say much, just a few pleasantries and when the tea and toast had disappeared, the man thanked Ben and said he just had to get some sleep.

As the man left the kitchen, Ben threw a question at him. "Emma Parker?"

"Bitch should be in her room. She missed her shift last night. Number four."

It was interesting what reactions that name threw up.

*

He thought about tapping on the door, but then she might have been in one of her alcohol or drug induced states and would not hear it. Instead, he gave it the full hammer treatment from the start. It had the desired effect.

"Who is it?"

"Ben Price."

"Ben? What do you want?"

"Come to see you, Emma."

He heard a crash from inside, something solid, maybe a shoe or a bag, and then shuffling feet making their way to the door. "What do you want, Ben?" she asked again, more quietly.

"I told you. I've come to see you. Told Lynn I'd give you a Boxing Day visit. Giving me instructions from the grave." Of course he'd lied. He needed to get into her room, but didn't want to create a fuss. A visit from Security was the last thing he wanted.

There were a few hesitant attempts at conversation from the other side of the door until she eventually said, "I'm not too good this morning, Ben. Can we leave it for another time?"

"We could do," Ben replied. "I've just got a little something that I know she would like you to have." Closing his eyes for a second, he thought, 'Please Lynn, forgive me for using your name in vain, but in this case, the end will justify the means. I promise.'

The door opened. Emma was the third person today who looked far from well. She was, by a long distance, the worst of the three. Her legs seemed removed from the rest of her body, swaying from side to

177

side. Her eyes refused to focus, her once beautiful blonde hair a variety of shades, none of which had been put there by a hairdresser.

"Can I come in?" Ben asked, looking over her shoulder. Clothes were strewn all over the room, along with shoes and bags. She wore a dressing gown, open at the front, revealing a cute nightdress with Minnie Mouse on the front.

Despite her appearance, she had managed to recover her vocal capacity. She answered remarkably strongly. "I'm afraid it's a bit of a mess. Having a tidy up."

"I'm used to mess. Have you seen my house recently?" Before she could stop him, he moved her out of the way and walked in. He invited her into her own mess and closed the door behind her. Looking specifically for one thing, his eyes scoured the room and he was pleasantly surprised to find no bottles and no stench of alcohol. Although this was a good sign, Emma was still under some kind of influence and that could mean only one thing.

"I've not come here to pass judgment, Emma," Ben said. "You can lead your life how you want to. I've just come for a few answers."

"What about?"

"I was in a very nice apartment this morning. In the apartment was a photograph of a very striking lady. Dark shoulder length hair, regal features. Ring any bells, Emma?"

"No. Should it?"

"The apartment was simply furnished, yet classy. Same as the lady. Kitchen, living area, bedroom with bathroom leading off. Wardrobe crammed full with expensive clothing."

He waited for a response. None.

"Perhaps a few more specifics would help. New development of apartments for the well-to-do. 'The Kings,' near the university. Know it Emma?"

"I think I've walked past it a few times, but I'm not sure."

"The photograph, shot in the apartment, was not of the lady alone. There was someone else alongside. They faced each other, noses touching, lips making gentle contact. The other person was a girl also. She had the most beautiful creamy complexion. Her blonde hair was full of life, her smile full of happiness. It was you, Emma. It was a photograph of you and another girl very much in love."

Emma sat on the bed amongst the clothes. She sat like a small girl, lost. Her knees touched as did her toes, her feet turned in. She played nervously with her fingers, wrapping them around each other, constantly changing their position. She looked at them, but saw nothing. Her eyes were elsewhere, lost within her memory. Ben had expected tears, but there were none.

Suddenly, she threw her hair back and laughed. "That was a long time ago," she said. "Last summer when the sun shone and everyone was happy."

"That's not so long ago," said Ben.

"It was a lifetime ago. And then the light from the sun dimmed and the darkness enveloped our lives. And now it's come to this." She stood up and waved her hand around the room, twirling her body in full rotations, spinning more quickly with each turn. It was when she began to whoop that Ben felt he had to intervene, stepping in and holding her tight. She lay limp in his arms. He held her for a moment and then placed her body gently down as he had done on the night Lynn died.

"Come on," Ben said, tapping her cheeks with his fingers. "Wakey, wakey. Don't go to sleep on me. I haven't finished with you yet." He lifted her up and walked her round the room. Her legs were dragging behind her, but slowly her eyes opened and showed signs of normality.

"Why did you have to remind me?" she said. "Why did you have to take me somewhere I didn't want to go?"

"Because I'm worried about her, Emma. If you have any feelings for her, you should be worried too."

Ben was beginning to tire, but she was gradually coming round and eventually, the soles of her feet made contact with the ground and she began to walk with him across the length of her room and back. Time after time.

"She was my life," said Emma out of the blue. "There had been no others before her and none since. And you know what, Ben, I was her life too. I know you'll find that difficult to believe. Young tart and rich lady. But it worked."

"I know it did," Ben replied. He wanted her on his side, but speaking the truth made it easier. "I saw the photograph. You can't fake the look between you, the intimacy, the love."

Emma was now walking on her own, with only the slightest touch on her elbow from Ben. She was regaining her strength, both in body and mind. But she was still inconsistent, various expressions dashing across her face reflecting the mood swings she felt. Her voice adopted an aggressive tone.

"I suppose you want to know the details. Men always do with lesbians. Is that why you're here?"

"Just who she is, Emma. That will do."

"Why?"

"As I said before, I'm worried about her."

"Why should you be worried? You don't know her or you wouldn't be asking who she is. Unless you've been with her, for a fling, no names, just the sex. But she wouldn't do that. She's not like that at all. Doesn't like men, doesn't like flings." She was ranting, tossing conflicting arguments out of her mouth that were floating around her head. "And another thing, Mr Goody Two Shoes Ben Price, what were you doing in her apartment? And how did you get in? She give you a key? She give you what you wanted? She give you the sex, Ben? Bet you haven't had any since Lynn, have you? Bastards. I hate the both of you." She threw her arms away from Ben, catching him on the chin with her elbow, and collapsed onto the bed, face buried deep in her clothes.

Ben gave her time, a few minutes, to calm her stifled sobbing. He thought it best not to touch her, she would have reacted physically, so spoke quietly by her side. "I can promise you that I don't know your friend at all. I've never met her. The photograph is my only contact with her and the only reason I'm interested in her is because you were on the photograph too. It's true, I was in her apartment and I can tell you why later, but for now let me ask you this. Do you think Lynn died in a car accident?"

The switch in conversation had the desired effect. Pushing herself from the bed, she turned and sat, facing Ben, wiping a few streaks from beneath her eyes. He could tell she was puzzled. What was the connection between Lynn's death and her lover?

"No," she replied.

"How do you think she died?"

"She was killed by that bastard Jimmy Buller."

"Well, I think your friend is in just as much danger as Lynn was. I think she's an intended victim." Ben preferred to keep his involvement in her planned demise out of the conversation for now. He needed Emma on his side.

"From Jimmy Buller?"

"No, not from him. I think he's otherwise engaged at the moment. From a different source." Of course, the Donors were involved in both cases, but it was all too complicated to explain to this fragile creature.

"Her name is Jennifer," she offered. "Do you know the bars on Deansgate? La Tasca?"

"Never been there, but walked past it. A bit up-market for me."

"I had a job there, making a bit of extra cash to pay my way through university. One night, Jennifer walked in with some of her friends. She asked for drinks, I served them. There was something between us right then. Sounds crazy doesn't it? Every time I looked across at them, she was watching me. When all her friends left at the end of the night, she stayed. I finished my shift and we moved down the road to another bar. We chatted, she bought the drinks and we went our separate ways. The following night, she was there on her own, waiting for me to finish. Same thing. A few drinks, a lot of talking, a lot of laughter. We went to her place, I spent the night. It was crazy. It had never happened to me before, falling for another woman, loving someone else. I was always such a selfish cow, loved myself and no-one else. Jennifer changed all that."

"Are you still with her? Do you still go to her place?"

Emma looked at her hands again. Twisting her fingers, pressing her palms together once more. Ben waited for another mood swing, but it didn't come. She had regained control. Ben got the feeling that what she was about to say, she had said to herself a million times before, had run the questions through her mind and accepted the outcome, however reluctantly.

"It's over. The last time I was in her apartment was two months ago. First of November, to be exact. That's when we decided it had to be over."

Her words were confirmation for Ben. It was Jennifer, not Emma Parker, who was the intended target. No matter how much he despised Sebastian, Ben admired his organisational skills. He would not have planned to kill Emma in an apartment which she had not visited for two months.

Ben sat next to her on the bed. He had found the answer to his question. Emma was not at risk. Lynn would be happy and so that was the end of it. He could go back to leading a normal life and leave the events of the week behind. That's how he wanted it to be, but he knew it was impossible.

He was too deeply involved for such a simple escape. Using the death of Lynn, Sebastian had satisfied Ben's lust for vengeance and drawn him into his world. Then the second job. Ben had bucked the plans and now it was Sebastian who wanted revenge. The tables had turned and Ben felt suppressed by the weight of it all.

He wanted to end his conversation with Emma, but was desperate for more information that might give him a chance to get out of this mess. Also, his old friend, Mr Curiosity, had reared his head again. There were too many loose ends that had to be tied or cut. So the only option was to bite the bullet and search for more.

"I don't wish to pry, Emma, but why did it end? You were so much in love."

"We still are," said Emma. "It was her father. He found out and that was it."

"Jennifer finished the relationship because her father told her she had to? She looks to have been too strong a lady for that, having Daddy tell her what to do with her life."

"She was strong. So was I. We fought it, tried everything, did everything, but in the end, he was more powerful than us, too powerful. Stronger than we could ever be."

"It doesn't make sense, Emma. From what you say and from what I feel, you had everything. Okay, Daddy may have provided her with a swish apartment and money for expensive clothes, but if it was perfect for the two of you, then all the rich living would have meant nothing."

A faint glimmer of a smile appeared on her face. "The nights we spent, planning our escape. Where we would go, what we would do. And we could have done it, but for him. Wherever we had gone, he would have found us and dragged Jennifer back and me as well."

"But you were two consenting adults. You weren't his slaves, Emma. He couldn't have simply brought you back from wherever you had gone."

The smile faded. Her expression changed in a moment. "It's my favourite expression."

"What is?" asked Ben.

"And then the light from the sun dimmed and the darkness enveloped our lives."

Ben remembered her using it earlier. It made little sense then, thinking it was some transcendental expression from some long forgotten religion, now in vogue with the great and good. It made less sense now. He waited for her to continue.

"I say it often, to remind me of how it was then and how it is now. Our life wasn't as perfect as you think, Ben. There was one tiny flaw. We'd been seeing each other for a few weeks before I realised, but by that stage, I was too much in love, too far gone in our relationship to do anything about it. One morning, as we lay next to each other, we were playing, toying with each other as to who had lectures first. I rolled on to her, she fought back, I grabbed her arm and noticed the marks. At first, I thought she'd banged herself on something, but when she saw me looking, she pulled me off and admitted her addiction. 'I'm a rich kid with a bad habit' were her words. I should have tried to get her off it, but instead we went the other way." She lifted her frame from the bed and drifted to the window. Ben let her go. She was stronger in mind and body than when he had hammered his way into her room. Staring into the past, she carried on. "We made excuses like 'Everybody's got some kind of addiction.' Yours is work, Lynn's was healthy eating, mine was the odd pill to keep me going. Jennifer's was heroin, but by the time I met her, she had moved on to cocaine. It was so fucking available. In the circles she moved in, it was cheap and it was there – on tap. We never had to wait. And then the light from the sun dimmed and the darkness enveloped our lives."

"So, the sun was your relationship with Jennifer, and the darkness was the drugs?"

Emma laughed and turned to face Ben. "No, Ben. You don't understand. The drugs held no fear for us. It was something that we did together, something that enriched our lives. Cocaine was the sun."

Ben was trying to understand, but found the whole business so alien to him, he could not. "Then what was the darkness?"

"Not what, Ben. Who? Her father was the darkness. He found out about the sun and he found out about me and he enveloped our lives."

Ben stood and turned away from her. None of this was anything to do with Lynn or Jimmy Buller or the mess he was in. This was not what he expected. He had hoped for an answer to his problems and was getting more deeply involved in Emma's. Was this why Lynn was so protective of her? Had she caught Lynn on the same pitiful hook?

Moving the conversation away from Emma, he asked, "Can you think of anyone who would want Jennifer killed?"

She laughed again. "Oh, yes, I know someone who would want Jennifer dead. Her father."

"Her father?" asked Ben.

"You're finding all this a bit difficult, aren't you Ben? You don't understand that a girl can love another girl or that a loving relationship can involve the habitual taking of cocaine or that a father could wish the death of his own daughter. I think you'd better sit down."

"And why would I want to do that?" asked Ben.

"Because if you're having trouble with that lot, then you're never going to believe this next bit." Ben resumed his place on the edge of the bed. Emma continued. "Jennifer's father had long since suspected his daughter's persuasion for women. They'd had disagreements about it, sometimes a bit physical. You were right when you said that Jennifer was strong willed. She'd had enough of her father's bullying, so when she left home for university, she decided to break free. She was a brilliant student, four grade As at A Level, but refused to go on to King's College in Cambridge, the fine establishment her father had attended. She chose Salford University and studied Computer Science. Daddy was not pleased and threatened to cut her allowance. She rebelled, got a secret allowance from her long suffering, equally wealthy mother and broke free. So she thought. First he found out about the allowance. He couldn't do much about that – her mother had independent means. Then he heard of her cocaine habit and then he heard about me."

"But none of this is an excuse to kill his own daughter. It's a pretty big jump from disliking his daughter's sexual persuasion and cocaine habit to wanting her dead."

"You don't know the man." Emma's fingers were on the move again. Moving slowly across her room, her voice dropped a level so that Ben could barely hear. "When her father found out about us, he used his influence and contacts to discover Jennifer's supply route and cut it off. You may think that finding another supplier would be easy, but we were used to good stuff by now and street cocaine is shit. Not to mention dangerous. We couldn't get our hands on what we wanted. Both of us suffered. The shakes, the sweats, everything. Just when we thought we were coming through it, I got news of a supplier with good stuff. He said he knew Jennifer, heard she was suffering and wanted to help. But Jennifer was never to know where the stuff was coming from."

"Why didn't you say no? You'd done the hard bit," Ben said.

"I was on a course once where some ex-junkie was giving a talk. I remember him saying, 'Once an addict, always an addict, even when you think you're clean.' I thought he was speaking a load of crap. But he wasn't. You don't know how the stuff gets you. The temptation is always there. If the offer had been made a couple of weeks later, then perhaps we'd have had more chance to resist, but it was still in our blood. We still remembered the sun, Ben."

"So you started taking again?" Sweet forlorn Emma, walking the floor of her room, did not need to respond. She was living proof of what the ex-junkie had said.

"I got a knock on my door one day. I was expecting one. The supplier had called and made an appointment. I opened the door and there was Jennifer's father. Smartly dressed, smiling that pathetic smile, he walked in. I was too surprised, maybe too afraid, to stop him. We'd never met before, yet he knew everything about me. He closed the door behind him."

"What did he want from you? To finish with Jennifer?"

She laughed again. "Ben, you are so naïve. The supplier was his man. He'd set the whole thing up. He said he was willing to continue with the supply. He wanted two things in return."

"Which were?" asked Ben.

"He demanded a slow end to the relationship, so Jennifer didn't know of his involvement, and he insisted that when he provided the drugs, I would provide the sex."

Ben was dumbstruck. It was one of those moments when words fail you, like when your best friend tells you that his mother has died. The obvious response would have been 'I'm really sorry,' but it didn't seem appropriate in this case. He was relieved when Emma began to continue, but regretted it when he heard what she had to say. "So, he raped me there and then and threw a bag of cocaine on my face as he left."

"My God, Emma. Nobody can treat another human being like that. You went to the police, didn't you?"

"To say what? I'm a cocaine addict and my supplier just raped me. They'd laugh me out of the station. It's like reporting your sixteen year old daughter has run away from home. It's an everyday occurrence."

"What did you do?"

"I took the bag to Jennifer and we followed the sun. It was good stuff. Jennifer was back to being happy. No more shakes, no more shivers, no more worrying where the next bag was coming from."

"And the sex?"

"I just lay back and took it. All I could see as he banged away was the sun shining on Jennifer's face and it was worth it. It got to be routine. Even when he called me bitch and slut and whore, it was worth it. I had something he would never have. The love of his daughter."

Ben shook his head in disbelief. "How long did this go on for?"

"Till Jennifer became inquisitive. She wanted to know where the stuff was coming from. At first I didn't tell her, just said it was a present from me to her, but she was persistent and one night as we lay in each other's arms, she asked again. It seemed the right time to say, so I did. Everything. It was the beginning of the end."

"How did she react?"

"She said I was stupid to have kept it from her, the first time she'd said anything nasty to me. From that moment, she feared for my life. You see, the darkness had enveloped our lives. I know she still loves me, Ben. It's just that we can't be together."

Ben walked to the window and opened it to get some air. He felt the cool breeze on his face and shivered involuntarily. He had heard tales from a world far removed from his own, but recounted with such honesty that he had to believe them. He turned to face her. "Emma," he said, "I'm so sorry." Even at this stage, the words seemed so inadequate.

Emma had not yet finished. "Earlier, when you said it was a big jump from disliking his daughter's sexual persuasion to wanting her dead, I said that you didn't know the man. That much is true, but you do know of him. And you've seen him. Jennifer's surname is Ashcroft. Her father's name is Charles."

"Charles Ashcroft," Ben confirmed, although the significance was as yet beyond him.

"Charles Ashcroft," repeated Emma. "The Right Honourable Charles Ashcroft, Home Secretary."

*

An eight year old girl abducted from her own birthday party. Five days later her body was found two miles from her house in a shallow grave covered with leaves.

Charles Ashcroft, appearing on television, expressed his resolute determination to catch the killer. Within two days, the girl's uncle was arrested and DNA tested. Having pleaded guilty, he was convicted of the girl's murder and sentenced to life imprisonment. For the police, it was a perfect investigation without flaw. For Charles Ashcroft, it was a perfect beginning in his recently appointed role as Home Secretary. Unsmiling, determined, he had driven the case from the front. He was sympathetic towards the girl's family and supportive of the police. He said all the right things at the right time. Even the opposition praised him in the House of Commons.

Ben was not a great fan of politicians. Whenever he heard them spouting forth on the television, he would repeat his favourite political adage. 'Would you buy a secondhand car from him?' But Ben had warmed to the endearing face of Charles Ashcroft, even admired him. His view was shared by many.

"I know what you're thinking," said Emma. "You've seen him on the television. He's a good guy, you think. But sometimes the public persona can be very different from the private man. Charles Ashcroft is not the first to woo the public while being the holder of dark secrets. Remember Harold Shipman?"

How could anyone forget Harold Shipman? A doctor of some renown in his local community, people were confident they could trust Harold Shipman with their lives. Unfortunately, some of them paid the price. He killed them either in his surgery or at their homes. Many of his victims had left money to him in their will. His dual reign of mild mannered doctor and undisclosed murderer went on for years. He was the most evil serial killer, yet he lived day to day amongst the families of his victims.

Emma continued. "As much as anyone can actually hate their own father, Jennifer did. The hatred was reciprocated."

"It's obvious why," Ben interrupted. "If you don't mind me saying so, a Home Secretary can't afford to have a drug-taking, lesbian, anti-establishment daughter shouting her mouth off. It's what political resignations are made of."

"So, they made a pact. Jennifer promised never to embarrass him in public and he promised to let her get on with her own life. Jennifer was eighteen when the pact was made. They've never spoken to each other since."

"Sounds as if it suited both of them."

"It did, until he made contact with me and I told Jennifer. She went berserk, throwing stuff against the wall, calling me stupid. He had invaded her life and reneged on the deal. I'm sure I came off lightly because she was so annoyed with him. After she had calmed down, she talked about us being over, that she couldn't look after me twenty-four hours a day. I said it would be okay. We stumbled on for a while longer, but it was never the same again. Everywhere I went, I had to call her to tell her I'd got there safely. She'd phone me at all hours, while I was on duty, leaving messages for me to contact her. She became obsessed by my safety."

"Do you think she was justified?"

"Not at the time, but looking back, yes. The final night we spent together, she told me about Mr Steven Cross. Mr Cross had died following a stroke and Ashcroft replaced him as Member of Parliament. She recounted a conversation she had overheard between her father and his campaign manager where Ashcroft laughed as he said, 'It was worth putting the frighteners on old Crossy.' Ashcroft saw his daughter climbing the stairs, followed her to her room and beat her, threatening that if she ever told anyone what she had heard, then he would kill her. At that time, he ruled Jennifer through fear. It was one of the many times that she witnessed just how ruthless her father could be."

Ben shuddered. All his working life he had heard stories of brutality within the home. People assumed it only occurred in working class environs. Through his studies, he knew better. Still, it was the first time he had heard first hand evidence of it.

Ben felt the cold on the back of his neck and saw Emma shiver as she knotted her fingers, one over the other. He closed the window and placed a coat that was lying on the bed over her shoulders.

"And you never saw him again after you and Jennifer finished?" he asked.

A tear hung at the corner of her eye, but had no energy to fall. "I needed the stuff. Couldn't live without it. So our arrangement carried on for a while, but he soon lost interest. If I no longer had his daughter then he no longer needed me."

Ben sat beside her and placed an arm around her. She sank into his chest, allowing her cheek to rest on him. "You said that Jennifer feared for your life, but did she fear for her own as well?" he asked.

"She should have done, but I don't know. I haven't spoken to her since the night we split."

"We're back to the same question. Why would he want his daughter dead?"

"Apart from him being utterly vicious and vindictive. Apart from her being a lesbian. Apart from her rebelling against him. Apart from her being a cocaine addict. Not a lot there for him to be annoyed about. But in the end, it's all very simple. He would do anything to anybody if he could profit from it. Remember Mr Cross?" She paused for a moment, then said, "Did you hear the radio on Christmas Eve?"

"No," he said, "I was busy." In Germany, thought Ben.

"I laughed when I heard the Prime Minister calling for a clamp down on the supply and possession of Class A drugs. It wouldn't look too good for Ashcroft if it got into the public domain that his own daughter was a cocaine addict." Ben raised his hand to ask a question, but Emma pointed her finger and stopped him. "But," she said, "if he could disclose that his dead daughter had been killed by inhalation of an illegal substance, what sympathy would that generate?"

Ben shook his head. "I'm not so sure, Emma. Even after hearing about the other life of Charles Ashcroft, I still can't believe that he would have a hand in his own daughter's death. It's just too absurd."

"But he didn't have a daughter, Ben. Remember, he disowned her when she was eighteen. She meant nothing to him, unless she could be a pawn in his political game. She would be more use to him dead than alive." Ben was surprised to hear her laugh. "It will never happen though," she said. "Jennifer's stronger than him. Cleverer too. He would never get near her to do her harm."

"I think that's where I come in," said Ben. "I was in her apartment this morning for the sole purpose of killing her."

*

If someone had taken a photograph of Emma's face, they could have placed it on the Internet under the heading 'Total Disbelief' and sold a million copies of it. It could have adorned offices around the world and been referred to, pointed at, thrown darts at when one of those insane initiatives, which everyone knew was doomed to failure from the start, was implemented by highly paid executives from above.

The expression remained on her face for twenty seconds or more, so there would have been no need for high-tech camera management. Just point and press. Emma shook her head and grew a smile. "I look at you sitting here and I think, 'What a load of bollocks, Ben Price.' You couldn't kill a fly. It's just so far removed from your personality, it's a ridiculous notion." She became more serious. "But then I think of your arrival here and the questions you've asked and I think maybe you're telling the truth."

"Unfortunately, I am." He looked away, ashamed of the admission. Emma was the first he had told, something he had not planned. He would rather Tom had been the first to know, but circumstances had changed that. The ball was rolling and at that moment, Ben had no way of stopping it. He was desperate to find his escape route and would try any one that was on offer.

The lives of Ben Price, Emma Parker and Jennifer Ashcroft had become inextricably linked. Any one of them was dependent on the other two for survival. It was just that Emma and Jennifer didn't realise that yet. "Was Jennifer due back at her apartment today?" Ben asked.

"I don't know. I told you I haven't spoken to her since we split."

"If she's not there, any idea where she will be? I think she may be in real danger."

"Last year, she spent Boxing Day with her mother and if she's there, then she's in the safest place."

"But if she's staying with mother, then she's with her father as well."

Emma had the appearance of a little girl, but, on the street, she was old beyond her years. "Ben, will you stop thinking that every family has a mother and a father and that their marriage is perfect in their sweet, rose-covered cottage in the country. The Ashcroft's marriage is a sham, ever since she caught him with his trousers down screwing the flower girl who had just delivered a beautiful bouquet sent with everlasting love from husband to wife on their wedding anniversary. She's by his side at all the political rallies, but she lives in her own apartment in their so-called family home. Jennifer can come and go unnoticed. Her mother is independently wealthy, self-made, something else which irks Ashcroft. She's a tough cookie, a trait she's obviously passed on to her daughter."

"You need to contact her and tell her to stay there."

"I can't. Jennifer's changed her mobile number. I don't even know where the house is."

"Okay. We'll try and find out for tomorrow. In the meantime, get some clothes off your bed and into a bag. You're coming with me."

"Are you mad? Why would I come with you?"

"Because if you don't, you may not even see tomorrow."

*

Ben leaned his head against the cold window. Emma's frail frame leaned against him, her body asleep, her breathing slow and regular. He smiled as he heard the occasional sound emanating from her nose, a restricted sound trying to become a snore, but not having the strength to succeed. Bordering on exhaustion, Ben found sleep impossible. Too many questions and not enough answers.

The streetlights had changed from a red glow to a deep orange. The bus on which they had been travelling had been illuminated by its severe internal lights, disguising the changes occurring on the outside. Without Ben realising, night had crept over them.

Ben gently woke Emma. He led her down the step and onto the pavement. He wrapped his arm around her, holding her against him, for support or warmth or both. It was a short walk.

As Ben rang the doorbell for the second time that day, he saw no sign of anyone being there. The front curtains remained open, the standard lamp in the corner illuminating the Victorian features within. Ben leaned across to take a closer look through the window, but almost fell from the step as he heard a voice from behind the front door. "Who is it?"

"It's Ben."

The door opened until the chain brought it to a halt. Suzanna stared out from the hall's darkness into the glare of the streetlight, the brown of her eyes contracting against the stronger light. The chain slipped from its lock and the door opened fully. Taking Ben by surprise, Suzanna threw her arms around his neck and held him tight, her cheek pressing against his. "What the hell is going on, Ben?" she whispered in his ear. Kissing his cheek, she pushed herself away, clinging onto his arms in the process. "Where've you been? You've been gone ages. We were getting worried."

The only word Ben heard was 'we.' She had managed to get to them and bring them to safety. And they had not been followed. If they had been, Sebastian and Delaney would have been keeping them company. And if that was the case, Suzanna would not have appeared so … Suzanna.

Looking directly at Ben, she continued, "I need an explanation. I've got Doris in the kitchen not knowing what the hell is happening. Tom says he can't say anything, although he obviously knows more than Doris and me. And talking of me, well, I'm scared shitless here, Ben."

"Jo?" asked Ben. "Where's Jo?"

"Jo took an early morning train to Cornwall to see an old school friend of hers. Pre-arranged. She's fine. But I'm not, Ben. I'm not and, shit, what the hell is *she* doing here?"

Emma had been next to Ben the whole time, but it was the first time her presence had registered with Suzanna's brain. She had been so focused on Ben's safety and her own anger that pathetic little Emma was an irrelevance. Ben's apology was mistimed. "Oh, sorry. This is ...."

"I know who she is. She's Emma Parker and if she could look after herself like any other twenty something year old, Lynn would still be alive today."

"Suzanna, calm down," Ben said. "Let's go inside and I'll explain everything. I feel a little conspicuous having a conversation on the doorstep."

Reluctantly, Suzanna moved to the side and allowed her guests to enter. Emma tried a smile as she entered, but Suzanna wasn't even looking at her and had no intention of doing so. Taking a last look up the length of the street, she saw no-one suspicious, as if she knew what suspicious people looked like, and closed the door behind them. Clicking both locks closed and sliding the chain into place, she followed them into the kitchen.

There was an embarrassed silence. Both Tom and Doris knew Emma, Doris more so as Lynn had off-loaded Emma's plight onto her mother, using her as a sounding board. Doris had found it difficult to be sympathetic. Neither Tom nor Doris blamed her for Lynn's death, but she was the catalyst for everyone's actions that night and that was difficult for the grieving parents to ignore.

Suzanna had been wise to keep them away from the front room, just in case. Her car was parked in the back yard and they had everything they wanted in the back rooms. She had been the perfect host, plying them with cups of tea and biscuits and even switching the television on so that Doris was more occupied. The sound was turned off, listening as they were for Ben's expected return, but it served its purpose.

It was Doris who broke the quiet, leaving her seat and holding Ben. "You don't look too good, son," she said.

"I don't feel too good either," he replied. He felt a hand placed at the centre of his back, a comforting touch from a dear friend. Neither Tom nor Doris appeared as angry as Suzanna, but they knew him more intimately than she did. They knew that when the time was right, he would offer his explanation of the strange happenings that had affected their day. In Ben's mind, there was no reason to delay.

"Please, sit down. You need to know everything. You deserve to know everything." They did as they were asked. Every face looked up towards him. Doris and Tom's loving look, Suzanna's subsiding anger and Emma's vacant features. Of them all, Tom knew most and Emma knew some. All the events would be completely new to Doris and Suzanna. "I'm afraid I may have placed you in a certain degree of danger. I'm not sure how you're going to react. Not even you, Tom. Things have moved on since we last met."

"Then, what do you think, Ben? Shall we do a double act? Do you want me to lead off, tell them what I know? We can get that bit out of the way, Doris can curse me for not telling her about it, you can all observe a real marital dispute and then you can fill us in on the rest."

As always, Ben was grateful for Tom's remarkable knack of understanding a situation and offering a helping hand without dominating. It was a rare gift. "Thank you, Tom. That will help a great deal," Ben said. It would give him time to organise his mind, sift the facts into some kind of order.

Tom was succinct but detailed, leaving no stone unturned. There was an initial incredulity, similar to the feelings Ben had experienced when he first listened to Sebastian's plan, but the gasps became fewer as they began to realise the enormity of Ben's decision. At the most controversial stages where Ben's actions might have been the most difficult to understand, Tom offered his overwhelming support, placing himself squarely on Ben's side. And when he had finished, he passed quickly over to Ben for an update.

Ben continued, using Tom's successful method. He had said they deserved to know everything, so that is what they got. He thought the involvement of Emma would be the biggest hurdle, but there was a deal of sympathy, not least when he revealed Lynn's determined quest to help her. Empathising with the struggles he had faced, none of them offered any condemnation of his actions. This was surprising; he had expected some reaction from Suzanna in particular, but pleasing all the same. By the time he was nearing the end, they had got so accustomed to the abnormality of the proceedings that the final revelation that Charles

Ashcroft might be involved, was greeted with resignation rather than surprise.

When he had finished, there was a momentary silence before Suzanna spoke. "I don't know if this makes you feel any better, but if I had been given the opportunity you had, I'd have accepted their offer. I just don't know if I'd have been strong enough to carry it through."

"And full marks for rebelling against them, Ben. This Jennifer girl doesn't deserve to die. Lynn would be proud of you," Tom added. "But we now have a problem. Where do we go from here?"

It was a question Ben had no answer to. He had run out of ideas. There had been no adverse reaction to the choices he had made, so he was hoping that there might be some suggestions from his friends. There were none.

Ben threw out a possibility, but hoped they would reject it. "All of us in this room have failings, but on the whole, we're law-abiding citizens who try to steer clear of trouble. We also have morals. We know right from wrong. What I did to Jimmy Buller was wrong. I killed someone. All things considered, I should turn myself in to the police, tell them the whole story and face the consequences."

Tom replied without hesitation. "Too hasty, Ben. Let's think about this for a while. Anyway, I'm an accessory, so it would be a hard bed and bread and water for me as well as you. Doris might enjoy the peace, but I plan on being a pain to her for a good time to come."

"And who would believe you?" Suzanna chipped in. "Morning officer, I've just come to confess to murder. It was planned by an anonymous group calling themselves the Donors. An ex-Prime Minister knows about them. Oh and by the way, the Home Secretary may be involved. They'd find you guilty and send you to prison, while the real bad guys get off scot free."

"Everyone else has covered their backs, Ben," said Tom. Suzanna agreed.

"Perhaps we'd better sleep on it," suggested Tom. They all agreed, although Ben suspected that it was he that would get most sleep. Unlike the others, he'd grown accustomed to there being a murderer in his presence.

Suzanna ensured that the curtains in the front room were closed and that the light was turned off. She assigned them their respective rooms, beds or settees, for which they were all grateful. Blankets and pillows were distributed. It was like a wartime siege.

As they stood to leave the room, Emma suddenly let out a scream that energised the sombre proceedings. With one hand covering her mouth and the other pointing towards the corner of the room, she began to sob.

On the television was Charles Ashcroft, dressed in a striking black coat with black velvet lapels. But it was not the coat that drew everyone's attention. That dubious honour went to the black tie impeccably knotted at the centre of his white shirt.

*

Surrounded by similarly attired men to the rear and a mass of microphones to the fore, Ashcroft was composing himself before his speech. A man to his left was making an introduction, looking alternately towards Ashcroft and the members of the press that stood before him. He, like Ashcroft, wore a sombre expression, their faces gaunt, each line etched on their faces.

Occasionally, as the man continued to talk, Ashcroft would raise his gaze from the ground, attempt a straightening of the shoulders and neck to a more upright position, but it was all in vain. They would soon drop again. His eyes wore a permanent glazed look, moist and red. So distraught was he that he was unable to hide his despair.

Suzanna reached forward, took up the remote control and increased the volume just in time to hear the man say, "..... appreciate your co-operation at this very difficult time." He stood back from the microphones. Ashcroft took a few seconds in the silence, breathing deeply, to walk the short yard to take his place.

Ben glanced towards Emma. Staring implacably at the screen, she strove to hear what he had to say. She, like all those gathered, feared the worst.

197

Ashcroft began. "It is with the deepest sorrow that I have to announce the premature death at the age of twenty-two years, of our dearly loved daughter Jennifer." He paused, allowing the words to register amongst the assembled press. "Twenty-two years of age," he repeated. "She was so young, so vibrant, such a brilliant student. She had her entire life, a brilliant life, ahead of her. A life cut terribly short." Again, he paused. "Gentlemen, ladies, I will be perfectly honest with you. Our daughter had, in recent weeks, experimented with cocaine." There was a stirring amongst the crowd. This was big news. Ashcroft allowed them to settle before continuing. "All cocaine is bad, but this batch was particularly lethal. Our darling Jennifer," he lifted a handkerchief from his pocket and wiped a tear away, "like so many unsuspecting victims, died a horrible, painful death." Now he looked directly ahead at the television camera, rising up so that the cameraman had to re-position. His entire body language became more aggressive, his legs slightly apart, his shoulders leaning forward. Sadness had been replaced by anger. The microphone he held tightly in his clenched fist screeched its objection, but he ignored it and continued. "It is with an even deeper conviction that I will pursue the suppliers and, yes, the users of Class A drugs, if only to spare others this misery I am feeling at this tragic moment. Criminals, you will be sought, found and dealt with in the harshest possible manner. Users," he paused again, holding his bottom lip with his teeth, "I will help you to live your life again. Thank you." He was finished. He turned away and left. No questions were asked. The request for privacy was upheld.

All eyes were on Emma. Earlier, they had heard how much in love she was with Jennifer. Doris, in particular, had found this difficult, so alien was the concept of a woman loving another woman. Suzanna was more accepting. Different generations. Yet it was Doris who now held the quietly sobbing, murmuring Emma. Not one word she uttered was understandable, but Doris held her like she would have held Lynn, given a chance to do so.

She led her over to the settee and lay down with her, Emma's head buried in the soft comfort of Doris' bosom. Doris rocked her gently like a baby, singing quietly to her, a lullaby for a childlike adult.

Emma's eyes were closing. The full impact was refusing to register. That would be for another time. Tom nodded to Suzanna and Ben to leave the room, but as they turned away, they heard Emma's quiet voice issue the message loud and clear. "Get the bastard, Ben. Get the bastard."

The front room was in a grey darkness, a faint glimmer of streetlight invading through a gap at the side of the curtain. They liked it that way. Tom spoke quietly. "That's it then. It's impossible for you to go to the police now. They'll find evidence of you having been in Jennifer's apartment and you'll be prosecuted for double murder."

Suzanna continued. "You heard what Emma said. Ashcroft is ruthless. All powerful. Who would the jurors believe? Who would the public believe? After all, you haven't actually been the paragon of society since Lynn's death, have you?"

Ben knew they were correct in their assumptions. Going to the police would be a nonsense, something he had believed for some time. The death of Jennifer had confirmed it. Everything was stacked against him. Confessing to Jimmy Buller's murder would only be the start.

"So, we find another way," said Ben. Tom and Suzanna visibly relaxed, threw a smile towards each other.

"Thank God for that," said Suzanna. "I'd thought you'd well and truly lost it for a moment."

"I can assure you that my days of losing it are over. The more I think about all of this, the more annoyed I get. It's not the intrusion into my life, it's not the death of Buller, it's not the attempt to blackmail me into killing Jennifer, it's not even being hounded through the streets of Manchester by some control freak. There's something more sinister than all of that."

"Which is?" asked Tom.

"While Emma and I travelled back on Manchester's bus system, I had time to think and put things into perspective. For the first time in days, I had time to assess my actions. And when clarity dawned, I felt ashamed."

"But why, Ben? We're all behind you," said Suzanna. "You were brave enough to make the right decision. Buller was guilty. He deserved to die. Why should you feel ashamed?"

"Because I wasn't strong enough to resist something that was against my better judgement. Would Lynn really have been proud of me for taking the life of someone else? I don't think so."

"I disagree," said Tom. "I think she would have admired your actions, all of which were carried out for the right reasons. It's not that you have turned into a pathological killer. Take Jennifer. You knew it was wrong to kill, so you didn't."

"But I might have done if I hadn't seen the photograph of Emma."

Suzanna jumped in. "If you *had* gone ahead with it, it wasn't because of some mad crazed bloodlust you have recently acquired. It was to protect Tom and Doris. You knew they would have been in danger. You couldn't see a way out. All the right reasons."

Ben crossed the room and leaned his tired frame against the fireplace. His mind was divided into two vying parts. One part was of regret. It was impossible for him to turn back the clock, but if he hadn't agreed to Sebastian's proposition in the first place, then nothing that followed would have happened. This dilemma would not have arisen. His guilty conscience was too much to bear at times. The other part was an attempt at redemption, not from God or Lynn's parents, but within himself. He had always believed in looking forward and he was beginning to wonder what good, if any, could come out of this. Under the severe lights of the bus, it had started to become clear.

Tom interrupted his thoughts. "You said there was something sinister going on, Ben."

For a little while longer, he gazed at the tiles that surrounded the fireplace, composing himself. Turning towards them, he said, "Let's assume that nothing can be done about Buller's death. I'm just going to have to live with that for the rest of my life. But here's my dilemma. The Donors presented an opportunity to me and I took it. So it's the height of hypocrisy on my part to say that the Donors sicken me, but they do. They are not, as they see themselves, righting the wrongs of the justice system, they are, paradoxically, guilty as perpetrators of injustice. Not only do they prey on people when they're at their lowest point, like they did with me, but they also pronounce themselves as redeemers of justice. They are not. They are self-righteous and arrogant, sitting high above the rest of us passing godlike judgements. And that's what sickens me. It's the notion that a group of people exist who deem themselves so far above the law in this country that they can payroll murder." He moved away from the fireplace, suddenly more agitated, looking around the room, focusing on nowhere and no-one. "All the people that have been sanctioned to die by the Donors deserved to die, just like Buller. Agreed?"

They both nodded their agreement. "That is why the Donors exist," said Suzanna.

"Ah, but is it?" asked Ben. "It's what I presumed from the moment I knew of their existence. I presumed it because I was told that by Sebastian. I believed him. But what if he wasn't telling the whole truth? What if the Donors' power is more widespread? Is there any reason to believe that their sole purpose is to bring about justice to those who had escaped the system? These are the questions I asked myself as I leaned against the cold window of the bus. And at first there were no answers, but eventually they came. I relived the conversation I had with Emma and a question I had asked her repeated itself in my mind. 'Can you think of anyone who would want Jennifer killed?' And straight away, she threw out the name of Charles Ashcroft. Hours later, Ashcroft confirmed something I was beginning to suspect. He came on the television and announced the death of Jennifer."

Suzanna stood and moved closer to him. "I'm beginning to understand."

"Well, you're doing better than me, lass," said Tom. "Enlighten me."

Suzanna looked at Ben and continued. "At Luton, Sebastian told you you had another job for you. The next day, you go to Jennifer's apartment. Later, Emma reveals quite assuredly that Jennifer's father would want her dead. As you say, hours later Ashcroft announces the death of Jennifer. It's just too much of a coincidence. There's a direct link between Sebastian and Ashcroft."

"Correct," said Ben.

They both turned to face Tom, who was mulling through their thoughts, bringing himself up to their speed. "I'm not quite convinced yet. What if there was another party involved?"

"Impossible," said Ben. "You said yourself that Jennifer didn't deserve to die. That was before we actually knew she was dead. So, for a girl who didn't deserve to die, out of the blue come two separate assailants who want her disposed of. The idea that a second, totally different person or group, is involved is not at all likely. All roads lead to Ashcroft being involved in some way in the murder of his own daughter. And if he was involved, so was Sebastian."

"Which means," said Suzanna, "that Ashcroft must know about the Donors. If he doesn't, how else would he have known how to contact Sebastian?"

Tom piped up. "Which in turn suggests that Ashcroft may be one of the Donors. But not necessarily."

"Excellent, my dear Watson," Ben said. Perhaps it wasn't the right time to throw in some humour, but it reflected his feeling that there was some progress being made. He made his way back to the fireplace, his mood changing as he did so. He looked at Tom. "I'm afraid that none of this is the sinister part."

"There's more?" asked Tom. "Well, we'd better hear it, so all the questions are answered and we can get a good night's sleep."

"How many more Jennifers have there been?" asked Ben.

"What do you mean?" Suzanna asked.

"We said before that Buller deserved to die, like all the others the Donors have dealt with. But, again, it was another assumption on our part. We believed, because we were told, that all the victims had committed horrendous crimes and had gone unpunished. That's when the Donors stepped in. As far as I am aware, Jennifer hadn't cheated justice. She hadn't maimed or murdered anyone. She was an innocent victim, guilty of no crime whatsoever. All of which produces two further options. Either the Donors are diversifying from their supposed stand as upholders of justice. Or that is what they have always done: killed for price or reason as well as justice. How many more Jennifers have there been?"

Suzanna shuddered at the thought, linking Ben's arm as she did so. Tom remained seated, impassive. Ben enjoyed the quiet moment when Tom was in reflective mood. He gave him time. His logical mind was considering all the options. When they came, his words would be measured and calculated, unlike Ben, and now Suzanna, who reacted more emotionally and spontaneously. An exuberant duo and one wise head. Now the two waited for the wisdom.

Tom looked up. "There may well be some truth in everything you say. The problem is that it is all conjecture, apart from the facts that we have experienced first hand." He shook his head and sighed. "Too much of the Ashcroft side of things is based on what Emma said and, to be honest, if I bumped into Emma on the street selling the 'Big Issue,' I wouldn't buy, because I know the money would go to fuel her habit. She's irrational, a little unstable even." He paused and while he did so, Suzanna let go of Ben's arm and moved to the curtains. Her shoulders had slumped and she looked deflated, as if all their theories were about to be blown away.

But Ben knew Tom better. Tom's words were one side of the argument. Ben waited for the alternative. Tom continued. "She's also very emotionally involved. Take you, for example, Ben. Lynn's death was overwhelming for you. You wanted justice done. Though it may be difficult to imagine, Emma's relationship with Jennifer was just as important to her as you knew yours was with Lynn. She wants justice just as you did and what better way to get it than to blame the man who caused their separation and Jennifer's death. That's how her mind may be working. What do you think?"

Ben was disappointed to his core. He had expected Tom to support their ideas, if only because it was the only option they could think of, but instead he had destroyed them. Ben had been too hasty to believe Emma, just as he had been with Sebastian. In his search to find a way out of his crisis, he had allowed his emotions to blinker the truth. He was dealing with an addict and Tom's simple observations had never occurred to him, or if they had, he had brushed them aside in favour of a more palatable solution.

"But there is another view," said Tom. Suzanna turned from the curtains to face him. Ben took his finger from his mouth. They both looked at Tom, who had the beginnings of a glint in his eyes. He continued. "Like all of us, Emma has only just heard of Jennifer's death and, as yet, she has shown only surface emotion and displayed no deep vindictiveness. Emma told you about Ashcroft before she knew of Jennifer's death. Okay, she was hurt by the separation, but she knew that Jennifer had closed the door on her. She hated Ashcroft, but he was not about to allow Emma and Jennifer to be together again. So there was no reason for her to lie, no reason to stretch the truth. In her childlike state, she told you the truth as she saw it, as all children do. So all we can do is believe in what she said. Now, presuming Ashcroft hated his daughter as much as Emma said he did, I have no problems with the connection you made with Sebastian and Ashcroft. They are linked, in some way, through the Donors."

Suzanna moved towards Tom, leaned down and kissed him on the cheek. There were no words. She simply sat next to him. Tom spoke on. "If you don't mind me saying so, Ben, Emma's willingness to talk had nothing to do with your charm and magnetism. I think she wore an open heart because of her fondness for Lynn. And I get the feeling that she wouldn't have lied to Lynn. If Lynn had questioned her about the drugs from the hospital, she'd have been up-front and confessed. That's what I think."

Ben laughed quietly. "I think you're right," he said.

"But there is still one more question," Tom said. "Knowing all this doesn't make your situation any easier. Sebastian and Ashcroft are your only leads. I don't think Sebastian is going to come to you in the street and say, 'Sorry about all the problems, dear chap. Let's forget all about you making me look an idiot.' Neither could you ever get close enough to Ashcroft to question him and anyway, if you did, would he tell you anything about the Donors? Definitely not. All we've got is a link between Sebastian and Ashcroft and the Donors. This information doesn't make your life suddenly less precarious."

"I realise that, but there is a way of me getting out of this with my reputation intact and nailing the bad guys at the same time."

"And it is?" asked Tom.

"That's the problem," Ben replied. "I haven't thought of it yet."

27th December

Suzanna had found sleep impossible. A disturbed few minutes, now and again, was all she was able to manage. Her bed had never been so uncomfortable, the duvet never so heavy. The pillows had acquired lumps for no reason. She was too hot, she was too cold. It was too dark and that streetlight that she had never noticed before had become at first irritating and then annoying. She would just have to write to the Council to get it moved or dimmed or something.

Turning her body once more, this time away from the street, she lifted her head to check that the door was still closed. She had not heard anything since the creak on the stairs. Sitting up with a start, she had watched the door handle for signs of movement. There were none. On her left, the clock had shown the time to be quarter past two and when her mind told her that at least one hour had gone by, she looked again. It was twenty minutes past two.

Her door remained closed, the handle not turned. She made a mental note to have the creaking floorboard, which had never creaked before, checked and then lay her head back down on the lumps.

That injury she had picked up while playing hockey when she was seventeen, when the ball hit her left ankle, had not troubled her since, but after the floorboard creaked, she began to feel discomfort. Rolling her foot round a few times to ease the stiffness, there was an almighty crack, which was so loud she wondered if she had woken anyone. She hadn't thought about the injury for years, yet in the darkness and the quiet, it revealed itself again.

Sleep was one thing Suzanna normally found easy. She had always remained active, which helped. It would have been easy for her work to rule her life, but she was determined not to let this happen, as Ben had done before Lynn came along. She joined a gym, she played indoor hockey and went to yoga. She was extremely fit in mind and body.

Bad sleeps, she had never experienced before. She didn't realise that everything could be so exaggerated. At times, it was disturbing, almost frightening. Yet it should not have been. There had never been so many people staying under her roof before. No harm could possibly come to her. All these inner convictions made no difference. She had never turned as much and slept so little. It was a night full of nevers.

Setting herself targets in the darkening light or lightening dark, she wasn't sure which, she forced herself to pretend-sleep until three o'clock. So she lay awake, sleeping, wrapped in her uncomfortable duvet, watching the hour hand roll slowly, painfully, round.

The truth was, she liked to believe, that her body was filled with the excesses of the festive season and her normal fitness routine had been interrupted. Too much food and not enough exercise. Her stomach felt bloated, her body lethargic. That was why she could not sleep.

She also supposed that her sleep patterns were not enhanced by knowing that she had a killer in her house, although she tried not to think of Ben as one. He was a teacher, a colleague, a normal guy who had been placed in extraordinary circumstances. Anyway, she believed what she had told him, that she would have done the same as him given the chance. Hypothetical situations are always easier than the real thing.

Once she had capitulated to sleeplessness, she turned her attention to the task in hand: how to help Ben. A glass of water would help clear her mind, but that would have meant a trip downstairs and the creaky floorboard put an end to that idea. She didn't want to wake the whole house up. So she wrapped her dressing gown around her and paced the room in bare feet.

Incredible thoughts swamped her brain. The best possible solution to Ben's problem would be to dispose of Sebastian and Delaney. After that, Ashcroft had to be dealt with. All those that seemed to know of Ben's involvement needed to be killed in complete secrecy. Sebastian and Delaney were trained killers, so that might present a problem, and of course, no-one would miss a deceased Home Secretary.

And who would do the killing? Which one of this ragamuffin, besieged gathering would be the hero? None of them. As far as Suzanna was aware, they were all incapable and inexperienced in the art of assassination, unless Tom was an ex SAS agent. She doubted that.

The idea of a full frontal attack was not only absurd, it was impossible. There had to be another way. Having heard what Ben had said the night before, she was convinced that the only course of action was through the Donors. Maybe they were unaware of Sebastian's recruitment of Ben for the second time. Maybe they had not sanctioned it. Maybe Ashcroft and Sebastian acted alone under the guise of the Donors and if that was the case, the Donors surely could not condone their actions. Their policy, to right the wrongs of the justice system, would have been abused for personal gain. If only the Donors could be contacted, told the facts, there might be a chance for Ben to escape the despair he was in.

But a thought that had nagged at her wouldn't go away. Tom had told them that the only source of information on Ashcroft was Emma and therefore, it could be deemed unreliable. It was certainly unsubstantiated. In the same way, the sole witnesses to the very existence of the Donors were Sebastian and Delaney. Now that Sebastian had double-crossed Ben, gone back on his word, everything he had said could, potentially, be disbelieved. Perhaps the Donors did not exist, had never existed, and Ben's trip to Germany had been engineered by Sebastian and Ashcroft with the second murder in mind.

There were too many unanswered questions. Except one. What leads, however remote, did they have? There was a single answer. The Donors.

Suzanna's thoughts followed that path. Who, apart from Sebastian and Ashcroft, knew of the Donors existence? Delaney, Tom, Doris, Emma, Ben and herself were the ones she knew about. There may have been others from previous assignments, but they did not know of Ben's existence, so how could he know of theirs? There was no way to make contact with them.

Her feet were getting colder and her mind more numb, but she persevered, running Ben's words, his account of what had happened, around in her head. She was getting nowhere. Suddenly, it dawned on her. Out of frustration, she tapped her head with the palm of her hand. Ben was not the only person to recount the chain of events. Tom had been the one to recount the initial meeting between Ben, Sebastian and Delaney when the Donors had first been mentioned.

Immediately, a further name, mentioned by Tom, jumped out at Suzanna.

*

The Internet is a world wide phenomenon. In the late twentieth century, it grabbed the public's attention like no other, in a similar fashion to the advent of trains and road vehicles in previous centuries. To say that it changed the way the world works and lives and sleeps is to limit the impact that it had. It has, quite simply, revolutionised the planet.

Easy access to valuable information has transformed the way businesses, both local and global, are managed. On a personal level, it enables us to book holidays, buy cars, purchase our weekly shopping, all at the touch of a few buttons. It has made life ridiculously easy.

But, like all things all over the world, good things can so easily turn bad. The Internet is the greatest source of global pornography. Communication within and between terrorist groups is as simple as picking up the telephone, yet more discreet. Hackers from around the world can make their way along the corridors of the world's most secure buildings, into the White House itself.

Occasionally, an individual website can be used for good and bad, depending on the user's requirements. Research is one example. Relevant, detailed biographies of historical figures can be easily accessed for pupils and students. The same biographies can offer criminals and terrorists vital information they may require.

Sitting at her desk, staring at the computer screen, Suzanna did not know whether she should be classed as a student or a criminal. She settled for somewhere in between, inquisitive. Reading the details set before her, she felt intrusive, prying into someone else's life, but it was necessary, essential. She needed to know as much information as possible before she approached Ben with her thoughts.

She glanced at the notes she had made as she had scoured the biography in front of her. Born in 1932; father a miner; mother a housewife; gifted student; further education unaffordable; first job, miner; union representative; father, innocent bystander, killed by bank robbers; married late; two children; disillusioned with union movement and Labour party...

The voice from the doorway startled her. She had been so engrossed in the screen that she had failed to hear the door open. "You're supposed to be on holiday. Hope that's not school work," said Ben.

She swung round quickly and was immediately ashamed. Although she moved from the shock of interruption, she felt a tingle of fear, a quickening of the pulse, on hearing his voice. She had known Ben long enough to be comfortable with him, yet she could not hide the fact that the disclosure of recent events had left her a little perturbed. It was something she would have to overcome.

"Ben, don't do that," she said, hoping the rush of blood had not shown in the usual reddening of her neck.

"I'm sorry. Don't mind, do you? I saw the light through the gap under the door and thought you may be awake."

"For hours," she replied. "What about you?"

Ben nodded, a smirk crossing his face. "Slept surprisingly well," he said. "I was so exhausted, I just flaked out. I thought I may get the most sleep. I've been living with the circumstances for a few days now. It's all new to everyone else." He made his way across the room, looking at the screen. Suzanna moved across it, blocking his view.

"Don't look yet," she said. "Sit down." Immediately curious about Suzanna's secrecy, he placed himself on the spare chair with its high back and curling arms. He leaned back, relaxed. She continued. "While you were catching up on your beauty sleep, I did some thinking." She outlined her ideas, concluding with her theory that Ben's only chance was contact with the Donors.

"But that would be impossible," said Ben. "We have a few connections with the Donors, but all of them want me dead. There is no-one else who can give me any information about the Donors. They are a secret organisation after all."

Ignoring the sarcastic tone in his voice, Suzanna pressed ahead. "Wrong, Ben. There is someone you've forgotten about." She leaned to one side, revealing a full screen photograph on her monitor. Ben stood up and took a closer look.

The image was instantly recognisable. "You're a bloody genius," he said.

*

Perfectly combed, swept-back, grey hair topped a hardened sun-baked face, a multitude of lines stretching across from his eyes and mouth. Ben guessed he was in his late sixties, but his eyes showed an alertness that defied age. Clear and compassionate, they exemplified the man and his reputation.

Suzanna revealed more information. "Apparently, it was the gunning down of his father that directed him. From that moment, his life changed. The Trade Union movement, which had been his life, became too restrictive for a man who was looking towards the bigger picture. He was no longer interested in workers' wages and rights. He felt he had gone as far as he could with that, so he branched out and at the same time, ironically, you could say that he became more obsessed with more definitive things. He specialised more."

"How do we get to him, Suzanna?" Ben asked.

"Easy. His address is on the Internet."

"You're joking," Ben said. "He was a leading figure in the country. You're not telling me that every gangster and law breaker can find out where he lives from an Internet café."

"So which am I, a gangster or a law breaker?" asked Suzanna.

"No, not you. He must have loads of enemies, nutters who would give anything to get their own back."

"Well, that might be true, but they can find him as easily as I did. Protection is a bit limited as well. He gave up his right to that when he ceased to become a public figure."

211

"Do you mean we could just walk up his drive and ring the doorbell?"

"Not sure," Suzanna replied, "But it's got to be worth a try."

*

It was Tom who came up with the idea of hiring a car. That way, if things went wrong, if they were spotted, Suzanna's car, which was now parked at a car park in the town, could be their escape route. Somewhere to aim for, to rendezvous if they had to split up. It all sounded a bit cloak and daggerish, but Suzanna was the only one of them who was still unknown to Sebastian, Delaney and Ashcroft.

Reluctantly, Suzanna had agreed to stay with her car. There was no point in allowing her or it close to their final destination. She was too important as the silent partner. If things did go awry and they had to leave the hire car, Suzanna's car was within walking distance and could be easily reached.

Suzanna was not so agreeable to taking Emma with them. As the plan unfolded further, she became more agitated, totally opposed to the idea that Emma should continue with Ben while she, Suzanna, remained alone in the car park. She felt her importance was being undermined. After all, none of this would have been possible without Suzanna's prowling of the bedroom floor during the night while Emma slept downstairs, wallowing in self-pity.

Doris had talked to Suzanna while they were making the breakfast together. Her measured argument was entirely convincing. Emma was unstable, she had to be watched at all times, she could not be allowed to leave the house on her own, yet it would be impossible to keep her a prisoner there, Ben understood her better than anyone, she couldn't be left alone with Suzanna's car. So, she had to accompany Ben. Emma was also the only one of them who could offer a first hand account of Ashcroft's involvement should the need arise. Her pitiful frame might be the deciding factor. Besides, Doris said with an attached hint of blame, Ben brought her here, so Ben could look after her. Suzanna smiled at that.

Communication was important. Tom and Doris were left in the house with Emma's mobile, Suzanna had her own, as did Ben. Tom suggested that Suzanna's name be changed in Ben's contacts list, so as not to draw attention to her if Ben was caught. Suzanna got to choose her own contact name. She thought Brian was appropriate as she had once taught a boy called Brian, who had little between the ears, so much so that he always spelt his own name Brain. As she was the brains behind the operation, she thought Brian appropriate. Tom said he didn't understand the mind of the female.

Suzanna tapped the steering wheel with her fingers as she watched the blue Ford Fiesta leave the car park. Emma's head could barely be seen above the side window. She rested her head against the back of the seat, sideways on, looking inwards. Facing directly forward, Ben did not look back.

It would be a long wait. Suzanna looked around her.

Wilmslow is a nondescript town on the outskirts of Manchester. Its residents like it that way. They also like the idea that footballers and television celebrities choose nearby Prestbury as a place to buy and build their luxury mansions. Wilmslow is able to slide out of the limelight and into obscurity, hiding the affluence that exists there.

Add all the bank balances of the inhabitants and compare the two places, Wilmslow wins hands down. But only they know that. It is a place of unannounced wealth. The Porsches and the Bentleys are kept in the garages away from sight until longer journeys are required. The Golfs and the Mondeos are driven to supermarkets, on show, in full view of the masses.

There is a further disguise. Wilmslow has its middle class areas and many of them. Bank managers, owners of small businesses, accountants are all drawn to the school catchment area and for that peace of mind, they are willing to find the extra 10% on the house prices.

But not all the inhabitants are the same. The wealthy of Wilmslow are not interested in school catchment areas. Their children attend private schools, mix with the right people there, make life contacts, set up their future, just as their fathers have done before them. The wealthy of Wilmslow have been wealthy for a long time, and they will be wealthy for a good time longer. Much longer than their flashy neighbours in Prestbury. They are happy living in the comparative anonymity of Wilmslow.

Glancing at her watch, Suzanna suspected that the rest of the day would travel just as slowly as the night had before. Noticing a McDonald's at the end of the road, she thought she might perhaps pay a visit there. She was certain that, in the circumstances, health conscious Lynn would not mind. She would always have her mobile with her and the big clown was within a thirty second run from her car, so a change of scenery would break the day. Perhaps even a couple of visits, she thought.

She opened her handbag and lifted the book which she had brought with her. At first, she thought it would distract her from she didn't know what, but she had been persuaded to take it by Tom. It was a good decision. One hundred and fifteen pages read, three hundred and eighty-four still to go. That should keep her going.

It was going to be a long day.

*

Ivy ran snakelike up the front walls of the grand house. Symmetrical in design, there was a huge door at the centre, flanked by four windows on either side. A deep arched window was centred on the second floor, revealing an inner staircase that turned in on itself. Reaching out to the sides were four more windows, reflecting the ones below.

Separated from the main house by a concrete roadway, outbuildings of variable sizes stretched towards the myriad of fields, almost manicured in the winter break waiting patiently for the growing period in the spring. Neatly trimmed hedges, leaves long gone to the winds of the autumn and branches taut against the expected frost, lined each field.

Two tractors were parked alongside each other in an open barn. Ploughs and planters stood next to them, forming a perfect line like some agricultural Le Mans, awaiting their drivers. They would not arrive until the frosts had departed and the soil was ready. Despite the cleanliness and the orderly nature, the machinery was well used. This was a working farm making its way, earning its living.

Leaving the car in a parking bay at the beginning of the drive, Ben and Emma crunched their way along the gravel which led to the front door. It seemed an endless distance, it always does when you think you're being watched, but as Ben looked round, he estimated that they had only walked thirty metres or so.

Ben was surprised that Emma appeared undaunted by the whole events. She'd followed him like a lamb. 'You're coming with me, Emma,' and 'Get in the car, Emma' and 'Let's go to the front door, Emma.' She had drifted along with Ben's every demand. Maybe she was still under some kind of influence. He didn't know. He'd looked across at her a few times, asleep in the car, but there was no emotion in her rag doll features. No reaction at all.

Ben's attention moved to the corner of the house. "Maybe we won't have to ring the doorbell after all," he said.

Dressed in a Barbour jacket and corduroy trousers, his hair perfectly combed and his tie Windsor knotted at the centre of the collar of his shirt, an elderly man strode towards them, his determined stride defying his age. Ben knew how old he was. He also knew about his background, his popularity and the rise of his wife's organic farming interests which by chance, dovetailed with his own business interest of distribution. Suzanna had drummed the details into him over breakfast.

Oscar Baker was wealthy long before his wife turned her hand to the land. Now they were reaping the rewards of being there at the beginning of the organic produce revolution. They had the experience and the know-how and the name, all of which, combined, put them in an enviable position.

Despite the grandeur of the surroundings, their lifestyle was simple, but productive. Although the businesses were extremely profitable, Baker refused to forget his roots. One of the less talked about aspects was their weekly food delivery to the Salvation Army, who fed the homeless and needy. This rare kindness amongst ex-politicians was not talked about because Baker did not want it talked about. So it was kept quiet by the Sally Army and by the local press who once stumbled on the story. They approached Baker for confirmation, were given it, but then asked not to print. He did not want his generosity in the public domain. They did not print. That was the stature of the man. It just so happened that Suzanna's uncle worked on the local paper. He was the journalist who kept the story quiet, except to his trusted family of course.

There was a mixture of myth and fact surrounding Oscar Baker. Within the corridors of power, he was respected for his dogged determination to bring law to an often lawless land. In this, he showed a ruthless persistence which made him enemies, all of whom were angered by, or was it envious of, his pursuit of justice. Many rumours circulated. One was of a particularly nasty encounter with a fellow Member of Parliament who was evicting tenanted families from his land to make way for luxury cabins surrounding a new golf development. The evictees could keep their jobs on the estate, but had to find places to live. The argument rumbled onto the front pages for a time, but then disappeared. The families were never evicted. It was never printed why the MP had such a sudden change of heart, but most people knew. Such stories, although unreservedly denied, struck a chord with the public and won Baker massive support. Various nicknames from 'Robin Hood' to 'Father Teresa' were penned and once they were in print, they stuck. Further stories surfaced surrounding his overwhelming generosity, but could never be proved. He became somewhat of a living legend.

The indisputable fact was that he had risen from the shadows of the mines to the dizzy heights of Westminster, taking his down to earth manner and upbringing with him. For years, he defended the downtrodden and the victims of a society that often ignored the simple humanity that was in everyone. If there was a cause of injustice worth fighting, then Oscar Baker could be relied upon to assist, less so in his retirement, but even age could not destroy the collective roots of his mining community. Which all made Oscar Baker, ex-miner and ex-politician, respected by friends and foe alike.

America praises those who rise from nothing to something. Britain, on the whole, envies them, even despises them. In Oscar

Baker's case, the great British public willingly shed their usual envious hatred. That he lived in a house such as this was of no consequence to the public. Oscar Baker was a rare breed. It's a cliché, but he truly was a man of the people.

It was impossible for Ben to imagine the figure striding towards him ever wearing a blackened face and steel helmet, emerging from the cage after its ascent from the dark depths. Perhaps it was the grooming of the man or the clothes he wore. Maybe it was the Springer spaniels who raced away from him, tails reaching out behind them, noses pointing forward. Or the magnificent surroundings. It was all of these things and more.

Over his arm, he carried a shotgun, the double barrel lying over his arm, cocked open, brass heads of the two cartridges displayed with bravado. It lay with perfect nonchalance in position, as if it had been born at the same time as its owner, attached at birth like Siamese twins. It was comfortable with its owner and he was with it. With an expert flick, the gun could be quickly closed and used against some unsuspecting grouse or pheasant.

Oscar Baker moved towards them as a fully paid up member of the quintessential landed gentry fraternity.

As he came ever closer, Ben released the tension he was feeling with a few deep breaths. He'd practised his chat up line in the car, but he had imagined delivering it at the front door or in the house. Now, they were out in the open, exposed. They were on Oscar Baker's territory.

Ben reached out with his hand, offering a handshake, but to accept, Baker would have had to release his right forefinger from the trigger area and he was not yet prepared to do that. He stopped a few metres away.

"Good morning," Baker said politely, dropping his head with a quiet nod in Emma's direction. "What can we do for you?"

Ben noticed the use of the word 'we.' Did that mean they were being watched by a silent partner, or was it simply a variation on the royal 'we'? "Good morning," Ben replied, all politeness in return. "We're very sorry to trouble you, but could we take a few minutes of your time?"

217

"In what way?"

"To ask a few questions."

Baker took some time to look them up and down. "I've seen a lot of reporters in my time, but you just don't fit the mould. No appointment, no notebook, no tape recorder, although I don't know what new-fangled listening device has hit the market recently. You're not, how do they say, 'wired up,' are you?"

"No, no," said Ben quickly. "We're not reporters."

"Then who are you?"

"My name's Ben Price and this is Emma Parker," Ben responded naïvely.

Baker chortled quietly, scraping the gravel on the path with his shoes. He spoke in kind tones. "What I mean is, what are you? If you're not reporters, what are you doing here, why are you on my land? It's called trespassing, you know."

"Yes, I know, sir. I do apologise." This was not going well. Ben's intended speech was in disarray. He had been forced gently on to the back foot by the man's charm and status. But that was no bad thing. At least he had brought the spaniels out. Suzanna had warned him that Baker bred Dobermanns as well.

Ben continued. "I'm in a spot of bother, Mr Baker. And I was wondering if you could help."

Baker took a second, longer look at Ben before turning his attention towards Emma. She had not said a word and did not seem to be capable of doing so. "Well, neither of you look too grand, but if I had to choose, I would say that your friend is the one who needs the help." Ben recalled what had stared back at him from the mirror when he woke that morning and compared the image with Emma's present appearance. He had become accustomed to Emma's waif-like, drawn figure, but Baker had reminded him of how pathetic she looked. She could barely stand, let alone communicate.

Baker's voice broke the silence. "Come. Sit down over here." With the barrel of the shotgun, he pointed to one of the benches that lined the driveway. "But please, keep your hands in full view. As a precaution. After all, I still have no idea what you are."

While Ben and Emma sat down, Baker remained standing a few metres away, keeping his distance. "Now, tell me why you are here."

Ben began his tale, part invention, part fact.

"I'm being followed by two men who are threatening to kill me. I don't know who they are or why they are after me. It started a week ago. I was having a quiet drink in a bar, relaxing after work. They sat either side of me. Only one of them did the talking. He said I was going to die and that his silent friend would do the killing. I laughed it off at first, but there was something in their eyes that frightened me. I asked why they were going to kill me and they said they couldn't tell me. They just had to do it. The pressure has been relentless. They warned me that if I went to the police, then they would kill my girlfriend." He placed his arm round Emma's shoulder in a show of unity. "Yesterday, we were walking through Manchester, doing some shopping in the sales, when I noticed them. All they were doing was staring. I looked behind me and they were there. I looked in the shop window and they were in the reflection. One of them even stepped onto the escalator in Marks and Spencer and when I was about to step off, he just touched me on the shoulder. Nothing more. Just touched me. I was terrified. Emma was looking at some lingerie and when I got to her, there was the other guy, right next to her. We stood by the underwear, the four of us together, side by side. They didn't say anything, they didn't do anything. Just stood there. Emma didn't know anything about them at the time, but she felt their closeness and, after they had gone, mentioned them to me and said they were weird. She felt uncomfortable, I was terrified. I thought she had a right to know, so I told her." He held her tighter, squeezing her towards him. "We don't know what to do, didn't know where to turn. Our parents are dead, we've no family, we can't go to the police." Ben's voice was quivering now, displaying the fear he felt, both in reality and fiction. "My Dad talked about you a lot, Mr Baker. He said you were a man of the people, a man of scruples, a man of the law. I'm sorry to disturb you at your home, but you were the only one I could think of. I need your help, Mr Baker."

Ben even impressed himself. He had done a spot of amateur dramatics in the past, carrying the odd tray on to stage, but this was quite a performance by his standard. The truth was that most of it was not acting. Deep down, he was terrified, not only for himself but for those around him. That terror had surfaced in the tale he told to Oscar Baker.

Baker listened intently. Ben could tell that he had got his attention, that the relentless battle for the underdog on which Baker had made his name was still alive. Ben could see it in his eyes. Baker raised his finger from the trigger and held it by his lips, in pensive thought. Scraping the gravel with the sole of his shoe, he gazed at the indentation he had made. Minutes passed, but Ben had learned the art of waiting. Timing was the key. He waited for the response.

Looking up from the ground, he said, "Ben, you have no proof of any of this, except for your dishevelled appearance and the fear in your voice. But I'm willing to believe you at this point. However, there is nothing I can do for you personally except to make a few phone calls to the Greater Manchester police. As you will imagine from your father's comments, I have contacts there. Influential contacts. You must go to the police and tell them everything. Trust me, you will both be perfectly safe. They will protect you."

Baker's response was what Ben had expected from the law abiding ex-politician. Of course, he could never follow the advice. Ben knew that to tell all, the real truth, to the police would be to condemn himself to a prison cell for a very long time.

Ben felt the first drops of rain on his hands. It was not heavy, but the drizzle increased as the three waited for each other to speak. "Bloody rain," said Baker. He held his hand out in Ben's direction, signifying that the conversation was at an end. "I have a phone call to make," he continued. "Drive straight to a police station, any station in Greater Manchester, and mention my name. By the time you get there, the wheels will have been set in motion. I promise you."

With his arm around Emma's shoulder, Ben rose from the bench and took the offered hand with his free hand. "I can't thank you enough, Mr Baker. Everything my Dad said was true." Shaking Baker's hand vigorously, he continued. "You don't know anything about a group of people called the Donors, do you? Only the talkative one mentioned them at our first meeting."

Timing. Perfect. If Ben had not been expecting some reaction, he would have failed to notice, but there was a definite split second pause in the hand shaking and a change in the look in Baker's steely eyes. Briefly. Very briefly, but it was there.

The rain became more persistent, the drizzle becoming thicker. Baker released his hand from Ben's and began to turn towards the house. He whistled to the spaniels who were chasing the raindrops, reaching out and snapping at them. With his back towards Ben and Emma, Baker raised his arm to his side and flung the palm of his hand in the direction of the house. "Come on, you two. Let's get in the house or we'll get soaked." He began to break his seventy year old body into a run. Ben and Emma followed.

And it was then that Baker's mobile phone rang in his pocket.

*

To put an age to the man was not easy. The grey hair that hung over his collar placed him in his fifties, but the ease with which he moved put him in his forties, perhaps even younger. There was a bounce in his step, fluidity in his turn, speed in his sidestep. Sure, he had the beginnings of a paunch around his middle, emphasised by the whiteness of his shirt, but there was a straightness to his back and a width across his chest that suggested he kept himself reasonably fit.

Suzanna had first noticed him when she had succumbed to the temptation of a vanilla milkshake. As she made her way across the car park, he had watched her. This was nothing new to Suzanna. Men did look at her, found her instantly appealing. In her unassuming way, she believed her glossy hair and neat clothes were the main reasons, but Lynn had mentioned many times how the eyes focussed on her pert little bottom as she passed them by. Suzanna blamed Lynn for the admiring glances and the hopeful smiles. Many times they would smile in return, then link their arms like two schoolgirls and attack the next shop on their list. She'd grown accustomed to men taking second looks.

Sitting in her car, sucking at the straw, she could see him through the rain that was now falling on the windscreen. He was leaning against the wall under the canopy outside the supermarket. There was no staring in her direction, but whenever she looked across, he seemed to be turning his head away from her.

He disappeared for a while, but occasionally returned to his wall, turning away every time she peered through the rain. A sense of unease drifted through her. She had the feeling that she was being watched, rather than looked at. Studied rather than admired.

She decided to move on. Bringing the car to life, she slowly pulled out of the parking bay, glancing in her mirrors at the same time. He watched the rear of her car for a while, then left his wall and returned inside.

Being a little old-fashioned, she viewed uniforms with a certain amount of respect. The wearers were there to do a job, to protect something, whether it be people or property. But in the present circumstances, waiting for Ben and Emma to return, the man in the security uniform with the grey hair and the slight paunch at his waist, the man who found her so interesting, could only be regarded as a threat.

Maybe her imagination was playing tricks, but better to be safe than sorry. For her own peace of mind, she had made the right decision to drive away. She would have to return later, to meet Ben and Emma, but then she would be more alert and park up a little less conspicuously.

She drove away from town, down a winding country lane that led past dog kennels on the left and riding stables on the right. Speed limits were not broken and she was certain she was not followed. It was a good fifteen minutes before she cast her mind back to the kennels and the stables. She'd seen them before. Not in reality, but on a large scale map that she had been looking at that morning while the rest of her house slept.

Maybe it was subconscious thinking, maybe it was sheer coincidence, but the country lane was taking her in the direction of Oscar Baker's house, a place she did not really want to be near. Ben was perfectly clear when he said that she was their secret weapon, the one person in their group who was unknown to Sebastian and Delaney and she had to remain so. That was why she had spent hours away from the action getting progressively colder in a car park by McDonald's.

Pulling off the lane into a lay by, she manoeuvred her car through a three point turn and made her way back to the heart of Wilmslow. Because of the narrowness of the lane, she remained in third gear, driving slowly, and that is probably what saved her life.

She had a split second to react. It appeared from nowhere, on her side of what little road there was, travelling at a reckless speed more suited to a motorway. Taking in the obvious details, it was a black 4X4 with a huge grill at the centre front. The driver was leaning forward, almost shoving the steering wheel forward as if it would give him more speed.

One thing was obvious: he was making no attempt to avoid a collision. He didn't need to. There would be only one winner in this contest and it would not be Suzanna. She would be rammed into the ditch at the side of the road, her car a write-off, and he would motor on with barely a scratch on his chromed grill.

She moved quickly and instinctively. Swerving to the left, her tyres spun on the wet grass that bordered the tarmac of the road. She was sliding rapidly towards the ditch. She yanked the steering wheel back to the right, but struggled to change the car's direction. Her back wheels were edging ever closer to the final drop which would send the rear of the car tumbling down the small embankment, either flipping the car over or becoming permanently wedged with the front wheels in the air, spinning wildly.

Front and rear wheels seemed to be working against each other, one set resigned to the plunge into the approaching ditch and the other set attempting to keep their head above the water, struggling for survival. If the car had been more flexible, it would surely have stretched and then broken.

Suzanna could hear the grit from the side of the road hitting the underside of the wheel arch, thrown there by the velocity of the spinning front tyres. She eased her foot off the accelerator pedal and immediately felt more grip at the front of the car. The tyres were beginning to bite, but she was still sliding on, more sideways now as the anarchic rear of the car fought against the control being gained at the front.

Suddenly the struggle was over. Her body jerking against the pull of the seat belt, she held on to the steering wheel as the car lurched forward away from the ditch. The 4X4 had not yet fully passed her and the front of her car now raced towards the enormous bumper on the back. Pulling the steering wheel to the left, she felt an immediate response and pulled clear. Almost. There was a slight collision, one that administered a dent to the front of her car, but, she presumed, little damage to the 4X4.

And why did 4X4s have to have that enormous spare wheel, covered in customized metal, protruding from the back? The impact lifted her car up at the front, but she was soon back down on the road with a thud that threw her body forward against the seat belt. The opposite hedge appeared from beyond the 4X4. Demanding further response from the front tyres, she slammed her foot down on the brake pedal. There was no ditch on this side of the road, so she came to rest with the front part of her bonnet merging into the leafless hawthorn hedge. The scrapes from the thorns on its branches made her shudder, like fingernails dragged down the blackboard at school. Her whole body shook. It was a few seconds before she realised that her car was at a standstill and the 4X4 had raced away with barely a backward glance.

In the silence, she first reached to the side to undo her seatbelt, to inspect the damage imposed on her car, but thought better of it. Departure was the better option. Having witnessed the arrogant ferocity on the driver's face, she doubted whether he would return to check on her health, but she could not run the risk. If he did return, then he might insist on phoning for an ambulance, maybe even the police. Then she would have to lie and she had never been very good at that. They would ask her questions that would be impossible to answer. Simple ones like, 'Why were you travelling down this narrow country lane that leads to the residence of Oscar Baker?' No, much better to flee the scene.

Gingerly shifting the gearstick into reverse, she prayed that the damage was not so great that she would not be able to move. She need not have worried. The willing front tyres gripped the grass immediately, the thorns retreating down the path they had previously created on the bonnet. The scraping sent shivers through her entire body, but the car slowly moved away from the hedge and back onto the road.

Engaging first gear, she pulled away in the direction of the kennels and the stables. To her untrained ear, the engine sounded the same as it always did and the car seemed to be rolling along with no flat tyres or bits of car hanging off. She tried second gear and then third, but resisted the temptation to increase speed. There might be another 4X4 just around the corner.

It seemed like an eternity, but the stables on the left and the kennels on the right appeared and passed. She knew that beyond them, the road would widen enough for her to stop and inspect the damage. There could be no attention drawn to her, so if the car was too conspicuous with dirt and dents and scrapes, then she would have to park up somewhere else and walk into town to meet Ben and Emma.

No-one was following her. Passing by woods on her left, she pulled off the road into a parking space normally used by ramblers and dog walkers. Flicking the catch to her seat belt, she opened the door and moved to the front, where she presumed there would be most damage. She was pleasantly surprised. Okay, there were a few scrapes, but they were not too obtrusive, and there were a couple of dents on the front wing of the car where first the bumper and then the spare wheel of the 4X4 had made contact, and there were splatterings of mud along the left hand sills, but overall the paintwork was still intact and the car still looked like a road car and not a stock car.

It now resembled a vehicle that the wealthy of Wilmslow would buy for their sons after they had passed their driving test. A car in which they could have their first speeding fine and their first accident, without damaging Daddy's little baby which stayed in the garage. It was cheap and cheerful and driven to be destroyed. It could be parked in the town's car park without too much attention.

Suzanna drove on.

4X4 drivers. They think they own the road. Some rich plonker with his long hair who just happened to make it big in the music industry. Probably high on drugs after a party. He never even saw her, she guessed.

*

In contrast to the exterior of the house, the interior was modest. The central staircase was impressive, rolling back on itself towards the window at the front of the house, exposing the height of the entire house above the large hallway. It was how the house had been designed and how it had been built and how it had stayed. A chandelier hung from the ceiling on its elaborate chain. Decorated corniche ran along the angle of the wall and ceiling. Beyond the staircase, logs of every size and description adorned a huge open fireplace that had at one point been the focal point of the house's revelry, the pig turning on the spit, the guests drinking their grog after the completion of the hunt.

The modesty lay in the touch that the Bakers had brought to this part of the house. Pictures, furniture and the odd table were similar to those Ben would have bought himself. There was no snobbery in their simplicity, even though Ben thought that he could probably fit his entire house into this hallway.

As Baker motioned them to remove their wet coats and place them on the coat stand by the front door, Ben noticed a miner's helmet hanging on a nail to the side. It was coated with a scattering of dark coal dust, interrupted by the odd finger mark. It had never been cleaned, never dusted. Ben imagined the finger marks were Baker's, touching it on his way out of the house to remind himself of his humble beginnings.

Baker pointed at the hallway settee. Ben and Emma sat down, waiting for their host.

"Okay," Baker said. "No problem at all." He lifted the phone away from his ear and clicked the off button, returning the phone to his pocket. "Sorry about that. No peace for those in business. Fancy a cup of tea or something stronger perhaps."

"No, it's okay," Ben replied. "We don't want to take up too much of your time. You've been very good to us already. We don't want to overstay our welcome."

Baker removed his coat and sat close to them on an armchair. He leaned forward with his forearms resting on his thighs. "Now, what was it you asked me before the rain came?"

"I asked you if you knew anything about the Donors."

Baker stroked his chin with his hand, rolling his fingers through the dimple that stood in the centre as if deep in thought. Slowly, he began to shake his head. "No, never heard of them. Sounds like something to do with blood or sponsors of football teams. What are they?"

"Well, to be honest, I don't know if they really exist. It's just that one of my stalkers mentioned them."

"In what way?"

Ben had reached the point of no return. He could either end the conversation now or he could reveal more. He had no idea of the consequences of pursuing the latter course, but this was why he had come here. Baker was his only hope, as Suzanna had repeated on more than one occasion.

Taking a deep breath, he began. "When you left your Westminster office, you were approached by the Prime Minister to research the possible instigation of a secret organisation which could right the wrongs of the justice system. He felt that too many of the guilty were being released without charge. Although the concept floundered, it never went away and eventually the Donors were formed. They now finance, through taxpayers' money, the killing of those who have evaded justice. They financed the death of Jimmy Buller, the killer of my fiancée, and I killed him."

Baker remained motionless on the chair, staring passively at Ben. When he spoke, it was with the succinct political directness for which he was famed. "Go on," he said.

"I am not blaming the Donors for what I have done. I had the choice. I chose to kill. But then there was more, something I had not agreed to. A second killing was demanded and if I did not comply, then proof would have been revealed as to how I killed Buller. I was being blackmailed. Kill someone I didn't know or spend the rest of my life in prison."

Ben paused, allowing Baker time to respond. Surely Baker would ask how he knew so much. After all, clandestine discussions between Prime Ministers and former Members of Parliament were not exactly out there in the public domain. They were the stuff that newspapers would pay a fortune for, the intrigues of government, especially the contents that Ben was privy to. "Go on," was all Baker said.

"I couldn't kill the second time. As you can imagine, this didn't make me very popular and that's why I'm being followed and threatened."

"So, the story you told me outside was untrue," interrupted Baker. "There was no chase through Manchester and Emma is not your girlfriend."

"The chase took place, but Emma is not my girlfriend."

"So, what has Emma to do with all of this?"

Ben quickly switched to lying mode again. He was getting good at it. Instinct told him that bringing Charles Ashcroft into the tale was inviting more controversy, something he could do without. "I've known Emma for years," he replied. "It's just that she was with me yesterday, doing some shopping. Those who were following me have seen her now. They know who she is. I thought she'd be safer with me."

"Very noble of you," Baker said. He pushed his frame from the chair and strolled towards the staircase. Ben watched him carefully. Even Emma raised her head. Standing with his back to them, he continued. "The Donors, as you call them, do not exist. They never have done. I admit that in the dim and distant past, I looked at the possibility of the formation of such a group, but it was an ill conceived, hideous idea that was born out of general conversation amongst a group of drunken parliamentarians. If the plan had gone ahead, it would have signalled the end of the law and, some might say, democracy. The notion that a group of people could have been above the law appalled me. The idea sank so quickly, it never had a chance to flounder first." He turned quickly to face his guests. Walking towards them, leaning forward, he said, "The Donors do not exist."

Baker stood over them for some seconds, which seemed like an eternity, before continuing. "Now I need a cup of tea. You must join me."

Ben was stunned by the sudden change in Baker. Standing over them he was dominant and aggressive, the old headteacher admonishing his pupils, but now he was the charming host, offering light refreshment at a summer garden party. Disappointed by Baker's dismissal of the Donor's existence, Ben struggled to drag the conversation back. "The Donors don't exist?" was all he could manage.

"Exactly. Do you take sugar?" Baker began to turn away.

"Mr Baker, the Donors do exist. I can prove it."

"Go on then. Tell me. Prove to me that the Donors exist," Baker demanded.

"I've told you already. If it wasn't for them, I wouldn't be in this position. They forced me into everything."

"And I only have your word for that. The word of a grieving fiancé who has killed the man he perceived to be his fiancée's killer." Slowly, he turned to face them. His demeanour had changed again. He opened his mouth to speak, but was silenced by the ringing of his mobile phone. Quickly, he turned and held the phone to his ear. He said nothing during the brief call. Clicking off the off button, he faced Ben and Emma for the last time. "Business," he said. "Something that requires immediate attention. So, forgive me. I repeat to you what I said outside. Go to any police station in Manchester. They will be expecting you. Give yourself up. No-one is above the law, Ben. Not even you."

Ben helped Emma from the settee and held out his hand. "Thank you, Mr Baker. You have been a great help. I believe I have to consider my options."

"There is only one option." Baker ignored Ben's outstretched hand and opened the front door.

Ben walked through, supporting Emma with his arm around her shoulder. He heard the door close behind them and sensed the eyes watching them as they made their way towards the rental car parked at the end of the drive.

Ben turned the key in the ignition and smiled.

*

The uniform was the same, but the man was different. The grey-haired man with the beginnings of a paunch had been replaced by an obviously older man. He leaned against the same wall, but as he pushed himself away, Suzanna noticed him roll his neck and stretch his back before he moved inside. And he smoked. Whether that made him less observant than the first man, Suzanna did not know. She just thought she could get away from him more easily if there had to be a foot race.

As she pulled to a halt, her mobile phone began to ring.

"Just thought you'd like to know we're on our way back," said Ben, as calmly as if he was returning from a football match and would she put the kettle on.

"How did things go?" Suzanna asked.

"Good. I'll tell you later. See you in about twenty minutes."

"Okay," said Suzanna and the phone clicked off.

*

Ben had much to ponder. He was pleased with his meeting with Oscar Baker. He was the man his father told him about and more. A living legend was how his father had described him, a man loved and respected by the people, which was rare indeed amongst the conniving group of politicians that ran the country. Distrust of them had become an epidemic in the country, but amongst them Oscar Baker stood alone, a beacon of light for the average Joe, fighting grievances that other politicians chose to ignore for fear of upsetting their boss, or his boss, and losing their own credence within whichever political party they associated themselves with. It didn't matter which one. They were all the same nowadays.

Oscar Baker was a man to be admired and Ben's ten minutes with him had done nothing to diminish his legendary status.

He was a man who would do everything for the right reasons and Ben was convinced that the conception of the Donors was not an exception to this. It was just that, well, the whole concept had got out of hand. Oscar Baker was no longer at the reins and the horse had galloped away from him. Legs stretched to the limit, mane flowing back, nostrils flaring, the Donors were out of control and not even Oscar Baker knew which direction it was travelling in.

Oscar Baker did not know how to help Ben Price. The hopelessness was there in his eyes and in his reactions. The only solution he could muster for Ben was to go to any police station in Greater Manchester. Forlornly, Baker still held on to the notion that had kept him going all these years. Ben Price could rely on the law. It was just that Ben didn't believe that. And with a heavy burden of sadness, neither did Oscar Baker anymore.

Ben was running these thoughts through his mind as he made his way back to the car park in Wilmslow, where he would meet Suzanna. They would return to her house and discuss with Tom and Doris their next course of action.

But sometimes in life, things don't turn out the way you expect them to.

At first glance, the accident did not look serious. Still on all four wheels, the 4X4 was stretched across the width of the road at ninety degrees, as if it had been parked there with extreme precision. There was no obvious damage to the bodywork and everything seemed to be in the right place.

It was the detail that revealed the true picture. The front wheels of the car lay at an angle which suggested the driver had attempted to retrieve an impossible situation. Wisps of smoke rose from the tyres. Steam crept out from beneath the bonnet.

And then there was the noise. The horn was blaring, set into operation by the head of the driver which lay against it. Ben could see a mass of hair straggling its way around the steering wheel.

All thoughts of Oscar Baker and Donors disappeared. Ben's reactions were instinctive. As he rushed out of his car, he smelt burning rubber. On the other side of the 4X4, black tyre marks reached out along the road at impossible angles. Even to the uninitiated eye, the reason for the crash was quite obvious. The driver was driving too fast for any road, but on this narrow country lane, it was mindless.

Racing round the rear of the car, Ben brushed past the protruding spare wheel. First checking that there was no-one else in the car, he wrenched the driver's door open. There was no movement from the inert body. Clothed in a baggy coat, protection against the winter chills, it was

231

impossible to tell if it was male or female. Arms hung loosely on either side of the legs, the whole weight of the driver against the steering wheel.

Basic first aid ran through Ben's mind. The head was the most important. Keep it as immobile as possible. But that was difficult if the whole upper body was to be moved. There was a slight gap between the chin and the chest, big enough to slide his arm through. Then maybe he could support the head and lift the shoulders away into a more upright position.

As Ben reached forward, doubts emerged. Should the body be moved at all? Was he only moving the body so that the incessant noise from the horn would stop? An ambulance. He should phone for an ambulance. But if he did that, then the questions would start and Oscar Baker would be drawn into it and he would have to tell Ben's story to the police and then there would only be one option, as Baker had said earlier.

From his position by the open door, and unable to distinguish any breathing because of the heavy coat, Ben could not even tell if the driver was alive. Perhaps immediate help was needed. An ambulance would be too late. The driver had to be moved. It suited everyone: the driver, Ben and Oscar Baker.

Sliding his hand under the driver's chin, Ben could feel the driver's stubble. Confirmation that the driver was a man. It made Ben feel better. There was less reason to be gentle. He felt he could manhandle a man's body more readily. Crazy thoughts in a life or death situation, but that's how Ben's mind worked.

He took a firm grip on the man's chin, ensuring that it remained in its exact position. He placed his free hand at the front of the man's shoulder, palm down, fingers in the cavity by the collar bone. To minimise movement from the spine, head and neck, he would have to move both head and torso at the same time. Gently he began to lift the body into an upright position.

Immediately the blaring from the horn ceased. It brought a calmness to the whole event, the silence a little unnerving at first, but a relief all the same. Centimetre by centimetre, he raised the body away from the steering wheel, keeping the head facing forward and down, unwilling at this stage to raise it for fear of damage to the neck. The movement of the body revealed gaps around the waist. He looked the body up and down for blood. In accidents in the movies, he'd seen blood gushing from unseen places at the merest hint of movement, but here there was no such thing, not even a trickle.

The man's back was slowly making contact with the seat, gently as if placing a baby on the changing mat for the first time, ensuring every part was straight and relaxed. The torso was securely in place. Now came the bit he was dreading. The neck and head. Paralysis is incredibly debilitating for the victim, but to be the cause of such a thing would be worse. Perhaps he should leave well alone, pull the unused seat belt across the man's chest, leave him immobile with his head resting against his chest, call for an ambulance and go. But it was in Ben's nature to help if help was required. Anyway, his old friend curiosity had made its appearance again.

Leaving one hand supporting the near shoulder against the seat, he began to raise the man's head, listening for any cracking of joints, feeling for any grating of bone. He heard nothing, felt nothing. The man's hair was slowly falling away from his face and back into place, each dreadlock following the previous one in perfect rhythm.

And for the first time, there was life. Ben's hand, lying over the collar bone, felt the rise and fall of the man's chest through its fingertips. There was a living being to communicate with. "Come on," said Ben, "let's straighten you up." He knew there would be no response from the man's mouth, but if he was conscious, he would know he was no longer alone. There was someone there to help. "Gently now," as another dreadlock fell backwards to his shoulder. "Come on, Bob." Ben smiled that he had instantly named the man after that great hero of reggae, Bob Marley. "The last time I saw hair like this was …."

Before he could finish the sentence, something struck him hard in the midriff, taking all the wind from his lungs. He fell back, holding his stomach, gasping for breath. He felt his lungs react, expanding and contracting rapidly, struggling for just a little of the oxygen that surrounded him. But they were failing. Another blow struck him just under the rib cage, lifting him from the ground for an instant, forcing his upper body forward. And then another, this time with the palm of a hand, hard against his sternum.

Things were happening so quickly that he could not tell from which direction the attack had come. The present had become a blur. He was staggering like some drunken oaf in the middle of the road, hands gripping his stomach. He tried to lift his head, but it was too much effort. Only his eyes moved, blinking ferociously with the pain, hazily searching for his assailant through distorted eyelids.

He did not have to look far. There he was, directly in front of him, like some demented Yeti, arms raised at the side, legs stomping towards him in huge, deliberate strides. Ben shook his head, attempting to clear his mind and his vision, but before he could react, the man leapt on him and forced him to the ground. He felt a fist strike him again, taking more air from him. And another, until he lay impotent on the road waiting for the final blow that would end it all. There would be no more pain and no more problems. Sebastian had won his bout with the amateur and the Donors would continue to rise above the law. He didn't care anymore. He would be with Lynn and they could look down together at this corrupt, god-awful planet that was created by God and destroyed by Man.

Instinctively he protected his face with his hands and raised his knees. He had to look his best for Lynn. After all, they had their own wedding to attend. He heard himself whimper, like a terrified dog at the hands of a vicious master, lying there waiting for the next assault.

Without warning, a hand pushed into his chest and the weight lifted from him. The danger was still near. Though there was no sun to create a shadow, he sensed a presence hanging over him from above. Ben knew he still had company, which made him petrified of doing the simplest thing, like opening his eyes.

How the hell had Sebastian found him? Ben ran through locations and people. He was convinced there had been no sign of him at Suzanna's or Emma's. The numerous buses he had travelled on had been Sebastian-free. Tom would not have placed Doris at risk if there was any chance of them being followed from their home to Suzanna's. Was

Sebastian that good, that inconspicuous, that he could hide his presence from them all?

Ben had to face him sometime. Through widening fingers, he looked up. Standing above him like some prehistoric caveman, his assailant swung one arm in front of his chest and one arm behind him. Both hands were holding something long and hard. The arms began their descent, bringing with them a wooden baseball bat aimed directly at Ben's head.

Ben swung to one side and felt the blow crash against the back of his shoulder. Severe pain shot uncontrollably down his arm, his whimper turning into an anguished cry. He continued to roll until he was face up. Down came the baseball bat again, but the movement was more frantic this time and the aim not so true. Ben threw his head to one side and the bat smashed against the tarmac of the road, sending splinters of wood bouncing into the air.

With each swing, the man shouted uncontrollably, willing the bat to land the final blow, but Ben was moving more quickly now, his mind more alert, his increasing desire for self preservation taking over. He rolled back towards the man's legs and knocked him slightly off balance.

Stumbling, almost falling to the ground, the man raised the bat once more, but he could only manage a glancing blow to Ben's upper arm. Ben felt the bat linger there. He spun round. Reaching for the bat, he wrapped both hands around the thicker end and pulled hard. Taken by surprise, his assailant fell towards him. The bat, now with four struggling hands upon it, battered between them, digging into their ribs at awkward angles until, with their bodies rapidly coming closer together, it finally flung itself to one side, away from grabbing hands, clattering on the road by their side.

The full force of the man's body landed on top of Ben, but this worked in Ben's favour. Momentum carried him beyond Ben, his hands reaching out in an attempt to break his fall on the road beyond. Ben used the continuing movement of his assailant to slide his upper body away, frantically kicking his feet against the man's legs at the same time.

Without hesitation, he began to push himself from the ground, glancing over his shoulder in time to see the man's head make contact with the ground, wincing as he saw the man's cheek scraping along the grit of the road. He momentarily thought of running, but he was still struggling to get air into his lungs and his body was so badly shaken from the beatings that it was refusing to stand upright. He remained on all fours, chest heaving, mind numb.

He reached for the baseball bat by his side and grabbed it in both hands. Lying on the ground, the man was beginning to turn towards him, eyes glaring through the dreadlocked hair, skin hanging loosely from his cheek. Ben swung the bat down, but there was no room to create any force and it landed limply on the man's padded coat. A hand at either end, Ben grabbed the bat and threw his body on top of the man who was by now lying on his back pushing himself up on his elbows. Forcing the bat against the man's neck, Ben pushed hard, driving the wooden implement closer to the ground in the hope that the windpipe would be strangulated. It looked for a moment that he would succeed, the man at first struggling, then letting out a long gasp of air from his nose. Ben felt the body underneath him relax.

Was it that easy to kill someone? A wave of guilt ripped through his body. He had taken the life of another human being, albeit the life of someone who was trying to take his. The guilt was as short-lived as it was premature.

Suddenly, hands forced their way between their chests and before Ben could react, four hands wrapped around the baseball bat that still lay across the man's neck. He felt the downward force weaken. The bat began to lift, releasing the pressure on the neck and eventually rising from it. Ben pushed hard against its movement, exerting as much force as he could, but it was a hopeless attempt. The force from below was greater than the force from above.

The bat came to a halt in mid-air between the two faces. There was laughter from below. The man's mouth began to open and the clenched teeth appeared in a sadistic smile. Finally, frighteningly, the eyes opened wide, staring up at Ben. He struggled to push the bat back down, but he knew he had lost the fight, knew that the last remnants of resistance had been battered out of him.

And in his final moments, he realised that his attacker was not Sebastian at all. It was the dreadlocked hippy who, before the nightmare began, had offered him a drink and bragged about being pissed on at Glastonbury. Peace, man. Peace.

The end came quickly. The laughter increased, an inhuman laughter. The body below him began to shake and those wide eyes stared up at him. He felt himself being turned to one side and he could not resist. As he began to fall off the body beneath him, he felt his grip loosen on the baseball bat.

Out of the corner of his eye, there was a sudden flash of movement by his face. Blinking rapidly, but unable to look away, he did not know what to expect. He caught a glimpse of metal pass him closely by and those eyes looking up at him from below changed in an instant. The arrogance drained away, to be replaced by fear. The brown pupils dilated as the metal made contact, piercing the iris in the centre. Natural reaction forced the eyelids to close around the metal which held its position, protruding from beneath the eyelashes.

Loud cries of pain and anguish came from the man. He let go of the baseball bat and reached for the metal that was lodged in his eye, but before he could release the pain, the bat was lifted from between the two bodies and brought down with such force that the man's skull cracked instantaneously. The bat descended a second and third time, each blow measured and direct. Ben rolled away. He could still hear the sound of wood on bone, time after time, even after the cries of pain had stopped.

And then there was an eerie silence. It had all happened in such a short time, yet each second seemed like an eternity, each miniscule part of the action engraved in detail in Ben's mind. He pushed himself from the ground and looked around. His assailant was undoubtedly dead, his skull cascaded in three places, his face distorted from the constant beating. His eyes were open. From the centre of one of them, a hypodermic needle stood proud and erect, buried deep into the brown centre.

Ben turned away and wretched loudly by the side of the road, his entire body shaking. When he had recovered, he turned back to the body. Emma was still standing there, baseball bat in her hands. She looked over to Ben. "Okay?" she asked.

Releasing the grip of one of her hands on the bat, she leaned over the dead body. Reaching down, she held her forefinger against the inside of her thumb, released it quickly and flicked the needle. It moved rhythmically from side to side, like a metronome, with the point firmly attached to the eye. "Always keep one in my bag," she said. "Never know when I may need it."

*

It had been a long twenty minutes. Suzanna looked at her watch. Twenty-three minutes in fact.

She was certain that Ben had not returned to the car park. She was parked in a good spot, less obtrusive than before, yet with a clear view of the entrance. There was only one entrance.

She had shown all the signs of increasing irritation, the fingers tapping on the steering wheel, the constant reference to her watch, the inconsequential flicking of the gear stick to check it was in neutral. She was not very good at waiting. She was better at doing.

Ben's instructions had been logical. "Watch for us driving in. We'll park as far away from the entrance as possible in the middle of a few cars. Give it a good ten minutes to check if we're being followed and then make contact." Ben was not too pleased that Suzanna had smiled at that point, but relaxed a little when she explained that he was beginning to sound like a true professional. "Are you sure you haven't been doing this stuff for years?" she'd asked.

Twenty-four minutes and Ben had not returned.

The sudden ringing of her mobile made her jump. She patted her chest and breathed out before taking the phone from the seat next to her. 'Emma,' she thought. 'I bet it's Emma who has delayed them. I knew he shouldn't have taken her with him. A liability, that's what she is. No good to anyone, not even herself. She's probably collapsed or had a fit or gone all pathetic, saying she's desperate for a fix and can't live without it.'

"Hello," she said aggressively, thoughts of that stupid girl still in her head.

"Suzanna?" She had expected to hear Ben's voice, but it was not. She became concerned and defensive at the same time.

Not wishing to reveal her own identity to an unknown person, she repeated, "Hello?"

"Suzanna, it's Tom," and the relief swept through her body. "Just wondered how things were going." In the midst of all the worry and the irritation, Tom was his usual self, talking calmly, giving nothing away. Perhaps he thought people were listening.

"Okay," she replied. "He said the meeting had gone well and that he would be back in twenty minutes." She thought it best that she didn't reveal that that conversation had taken place twenty-six minutes ago.

"That's good," said Tom. "I'd better get off in case he phones you again."

"Okay, Tom. Thanks." She clicked the off button.

Her eyes had never left the entrance and they had still not arrived. The fingers resumed their incessant tapping on the steering wheel. "Come on," she said to herself. "You were never this late when you were picking Lynn up. Why should an appointment with me be any different?"

She realised her left hand was moving the gear stick from side to side, so raised it quickly. Out of embarrassment really, embarrassment that she was getting more annoyed and for no reason. The number of times Lynn and she had been delayed by a summer dress that they just had to try on and no, it didn't suit Lynn's colouring, but it was perfect for Suzanna, and after the purchase they returned to their arranged meeting point at the café to find Ben reading the sports pages of the newspaper. Lynn would kiss him on the cheek and offer her apologies and Ben would look at his watch and express his surprise and they both knew that he knew exactly what time it was. And he was incredibly calm about it.

There was no reason to panic now that he was a few minutes late.

But Suzanna was worried about him. He had found himself in an unreal situation, dragged along by events which were alien to him. Now he was as deep as he could possibly get, with unknown assassins waiting round every corner.

Suzanna was no longer involved out of a sense of duty to Lynn. She was not waiting in this car park out of some strong allegiance to her friend, nor because she felt a compulsion to look out for him now that Lynn was gone. It was more personal than that. Suzanna was worried about Ben because she wanted to worry about him. And now he was late and it was because of poor little Emma who couldn't look after herself.

Suzanna didn't realise just how wrong she could be.

*

"Was there anything in that?" Ben asked, pointing to the needle that was still embedded in the man's eye.

Emma laughed and shook her head. "Why should I waste any stuff on him?" she asked.

Still holding the baseball bat in her hand, she stood over the body inspecting the damage. The skull, lying face up in a thickening swamp of blood, was battered beyond recognition. Each dreadlock fell backwards, wriggling towards its final resting place in the increasing coagulation. Streams of red rested in the lines around his forehead, eyes and mouth. In contrast, his torso and legs were as normal, in some macabre way emphasising the violence that had been unleashed on his skull.

Ben made his way over to Emma and took the blood-splattered bat from her hand. He had seen enough of the corpse on the road, but Emma seemed to be transfixed, unable to tear her eyes away, moving her head to get a closer look. It was an abnormal reaction to something so sickening, especially when Emma's recent fragile state was taken into consideration.

Fearing that she was close to hysteria, there had to be some adverse response at some stage, he calmly said, "It's too repulsive to look at, Emma. Come on, let's get you back to Suzanna's."

Placing an arm around her shoulder, he expected that she would come along with him as she had always done, but she shrugged him away and crouched down, inspecting the damage she had created. When she spoke, it was with a strength Ben had not heard before. "Have you ever been to Accident and Emergency on a Friday night, Ben?" she asked, but didn't wait for a response. "Now that's enough to make you puke. Never buy a motor bike, Ben. Motor bike accidents are the worst. Smashed hips, legs, arms, you name it. Anything can get broken when you get flipped off one of those things at a hundred miles an hour. And it's rare that there's a full recovery. A man with a severe limp or one leg has more trouble finding a decent girl, you know. And you wouldn't believe how many times the crash helmet comes off. They think it will protect them against anything. Well, I can tell you, it doesn't." She flicked a finger in the corpse's direction. "This is minor. Severe head injuries, smashed skull. Even if he had lived, there would have been permanent brain damage. Better for him that he's dead. Anyway, it was either him or you, Ben. And I didn't fancy much for my chances if you'd been the one to die."

Ben realised that Emma had not been close to hysteria at all, far from it. She was simply doing what came naturally to her, examining the body, assessing the injuries so that she could use this experience in the future. She had seamlessly slipped into professional mode. And she was good, very good. He could see why Lynn thought Emma so special, why she did not want her to waste her life.

There was one other thing. She had saved his life.

"I don't know how to thank you, Emma," he said.

Rising from her crouched position, she looked Ben up and down. She lifted her hand to his cheek and stroked it gently. Despite his dishevelled appearance, he was still a good looking guy. "I do," she said. She nodded in the direction of the open door of the 4X4. Taking a step back, Ben recoiled from the thought. He didn't expect such a reaction. Emma grabbed him by the arms, the baseball bat falling to the ground.

"Emma," Ben said. "I don't think ...."

"That's right Ben. Don't think. Just do." She pulled him closer, reaching her hand around the back of his neck and pressing her cheek against his. It was all too crazy for Ben. The corpse was lying on the road and here was its killer taking her reward. He felt an obligation to go through with it, but was repulsed by the thought.

"You know what?" Emma whispered in his ear.

"What?" Ben responded, lamely.

"It's bloody great," she whispered seductively, "when you can get a man not knowing if he is coming or going." She withdrew her hand from his neck and her cheek from his. Placing her palms on his chest, she pushed him away, laughing lightheartedly. "Don't look so worried Ben. It's the going that you'll be doing, not the coming."

Ben was unsure how to react. He was surrounded by a hired Ford Fiesta, a crashed 4X4, a nurse who was taking the piss, oh, and a dead body with a needle sticking out of its eye. He just could not think straight. Emma came to the rescue. "And by the way, I know how you can really thank me."

"How?" Ben stammered.

"Stop treating me like some kid who doesn't know what's happening. I am an adult you know and I've got some interest in this. You're not the only one who's had their love taken from them. Now, I think it's best we get out of here. You have a habit of attracting trouble."

She took hold of his hand and led him back to their car. Opening the driver's door, she led him to his seat, like some doting granddaughter leading her Grandad, and made sure his seat belt was fastened. She pulled his face towards her, forcing him to look at her. "Are you okay?" she asked. There was no response. She landed a quick slap across his cheek. "Are you okay?" she repeated. "Because I bloody well need you now, Ben. I haven't got a clue how to drive this thing and I'm coming to the conclusion that this is not a healthy place to be. So, accept I've killed someone, get over the shock and drive." She slapped him again.

His reactions were sharp. Grabbing her wrist with his hand, he held it tight until it hurt. Grimacing with the pain, she shouted for him to let go and tried to wriggle away, but it was no use. His grip was too strong. Slowly she relented and was pleased to accept that he was back in control, not of Emma, but of himself.

They looked each other in the eyes and knew that what they had been through had drawn them closer together. Ben had Emma to thank for saving his life and, in a different way, the reverse was true. Ben honestly believed that Emma was on her way back from the depths to which she had sunk. Whether it was because of her respect for Lynn or whether she was accepting that not all the world was against her, he did not yet know, but the main thing was that from this moment, he would treat her like an adult and not some kid who didn't know what was happening.

"Thanks," he said quietly.

"Drive," she replied. She ran round the front of the car and jumped in. He set off slowly. With the right hand wheels on the grass and the thorns of the hedge making horrendous sounds down the side of the car, he eased them through the gap at the rear of the 4X4.

"Which one was he?" asked Emma as he pulled the wheels back onto the road and accelerated away.

"What do you mean?"

"The dead guy. Was he Sebastian or Delaney?"

"Oh, neither."

"Neither?" Emma exclaimed. "According to your story, there were two guys chasing you up and down the streets of Manchester trying to kill you, Sebastian and Delaney. Please don't tell me I've just killed someone who just happened to have an accident in a 4X4, an innocent passer-by."

"No, no, not at all," said Ben apologetically. "I've met him before when I was out on one of my many evening benders. We got talking about Glastonbury and all sorts of rubbish. I soon got tired of the conversation and left."

"So, I've just killed one of your ex-drinking partners?"

Ben swung the car round a tight corner, the steering wheel alive to his every touch. He laughed. "He wasn't simply a drinking partner. He was planted there by Sebastian, to lure me into their game, before the brawl outside the pub when I was arrested."

"Is that some theory you've got or is it true?"

"It's true. Sebastian told me he was one of his."

243

Emma looked out through the window, but she was seeing nothing. Her head hadn't been this clear for months. She was totally focused on the events of the day. Entering the fray, as it were, as a late outsider, she was able to bring a new perspective to everything. As is often the case, people close to the events cannot see what is right in front of their nose.

"How about this then?" she said to Ben. "Sebastian is the dead dreadlock's boss, so there is a connection between the two of them." Ben nodded. Emma continued. "We can only assume that Sebastian was not close enough or he would have been here himself. I think it's fair to say that you have got right up his nose, so he wouldn't let someone else kill you if he could have done it himself. So, he sends the dreadlocks. Now, if you were Sebastian, what would you do? Just leave dreadlock to it, or would you get to the scene as quickly as you could?" There was no need for Ben to reply. The answer was obvious. Emma continued. "So, we can assume that Sebastian or Delaney or both are on their way."

"Why do you think I'm driving so fast?" asked Ben.

"Okay, wise guy. So you had figured that out already. What about this? How did Sebastian know we were here?"

Ben raced past the kennels and stables, willing the car to reach the safety of the junction by the main road. He knew this was the direction from which Sebastian would come. There was no other route, no other option, not if Sebastian was still in the Manchester area.

Although he was unused to the car, he found the drive relaxing. He had always been able to drive and think at the same time. He couldn't understand why some people had to have full concentration when driving. If something happened, required his attention, he reacted instinctively, found it easy. He could easily switch his thoughts to the moment if need be.

And at that moment, his mind was on what Emma was saying. The only people who knew he was going to Oscar Baker's house were Tom, Doris and Suzanna. He could trust them all. The only reason one of them would talk was if Sebastian had got to Suzanna's house and had threatened Doris' life. Tom would have had to relent, much to the annoyance of Doris. But he was certain that Sebastian could not know about Suzanna, so the house was safe and so was Suzanna. Of course, Emma knew they were going, but Emma had more than proved herself. So, back to Emma's question. How did Sebastian know where they were?

"Tom, Doris and Suzanna can be trusted," said Emma, "so they wouldn't have said anything. But there was one other person who knew we were at Oscar Baker's house."

Ben increased his speed as the lane widened. That was the easy bit. The difficulty lay in finding the answer to Emma's conundrum. "Who?" he asked timidly. He had the feeling he was just about to be made a fool of.

"Ben Price," she said sarcastically. "Teacher extraordinaire. If you asked one of your kids to name the factors of, say, twenty-four, which factor are they most likely to forget?"

Without hesitation, he replied, "One."

"And the factors of thirty? Which one might they forget?"

"One."

"Correct," said Emma, with exaggerated pride that she was still one step ahead of the teacher. "The kids are most likely to forget the only number that is a factor of all numbers, the number that is constant. They forget the obvious." She gave him time to contemplate, but there was still no response. "So, who are you most likely to find at Oscar Baker's house?"

Ben banged his hand down on the steering wheel, but smiled at his stupidity at the same time. "Oscar Baker," he said.

"Well done, teach," she said.

"But Oscar Baker didn't know we were going to his house, did he?" asked Ben.

"Not when we arrived, hence the gun, which personally I thought was a bit over the top. But there were two phone calls while we were there. Business, he said, but what type of business?"

Ben was thinking back, reliving the events from the time they had first seen Baker emerge from the side of the house to the time he had dismissed them.

Emma was ahead of him. "As soon as you mentioned the Donors to Baker, he changed. Up till then, he was willing to help, use his influence. But then the rain began to fall and he told us to follow him to the house. I don't think he was protecting us against the rain, I think he was protecting himself. He didn't dare let someone leave who knew about the existence of the Donors."

"And that's when the phone rang for the first time."

"That's right."

"Who do you think?"

"Could have been anyone, but one guess might be that it was Sebastian, because after that Baker did everything to delay our exit. He even offered us a cup of tea for Christ's sake. Twice. Five minutes before, he had his finger on the trigger of a double barrel shotgun. Now that's some change in approach."

"Then there was the second call."

"Sebastian giving him the all clear to let us go. Our exit was pretty rapid, you must admit. No tea being offered now. Their man, good old dreadlocks, was in place and ready. Baker wanted us off his land as quickly as possible."

"So you think Baker is a member of the Donors."

"Maybe, but maybe not. My opinion, for what it's worth, Ben Price, who thinks I'm a little kid, is that Baker knows about the Donors, but wishes he didn't. He was there in their infancy, but wanted out when he realised they were so much above the law. He near enough said that himself. So he distanced himself from them with no strings attached. And the price for that? Silence about the Donors' existence from Oscar Baker. Up until now, it has been easy for him to keep his part of the bargain. But then you came along, upsetting the apple cart."

"It all sounds reasonable to me, Emma. Except one thing. Why would Sebastian contact Baker if he was no longer part of it?"

"Why did *we* contact him?" asked Emma.

"He was our only link to the Donors. Our only option."

"Perhaps it was the same for Sebastian. Might have been his last throw of the dice. He couldn't find you and had nowhere else to turn. Baker was his only option as well."

"There's one other thing that makes your crazy idea not so crazy. Sebastian knew that I knew about Baker's connection with the Donors. Sebastian was the one who told me. Maybe it wasn't anything to do with throwing dice, maybe it was logic."

"And if that's the case, then maybe we're not too far ahead of him."

"Not far enough is my guess."

*

"Suzanna?"

"Ben, where the hell are you? Twenty minutes you said and now it's thirty-six."

"Sorry about that. We got a bit delayed."

"Delayed? Well, why the hell didn't you phone me and let me know."

"You could say we had our hands full."

"Had your hands full? What the hell are you talking about?"

"We got a little distracted."

"Well get undistracted and get back here. I've been worried sick about you."

"No need to worry. Not at all. And there's no reason to hang around. There's been a slight change of plan."

"Change of plan?"

"Go back to your place and wait there with Tom and Doris. Emma and I have to make ourselves scarce for an hour or two. We're both safe, but we need to make doubly sure that we're not being followed. We're making a slight detour, but all being well, we'll meet you at your house this evening."

"All being well? Are you sure you're okay?"

"Yes. Sure. Go back to yours and we'll see you later."

The phone clicked off.

"Men," said Suzanna aloud. "Do this, do that. No explanation." Clicking to the contacts list, she looked at Ben's number on the screen in front of her. Shaking with annoyance, she held her finger over the 'call' key, but thought better and refrained from phoning him. She tossed the phone onto the seat by her side and turned the key in the ignition, pulling away from the car park, faster than she had intended.

It took a while for her heart rate to settle, mainly because certain phrases he'd used kept jumping out at her: 'Making a slight detour,' 'Make ourselves scarce,' 'Got a little distracted,' and 'Had our hands full.' Her imagination ranged from Ben and Emma being discovered and followed, to them making wild abandoned love in some barn on bales of hay.

By the time she was driving down the familiar road of Victorian terraces, sanity reigned and Ben knew what he was doing and Emma had ceased to be a raving nymphomaniac. She was a lesbian after all. So what was Suzanna worried about?

*

Police Constable Simon Austin was still, metaphorically, in short trousers. He'd done all the training, passed with flying colours, but was now learning on the job and was expected to make mistakes along the way. He was determined not to. In the two days since becoming a fully fledged member of the Constabulary, he had managed to avoid any jibes from his new colleagues, although on one occasion, filling in a 'theft of bicycle' on a 'rape' form was very nearly the catalyst for much deserved, well meaning, abuse. Fortunately, he spotted his mistake before anyone else did.

His sergeant had protected him from any disasters, kept him away from any flash points or trouble spots and so far had put him with an experienced copper who knew the ropes.

Now he was on his own. It was nothing special, a routine job, but he was flying solo for the very first time. It felt strange, like driving a car for the first time with no-one next to you in the passenger seat. Nervous as hell, yet when it was over, he would feel like he could conquer the world. Unless he cocked up and then the shit would really hit the fan.

"Nobody should be allowed down here unless they can show official ID," the sarge had said before he drove off and left him standing in the middle of a country lane with just a few cows for company. The only sound he could hear was the barking of the dogs from the kennels they had passed on their way.

Of course, Constable Austin had no idea what mayhem lay beyond the double bend ahead of him.

Minutes after the sarge had left, a blue Mondeo approached, registration PC 05 CND, two men in the front, rear seats vacant, driven at normal speed. He was already compiling his report in his mind. Standing in the centre of the road, he raised his arm, right palm facing the Mondeo.

The car pulled gently to a halt, and Austin made his way to the driver's side. The electric window slid down. "I'm sorry, sir, but I have orders that no vehicles should be allowed beyond this point. You will have to find an alternative route."

The driver was already raising his hand, but he allowed the constable to finish his sentence before handing over his ID. He had always been taught that it was rude to interrupt. Good manners are the essence of civilization, his father had said.

Austin read the details on the card. There were a few abbreviations and initials on there that he didn't understand, but it looked official enough and the photograph was that of the driver. He handed it back. "Thank you so much," said the driver. "I hope you don't get too cold. We'll be as quick as we can. If we take too long and the winter chills begin to bite, it's me you should blame. I'm the one who put you here."

The car pulled around the first of the double bends and disappeared from view.

'Well, that didn't go so bad, did it?' thought Austin. 'What a nice man.'

*

"Turn right at the next junction," said Emma.

"Park here on the left." Ben was unsure where Emma was taking him, but had followed her every direction. His concern increased when she took him along some unsavoury streets, and then there was that brick that narrowly missed the car thrown by a bored child with nothing else to do, but now they had stopped, Ben had to admit to being surprised.

The apartment block was modern in architecture and materials. Huge picture windows adorned the front fascia, each apartment distinctively separated from its neighbour by beautifully crafted steel girders. Striking though it was, Ben could not have lived there, even if he could have afforded to. The outside world could see everything that every apartment had to offer, yet each occupant was ignorant of what was happening above and next to them. It was like Big Brother without the cameras.

Emma led the way to the front door where eight door bells sat next to each other, some with names attached, others not. She pressed one of those that remained anonymous.

"Yes."

"Emma Parker." The door clicked open and they walked through. Emma chose the stairs and Ben followed.

Number eight on the top floor was no different from the other seven, at least from the stairwell. All had bland, brown-stained wooden doors with the obligatory peep eye in the centre. Emma rang the bell.

"I hope I can trust your friend," came a voice from beyond the blandness.

"More than me," replied Emma.

"That would not be difficult," said the voice.

The door opened slowly, allowing Emma and Ben to enter. They were greeted by a smartly dressed man, aged about early thirties. He took Emma by the arms and kissed her cheek, then held out his hand towards Ben, which he shook. "My, my, Emma," he said, "you look dreadful, my dear."

"Thank you so much. And you," she said looking him up and down, "look magnificent."

He reached forward and held Emma close to him. Quietly he whispered, "I'm so, so sorry, my dear. She was an angel and a rebel and we loved her for it."

Until this moment, Ben had not known where he was heading or who he was meeting. Emma's new confidence and assertiveness had convinced Ben that he could trust her. Now he felt like an intruder into a world he did not understand.

He turned away and was surprised to see that his view was not of the outside through a large picture window, but of a beautifully designed interior room with light streaming from the skylights above. The apartment was much larger than it had seemed from below. If the owner wished privacy, he could retreat to one of the many back rooms that it held, such as the one they were now in. Privacy was indeed controlled by the occupier. Big Brother was not watching unless the occupier wished him to. Such privacy cost money and lots of it.

"I'm David. I'll introduce myself, seeing as Emma has temporarily lost her manners."

"Ben Price." They shook hands once more.

"Drinks?" David asked.

Emma was quick to respond. "G and T please."

"Ben?"

"A beer would go down just fine," Ben replied. One drink would not do him any harm.

Emma, a little belatedly, introduced David in more detail. She did not hold back. "David is a well respected accountant earning so much money he doesn't know what to do with it. He owns this fantastic place, amongst many others, and is the type of person who sits back and waits for the offers to flood in. He never, ever seeks work. It finds him. True?" she asked in David's direction.

David tilted his head to the side and handed the drinks over. Emma took a sip and continued. "He is also the most decent human being I have ever met. He is my rock and, until I got to know you a little better, Ben, the only man I could trust. Without David, I would have been either in the gutter or in the mortuary."

"That's quite a eulogy," said Ben.

"And all quite true," David replied, raising his glass in Ben's direction.

"So, David, if you are such a decent human being, how could you let Emma get into the state she is in? You obviously like her, judging by the reception you gave her."

"Can I answer that?" asked Emma. David gave another tilt of the head. "He also believes in people helping themselves. Sure, he could give me loads of money to get myself out of this hole I'm in, but he won't unless I can give him my full time commitment to rehab. It's the carrot he dangles tantalisingly in front of me." Ben had to agree with David on that. It would have been like pouring money down the sink. Emma continued. "I could never promise him that. So, every time I needed help, he was there. He's fed me, watered me, sat with me through the night while I shouted obscenities at him and called him all the foul-mouthed names under the sun. So, he's my rock, aren't you?"

"I most certainly am, my dear."

"Can I assume that you are also Emma's supplier?" asked Ben. The words just came from his mouth. There was no proof, just an inkling. Emma was so smarmy when she spoke of him, so sickly sweet. There had to be a reason. Apart from his obvious arrogance, this David man was too good to be true. And no accountant could be this wealthy, could they? There had to be another source for his income.

"Ben, where are your manners?" asked Emma. "That's not a hint of jealousy I can hear in your voice, is it?"

Embarrassment flooded through Ben. He hadn't meant it to show. Envy was probably the better word, but jealousy came pretty close. Ben apologised. "I'm sorry, I didn't mean to assume. The words were out before I thought."

David spoke. "A reasonable assumption on your part. I would think the same way. I'm no drug supplier and I am not Emma's lover. My male companions would find that rather absurd."

With the initial masculine foreplay out of the way, Ben visibly relaxed. There was no reason for the way he reacted, he couldn't explain it himself. If David was the knight in shining armour that Emma was suggesting, he would have Ben's full backing.

Ben reached out his hand once more. "I'll start again. My name's Ben Price and I'm not usually as big a prat as I've just been."

"And I can vouch for that," said Emma.

David laughed out loud and took Ben's hand. "Now, my sweet Emma, what can I do for you? For all my protestations of you looking dreadful, you don't actually look too bad."

"No, I'm not. In fact I'm feeling pretty good. Still off the hard stuff, although I have my ups and downs. The downs are so down I feel like some distant mutant relation to a human being. But I'm getting there. I'm nearly ready to take your money."

"That's excellent news," said David. "It will be there when you need it."

"There is something else," said Emma. "We need a place to stay for a couple of hours. Out of sight."

"And why would that be?"

Emma looked across at Ben. There was quite a story to tell if she wanted to, but she couldn't. Not yet. "David, I would be really grateful if I didn't have to say." She was struggling to keep something from a man who was prepared to give her everything.

Ben interrupted. "Emma has been a great help to me, David. You may find this hard to believe, but she has saved my life. Can I just say that it has something to do with a lady who was an angel and a rebel, and leave it at that for now?"

David turned his glass between his forefinger and thumb before responding. "That's good enough for me. If there's anything I can do to help, let me know."

"You may be sorry you said that," said Ben.

*

Delaney had witnessed extraordinary scenes in his life and this compared with the worst of them. It wasn't the most violent and certainly not the bloodiest, but he knew the events leading up to this, knew the characters involved, and he was astounded by the carnage that had been inflicted.

That two normal people with no specialised training could wreak so much havoc was extraordinary. The ferocity of the attack

253

overwhelmed him. The skull had been assaulted with such force that it was difficult to recognise its separate features, lower chin merging with upper jaw, cranium caving in towards them. And the needle in the centre of the eye. Was it an afterthought or an integral part of the attack? Whatever it was, it was pure theatre. They had left their calling card.

Looking at it from a professional perspective, he was full of admiration. The job was done, the victim deceased. He would have been proud of it himself.

Sebastian stood apart. Paying little attention to the detail, he was more interested in the consequences. Ben Price had outwitted him again. First in Jennifer's apartment, next on the streets of Manchester and now this killing. No-one had ever done that to him before. Three times. He was beginning to get annoyed.

Control was his forté. He liked to organise, perfectly of course, and then see it all come together. He was not used to chasing someone, following in their wake. This was a new experience for him and he didn't like it. Delaney could look at dead bodies all day long, but dead bodies for which he was not responsible proved one thing only. He had lost control.

It was time to get it back.

"Mr Delaney," he said to his colleague. "It's time we seized the initiative. Ben Price has had it his own way for too long. I'll draft the whole team in, holidays or not."

Delaney laughed out loud. "I must see this. There'll be some sore heads and sour faces amongst them and I wouldn't miss it for the world."

Sebastian ignored him. "You go and see Oscar Baker and I'll do the phoning. We'll all meet at the station, back door, back room. I'll make sure it's not being used."

*

Doris was the most annoyed. "What is he playing at?" she asked.

"I have no idea," Suzanna replied. "I've told you everything I know and still don't understand."

Tom was sitting quietly, watching the television. "Perhaps we should take what he said at face value and not read anything into it," he said, not quite knowing if his comment would calm the situation or fuel it. He should have known that the best course of action would be to keep his mouth firmly closed, allow the ladies to vent their feelings, but he thought he had some responsibility to support Ben's actions in his absence.

"What do you mean?" asked Doris, refusing to diminish her anger.

"Well," he explained, "he said they were safe, but they needed to be sure they weren't being followed. Perhaps what he said was what he meant."

"Then why didn't he explain that to Suzanna? I can't use one of those damn mobile phones, but he can, so why not use it?" Doris queried, all questions and no answers.

"In answer to your first question, that's exactly what he did explain, and in answer to your second, perhaps he doesn't need to phone us as he has already told us. Perhaps he trusts us to believe him."

Placing a mug of tea on the table by Tom's side, Doris said quietly, "I know I held her in my arms last night, but I still don't like the idea of him being out there alone with that Emma girl."

Ah, thought Tom. Now we're getting to the real issue.

*

The trousers were too long and the sweatshirt too baggy, but it was great to feel clean clothes against his skin again. Standing in David's bedroom, Ben looked at himself in the mirror, showered and freshly shaven. What a difference the basic needs of man make to one's soul. Maybe even Sebastian would not recognise him now.

Making his way to the back room where they had first entered the apartment, he saw Emma talking to David. Unnoticed, he stopped and stared.

She was revitalized. Her hair was shiny like on the photograph and her complexion had a glow to it. She too was wearing clean clothes but, unlike the ones Ben wore, they fitted her perfectly. Floral skirt just below the knees, tee shirt beneath yellow cardigan, she was the Emma that Lynn must have first met. An English rose not fully bloomed, but no longer pruned to near extinction.

"I think we have an intruder," said David. Ben walked towards them, holding his arms out at the side.

"Not quite as muscular as your friend David here, but not bad all the same," he said.

"And what about our dear Emma?" asked David.

"A picture," Ben replied, almost regretting his obvious enthusiasm. "But where did the clothes come from?"

"David bought me a few items and keeps them here for me."

"I like to see her leave my place looking good," he said. "In the hope that one day, Emma will accept that she truly is an intelligent, beautiful woman."

Emma curtsied, shy look on her face, eyes sparkling. "One day," she said, "I'll make both of you proud."

"I'm sure you will, my dear," said David.

Ben wondered how many times David had said his goodbyes to Emma and how many times she had let him down. Of course, David would say that she was letting herself down, not him, and he would help her for as long as it took. There was something between them that could not be intruded upon, but they had allowed him an insight. He did feel like a gooseberry, but a welcome one now.

"I've been checking the front while you've been showering and there is definitely no-one the least bit interested in this apartment," said David. "It's time to go, I think."

Ben noticed that his coat, which had been hanging on the stand had been replaced by another. Automatically, he put it on. It would go with his new attire. "David," he said, "can you do me a favour?"

"Sure," he said.

"The old coat, don't throw it away. Sentimental value."

"Consider it safe, my dear Ben."

Emma reached up and kissed him on the cheek, holding his back tightly with both her hands. Ben made out her whispered words to him. "My rock," she said.

Ben shook hands and they left.

Descending the stairs, Ben was unaware that Emma had linked his arm with hers. She rested her head against his shoulder and they left the apartment block, returning to the car. They sat in silence for quite some time, looking ahead, before Emma asked, "So, what did you think of Jennifer's illegitimate brother?"

*

Constable Simon Austin had been listening to the sounds of winches and chains for ten minutes, since he had allowed the lorry and the van with the blackened windows through. The man with the ID had been there when they arrived. There was no way to ascertain how many people were in the van and that might give the sarge cause for concern when he submitted his report.

Suddenly the noise stopped and the dogs could be heard.

A police car drove up the road and stopped in front of him. His sergeant executed a three point turn in the narrow lane and opened the passenger door. "Get in, son," he said.

Austin leaned over, talking as he did so. "But there's still a lorry and a van down there, sarge. God knows what they've been up to."

"That's okay, son. Get in."

Constable Austin was about to learn a valuable lesson, one that would have to stay with him if he was to make a career and seek promotion within the Force. Driving steadily down the road, the sergeant advised him. "There are times to ask questions and times to keep your mouth shut. Guess what kind of time this is?"

Austin caught on quickly. "Time to keep my mouth shut."

"Perfect answer. Now here's another couple for you. What lorry and what van?"

Austin was a bright lad. He would go far. "Been as quiet as a graveyard, sarge. No-one came down the lane all the time I was here, sarge."

"Good lad."

"I take it you don't need a report, sarge."

"Not necessary, son."

It was the beginning of a beautiful friendship.

*

Ben hitched the sleeves of his sweatshirt up to his elbows. It was one of his foibles, not liking anything around his wrists, except the watch that could not be relied upon. He looked down at the creases stretching along his lap, more than normal because of the bagginess of the trousers. David was a decent chap. He could see why Emma liked him so much and, following Emma's revelation, he could understand why there was an invisible bond between them.

Leaving the city lights behind them, they headed towards the sanctuary of Old Trafford where there would be some explaining to do. A lot had happened since they had left Suzanna in Wilmslow. As if the meeting with Oscar Baker hadn't thrown up enough, there was the 4X4 and the accident and another killing and David, although Emma might want to keep him out of it.

"You're dying to ask me, aren't you?" said Emma.

"Well, I am a bit …."

"Curious?" Emma offered.

"Curious. And a little confused," replied Ben.

"If you're sitting comfortably, then I will begin. Elizabeth Ashcroft had been consumed by guilt for years. She'd had a fling with the plumber. Just the once, but it was enough. The plumber was happily married, regretted what he'd done, said he didn't have the finances to bring up the child. Elizabeth agreed. Not once was abortion mentioned by Elizabeth or the father. It never entered the equation."

"So what happened during pregnancy?" Ben asked.

"Elizabeth has a sister living in the Scottish Highlands. Very remote by all accounts. She was having a difficult time with her first pregnancy. That's what Elizabeth told Ashcroft anyway. Elizabeth stayed with her for six months and then, hey presto, her sister has a child. Ashcroft had no elections coming up, so no requirements on his wife, so was more than willing for her to go to the Highlands to help. God knows how many women he shagged while his wife was away."

"Did she know what her dear husband was like?"

"Oh yes. According to Jennifer, she had done for years, way before the plumber arrived. Finding the proof was the problem. Then she caught him deflowering the flower girl and that was that. Separate flats. There could be no complaints from Ashcroft. He needed her more than she needed him. She was the perfect politician's wife, loved by the public. It was claimed that she won more votes for her husband than he did for himself. Their marriage of convenience remained as convenient as it always had."

"And David? He obviously knows that Elizabeth is his mother."

"On his eighteenth birthday the two sisters sat down and told him the news. They needn't have bothered. When he was eight years of age, he'd been rummaging round the attic for an old Meccano kit his uncle, who he called Dad, had told him about. In a wooden chest he found a stack of letters from Elizabeth addressed to him. She wrote to him once a week from the time he was born. The letters were meant to be shown either if Elizabeth died or when he reached his eighteenth birthday."

"So, he'd known about it for ten years?"

Emma nodded. "And made a trip to the attic every month to keep up to date. What he liked most of all was seeing his younger sister growing up, each photograph sent by Elizabeth absorbed into his mind."

Ben was flabbergasted. Put in a similar situation, he imagined himself being destroyed by such news. It would be the reason behind everything he did wrong. He could lay the blame on his background and everyone would be sympathetic and support him. David had chosen to live with it. To say he was mature at the age of eight was an understatement.

Emma continued. "David has always said how lucky he has been to have two fathers and two mothers. He loves them all dearly."

"Two fathers?" asked Ben. "Does he look on Ashcroft as a father?"

Emma could not contain her amusement. "Ashcroft as a father? You must be joking. Charles Ashcroft doesn't even know David exists and what's more, he doesn't need to. Elizabeth didn't need his money. She supported David and her sister completely. They wanted for nothing."

"She's that rich?" asked Ben.

Emma nodded. "But none of David's wealth comes from her. She gave him a great start, but it's all self-made."

"I don't doubt it," said Ben. "But what about the two fathers?"

"Well, there's the one who he lived with, his uncle in reality, and then there is his biological father."

"The plumber? I thought he didn't want anything to do with him."

"I didn't say that. I said he didn't have the finances to bring him up. What do you think of David's apartment?"

Ben glanced across at Emma. "Very nice," he said, somewhat bewildered at the swift change in conversation.

"His Dad did that. He's moved on since his plumbing days. He's now a builder of some renown. His business kind of took off when he met his silent partner."

"David?"

"That's right."

"Does the plumber know that David is his son?"

"Absolutely. It's all out in the open, but only to a select few. David, Elizabeth, her sister and brother-in-law, David's father, Jennifer, me and now you. The secret's been safe for years, so if it gets out now, we'll all know who to blame."

"I wouldn't dare," said Ben.

The house with the red sills and white frames appeared at the end of the road. Ben pulled round the back and parked alongside Suzanna's car. "We'll have to explain everything, you know," he said to Emma.

"But David is kept out of it. We've been to one of your friends, that's all. No names mentioned, okay?"

Emma looked at him through sparkling eyes. "It's a good job. I wouldn't have wanted to swing a baseball bat in your direction as well."

*

When the two of them arrived, the rest were there. Every single one of them. There's something about the demise of a colleague, even if the colleague is not known to them personally, that results in a unity that does not normally show itself. It's that oft quoted, but true, phrase: it could have happened to any one of us.

They were as different in appearance as they were in nature. Some had spent their Christmas with family, some on their own and others with friends. It was obvious by their appearance alone which was which. A clean cut, small framed man dressed in open shirt and corduroy trousers sipped tea from a cup; two almost identical men sat in opposite corners, heads in hands, looking monumentally hung over; a pretty young girl with blonde hair and legs crossed read a magazine with intense concentration; a flashy, tarty looking girl with heavy make-up, some of which had run down her cheeks, leaned against the wall.

There was no conversation. There wouldn't be. They had never met before. Theirs was a secret world where it did no good to get to know a colleague. They were all professionals doing their own part, knowing that others would do their part and the parts fitted together.

Sebastian did the fitting together.

He regarded them all as his personnel, there to follow his orders, although he had never met them before. Applications and interviews for the job had not been necessary. They had been chosen for their expertise rather than their ability to get on with the boss. And they were good. For that, they were well rewarded, but they were also on call, twenty-four hours a day.

They looked up as Delaney spoke. "What a right fucking motley crew we've got here, but I must admit, I was expecting worse. Only

261

three of you dead on your feet. A sobriety rate of forty per cent is bloody good for this time of year."

There was little reaction to his comments, except for a grin from the girl reading the magazine. Sebastian spoke. "Allow us to introduce ourselves. I am the one who gives the orders and my friend with the charming way of expressing himself is my associate. We organise the little adventures that we send you on from time to time."

Delaney moved towards the radiator, felt it with his hands and appeared to be satisfied. Leaning against it, he faded into the background. The floor was Sebastian's.

"It was never our intention that we would ever meet, although some of you will have bumped into each other on a few occasions out of necessity. So, as you may have guessed, a highly unusual situation has arisen." He placed a photograph on the board. "This is Emma Parker. A nurse and an addict. Knowing her whereabouts may help us, but she is not the main player." A second photograph appeared next to Emma's. "This man is the target. He is a loose cannon who has become a danger to our organisation. Ben Price, schoolteacher. The two of them have gone walkabout when they shouldn't have." He strolled round the assembled group handing them each a folder. "You will glean more information about the two in here. The first thing we have to do is find them, so I'm afraid that this won't be the assignment that we normally ask of you, not yet anyway. It's hard graft and lots of research, hence the computers in the room. We need connections, associates. Anybody that may be hiding them. Also in the folder are details of a Lynn Thomas, Price's fiancée who died in a car crash. He believes she was murdered. Tie the three of them together with a place or person who may be helping them and we've got him."

Sebastian paused. "I can see why I hired you," he said. "You have given nothing away to one another, yet you all know that you have met Ben Price before." He looked at each in turn. "The driver who took him to Luton Airport, the two drunken men who started a pub fight, the girl who sat next to him on an aeroplane destined for Dortmund and last but not least, a girl who once rammed her crotch into his. Well, he has shat on us all from a great height, my friends. And no-one does that to us. My charming associate will remain here with you and will co-ordinate from this end. Any questions?"

There were none. From his people, he wouldn't have expected it.

*

There was tension in the air, more than he had expected, when they entered through the back door. It did not take a man with ESP to spot it. Doris glanced up from the kettle, Suzanna turned her back and left the kitchen. Neither of them said a word.

Ben immediately thought that something dreadful had happened, but it was not quite that type of atmosphere. It was more of a collective display of unhappiness and as Ben seemed to be the focus, he took it that it was he who was the target of discontent.

He followed them into the back room, where Tom threw him some much needed support with a casual nod and a wry smile. "The ladies are a bit put out," he said in his distinctive sarcastic tone. "They think you should have informed them in more detail about what you were doing. Three pages of A4 might have done the trick."

"But I said we needed to make sure we weren't being followed," said Ben in his own defence.

"You certainly did," said Tom.

"I told you on the phone."

"You certainly did," Tom repeated.

"Oh, shut up Tom," said Doris. She looked across at Ben and then at Emma. "We were worried about you."

"You needn't have been. We were in safe hands." He looked at Emma, a grin on his face.

Suzanna rose to the bait. "And exactly whose hands are you talking about?" she asked.

"A friend of Emma's. It was safe there. Look, I'll tell you everything if you give me a chance."

Suzanna remained quiet, turning her head away, looking anywhere except towards Ben. She was clearly annoyed with him and she wanted him to know it, exaggerating every move. Ben thought it was a simple misunderstanding. He thought he'd explained. She obviously didn't. It was a classic example of a lovers' tiff, except they weren't lovers.

It was Emma who broke the silence. "God, I am enjoying this."

"Enjoying what?" asked Ben.

"Me being at the centre of this sexual tension thing. Never happened to me before. I could let it go on for hours, I'm loving it so much. But time is against us on this so I think we should get a few things straight. Close your ears, Doris, this may be a bit earthy for you, but there's no other way to say it." And earthy she was. "Suzanna, I've not shagged Ben, I have no intention of doing so. I love him to bits, but he's a man and right now, I'm off men big time. He's a friend, a real close friend and that's what I need from Ben, nothing more."

Suzanna shuffled in her chair, Doris held her hand over her mouth and Tom laughed. Emma continued. "In fact, I think I rather fancy you to him, Suzanna. What do you think?" Exaggerating, she winked at Suzanna.

Suzanna shot an angry look in her direction, but this time resisted the intimidation.

"Look, ladies, fascinating though this is, can we save it until another time?" It was Tom. "Maybe we should let Ben and Emma tell us what they've been up to."

As there was no response, Ben told them everything from the meeting with Oscar Baker, through the attack by the man with dreadlocks and the visit to Emma's friend, whose name and details he omitted.

Doris asked if they were sure the man in the 4X4 was dead. Emma replied with a definite affirmative. Doris gasped out loud. "I'm sorry, Doris," said Emma, "but it was either him or me. Self-defence. And anyway, I'm too important to lose." Sitting next to Doris, she held her hand.

"And what do you think of Oscar Baker?" asked Tom.

Since leaving Baker's house, Ben had untangled his thoughts and had come to his own conclusion. During the ten minutes Ben had known him, Oscar Baker had leapt back and forth from one side of his character to the other. He had appeared, in turn, charming and aggressive, polite and dominant, understanding and questioning. He had vociferously denied the Donors' existence and yet, more importantly, happily revealed its embryonic concept. There was no reason why he should do that. He could have dismissed Ben's ramblings with a sharp denial of their existence, but he felt a compulsion to justify their conception.

And he was too defiant. 'The Donors do not exist' was his forceful retort. He was taking a sledgehammer to hide the truth. Ben had seen enough denials from children to know when there was room for doubt. Adults were just the same. Add all this together and what did the visit reveal about Oscar Baker?

Ben delivered his synopsis. "I think the Donors are a noose round his neck. It was just a question of time before the noose tightened."

"What do you mean?" asked Tom.

"I think everything Sebastian said about the concept of the Donors is true. Baker was in on it at the start, but he quickly saw the warning signs. He was 'appalled,' his word not mine, by the thought of a group of people being above the law, so withdrew his support without penalty as long as he kept his mouth shut. He's been quite happily kept in the dark about the Donors' activities for quite some time. Then I came along."

"So, Baker knows about the Donors but isn't involved now."

"That's the theory," said Ben. "God knows what the reality is."

It appeared that no-one was willing to ask the question. Of course, it was Tom who did. "So, what happens next?"

"Well," said Emma a little reluctantly. "I have a phone number I could ring."

*

A third photograph had been placed alongside that of Ben's and Emma's.

The photograph was of Ben Price enjoying a Starbucks with one man and two children. The background was undoubtedly the Arndale Centre, Manchester.

From the photograph, Delaney had drawn a squiggly line with an arrow at one end and a bubble at the other. Inside the bubble it read 'Who is this man?' written in Delaney's scrawly handwriting.

The blonde-haired girl now knew. Looking back at her from her monitor was the smiling face of Edward Holton. It was just a hunch, but then she was good at hunches, to have a look at the website of Ben's school. Under the name of the school, centre page, was Edward Holton, proud headteacher.

It was tempting to call Delaney across, but she thought she'd delve a bit more first. She just couldn't put Holton and Price together as bosom buddies, couldn't imagine Holton protecting Price. Perhaps there was more to be found.

She scrolled down.

A list of the names of teaching staff. That might prove more interesting.

*

"Too dangerous," said Tom. "Far too dangerous."

"Well, what else have we got?" asked Emma. She knew there would be no response. "I could pick up the phone, arrange a meeting and then take it from there."

Ben was pacing the room, looking agitated. "I agree with Tom. Besides the danger, what else would it achieve?"

No answer again. They were a bunch of amateurs clutching at straws, stumbling from one idea to the next and sinking deeper into the mire. From the optimism surrounding the Baker theory to the pessimism of what to do with it, they were on a never ending roller coaster driven by that most uncertain of drivers: hope.

Emma's hope lay in the phone number that she had memorised and kept locked in her head. If she phoned, if she arranged the meeting, maybe she could get a confession, but like everything else they tried, it was shrouded in uncertainty. And then there was the risk. High risk.

Suzanna had remained silent since her locking of horns with Emma. But she had listened well. "Do you have to meet?"

"What do you mean?" asked Ben.

"If you meet face to face and get some proof, you will need evidence of what was said. It's much easier to obtain that over the phone."

"Record the conversation? How will we do that?" asked Ben.

"Leave that to me," Suzanna replied. "And you," looking towards Emma, "get practising what you are going to say. You'll get one chance at this. One chance to nail Charles Ashcroft."

*

Sebastian knew he had to make the call. Ashcroft wanted to be kept informed and what Ashcroft wanted, Ashcroft got.

It was a new experience for him, having to confess not only to failure, but to continued failure. He dialled the number, the private one he had been given. The phone rang for some time before it was lifted. There was no voice from the other end, as he expected.

Sebastian kept it short. "The couple we are pursuing remain free. The whole team has been drafted in. I expect success tomorrow at the latest."

Ashcroft was breathing heavily. "Tomorrow. At the latest."

"Without doubt."

"One more thing. The girl is mine. Alive."

"Of course. I'll see to it."

"I hope so. I sincerely hope so."

The phone went dead.

28th December

In the early hours, Suzanna found what she was looking for. It hadn't taken long, just twenty minutes once she had typed the correct wording into the search engine.

As always, she was amazed with what could be bought over the internet and the ease with which it could be purchased. As she scrolled her way around the website, she couldn't help but think that surely it was illegal to sell these things on the open market. But apparently not. Not only could you get them posted to your door, you could, in some cases, buy them over the counter.

That's the part that interested her. They didn't have time to order it and wait a few days for it to arrive. They wanted it today. Or it might be too late.

So it was that she visited various websites and ignored most because they didn't show a real address. Website addresses were no use to her. She required the old-fashioned ones that have a street and a number and a town. But then it couldn't be any old town. It had to be within driving distance.

Prestwich, Manchester. An ordinary looking shop, quietly informing any passer-by that it was 'Manchester Surveillance.'

And that was how she and Ben came to be standing outside the shop wondering if they were being surveyed upon. They obviously were.

Ben opened the door and Suzanna followed. There was no bell to sound their coming, but they were met by a man who arrived at the counter at the same time as them, but from a different direction. He was an ordinary man wearing ordinary clothes who spoke in an ordinary voice.

"Now, what can I do for you at such an early hour of the morning?" he asked.

"We were wondering if ..." Ben stuttered as if he were a teenager buying condoms for the first time, red-faced with embarrassment.

Reaching into her bag, Suzanna brought out a print-off and handed it to the man. "Ah," he said, looking down at the paper, "you'll be wanting a telephone recorder then."

"That's right," said Ben, natural colour returning to his face.

"Ever done this sort of thing before?" the man asked. They shook their heads.

"Okay, it's easy," he said matter of factly. They could have been indulging in any kind of illegal activity. The man didn't want to know. He sold. They bought. "Plug this phone cable into any phone outlet in the house. When the phone is lifted, the unit will automatically click on and record both sides of the conversation. I say click on, but the playback will reveal no clicks and the people on the phone will not hear anything different to normal. It's foolproof. When the phone is placed back in the receiver, the recording will stop, again automatically."

"That's incredible," said Ben.

"It will record any phone in the house, so if the husband is talking to the mistress downstairs, the wife can plug into the upstairs outlet and the conversation can be recorded while the wife is having her bath. It works perfectly, as long as the husband doesn't know about it being plugged in. One word of warning. It won't record from mobiles."

"That won't be necessary," said Suzanna. "Both phones are landline."

"Then, that's the one you want," he said pointing proudly to the unit lying on his counter.

And so, for the cost of a round of golf, Ben purchased a telephone recorder. It was easier than buying a bunch of flowers for Lynn. The man slid it into a bag, Ben handed over the cash and they left.

Walking away from the shop, Suzanna began to laugh in equal measures of excitement and embarrassment, which set Ben off and they dived into the car giggling like two school friends who had experienced their first sexual encounter. Suzanna could not contain herself. "Did you see what was on the shelves?" she said excitedly. "Recording briefcase, bug detectors, tracking equipment, miniature pinhole cameras."

"Well spotted, Q," said Ben, attempting a very poor impersonation of Sean Connery.

It didn't take long for the jovial moment to pass. As they journeyed back to Suzanna's house, the quietness returned and they sank into their own thoughts. Ironically they both thought of Emma. They were relying on her now. Having seen her performance with a baseball bat, Ben was confident.

Suzanna, on the other hand, was worried as hell.

*

The two pints of Guinness stood proudly at attention waiting for the head to form and the cloud to settle. Delaney, reaching across the table between them, took her hand in his and stroked the back of hers with his thumb. Surprisingly gently for a man who could be so ruthless.

But then she didn't know he could be ruthless. She knew him simply as the mechanic who had appeared on that lonely country lane and fixed whatever was wrong underneath her bonnet. She'd offered to buy him a drink. He'd accepted. They both drank Guinness and hit it off. They met as often as they could, a bit hit and miss considering his real job, but she stuck by him and didn't ask too many questions.

She liked men who had more under the surface than they showed. It added to the mystery.

The Guinness was not the only thing they had in common. It didn't take long for her to discover he was IRA. Although not active herself, she was a sympathiser. Seeing your boyfriend being shot by some spotty teenager dressed in a uniform was bad enough. Seeing the murdering bastard escape retribution was worse. Her boyfriend was reaching across the front seat of the car for her daughter's doll. Spotty teenager said he thought it was a gun.

How the hell can it be lawful to kill an innocent man for picking up a doll? She couldn't come to terms with that. She hated the Brits, even though she was one herself, but that's as far as it went. On the other hand, she didn't mind her men going that bit further, even admired them for it.

It was all going so well until he disappeared. She thought he'd been killed in action, but the IRA didn't come calling as they usually did, offering sympathy and help. The Good Friday Agreement was just around the corner. She never saw him again.

She wasn't to know that Delaney had become invisible. He didn't exist anymore. His future, present and past were non-existent. No contact could be made with any aspect of his former life. She was the one regret he had. He missed her then and he missed her now.

At first it had made interesting reading. There was an Irish connection and anything Irish got Delaney's interest. But when he saw her face on his monitor, turned to one side, her long blonde hair blowing across her chin in the cold Irish wind, old feelings were stirred. He felt a quickening of the heart and the smoothness of her hand under his thumb, gently stroking her.

The photograph on the monitor left no doubt. It was her. And the details in the report matched perfectly. The dates, the ages, the places. They were his past returning to his present.

As Delaney reached out to touch her image, he knew that things had changed.

It had become personal.

*

"I think I may have something," she said as she walked across the room towards him.

Delaney quickly minimised his screen and met her halfway. He had spent years keeping secrets and old habits died hard. He gave nothing away. She looked up to see the usual Delaney scowl.

"What have you got, blondie?" he asked.

She was standing by the picture board, pointing at the group photograph. "Well, I've found out who your man is. Edward Holton, headteacher of the school where Ben Price earns his keep. I don't think he's got anything to do with this."

"Oh," Delaney said, sounding deflated. "So we can throw him in the bin then."

"Not just yet," the blonde-haired girl said. "He's nothing to do with this, but he is a connection." She placed a picture print-out on the

271

board. It showed a teacher enthusiastically at work with her children. She placed her forefinger on the teacher. "Suzanna Foy. Highly praised colleague of Ben Price. Drama specialist, but seems to be a good all-rounder."

"And you think that she has got something going with Ben?" asked Delaney.

"Don't think so, although that doesn't matter. The main thing is that our Suzanna is into keep fit and eating healthily. It's a big thing in the school and she's the prime motivator. Brings in visiting speakers on healthy eating and that sort of thing." She produced another photograph printed from the school's website. "Here she is with one visiting speaker, who she knows personally as they both attend the same yoga class and are members of the same gym."

Delaney recognised the girl in the picture immediately. "Now, that's one hell of a connection, blondie. Well done."

"My pleasure, sir. I think we'd better go and have a chat with this Suzanna Foy and see what she can tell us. I have her address right here," she said, holding a piece of paper in her hand.

Delaney stopped dead in his tracks. He pointed a finger at his colleague. "I'll only go," he hesitated, "as long as you never call me 'sir' again." Blondie laughed as they left, her monitor still glaring out an image of Lynn Thomas, guest speaker at Suzanna's school and murdered fiancée of Ben Price.

*

There had been more disagreement between Suzanna and Emma, the latter insisting that only Ben and she would be in the room when the phone call was made. Suzanna felt that she was being pushed to one side, despite the fact that she was doing all the research. If it wasn't for her spending the night hours surfing the net, they would never have found a place to buy the recorder. No recorder, no point in phoning.

For her part, Emma said that only she knew how Ashcroft could react and she had to be free to deal with it in her way. Ben would be there for moral support alone. If Ashcroft got any suspicion that others were listening in, then he would ring off and that would be the end of it.

Following a wasted few minutes arguing, Tom offered that he could see Suzanna's point of view, but asked her to remain with him and Doris so that Emma could get on with it. If it had been anyone else, she would have been more insistent, but she liked Tom and admired his balanced arguments. Still unhappy, she agreed to his request.

It didn't help that the telephone connection was in Suzanna's bedroom. As Emma followed Ben up the stairs, Suzanna felt a twinge of annoyance before returning to the back room and closing the door.

"Are you ready?" asked Ben. A test run had already found the device to be successful, so now, with the unit plugged in, everything was in place.

Emma's smile was a nervous one. She was remembering past encounters with Charles Ashcroft, brutal exchanges where her life had felt under threat and her confidence systematically destroyed. But this was different. Although anxious, she felt in control. She didn't need him for anything anymore.

Ben sensed her mood. He hoped she didn't lose her nerve. "This is the only way we can think of to get out of this," he said.

"And the only chance I have of getting the bastard back for what he did to Jennifer. Am I ready? Too bloody right I am."

Punching the numbers in, she heard the ringing of the phone. If there had been an answer phone attached, then it would have clicked in, but she just let it ring until eventually it was lifted from the receiver. There was no voice.

"It's me," said Emma quietly. She waited for a reply. None came.

"You know who I am. Speak to me." Again there was no reply.

"You know how you liked me to lie there with my blonde hair stretching across the pillow, lying there, waiting for you. I would place my finger in my mouth and move it in and out, slowly caressing the tip of it with my tongue."

It was all a bit unexpected. Ben covered his mouth with his hand, not quite able to believe what he was hearing. It was no surprise that

273

Emma didn't want the whole world to hear. He felt his body tense, not wanting to hear anymore, but having to in case Emma needed him.

Emma looked across at Ben. Shrugging her shoulders in apparent boredom and turning her mouth downwards in a show of distaste, she continued. "You would stand above me and remove your belt and I would spread my legs and show you what I had. And you would reach down to me."

"You bitch," shouted Ashcroft.

"And lie on me and take me, talking to me as you moved in and out."

"You fucking whore."

"Yes, that's what I am. I'm your fucking whore. Have you missed me?"

"Miss you, you slut? I only miss women who are some good to me."

"Then you must have missed your bitch, your slut, your whore."

There was no reply. All that could be heard was the heavy breathing of a grotesque example of a human being. Emma let the breathing linger in the quiet.

"What do you want? Drugs?" Ashcroft asked.

"I want you," Emma replied calmly. "And you want me."

"Why would I want you, bitch?"

"Because you've always wanted me, haven't you? I was the closest to what you really wanted but could never have. And now, you can never ever have because she's dead, isn't she Charles? She's dead."

"You fucking slut. You killed her with your lesbian ways and your drugs. It was you who killed her."

"Now you know that isn't true, Charles." She had slipped his forename into the conversation and he had not denied it. She was sucking him in like an expert. Her eyes were moist with tears, but her voice remained quiet and calm, the very opposite to the girl he had seen bludgeon the dreadlocked man to death. David had said she was an intelligent girl. Ben was beginning to realise just how intelligent. She had done as Suzanna had requested. She knew the difficulty of what she was about to undertake, but she had practised until it had become second nature. She was in complete control of the conversation, manipulating Ashcroft across a phone line. Ben was glad she was on his side.

He allowed her to continue. "I didn't kill your precious Jennifer, Charles. My precious Jennifer."

"She was never precious to you, you slut. She was precious to me. Only me."

"And then you lost her, Charles. You lost her because you couldn't accept the rebel in her, the rebel you had yourself created. It was because of you she turned to drugs, because of your self righteous brutality that she refused to speak to you, and because of how you, her father, had treated her that she could never trust a man again. And she found me, Charles. And we were lovers. We had something you could never share with your own daughter. We found love, Charles."

She let him digest those last few words. Ben could hear the breathing on the other end of the line becoming heavier, almost laboured. There was no attempt to intervene, no shouts of denial. Tears on her cheeks and a satisfied look on her face, Emma looked across at Ben.

Ben rolled his wrist around, urging her to keep going.

"Love, Charles. Something she never gave you. If I die, I know I will have had something irreplaceable from my Jennifer. I loved her so much, I could never kill her. You loved her so much, that you could, just to stop someone else from being with her."

Ashcroft's voice exploded from the other end of the line. "And the same will happen to you, you whore. If I can have my own daughter murdered, then killing you will be easy. Look around every corner, you bitch. They're coming to get you." The receiver was slammed down with such force that Ben threw his head back from the noise.

Emma placed the receiver down and threw her arms around Ben's neck. He held her tight as she sobbed into him. "Don't ever ask me to do that again you bastard," she said.

Ben did not think it was the right time to remind her that it was her suggestion all along.

*

275

"Drive on round the corner and let me out," said Delaney. "You've done well blondie, but now this is my time. Get back to the others. Tell them to go home and get the rest they deserve."

She turned the steering wheel to the right and pulled over. Delaney left the car and heard her accelerate away and home to her bed. Walking back to the house, he looked up at the window. Through the net curtains, he could see the outline of two figures entwined, the arms of one reaching upwards away from the neck of the other. Romantic. It was a pity he would have to spoil the party.

Silently, he entered the house through the front door. No key, but it was easy. He had done it a thousand times before. He could hear the dull tone of the television in the back room, occupying the others in the house. It was of no importance to him. It was the room up the stairs that required his attention.

As he took a step across the hallway, he heard the creak of a floorboard above. He stopped and listened and waited.

*

Suzanna was finding it increasingly difficult to keep still. Every time she shifted position on her chair, she looked across at Tom and Doris who were watching the box in the corner with intent, staring ahead, no communication.

How long does a phone call take? Not this long surely. Her imagination and jealousy were taking over again.

She rose from her chair and stretched her arms above her head, making the usual grunting sounds that people do when they stretch, or when they're nervous, or when they can't stand the silence any longer.

Oh, sod it. What the hell is happening? She made her way to the door and placed her hand on the handle.

At the same time, she heard the floorboard creak upstairs.

*

Her sobbing relented, but she liked the feel of his body against her so she held herself there, tight against him. Ben was a good man, someone she could see herself with for a very long time, if she could get over this lesbian thing. Perhaps it was just a passing phase. She held the back of his neck in the palm of her hand and kissed his cheek.

She opened her eyes.

The surprise was so overwhelming that her body refused to react. Looking over Ben's shoulder, she saw a figure enter the room, disturbing their privacy. Silently, he stepped in, half closing the door behind him. He placed a finger vertically across his lips, requesting her silence, and beckoned her towards him.

It was the gun that he held in his hand that convinced her. She knew nothing about them, but if the movies were to be believed, that was definitely a silencer on the end of it. Which meant he could kill them both and leave without a sound.

Slowly, she prised herself away, feeling the coldness on her cheek as it left his. His hands relinquished their hold on her back and her security had gone. Stepping to one side, she heard Ben say something, but the words did not connect. As she moved away from him, his gaze followed her and she saw the moment he realised they were not alone.

Reaching out towards her arm, his fingers simply brushed against her as she took a further step towards the stranger. There was hate in Ben's eyes, accompanied by increasing desperation. The danger was that they were so busy trying to help each other that they would both pay the price.

In limbo, between the two antagonists, she stopped.

Speaking quietly, she asked, "Which one is this then? Sebastian or Delaney?"

Her voice brought Ben back to her. Flashing glances between Emma and the man, Ben's eyes eventually focused on Emma. She was smiling. There was a madman in the room with a gun and she was smiling. Ben relaxed and took a long quiet breath. "Emma, allow me to introduce you to Sebastian, a kindly soul with impeccable manners."

Sebastian nodded in Emma's direction. "It is a pleasure to meet you at long last, Miss Parker, although I must say, you have been quite some thorn in our side."

"I'll take that as a compliment."

"Please do. Mr Baker thought of you only as a waif-like companion, but I fear you may have played some part in the demise of one of my employees. On his own, against my dreadlocked friend, Ben would not have stood a chance. Now come over here, my dear. Mr Ashcroft, with whom you have just had the most interesting conversation, would like to meet up with you again. Renew old acquaintances, I believe."

Emma hesitated, shocked at the mention of Ashcroft. At the end of a phone he was no threat, but now her skin crawled at the very thought of meeting up with him again. He had much to punish her for. He would be unrelenting.

Sebastian reacted quickly. Catching her off guard, he reached forward and took her arm, pulling her towards him so that she lay across his chest facing Ben, his free hand gripping her shoulder tightly, the barrel of the silencer resting against her temple. "That's a good girl," he said. "Now, a quick bullet in Ben's head and we will be away."

"No," said Emma. "You've got me, got what you came for. Leave Ben alone."

"I'm afraid you have things the wrong way round, Miss Parker. You are simply a by-product of this whole affair. It is Ben Price who knows things he should not know. It is Ben Price who cannot be allowed to share them with anyone else."

"I know them too," said Emma. "Ben told me."

Sebastian's inane grin fell, but only for a second. "Ah, that is such a shame, but not really a great problem. I'm sure I can trust Mr Ashcroft to dispose of you once his use for you is at an end."

As the gun began its journey in Ben's direction, Emma began to struggle but was held in place by Sebastian's overwhelming strength. Looking down the length of the barrel, Ben was surprised to feel the tension leave him. An old friend took the opportunity to visit.

"One thing before you pull the trigger. You know how curious I can be. How did you find us here?" asked Ben.

Sebastian smiled, thinking of similar requests to satisfy Ben's curiosity when the future was not so certain as it was now. "You know, Ben, under different circumstances, I could really like you. We could have been good friends, you and me. But it was not to be. Edward Holton also thinks very highly of you, Ben. We had a cup of tea while the kids played and he told me of your closeness to Suzanna Foy, who apparently regaled the staffroom with talk of mass shopping trips with Lynn Thomas. You know the food you kept finding in your fridge, Ben, after Lynn's death. That was not Mrs Robinson. It was Suzanna. Now that sort of information could not be ignored. It takes some kind of affection for someone to fill someone else's fridge." And as an afterthought. "By the way, Mr Holton and the kids are fine. I've nothing against them. It's just that he'll be a member of staff down in September, maybe two."

Suddenly, the smile dropped from Sebastian's lips and all Ben could see was the hole at the end of the barrel. "I'm so very sorry, Ben."

And that was when the floorboard creaked again and the door opened.

*

Casually, with one hand in his pocket and one hand holding a gun, Delaney entered the room. "How did you manage to beat me here, you bastard?" Delaney asked Sebastian as he took in the situation in the room.

"Never mind that, Mr Delaney. Let's get on with it before the assembled guests downstairs get worried. Pass me the tape from the recorder. I'm sure Mr Ashcroft will be pleased with its recovery."

Delaney reached forward and took the tape from its position, clicking the lid shut afterwards. Sebastian had the gun in one hand and Emma in the other, so Delaney slipped the tape into Sebastian's jacket pocket and returned to guard the door.

"So," said Delaney, "we kill Price, but what happens to Parker?"

"Mr Ashcroft has required her presence," Sebastian replied.

"Do you think that's a wise move?" asked Delaney.

"I certainly do. It will save our necks, bring back a little of our reputation."

"And what will happen to her?"

"Who knows?" questioned Sebastian. "Who cares?"

"I care," said Delaney as he raised his gun so that it pointed directly at Sebastian, who quickly swivelled his gun away from Ben and replaced it against Emma's temple.

"Ah, you found out," said Sebastian, grinning still.

Emma looked at Ben, confusion etched in the look on her face, but Ben could not help her. He didn't know what the hell was going on. His two enemies were having a disagreement about something, yet it was unclear what it was all about.

"How long have you known?" asked Delaney.

"A few days," Sebastian replied. "Ashcroft came to me and asked me to get rid of his nuisance of a daughter. I did a bit of research and found Emma Parker. If truth be told, she was not worth bothering about, but I found your connection, Mr Delaney, and thought it might be useful at some time. Apparently, this appears to be the time."

"I don't think it will do you a lot of good. Three against one is quite an advantage." Ben was baffled with what was unfolding in front of him, but one thing was gradually sinking in. Delaney had, for some unknown reason, switched his allegiance. He didn't know why. All he knew was that it had something to do with Emma.

"Not quite true, Mr Delaney. You see, I have the trump card in my hand, literally, so I feel the advantage is with me. Is that not the case?"

Delaney did not reply. He just looked at Sebastian with a glaring stare. Sebastian continued. "Whilst Emma Parker has a gun lying against her temple, you are powerless. You would not risk her life, not now you have been re-acquainted after all these years. If you would be so kind as to stand aside, I have a job to do and then Miss Parker and I will leave together. Mr Ashcroft will have such fun with her."

Ben was a useless observer, trying to clear his mind so that he might be of some help, mobile as a statue of granite stone, fearing that if he moved, Sebastian would pull the trigger. Emma was more aggressive. Displaying the resistance she had shown before, she kicked back in a vain attempt to escape from Sebastian's grasp, but she became frighteningly still when he pressed the barrel into her temple so hard that it caused her skin to pucker.

Delaney was motionless. His eyes were in another place, completely transfixed. Ben had seen him annoyed and impatient and exasperated, but this was something different. His whole persona had changed. Standing, staring, gun pointed directly at Sebastian and Emma, he was as Ben had never seen him before. Was this what he was like when his life was on the line? Is this how he had survived when he should not have?

Quietly, Delaney spoke. "You're dead right, Sebastian. Research is a wonderful tool. Ireland. A man suspected of planting bombs on the border is holed up in a house. Captain Ian McDonald goes in through the front door with his men. You're guarding the back door when the bomber backs his way towards you. He doesn't know you're there. You grab him, just like you've got Emma now, but he's got a gun in his hand, pointing towards the men as they burst in. You've a knife in your hand. You've had all the training, but a real body is different from a dummy stuffed with straw. You know what to do - thrust the knife upwards, under his ribs, through his lungs, save the men. But you didn't. You couldn't. The man's got his finger on the trigger, but McDonald is too quick for him. He shoots him in the forehead. One shot. Dead. I read the report. McDonald compliments your bravery, but I've seen enough reports to read between the lines. Did you ever work with him again? Never. He was your buddy from Sandhurst. Trained together, drank together, commissioned together. And you never saw him again. You left the army two years later." Delaney paused, allowing his revelations to sink in. "You were always big on organisation, Sebastian. The best. But when it came to the hand to hand stuff, you just couldn't cut it. You've never killed anyone in your life. Never looked into your victim's eyes and pulled the trigger, never plunged the knife between the ribs and

281

into the heart. You're no good face to face. And you know the worst bit, Sebastian? I am. I can kill without hesitation, given the right cause. Emma Parker is the right cause."

There was a puff of smoke to accompany the dull thud as the bullet left the barrel. Ben's eyes had never left Delaney, but now they swiftly looked towards Emma, fearing that she might have been hit. He need not have worried. Sebastian's head was thrown back against the wall. There was a hole in the centre of his forehead.

His gun slipped from his hand and fell to the floor. His body dragged its desperate path down the wall, his head leaving a trail of blood behind it. Emma fell with him, coming to rest on top of him, his arm still across her chest, unwilling to free his only hope. Throwing his arm to one side, she scrambled to her feet, reaching for the sanctuary that Ben could give.

"What the fuck was that all about?" she shouted as she threw her arms around Ben.

*

They must be on their way back down the stairs. Like a girl caught taking sweets from the cupboard, guilty as charged, Suzanna quickly resumed her place on the chair. She tried to look relaxed, assuming a position that might have been hers for quite some time. It didn't work. She felt awkward no matter where she placed her legs or any part of the rest of her body.

She waited for the handle to turn, glanced across a few times, but there was no more sound from outside the door or from above. Maybe she had imagined the floorboard creaking.

She almost made a complete fool of herself. Feeling the anger building up inside, she lost control and made to put a foot on the floor, with the intention of making her way upstairs. That's when she heard the floorboard for the second time.

Tom heard it this time. Maybe he had the first time, but hadn't reacted the way Suzanna had. Looking across the room at Suzanna, he said, "That's it then. Conversation over. How do you think she got on?"

Suzanna hoped the dash of red that flicked across her neck when she was anxious did not show. "To be honest, Tom, I don't hold out much hope. What do you think?"

"I think she'll have done okay, but I don't know what good it will do. I don't know what she will have got out of Ashcroft, but whatever it is, what are we going to do with it? Take it to the police is the obvious, but then there will be more questions for Ben. They'll need to know why he was involved and that would mean telling the whole story or inventing a completely new one. I think Ben's near the end of his tether. He can't cope with much more."

Suzanna pulled her knees up to her chin, arms folded across her shins. Tom was always so optimistic, but now he too seemed to have been affected by the never ending cycle of failure and dismay. He looked washed out, devoid of ideas.

The suddenness of the crash broke the silence. Suzanna raced to the door, threw it open and bounded up the stairs two at a time. What she witnessed when she pushed on the half-open door could never have been imagined.

*

Of course, Ben had no answer to Emma's shouted question. The last few minutes had passed him by. He could recall the sequence of events, but he understood nothing of what was said. One thing was for certain. Sebastian was dead and Delaney had shot him.

And Delaney still had a gun in his hand, finger on the trigger, ready to use.

Ben watched, impassive, holding Emma tight against him, as Delaney stepped towards the crumpled body half leaning against the wall. Reaching down, he placed his fingers on his neck, checking his pulse. Satisfied that the bullet had done its job, he reached down to Sebastian's legs and straightened them from the crooked state they had landed in. Taking a towel that had been lying on the bed, he folded it using one hand and the opposite arm, as if he had done this a million times before. The gun remained active, the finger on the trigger. He held the towel tight against the back of Sebastian's head, Ben presumed to prevent any of the brain from oozing out, before resting it gently on the rug that ran along the floor at the foot of the bed. Sebastian's body was now perfectly prostrate, ready for burial. It had taken seconds.

As the door burst open, Delaney spun round, gun rising to point directly at the open doorway. Suzanna made her entrance.

It was almost too much to take in, but there was a body and there was Emma and Ben in a clinch and there was a man pointing a gun directly at her. And all of this in her house, her bedroom. Gasping for breath, amazed eyes wide apart, she staggered back against the wall, pointing at the man lying on her rug in her bedroom with a hole in the centre of his forehead. "What the hell is going on?" she demanded.

"I think that's something we would all like to know." Silently, Tom had appeared, his arm round Doris, shielding her from the carnage, protecting her. It was a generation thing. Ben had not thought to consider Emma and Suzanna. He presumed they didn't need protection and would have resented it if thrown in their direction.

"I suppose I'm the one who can tell you," offered Delaney, placing the gun on the bed. "It's a bit cramped in here. Shall we go downstairs?"

They were all too unwilling to move. Scared. Delaney grasped the mood. "If you think I'm going to kill all of you, then think again. You don't deserve to die. Sebastian did." And with that, he squeezed his way past Tom and Doris, through the doorway and set off down the stairs, pausing only briefly to shout back. "Leave the dead guy where he is. I'll sort that out later."

*

The television was silent, the single colour permeating from the screen a dull, dysfunctional grey. Contrary to the usual English practice, there was no offer of tea and no politeness regarding seating arrangements. They simply entered the back room and sat where there was a seat.

Ben and Emma, the last to enter, were left standing. Suzanna sat on the arm of the chair where Tom waited patiently and there was the curious sight of Doris sitting next to an undercover operative of the British Army responsible for the deaths of countless IRA terrorists. If only she knew.

All eyes were on the stranger who had entered Suzanna's house, shot a man through the head and laid his body to rest with the care of the most skilled of undertakers. If any of the assembled were scared, they did not show it. In truth, they all had the feeling that they were about to be offered an olive branch, a way out of the mess. They were no longer alone.

The man sitting next to Doris seemed to be in control and for that, they were grateful. He had to be one of the good guys. After all, he had shot the bad guy and Ben and Emma seemed unperturbed by his presence. And the gun had been left on the bed, interpreted by one and all as a sign of peace.

This had been a long few days. They were quite happy to wait a little longer.

Of course, they did not know Delaney like Ben did. He was not surprised that Delaney began immediately the last of them was ready, which happened to be Ben leaning against the radiator. Delaney ran a smile across his face, which Ben was not quite ready to return.

"So, the explanation," he said. "My name's Delaney. It isn't my real name, but you can call me that for now. Sebastian is the corpse. Sebastian and Delaney, the two people who dragged Ben into this mess and, indirectly, all of you. We work, or worked, for the Donors, who I believe Ben has informed you about. I don't know for certain that he has, but I do know Ben, more than he realises, and I think that out of loyalty, he would have told you. Am I correct?" There was a circle of affirmative nods. Delaney continued. "We offered Ben the chance to bring justice to the killer of Lynn Thomas. He took that chance. You all supported his actions, albeit after the event. Another sign of loyalty between you. Then the shit hit the fan." He touched Doris on the knee. "Sorry about the language."

"Not a problem, young man," she replied, although she thought he was probably not much younger than she was.

"There was a second job, one I disapproved of. It's no concern of mine if you believe me or not, but in my defence, how was I in the car at Luton airport, Ben?"

"You never said a word, never made eye contact with me. I thought it was strange at the time."

"And what did I say to you when we separated after our run together in Germany?"

"That I'd never see you again."

"I said it because I honestly believed that at the time." Another question. "And where was I when Sebastian was following you in Manchester?"

"Never saw you."

"I was there, taking a few photos in case I needed them later on, but Sebastian didn't know that. You see, Sebastian's attempt to get you to kill Jennifer Ashcroft was different from anything we'd done before. Every killing to that point had reason behind it. Not this one. It was as if a coup had occurred inside the Donors and Ashcroft was using their power for his own purposes. I never knew anyone in the Donors, Sebastian had the contact with them, but suddenly Ashcroft's name was out in the open between the two of us. I thought it was the thin end of the wedge. Sebastian didn't see it that way. He became fanatical about it, having personal contact with Ashcroft, obeying his every command. I'm sorry Emma, but the dead man upstairs was the man who had Jennifer killed. He wouldn't have done it himself, he hadn't the guts, but he would have arranged it under instructions from Ashcroft. She was innocent of any crime, killed, in effect, by her own father. I wanted no part of it, but I wasn't one to be turning away from a good fight. I could tell the questionable ideological waters surrounding the Donors were getting murkier, so I hung in there, in case I was needed. In effect, I became your guardian angel, Ben."

"I've never known guardian angels to be killers before," said Tom. He raised a finger upwards in the direction of Suzanna's bedroom. "That must have been quite some shot."

"Like everything else," said Delaney with overstated nonchalance, "it's easy when you know how."

He looked around the room for further response. There was none. "And that, in a nutshell, is the explanation. The body will be removed, the room re-decorated. There will be no hint of what occurred there. Even the nosiest of neighbours will be ignorant of the events of this afternoon. So, that's it. I believe it when I say that you will never see me again." He stood up to leave, casting a final glance around the room.

But he could not leave. He wasn't allowed to. Emma stood in his way, blocking the exit to the room. Looking Delaney directly in the eyes, she said, "That's half the explanation. What was that crap about becoming re-acquainted after all these years and about Emma Parker being the right cause? Half an explanation, Delaney. Half an explanation. That's all."

Only the three of them, Delaney Ben and Emma, knew what she was talking about. The fourth person was lying dead in the room upstairs. Delaney laughed out loud.

"Your mother always said you were an intelligent, opinionated, rebellious young lady, Emma."

He sat back down next to Doris. Leaning forward with his forearms on his thighs and hands clenched, he took a deep breath and began. "When Ben and Emma couldn't be found, Sebastian called the whole team in to track you down. A smart young lady found the connection between Ben and Suzanna, same school, and Suzanna and Lynn, same yoga class, but just before she informed me, I had found my own connection, different from hers, nothing to do with Ben or Suzanna or Lynn. I don't know why, but I thought the answer to Ben's discovery might lie with Emma. If I could find Emma, I would find Ben. When I was researching you, Emma, in the depths of Secret Service files admissible by a series of passwords known only to a few people, I found my own past catching up with me." He paused a moment. "Let me explain."

Emma found herself engrossed in his voice, his words. Facing him, standing, she remained motionless, hanging on every word, waiting for the other half of the explanation. She listened as Delaney continued.

"While I was working in Ireland, I became involved with a lady who had a tragic background. Born and brought up in England, she met an Irishman on a weekend trip to his grandparents in Liverpool. Long distance love was no good to either of them, so she moved to Ireland and eventually they married. Tragically, he died at work, an accident. She thought she would never find love again, but she did, only to have a British soldier take her lover's innocent life. Then she met me. I never told her the truth, that I was working undercover. I didn't want to lose her and anyway, I was doing a job, one which required total secrecy, even to those you love. But she accepted that there was something I wasn't telling her. We never talked about it, but she knew I was connected to the IRA in some way. Perhaps incomprehensibly to all of you, she approved. She'd been a sympathiser ever since her boyfriend had reached over to pick up her daughter's doll and been shot dead." Shaking his head, he reached forward and touched Doris on the knee. Head angled to the side, he looked at her and asked, "What the hell is love, Doris? Well, whatever it is, we had it, for a short time. All too short. I was soon forced out of the country, my past non-existent, my future unknown."

Quietly, he was interrupted by Emma's voice. "She loved you so much you know. She still does. Still talks about her last love who left her without a word, without explanation. It must have been love, Delaney. She never says a word against you when she has every right to." Lifting her head, she spoke to them all. "The woman Delaney talks about is my mother. I am the daughter whose doll was the pathetic excuse for some army bastard to kill Gavin, the only man I knew as Dad. My real Dad died in an accident at work before I got to know him. Gavin brought me up. When he went, my Mam never allowed me to know any of her boyfriends in case I got too close again. In truth, there was only one other. I never met you, Delaney, until now, yet I feel I know you."

Taking the few steps towards him, they met as he rose from the settee and held each other. There was no sound from anyone else. It would have been inappropriate to disturb the moment.

A long few seconds later, they parted, but still held on to each other. Delaney seemed at a loss for words, something that Emma could not be accused of. She had become so positive about life since she found a purpose to it. "By the way, Delaney, that was some bloody introduction," she said. "Firing a bullet within a whisker of my head and killing a man. If that's the sort of company my mother keeps, then I'll have to have a word with her."

Delaney took hold of her again and whispered so that no-one else heard. "Nice to be re-acquainted with my past. What I told Sebastian was correct. You truly are the right cause Emma. Lynn knew that from the moment she met you and Ben came to know it. Now I know it."

Doris rose from her place and moved around them. "Shall I put the kettle on?" she asked and everyone nodded in agreement.

*

Delaney had asked for more time with Emma and the two of them made their way to the front room to catch up on old times and new futures.

Mugs in hands, the remaining four chewed the fat, mulling over everything they now knew, calculating if Ben was still in any danger. Attempting to eliminate the players, they all agreed that one threat to Ben, Sebastian, was gone. Delaney appeared to have switched sides, cemented by his relationship with Emma, if all that he said was true. There was no reason to doubt it, although there was a temptation to disbelieve everything. Oscar Baker had too much at stake to get more involved. Which left Ashcroft.

The perfect scenario would be to come to a nice friendly agreement that he wouldn't pursue them if they didn't disclose his involvement. But that was impossible from his point of view and theirs. They were convinced that, although Sebastian was dead, Ashcroft posed an even greater threat. He was powerful and ruthless with everything to lose, a dangerous combination to anyone who knew too much about him. And all four of them knew too much.

And there was the moral dilemma. They had an insight into the private world of Charles Ashcroft, Home Secretary, so different from the way the public perceived him. Should such a man hold such an office? But then, if the private lives of all the politicians were public knowledge, there probably wouldn't be anyone to run the country.

A few mugs of tea later, they came to their conclusion. They were at risk from Ashcroft and it was Ashcroft's abuse of power with the Donors that needed to be disclosed. Self preservation and morals, the two instruments that had brought Ben into this mess, remained at the forefront of their decision making.

Of course, their conclusion offered no answers to questions like how were they to survive Ashcroft's pursuit and how were they to disclose the Donors to the world, but by the time Delaney and Emma joined them, they felt they had made some headway.

"So," said Emma all bright and cheery after her time with Delaney, "where do we go from here?" With that simple question, Ben felt his enthusiasm drain away. There was no answer, but Tom attempted a less than convincing one.

"I suppose we bumble around like we have for the last few days," he said.

"Bumble?" cried Delaney. "You've had professionals running around like blue-arsed flies trying to find out where you were and what you were up to and you say you were just bumbling around. Everything in life is logical and what you did is choose the logical route. Ben, which city do you know better than Sebastian or me?"

"Manchester?"

"So you ran Sebastian ragged up and down escalators and according to Emma, round the transport system he had no knowledge of. Logical. Other than yourself, who knew of your involvement in Jimmy Buller's death?"

Ben thought awhile. "Tom," he eventually replied.

"So you brought him and Doris here, out of harm's way. Logical. Who else did you think might be at risk?"

"Emma. Because of her link with Jennifer."

"So you went and dragged her out of her stupor to bring her here. Logical. Now all those who could come to harm, who incidentally, might also have given you away to Sebastian, were here, under one roof. Logical."

"But the problem is that I've run out of ideas and so have all of us. We don't know the logical route anymore."

"Which is where I come in," said Delaney. "If you don't mind, that is. I know you're a merry little group and I'm an outsider recently arrived and I know you've done well so far, but you're at a crossroads, aren't you?"

Of course they were. "Please carry on," said Tom.

"The logical route. One. Does Ashcroft know you are here, at Suzanna's house? I didn't tell him, never met him, but Sebastian may have done. He doesn't know that Sebastian is dead yet, doesn't know he has failed, so there's still time to move. I know a nice safe house which is unknown to anyone. Except me. I've used it many times before and I've got the key. I suggest we move there. Agreed?"

Delaney sensed the hesitancy around the room. "Two. Can you trust me? I was the opposition a few hours ago. Now I'm suggesting rounding you up in a house where Ashcroft could be waiting with armed men ready to finish the job. Emma, what do you think?"

She took no time to answer. "I tell you, he knows so much about my mother, things he couldn't have got from any internet research site or secret files pulled from a locker. He's the genuine article. You know me, sometimes I'm so insecure that I have trouble trusting that I'm Emma Parker, but Delaney I would trust with my life."

Doris was the first to react by raising her hand as if she was in the front row at school. "I trust you, Delaney," she said and the rest followed her lead, some out of trust and some because they knew of no other way.

Delaney continued. "Three. The only way out is to reveal how Ashcroft used the Donors for his own purpose. But, nobody, save those involved, know that the Donors exist. If you revealed them to the world, it would seem so incredible in law-abiding Britain that no-one would believe you. Then you would have to convince everyone that the Home

291

Secretary had murdered his own daughter. Impossible. Especially as you, Ben, can be proved to have murdered Jimmy Buller. Would a murderer be believed?"

He allowed the reminder of that fact to sink in. "Four. The only logical route is to let the right people know in the right way. Quietly, so that it can be dealt with behind closed doors, like most important decisions. That way, Ashcroft will be revealed for the man he truly is and you will be safe. No recriminations."

Of them all, it was Tom who had followed most closely. "I was with you all the way until point four," he said. "I see what you mean, but the question is how? How do we let the right people know in the right way?"

"Leave that to me," Delaney replied. "I've learnt a thing or two about organisation from the master."

*

The decision was made to move house. Tom and Doris had already got a few things packed. Emma also. Suzanna could pack a bag easily, but Ben needed to buy a few things. The hire car needed to be returned, unfortunately a bit less pristine than when he had picked it up. The deposit would probably be lost, but that was the last thing on Ben's mind.

Getaway plans made, Suzanna raced upstairs to get a bag packed while the others got things together and made ready to go.

Without warning, there was a loud scream from above which made them all freeze. In the aftermath, they'd all forgotten that Sebastian was still lying on the floor. It must have been one hell of a shock when Suzanna opened the door and found him there.

Ben was the first to the door, bounding up the stairs two at a time. He knew what to expect, but still retreated to the wall as he entered. The unexpected is even more chilling when you think you know what should be there.

Three men stood, dressed in white paper boiler suits, staring at them. They each had a mask covering their mouth and the hood pulled over their foreheads. There was no movement. They held their arms behind them, leaning forward, almost threatening. Suzanna clung to Ben, waiting for them to react to her being there, but still they stared, motionless.

Appearing belatedly at the doorway, Delaney sauntered in as if he had come to bleed another radiator. "Hello boys," he said to the masked men in white and for the first time, the smell within the room hit Ben and Suzanna. Paint. The three men turned to the wall, brushes in hand. "Do the whole room will you fellas?" and then looking at the two frightened figures before him, "We aim to please."

It took some time for Ben and Suzanna to calm down. Suzanna packed a small bag with the necessaries, occasionally turning to check the masked men were still out of range, while Ben remonstrated with Delaney about how he should have warned them. "Didn't you hear them come in?" Delaney asked and Ben admitted that he had not. "When I was busy talking about Emma's mother. Silence is our middle name," Delaney said.

It was only when they were leaving that Suzanna realised there was something missing. She stepped back into her room and then back onto the creaky floorboard. "Where's the body?" she asked.

Delaney, halfway down the stairs glanced back. "Always the first thing to go," he said. "Difficult to do a good paint job when there's a dead body to climb over."

"You mean he's gone?" asked Suzanna.

Delaney made a movement with his arm, stretching it gently away from him, fingers twitching. "Flown away to God knows where. Wherever it is, I suspect I may be joining him there at some point. But not just yet."

They congregated in the back room. Delaney took control. "Tom, Doris and Emma, you go in Suzanna's car and I'll take Ben in the other. There's a few things we need to discuss on the way. Hope you don't mind." No-one was arguing with Delaney. They still held an element of fear in their minds and at the same time, they respected him. He was the professional at this sort of thing. It was good to have one around at last.

As if to emphasise the point, Delaney reached into his pocket and unearthed something that had completely slipped their minds, something vital in their defence, something Suzanna had spent hours researching and Emma spent minutes crying over. Holding the Ashcroft tape gently between finger and thumb, he said, "Where would we be without evidence?"

Making his way to the back door, Delaney waved some keys in the air. "Sebastian's Mondeo is parked down the road. I saw it when I arrived. We'll take the hire car back and then be on our way. I'll lead. I'm the only one who knows where we're going."

"And where are we going?" asked Tom.

"Cambridge."

*

The hire car returned, the deposit lost, they set off in convoy.

In the one car, Tom sat up front while Suzanna drove. In the back, Emma rested her head on Doris' shoulder and fell asleep.

In the lead car, Ben drifted in and out of sleep, head lolling against the head-rest and then falling forward with a start onto his chest, never fully achieving the rest he needed. Delaney let him drift. He admired the way Ben had survived this far. Didn't know how he'd managed it really. But he was still alive and, when he'd had a night's sleep, he'd be ready for the day ahead. There was no alternative. He had to be.

Cutting across country towards Uttoxeter, Delaney remembered when the journey would take twice as long, before the new road was built and the old one widened. It seemed to take forever.

Leaving Belfast behind, docking at Holyhead and travelling home to sleep for an eternity before reporting back to Command. The break was too short lived. He would soon make the tortuous journey back and filter false information to his IRA comrades, which they then acted on. And when things went wrong, he'd make sure that someone else got the blame. The secret was to survive when all the odds were stacked against you.

And that's why he admired Ben.

His attention was drawn to the lights flashing in the mirror. A toilet stop was required. He waved his response and the lights ceased to flash. The Little Chef, a few miles ahead, was strategically placed for both liquid disposal and liquid replenishment. It had been there for as many years as he had made this journey.

Entering the front door, they saw toilets to the left, café to the right. It was looking a bit tired and old now. A little out of touch. A bit dated. Like him really. Maybe it was time for Little Chef and Delaney to retire into the sunset and hand over to a new generation. Whether they would do the job any better remained to be seen.

Five of them took their caffeine intake and Suzanna her freshly squeezed orange juice. "Do you believe that, then?" Delaney asked Suzanna.

"Believe what?"

"That it's freshly squeezed."

"What do you mean?"

"Well, freshly squeezed, in my mind, means that it's just been squeezed. I mean now, recently. But I can't see any oranges in here. Not an orange tree in sight. What's the sell by date?"

Suzanna searched the outside of the bottle before finding the black print stamped on the side which told her that the sell by date was on 'the rim of the lid.' Holding the lid away from her, turning it this way and that to get the light, she read the indentations as 31.03, but the year was indecipherable.

"And that's another thing. Why do you need a stamp on one part of the bottle to tell you that the sell by date is on the rim? Why not put the sell by date where the stamp is in the first place. That bottle containing not-so-freshly squeezed orange juice is an analogy of life. Always make things difficult for the public to understand and they end up just going along with it, believing it."

And that's another reason why Delaney admired Ben.

He didn't just go along with things.

The journey resumed, reaching the outskirts of Peterborough and then heading south towards Cambridge. Light drizzle began to fall, the streetlights reflecting off the wet roads, making driving a little more treacherous. Delaney slowed his pace, keeping rigidly to the speed limit.

Ben, more alert since the sketchy sleep and the break, broke the silence. "Why was it so important that we rode together?" he asked.

"I wanted to outline a few things. Get your thoughts. After all, you are the one who has most to lose."

"Go ahead," said Ben.

"Some facts. Few people know of the Donors' existence. Others know of the concept, but are unaware that it's a functioning organisation. You and your friends hold knowledge and evidence that could get you killed and all that knowledge has to be disclosed, but it can't be done openly or heroically." Delaney paused. Ben waited. He was becoming an expert at waiting. Delaney continued. "I suggest we go to where the idea originated."

"Oscar Baker?"

"No," Delaney replied.

As Delaney outlined his plan, revealing most of the details, but not all, Ben could only sit and wonder why this whole mess went from bad to worse, from difficult to more difficult. No, not even that, thought Ben. "Impossible," he said aloud.

"But it'll be great fun trying," Delaney responded.

Just then, a telephone rang. Delaney looked towards Ben.

"Not my ring tone," Ben said.

"Not mine either," said Delaney, quickly followed by, "Oh, shit."

Fumbling around inside his jacket pocket, the car swerving from side to side, his hand pulled out a mobile. He pressed a key and said nothing. Ben could hear a man's voice, quietly at first, but then louder, shouting as Delaney made no attempt to respond.

Delaney ended the call as the voice continued to berate those who would listen. "Interesting," said Delaney. "Charles Ashcroft does not sound very pleased."

"Ashcroft?" responded Ben.

Delaney nodded. He held the now silent mobile in his hand. "I thought it might be an idea to borrow Sebastian's phone. After all,

Sebastian doesn't need it anymore. The dead have other ways of communicating."

"When did you get that?" asked Ben.

"The same time as I got his car keys. I didn't fancy his suit, not my style. Too much 'Men in Black' for me. All he needed was the sun glasses, a few aliens and a pump action shotgun. But as we know, guns and Sebastian did not go together."

"What did Ashcroft have to say?"

"Said Sebastian had promised him results by now, so why the fuck hadn't he been in touch? His words, not mine. When I didn't reply, he raised the decibels and the threats. I think the last one I heard was that the whole of the SAS would be after Sebastian if he didn't get Price and Parker."

"Why didn't you respond? He'll know there's something wrong by now."

"No, he won't. I've seen Sebastian give him the cold shoulder treatment before on the phone. Ashcroft will think he's gone off on one of his little sulks, but he knows his message will have got through. Well, it would have if Sebastian had been able to listen. A couple of things: the phone call confirmed he has no idea that Sebastian is dead, so no need to panic yet, and there's no way he knows that we're out of Manchester and on the road."

Ben looked ahead. It all made sense for a moment, but then he thought of the plan Delaney had outlined and he shook his head. Impossible.

*

Suzanna was getting anxious.

The A14 had drifted seamlessly into the M11 and they had already driven past two junctions that would have taken them to Cambridge. They were travelling further south where all the signs led towards London.

Delaney had said Cambridge, she was sure. It was true that she didn't know this part of the country at all. She was a Northern lass and proud of it. She'd passed this way a few times to watch her beloved Manchester United play 'down south' in important games, but then she usually went on the supporters' club coach which took them directly to the ground and then directly home afterwards. Most of the journey would be given over to sleep, so she wouldn't know how many junctions there were for Cambridge.

There was still a doubt in her mind about Delaney. That was what lay behind her anxiety.

Following behind him, watching day turn to night, in the quiet while Doris and Emma slept in the back and Tom kept his thoughts to himself, she had had time to think.

Running through the ever-changing path of events, one thing remained constant. Ben was in charge. He was the central figure around which this whole web was woven and he had taken the responsibility for that. The instructions came from him. Sure, they'd all had their say once they were involved, but it was Ben who made each final decision. Until Delaney killed Sebastian. Since then, they had all followed Delaney and believed everything he had said. Why?

Suzanna supposed it was because he had shot the bad guy. He had saved the hero and the distraught, pathetic damsel in distress. She still looked upon Emma in this way. He had laid down his weapon as a sign of peace and had taken control. They had let him. Every single one of them, including Ben, had allowed this self-confessed killer to issue instructions which they blindly followed. He was the professional who had taken a bunch of naïve amateurs under his wing and they were grateful for it. At last they had someone who knew what he was doing.

And now they had driven past junctions that would have led them to Cambridge.

Tom quietly interrupted the silence of Suzanna's worried mind. "He must be coming in from the south," he said.

"I didn't know you knew Cambridge," said Suzanna as calmly as was possible.

"Never been there in my life," Tom replied.

"Then how do you know …." but she stopped herself short as another blue sign loomed up indicating that if they wished to go to

Cambridge, then they should take the next junction. Out of the corner of her eye, she noticed Tom's raised finger.

Following Delaney off the motorway, they headed towards Cambridge along tree lined roads where the houses were set back, offering the privacy they required. Through traffic lights, most of them pedestrian, inactive at this time of night, they came to a halt by a roundabout, allowing a stream of traffic through.

Suzanna looked up at the building opposite. A true attempt at art deco style architecture, the white curves and the metal balcony rails would not have looked out of place opposite the warming waters of the Mediterranean. Three storeys high, each balcony ran into the next, occasionally interrupted by white walls offering limited privacy from fellow residents. At a quick calculation, there were six flats in all, perfectly symmetrical around a central heavily-glassed front entrance. White metal frames separated panes of glass which stretched upwards from the entrance the entire height of the building, revealing brown stained ballistrades curving elegantly round towards the top floor. Each front window was long and narrow, reaching to its curved conclusion at each side. It was a building born out of the opulence of the twentieth century, all Marilyn Monroe, now, sadly, crumbling around the edges.

Delaney edged forward across the roundabout and indicated right, turning in behind Ms. Monroe. Suzanna followed, blindly. There was a security code to be pressed and a single garage door rose. Delaney lifted his hand and waved towards the opening, indicating that they should follow, although there did not appear to be enough room inside.

Appearances can be deceptive. The narrow opening spread to an enormous cavern beneath the building, enough room for six or seven cars. Yet only one other car was parked there. Suzanna pulled in beside Delaney.

After the long journey, they emerged from the vehicles, stretching backs and shoulders in varying degrees. Tom strayed from the rest towards the parked vehicle, hidden beneath a cover which hugged the body as tightly as any of Marilyn's dresses. Moving slowly, his fingers playing playfully against the cover, he made his way round its entire shape.

Delaney joined him. Tom's eyes never left the car. "Beautiful," he said to no-one in particular. He crouched down at the front of the car and took a firm grip at the base. Smiling, he let out an amused chuckle. "Even better. Pre 1974. British craftsmanship at its best."

"I see you know your cars, Tom," said Delaney.

"MGB sports car. Classic British open topped sports car. This one was built after 1962 and before 1974, when rubber bumpers were introduced to meet American safety legislation. From a sales angle, it was a smart move. It became the most popular British car to be sold in America, always a tough market. Sales went through the roof, if you'll pardon the pun. But from a classic car perspective, it devalued the original design, watered it down. Ironically it was the beginning of the end. The final MGB rolled out just seven years later."

"It had outlived its expected lifespan by quite a few years though."

"True. And I suppose if they were still being built today, the original would have been diluted so much it would have ended up as pure water. No bite, no sparkle, no passion." He dragged his eyes away from the car and asked, "Whose is it then?"

"Mine. I tinker around with it when I've a bit of time on my hands. Now and again, I put the old Biggles hat on and take it out. Makes me feel good."

"I know what you mean. I've nothing like this, but mine's a 1999 TVR Chimaera. Drop the roof down, feel the wind, hear the throb. Nothing like it."

"Five litre?"

"No point," said Tom. "The four litre's a bit sluggish, the five's a bit twitchy and is no faster than the 4.5, so it was the 4.5 for me."

"When all this is over, you can take me for a spin," said Delaney.

"On one condition," Tom replied and there was no need to mention what it was.

"A deal," said Delaney and the two of them stood over the concealed car with their hands locked together in a firm handshake.

The silence was broken by an irritated Suzanna who tried not to show that the conversation was boring her to death. She failed. "Is there a way out of here?" she asked, lifting her bag from the concrete floor.

"Sure," said Delaney calmly. He made his way round a corner to a door. This too was security coded. "The cars will be safe. The garage is all mine and the code is changed regularly."

"What?" asked Ben. "Do you mean that no other cars use this place. What about the other residents?"

"They must park somewhere else, I suppose. Never asked them. Never met them."

"Seems a bit opulent for a man of simple tastes," said Ben.

"Necessity, not opulence. On more than one occasion, the place has been full of all sorts of vehicles from motor bikes to camper vans. I'll tell you about it sometime." He punched in the four digit code and the door opened. "Don't bother trying to remember, the code changes now until the next use, when it changes again. I'll let you know if you need to."

They climbed the stairs, hearing the click as the door below glided into place. Another door, another security code, another entry which led into an open plan living space.

It was a typical man's place. Television, a few comfortable chairs which had seen better days, microwave, a few mugs in the sink and a table, all within the same large room which was dominated by the large curved window that Suzanna had noticed from below.

"Make yourselves at home," said Delaney throwing open a cupboard door. "There's blankets, sheets and towels in here, food in the fridge, water in the tap, all you need at your finger tips. I'm sure you can sort out the sleeping arrangements between you." He opened one of the five doors that led from the main room. "This is my room. I've more work to do, a few things to check up on, so it's a bit of privacy for me if you please. And then bed. Get some rest, especially you Emma. You're coming with me tomorrow morning. Be ready for eight o'clock with your breakfast inside you and your training shoes on. We've a bit of walking to do."

And with that, Delaney disappeared from view and left his guests to fend for themselves.

*

He'd heard nothing from Sebastian.

Nothing at all.

He'd expected contact by now.

None.

Trusted him though. Knew he would get the job done.

He'd give him till the following morning.

When he flicked the light switch, the room was engulfed in complete darkness. He lay with his eyes wide open. The dark held no fear for him. Not like some people who worried with every creak, every sound. Wimps, all of them. It was the same with sleep. He always slept well. No matter what he had done during the day, no matter who he had manipulated, even destroyed, he slept well. No conscience, you see. No conscience at all.

He closed his eyes and was fast asleep within seconds.

29th December

Surprisingly, Suzanna slept well. It was one of those sleeps that she used to have when life was a routine and she knew what was happening that day and the next. She put her head on the pillow and fell into an immediate sleep. Eight hours later, she woke, opened her eyes, swung her legs off the edge of the bed and went to the bathroom. Routine-like.

There were no dreams she could remember, no tossing, no turning. Lying on her side, foetal position as she always did, she fell asleep facing the door and woke up in the same position facing the same way. It was a great sleep.

Yet it shouldn't have been. The events of the previous day were not part of her everyday existence. Dead bodies in the bedroom, bullet holes in the middle of foreheads, fleeing her own home for her own safety, following a killer's car to Cambridge. Christ, she didn't even know his name, not his real one anyway.

Life was so uncertain that she should have spent the night pacing her room trying to make sense of it all. And yet she slept like the proverbial baby. It must have been complete exhaustion. That was the only explanation.

And if she was exhausted, how must Ben have felt? He looked peaceful now, lying on the settee which he insisted would be his sleeping quarter, despite protestations from them all that if any of them needed a restful night, it was him.

"Two single rooms for the girls," he'd said, "and one double for Tom and Doris, which leaves the settee for me. It all makes perfect sense." Truthfully, they were all too tired to argue.

Pulling the curtains to one side, Suzanna looked out of the window at the couple walking away from her, leaving footprints in the frost that had visited whilst they slept. The girl linked the man's arm, leaning in towards him, occasionally lifting her head to look at him, laughing, her breath leaving staccato traces in the chill of the air. Both wore woollen hats, pulled low to protect their ears from the biting cold.

The man held both his hands in his coat pockets. Men do that, don't they? Ignore the girl's frozen hand as she links him while his hands stay warm within the confines of his pockets. On closer inspection, Suzanna noticed that she wore gloves, floppy, a little too big for her. Perhaps she'd got him wrong: the girl had no gloves, so he had offered his. Chivalry was not dead.

Slowly they disappeared from view. Delaney and Emma.

She couldn't bring herself to trust either of them.

*

Ten minutes' quick walk and they crossed the road, leaving the buildings behind them on their right. In their place was an expanse of white starched grass, each blade reaching razor sharp towards the sky. An illusion of course. Emma dashed forward, hearing the subdued crunch as her feet padded the grass, leaving behind a trail of wet footprints flattened to the ground.

So many times, things are not what they seem. Strength becomes weakness in an instant, the reversal of which takes a greater length of time. But she had managed it. She felt strong and all the stronger with Delaney by her side. For a fleeting moment, she wondered if he was all that he seemed, but she dared not linger on the thought. The consequences would be too great.

Running back towards his laughter, she linked his arm again and leaned against him. Be what you said you are, Delaney. Please.

"Are your feet wet?" he asked.

"Not with these trainers. Dry as a bone. Jennifer used to tell me that you get what you pay for. She bought these for me on my last birthday. The most expensive pair of shoes I've ever had. I saw the receipt in the bin. I told her she was barmy for paying that much, I could have got them for a quarter the price. Not like these, she said. The best combination. Light and waterproof, you get what you pay for. As always, she was right." She lifted a foot in the air. "Dry as a bone."

They passed the parked cars lining the side of the road and the silver-shrouded trees. Through the leafless branches, she caught glimpses of grand buildings peering at her through the mist which dispersed as it rose high above the cold earth. Towers topped with flags emerged, each of them different, each imposing in their own way.

Emma was experiencing the awe of visiting this city for the first time, one of the two great seats of learning in the country, known the world over for its Englishness and tradition. If only people knew the truth, Delaney thought.

He allowed her her silence. It was only natural. What he would not allow her was the intimidation that Cambridge sometimes brought, as if their students were somehow better educated, above the rest. It's true that, along with Oxford, it had provided the backbone of British society for hundreds of years, the stiff upper lip, the upper class that ruled the country through two world wars, but this was mainly because of connections, rather than intelligence. It had been known for royalty to enter the hallowed halls despite not having the necessary qualifications demanded of the masses. That way, the future of England was intact within their own select group. Proof of the immortal words of George Orwell: 'All animals are equal, but some are more equal than others.'

But times had changed. Some highly intelligent students were actually refusing places at these famous institutions, preferring to attend universities that would give them real experiences for the present century, not the previous five. And as yet, the high and mighty in the gilded halls of Cambridge had not risen to the challenge.

"What do you think?" asked Delaney.

"It's beautiful," Emma replied as she leaned against his shoulder, passing an arm around his waist. "In a different way to the living greenness of Ireland, but still beautiful. Beauty in buildings is so hard to create with its inanimate stone, but here in this setting, there is no other way to describe it. It's quite beautiful."

"I have to agree with you," Delaney said. "It's what happens inside the buildings that's so bloody ugly."

Passing along the Backs, Delaney turned and led Emma over Garrett Bridge which crossed the River Cam, its punts hauled out of the water for the winter, emerging only if the milder weather returned or out of season tourists wanted to take photographs to show their friends back in Tokyo or New York or Shanghai.

Down the narrowness of Garret Hostel Lane where the buildings lean in towards you, they came to Trinity Lane and then Trinity Street. Looking right, Delaney pointed out Cambridge University Press Bookshop, the oldest publishing firm in the world. "Even they have their faults," said Delaney. "Some bright spark way back in their glorious history refused to publish one particular book. It was taken up by a rival firm. The bright spark could have been publishing the Cambridge English Dictionary. Instead the Oxford English Dictionary was born, one of the world's bestselling books."

"I wonder if the bright spark got the sack?" asked Emma, laughing.

"Not if he had connections," Delaney replied.

Walking away from the bookshop, Delaney led Emma round a curve in the street, stopping outside a huge stone archway. "Cambridge University is made up of many different Colleges, scattered around the city. This one is Trinity College, not to be confused with Trinity Hall," said Delaney. He pointed to a statue within the top of the arch. "That grand old man is Henry V111, a man of intelligence despite his reputation, and creator of this wonderful College. It's not what he's most famous for."

Emma interrupted. "Six wives, a few beheadings, a major disagreement with the Pope and almost continuous war with the French who were sometimes friends and often enemies. It was a kind of love-hate relationship."

"Clever girl," said Delaney.

A group of tourists, cameras swinging from their waists, stood with their guide, breathing in the cold air and wishing they had paid the extra money to come when it was a little warmer, but their enthusiastic guide was doing an admirable job. Delaney heard her hissing the name of Anne Boleyn as she offered a brief but graphic description of her beheading as he walked by. The punters loved it.

A man in a booth, wearing of all things a bowler hat, was collecting the entrance money. Emma fumbled in her pocket, but there was no need. Delaney flashed a card and was ushered through with a quick salute against the hat.

Meandering down the path between the grassed courtyard, Emma looked around her. Stone buildings surrounded her, at a distance, unlike the narrow streets they had recently walked. Symmetrically interspersed in the walls were old leaded windows as old, Emma imagined, as the walls themselves. Straight paths were edged by fine borders. Discreet notices warned visitors and students to keep off the grass. It was all meticulously well ordered.

It seemed that all the people working here had a bowler hat as part of their uniform, along with the tie and dark coat. They weaved their way along the gravelled paths and past the stone fountain, in hibernation, that rose at the centre, each with their own mission, each tipping their hat in acknowledgment as Delaney and Emma moved by.

It all seemed to Emma to be of another time or another life, another planet even, one you read about in magazines. A society that never invites people in, you are simply born into it or you are not. Emma did not belong here.

Delaney sensed her unease. He refused to let her be intimidated.

Delaney briefly threw his finger towards various points of interest. "The clock tower, the chapel, the dining hall, the porticoes. Look, it's too bloody cold to give you a full tour. We'll come back in the summer. Come this way." He led her into an archway, pointing out the dining room, set out like a banqueting hall, where professors in shorts ate their meals in the summer months. "The truth is the food is not so great, but it gets eaten. Wouldn't be right to complain. And that," he continued, looking upwards as they entered an adjacent courtyard, "is the library designed by none other than Sir Christopher Wren."

"How do you know all this?" asked Emma.

"They do let the odd pleb in here, you know. It's impossible to get used to this place, you just kind of drift along with it. Accept it for what it is and laugh at its foibles. Many years ago, I was a student here. Bit of a linguistic genius so they said. French and German at school, Italian and Spanish here, Russian and Arabic later. My pièce de résistance was that I could switch from one accent to another at the drop of a hat. It's what kept me alive in Ireland for so long."

"How long were you here?" asked Emma, more intrigued now that she had an insider for company.

"Longer than I should have been. Fifteen years on the pretence of being a student, attending the odd lecture, strolling the corridors, mixing with the rich and famous. A variety of parties to attend, everything from the black tie affairs when Mummy and Daddy came down to see how their little treasure was doing, to the black leather and whip affairs that Mummy and Daddy were not invited too. Hard as it may be for the little treasures to believe, Mummy and Daddy were hard at it when they were here too. Some things amongst the aristocracy and gentry don't change over the years."

"You said 'pretence of being a student,'" said Emma.

Delaney smiled. "I did, young lady. And now you demand an explanation. Let's get into the warmth. The library."

*

The envelope had just two words handwritten in black on its white front. Ben Price.

They sat around the kitchen table, the four of them, while Ben broke the seal and read the contents to himself. Occasionally he smiled, but for the most part, his face wore a stern expression. Suzanna was the least patient.

"What does it say?" she asked.

"It says we're to meet Delaney and Emma at an eating place called 'Ask.' I quote, 'A frequent haunt for all kinds, young and old, where nobody pays much attention to anyone else.' They'll be there for about eleven o'clock." He folded the paper and returned it to the envelope.

"Is that it?" asked Suzanna.

"There's a map on how to get there."

"And?"

"And I've to outline Delaney's plan to you."

And after Ben had finished, Tom said, after a good deal of thought, "It could work."

"Impossible," said Suzanna.

*

Emma looked through the window at the River Cam threading its gentle path alongside the expanse of lawn below. She could see the bridge over which they had walked, busier now as the city's spenders strode their determined strides towards the shops. In that respect, Cambridge was no different from Manchester. People in cities the world over love a bargain.

Crossing the library floor past the shelves of books resting on highly polished ancient wood, she overlooked the courtyard they had left. Three storeys high, the stone walls sat on porticoes that stretched along all four sides, their walkways offering scant protection in the cold.

A single figure braved the elements. His gait was slow, shuffling along well worn paths carved by endless shoes over endless centuries. Head bent low against his chest, wrapped from head to toe, his hat and scarf carefully placed to offer most protection. Emma guessed him to be an older man, a professor, roaming the buildings that were his life and his home. His books were his companion, his existence wrapped in cotton wool against the reality of the real world of Accident and Emergency on a Saturday night. An overwhelming feeling of envy engulfed her. He had no interest in the vagaries of the outside world. He had lived, and he would die, here and he would have a plaque with his name placed in the chapel as testimony to his intellectual accomplishments which had affected few, other than those in the cosseted world of academia.

Her imaginative thoughts were broken by the approach of Delaney. Sitting her down at one of the tables in the room, he began his explanation, talking quietly to prevent the empty spaces from listening.

"A quick history lesson. Between the two world wars, 1918 till 1939, there was an increasing distrust building up between the East and West of Europe. Russia had had its revolution in 1917 and was a fully-fledged Communist state. Not only did the West detest the notion of Communism with its 'everything for the State' approach, they feared its potential. It was a new doctrine and, as such, had to be kept an eye on. Good old Britain couldn't have its history of tradition and culture invaded by this hideous notion, especially as it was beginning to get a foothold within certain parts of society. Remember, the General Strike had occurred in Britain in 1926, the Jarrow Marchers in 1936 and all that unrest. People, especially those with no jobs and no prospects of getting one, were not pleased with their lot and were beginning to get restless. They were prepared to latch on to anything that would give them a better life.

"Of course, Russian leaders quite liked the idea of this peaceful revolution which might achieve European domination, with Russia at the centre. Ironically, Hitler came along with the same idea, just a different method, and scuppered the Communist advance, but before him, in the 1930s, Russia set out to gain as much information as possible about their European neighbours. So, they recruited spies sympathetic to their cause. They didn't look for the overtly Marxist boys handing out Communist literature in the street. They adopted a more subtle approach.

"Ironically, they found sympathisers in walks of society that, on the surface, had most to lose from the march of Communism. The upper class, the wealthy, the well connected. It shouldn't have come as a surprise. History is littered with accounts of the educated rich trying to make the world a fairer place and most often they failed. I suppose the French Revolution was one of the few successes, the movement to destroy the French monarchy driven forwards with the support of the affluent young, not those living in extreme poverty. When you haven't got the food, you haven't got the strength to fight.

"So, Russia found its spies here, in Cambridge, amongst educated establishments. King's College gained a reputation for the recruitment of Russian spies, but it always irks them that the big four came from just down the road: Trinity College. Burgess, Blunt, Maclean and Philby were active for the Soviet Union for over thirty years. Philby served the KGB for almost fifty. They were all eventually exposed, but never caught. That's how good they were.

"Imagine what damage was done, passing on secrets for over thirty years. It all sounds dashing and daring now, heroic even, but lives were lost because of these traitors. Good lives." Delaney paused, remembering names, those he had never met, but felt he knew. Men like him. Looking back at Emma, he continued. "The Cambridge Four were effective during the Second World War when the Soviets were supposed to be our allies and even more importantly after it during the Cold War. Blunt became the royal art advisor. He was on speaking terms with the Queen and eventually he was bestowed a knighthood and all the time he was spying for the Ruskies. Maclean's father was a Member of Parliament and in the Cabinet. He worked for the Foreign Office himself and the scary bit was that he acted as double agent for MI5 and MI6. Our dear Secret Service thought he was on their side while all the time he was spying for the Soviets."

"But where do you fit into all of this?" Emma asked.

"After their identities and backgrounds were exposed, everything hit the fan. That spies could be recruited from Trinity College was unbelievable. The feeling was that if such desertion could happen there, then no place, no person, could be trusted. Mass hysteria amongst newspapers and television followed, which over time calmed down. The public believed that if the story was no longer in the papers, then the threat of spies within our midst had disappeared. The truth is that when the press are no longer interested, that is when the greatest danger exists. So the Secret Services recruited agents to integrate with students with the specific aim of targeting prospective traitors. And that's where I came in."

"And what happened to your prospective traitors?" Emma asked.

"I passed the names on. They were investigated further. Some were innocent, so were never followed up. Some were borderline, so were monitored at regular intervals. Some were questioned, but found to be of no risk. Some were as guilty as hell."

"So, they were taken in and interrogated."

Delaney laughed. "No, Emma. They were allowed to run free, so contacts could be found, perhaps those who were running them, perhaps those on the other side. And when the moment was right, when all that could be gained had been, that's when they were brought in and interrogated."

"Tortured?"

"Quite possibly."

"Sickening."

"Hey, Emma, it's a dirty business, but someone's got to do it. It's just that I was bloody good at it. Caught quite a few and you can sleep safer in your beds because of it."

There was an uneasy quiet between them. Emma rose from her seat and moved to the window to view the calm outside. With her face turned away from him, she asked, "So if you were so bloody good, as you put it, why did you stop?"

"A little problem called Ireland cropped up. I was needed there. Besides, you can only get away with being a student for so long."

A door creaked open at the end of the library. Turning, Emma saw the man who had been ambling his way under the porticoes below. As he saw her looking, he stopped and allowed the door to close behind him. Only his eyes were visible, the rest of his body covered in a long coat and a long scarf and a floppy, wide brimmed hat.

He reminded her of Fagin, yet the clothes were fitted, expensive. He raised his hand to the creases at the front of his hat and raised it slightly so that it hovered above him, revealing grey hair pulled back from his forehead. "Good morning," he said, his voice strong despite the cold he had brought in with him from the outside.

Emma nodded, unsure of how to react. All she knew was that he had caught her stare and held it so that her eyes could not escape. They were fastened to him as he unravelled the scarf from around his neck, his grey hair falling at the back in an elegant pony tail.

Unfastening the top button of his coat, he said, "I was hoping to meet someone here."

Delaney, moving from behind the shelves opposite Emma, examined the man whose face was now revealed. His face serious, he acknowledged his presence with a simple nod of the head. He crossed the floor, gently held Emma's arm and said quietly, "Take a seat, Emma. I won't be long."

Sliding both hands into his coat pockets, he moved down the aisle in the centre of the room, between the rows of books, past the furniture designed by Wren, towards the man. She watched him hold out a hand, his left, his right remaining in his pocket, which was taken by the man, who then led him out of sight behind the furthest bookcase.

There was no creak of the door, just the simple scraping of chairs. They remained in the room. Emma was not alone in this high vaulted room with its ancient artefacts, so had no reason to feel afraid, yet a shiver worked its way through her body. In the quietness, she heard the wind whistling gently through the windows and the creaking of shelves under the weight of the books.

She remained where Delaney had left her. She tried not to reveal her nervousness, but the gentle noise as her feet shuffled along the floor beneath her chair cascaded around the library, reaching to the secret corner where the two men sat. Even her breathing could be heard, or was she just imagining that?

All had been fine when there had been Delaney and her, but the appearance of the old man had thrown her, disturbed her. There was something about him and something about Delaney's reaction to him. Respectful, certainly, but almost to the point of being deferential. Friendly, yes, as long as Delaney knew his place. There was a distance between them, yet a bond that could not be broken.

And why had Delaney used his left hand to greet him? Was he unsure himself? Did he need his right hand to be free, just in case? Nervousness was swiftly turning to apprehension. Unknown to the others back at the house, Delaney had brought a stranger into the equation. As if that was not enough, he could have come here on his own, to this pre-arranged meeting, but he had specifically chosen Emma to be with him.

He had forced her to become an intruder into his world and offered her details about his background that she had, at first, felt privileged to be told. But now privilege was being replaced by an unease that showed in the beads of sweat that she wiped from her forehead and the shuffling of her feet that she was unable to control.

But what could she do? There was no way out, save past the whispering men that she could not see. So, she sat and waited and tried to control her shuffling feet.

*

Breakfast was over.

He wiped the remaining grains of toast from his upper lip and cast a glance at his mobile.

Nothing. No contact.

Things must have gone wrong. Sebastian would have been in touch by now, even if he was embarrassed about revealing his failure.

Surely a bunch of amateurs couldn't continue to outsmart him. They would have to make a mistake at some point and that point should have been reached by now, if the right pressure had been applied.

Maybe something had happened to him, an accident. Unlikely. Not for a man with his reputation. He was just too well organised. Accidents didn't happen to people like Sebastian.

He could be dead, killed. But by whom? None of them would have the guts to pull the trigger or plunge the knife. No, he couldn't be dead.

But something was not right and he now had to consider the alternatives.

Enough of the waiting. It was time to take control.

*

Delaney waited for the man to sit, and then sat himself.

"You've put on a few pounds," the man said.

Delaney smiled and nodded. "Sorry to have let you down, but when you're not as involved as you used to be, it happens. I'm under some kind of self-delusion that experience will make up for a lack of fitness."

The man shook his head. "A combination of the two would be perfect, but there comes a time when you have to accept your age, I suppose."

"You never have. Still working?" asked Delaney.

"I'm here, am I not? And anyway, my work is, shall we say, less energetic than yours." The man looked up at the bookshelves. "The girl, is she active?"

"Not yet," Delaney replied, "but she shows promise."

"Shows promise?"

"Anyone who can stick a hypodermic needle into the retina of one of our operatives, then batter him to death with a baseball bat shows promise, don't you agree?"

The man turned away in disgust. "You know I'm not a violent man. I accept it has to happen, occasionally, but that part of the operation never interested me, as well you know. Stop trying to rile me."

A trace of a smile ran across Delaney's face. He always liked these exchanges between the two, especially after they had not seen each other for a while. It was a kind of battle of words, pupil against master, a battle he rarely won. He always thought of his mentor when he watched the 'Star Wars' films. Of course, he saw himself as the pupil, the rebel challenging the ways of the past. Fortunately, unlike Darth Vader, he had never crossed to the dark side, although there had been temptations to do so.

"The girl," the man continued. "Forget her aggressive qualities for now, if that is possible in your depraved mind. Let us look at the more admirable qualities that define the term 'shows promise.' Can she be devious, sly, persistent, intelligent and logical? Can she blend in so that she is unnoticeable? Is she convincing, and most of all, is she loyal?"

"I told you," said Delaney, "she shows promise. And in answer to your next question, no, you can't have an introduction. I know how persuasive you can be. Leave her be for now. I'll let you know when she's ready."

"So you think there's a chance?"

"I'll let you know. That's all I'm saying on the matter."

Unfastening the remaining buttons on his coat, the old man leaned forward and placed his fingers on the table, spreading them face down, a habit he always had, Delaney remembered, when enquiring about his charge. "And what about you?" he asked. "Are you still active?"

"Well sort of," Delaney replied in a resigned way. "The Cold War is apparently over, the IRA are no danger, at least for the next twenty years until the next generation of heroes emerge from the discontent. The world's a safer place, didn't you know? I'm obsolete."

"Not a bit of it," said the man. "I would have thought your sort is needed now more than ever."

Delaney looked across at him. "And what sort would that be?" he asked, trying not to let the growing irritation show. The master was winning the battle. He rarely let anything show. There was not a trace of emotion on his face.

"The world is full of extremists. I would have thought individual infiltrators would do more good than an entire army. Look at Afghanistan and Iraq. Disaster, both of them."

"The accent wouldn't be a problem. The colour might be," offered Delaney.

The man turned towards him and their eyes met for the first time. When he spoke, it was with an affection he showed few of his men. "You had a great brain. You could have done anything you wanted. I thought you might go in a different direction, but then the training affected you, the physical side, the buzz, the adrenalin rush got you. It hauled you in and kept you hooked. You were that rare breed: an intellectual with a penchant for death."

Delaney dropped his head against his chest. He always hated it when the old man turned back the clock and challenged him to justify the choices he had made. At times like this, he felt he had let his mentor down. There was only one answer. "The country got what it needed."

"Just about."

Delaney threw a hostile look in the old man's direction. "What do you mean?"

"At one point, we looked at the possibility that you might have turned, done a Maclean and Philby on us."

"Gone to the Russians?" Delaney said, the hostile look now a sneer of disgust that the notion had even raised its head. "You must be joking."

The old man laughed gently. "No, never the Russians. The Irish. You had a great deal of sympathy for them and their cause, did you not?"

There was no need to reply. They both knew it to be true, just as they both knew that Delaney's allegiance to his own country was absolute. It didn't stop him having his opinions though. He knew that most of the troops serving in Iraq and Afghanistan did not agree with the policy that put them there, but they were loyal to the Crown and that was all that mattered. They were doing their job. Impeccably.

Delaney changed direction. "Anyway, enough of me. What about you? Have you still got connections?"

"Not so much in my old age, but yes, I have."

"Good," said Delaney. "There's an envelope ..."

The old man quickly interrupted. "My dear boy, I'm an observer. You know I can't pass things on."

"I'm not asking you to. The envelope will be delivered by hand. Tell him he must read the contents. Not just for the country's sake. For his own."

*

The map was easy to follow, as you would expect. If an undercover operative could not give them appropriate directions to a restaurant, then what chance did the nation have?

The place was already half-full with students and professionals, the odd tourist scattered here and there, scouring the menu and understanding little, except the pasta and pizza dishes known by the same name the world over.

Ben found himself being led to a table for six, asked for by Suzanna, but not minding where they sat. He was more interested in the customers. Away from the security of the safe houses of Suzanna and Delaney and amongst the general public, his automatic reaction was to look for Sebastian, even though he knew he was dead and for Ashcroft, even though Delaney had reassured him that he could have no idea where they were.

When he saw neither, he glanced around the tables to see if he recognised anyone else. Perhaps the girl on the plane to Dortmund or the driver who took him to the airport. Or the girl who had straddled him in the pub a lifetime ago.

It was a trait that Ben had acquired over recent days. He had never felt less trusting in his life. Every new face was an enemy, every known face looked at with renewed uncertainty. Scanning each table, he recognised no-one, yet he remained unsure. A second, more detailed look searched for unusual movements, extra attention in his direction, couples that were less intent on each other than on Ben. There was nothing suspicious.

He sat down. "Well, this is very nice," said Doris looking around the room at the modern features mingled with the old style tables and wooden floors. It was suitably trendy, but not overly done. A place that Lynn would have taken them to, just to keep them up to date.

'Don't want you growing too old too quickly, do we?' she'd say and then proceed to tell them what was healthy on the menu and discourage Tom from eating anything with too much fat content. 'No, not that one, Dad. Too much cholesterol.' Doris could hear her now. She'd never stop listening to her and talking to her when she was on her own and Tom was in the garage tinkering with the car. She didn't want anyone else to hear. It was a bit embarrassing talking to the dead. People would think you were mad. Yet it was so comforting, talking to Lynn. Dear Lynn. She'd always be there. Always.

"Reminds me of a place Lynn took us to in York. Remember, Doris?" Tom said. It was extraordinary how telepathic you became after thirty years of marriage. But then, they had always been like this. Sometimes Tom wondered if there was any reason for conversation at all, they understood each other so well, but Doris always found an excuse. She liked a good chat did Doris, so Tom let her get on with it and uttered the occasional, 'yes' to keep her happy. Of course, she knew what he was doing, but she never complained. There was no point in doing so.

They ordered drinks, hot of course, and waited for the arrival of Delaney and Emma. Suzanna wondered if they would arrive at all. It didn't seem right, them going off on their own without any explanation. Delaney had become very close to Emma very quickly. Maybe there was an ulterior motive. For a fleeting moment, Suzanna thought about Emma's safety, but she was a grown woman despite her childlike tendencies. If she didn't trust Delaney, she wouldn't have gone with him, wouldn't have linked his arm and pressed herself close to him.

What was more worrying to her was their willingness to follow him. Out of desperation, allied with an ounce or two of belief, they'd gone along with Delaney's trip to Cambridge and the safe house, but now Ben had explained Delaney's plan to them around the breakfast table, her doubts had increased. Even if he was on the level, could his plan really work? Had their despair stretched to such a degree that they were willing to go along with anything, however absurd.

Lifting her cappuccino to her lips, she spoke through the steam emitting from the cup. "So, one of us is going to be put in extreme danger today. The question is, which one of us will it be?"

*

The sound of the chair scraping along the wooden floor caused Emma to renew the shuffling of her feet. She found herself wringing her hands and leaning forward to get a better look.

Emerging from behind the bookcase, the two men were ending their conversation, shaking hands, saying their goodbyes. The old man lifted his spare hand and placed it gently onto the arm of Delaney, gripping it tenderly and releasing it as he turned to retrieve his hat and scarf from the table.

Wrapping the scarf around his neck, Doctor Who style, he fastened his coat and placed the hat at a slight angle on his head. Finally, he lifted the collar of his coat, ensuring that his pony tail was tucked away from the vagaries of the cold.

They were talking as they had since they met, in low whispers, but as the old man placed his hand on the door handle, Emma heard his concerned voice say, "Take care of yourself, young man."

"I will," was Delaney's reply.

Emma saw the coat disappear from view and heard the creak of the door as it opened, so was surprised when he re-appeared and looked down the aisle at her. Slowly he lifted his hovering hat. "I hope to meet up with you again sometime," he said. "Maybe we can have a long conversation. About your future." Replacing his hat on his head, he smiled, turned and left, closing the door behind him.

Delaney stood for a moment, looking in the direction of the closed door, then turned and made his way towards her.

"What did he mean by that?" asked Emma.

"Oh, nothing," he replied. "He's an old man getting older. He doesn't quite know what he's saying sometimes." Delaney knew that this was so far from the truth, he felt embarrassed saying it, but Emma didn't know the old man and it would work.

"Bollocks," said Emma, blasting Delaney's theory to pieces. "His mind is as fit as mine and twice as active. Don't lie to me, Delaney."

It was at that point, when Emma held no fear in challenging him, that Delaney realised the old man was correct, as he always seemed to be. He had that enviable knack of spotting talent, even at a distance. There was no doubt. He would be meeting Emma at some point to discuss her future.

"He seems to think you could be a possible recruit," Delaney said.

"Recruit for what, although I think I can guess."

Delaney sat next to her. He wanted to hold her hand, to comfort her as he spoke, but knew that it wouldn't be proper and Emma would probably throw it off anyway. She wouldn't be satisfied until Delaney told her the truth.

Delaney obliged. "The old man is Randolph Buchanan Scott. He was a professor here at Trinity, but he hasn't lectured for over thirty years. He prowls the colleges looking professorial and attending lectures as an observer. He doesn't observe the lecturer, he observes reactions. The odd comment from the gallery, the facial expressions, the nods, the disagreements. Anything that shows those inner leanings that we all have, potential that may be exploited at a future date. For the good of the country." He allowed himself to pause and smile. "He's very good at it."

"And what does he do when he sees potential?" asked Emma.

"He has conversations with them. Long conversations to discuss their future."

"So, he's the same as you. He works for MI5 or 6 or whatever."

"In a way, yes, but we are opposites. In my time here, I looked out for anyone who might spy for the enemy. He looks for those who, potentially, could spy or work for this country."

"He recruits spies."

"Yes, and others."

"What do you mean?"

Delaney thoughtlessly reached forward towards her hand. Instinctively she pulled it out of reach. She was only accessible when she wanted to be. "You'll have guessed by now that he recruited me. Professor Scott is not known for making careless statements, so when, in one of our quieter moments walking along by the Cam, he said I had the potential to be one of the best, I was as proud as it was possible to be. Regrettably, I became one of his disappointments. I turned out to be one of the others, one that did not follow the spy route. I did all the training bit, but got more of a kick from the undercover side."

"But isn't that what spies do? Go undercover."

"True, but I had certain qualities that set me apart from others."

It would have been easy for Emma to ask what the certain qualities were, but that would have been taking the easy way out. That was not her style now. After a few moments, she stabbed at a guess. "You found killing easy."

"Not easy, Emma. Never easy, except for the right reasons and in the right circumstances. Then I would have no hesitation."

321

"I know. I've seen you in action, remember."

Delaney pulled his chair to one side and stared out of the window towards the manicured lawn below. The swans made their way along the frost-free grass, stopping awhile to take in the rays from the low winter sun. Willow trees hung their branches low over the water and the odd punt drifted by, its chauffeur, wrapped warm like the professor, struggling to be enthusiastic for his freezing customers. Delaney took in none of this grandeur. He was looking at nothing in particular.

He was struggling to find the words, but words did not come easily when he was attempting to explain the choice he had made. How could he ever justify his 'penchant for death' as the professor called it. He had told Emma that it was never easy, for that was the truth, but how could he tell her that he enjoyed it? Taking another human's life. Enjoying it. In that respect he was no different from everyone else. People always enjoyed what they were good at. It's just that Delaney was good at killing people.

Of course, he'd never had cause to kill for the sake of killing, never gone into a bank and blasted his victims for the sheer hell of it. All his victims, for one reason or another, deserved their death. So perhaps his conscience should have been clear. He only killed for the right reasons. That didn't stop him feeling guilty about the life he had led. When he suggested that he'd meet Sebastian in hell, he meant it. That was the only place for a man with his track record.

"I sort of drifted into it," he offered, his words escaping quietly. "During the training, I was streets ahead of the rest. Put a weapon in my hand and I could use it. Effectively, immediately. Pistol, knife, rifle, even the unusual ones like belts and rope. There was a different technique to them all and it all came naturally to me."

"Bare hands?" Emma asked, her voice sick with disgust.

Delaney did not hesitate. "Often. When there's you and him and one of you is going to live and the other will die and you're so close to each other you can taste each other's breath, then you put your hands round his throat and you watch the despair in his eyes as the last bit of life is squeezed out of him. You do it not just so that you can live, but so that you can live to kill again. When it's your job, that's what you do."

"I find that sickening."

"So do I Emma," he said, turning towards her. "In the cold light of every day, when I have nothing to occupy myself, I can't even look in the mirror. Images of the dead run through my mind. I can see them all, every last one of them."

"How can you live with that?"

"I blot it out, convince myself that it was necessary. That they all deserved to die because they themselves had killed and if they lived, they would undoubtedly kill again. Perhaps they would kill your mother or you. Bombs are indiscriminate, Emma. My hands are not. I have never killed an innocent."

"I get the impression that Professor Scott finds this all as disgusting as me."

"Amazingly, given the nature of what he does, Randolph Buchanan Scott is a pacifist. He's never killed another human being in his life. He couldn't. He regards his work as preventative. If we can obtain information, then deals can be done. Death and wars can be avoided. It's a bit simplistic, but nice in theory."

"He may have it right, you know."

"Possibly, but that's where we differ. He's one of the lucky ones. Cocooned as he is, he has never encountered the real world. If he ventured out, he might at some point, have to literally fight to stay alive. It doesn't happen to all of us, but it happens to some. Doesn't it, Emma?"

Immediately her memory threw her an image of a blood-soaked, battered head. Hair hung to one side as the head lolled its way towards the tarmacked road. He was no longer breathing. The baseball bat was in her hand. Four, five, six times? How many blows had she struck against his head? She didn't know. She battered him till he was no longer a danger, till he could no longer breathe, till he was dead. She had not lost control. She knew what she was doing. Either he would survive or they would.

"You'll never forget, Emma, but you'll learn to live with it," said Delaney, quietly returning to his chair. He held her hand gently. She accepted it. He stroked his thumb across the back of her hand, compassionately, from side to side. There was no need for words.

Minutes drifted by as they were lost in their own thoughts. Sitting within the peaceful confines of the library, Delaney had already turned his mind to the future, to the afternoon's work. Emma reflected on Randolph Scott. She liked his simple theory of information and deals. Maybe she *would* have a longer conversation with him about her future.

Speaking quietly, she asked, "How is Scott able to do it, move so freely around the Colleges and into lecture halls?"

Delaney's eyes smiled. "You should know by now that the University of Cambridge is a law unto itself. The world goes on around it, but here, nothing much changes. The Colleges are quite aware of what he does. They condone it, even promote it, for the good of the Empire and all that. He has full access and, incidentally, he never has to pay for a meal, despite the awfulness of the food."

"You like him a lot, don't you?" asked Emma.

"I do more than that. I love the guy. He's the greatest human being I've met in my entire life. Granted, I don't mix with the high and mighty that often, but I don't think there'll be many who can hold a candle to him."

"Then why did you shake his hand with your left hand? Was your right hand otherwise engaged?"

This girl never ceased to amaze him. She noticed everything. Telling a lie would be impossible. She'd recognise one immediately. So, he opened himself up again. "Old habits die hard," he said. "There was a gun in my right pocket, just in case. You see how pathetic I've become. I've adopted a lack of trust even amongst those I trust beyond anything."

Rising from his seat, wanting to cut the conversation short, he continued, "I think it's about time to have a hot drink. The others should be there by now."

*

He reflected on the situation.

The worst scenario was that his career could be over. No matter how far you rise, there are always ways in which you can fall. He had tiptoed along the thin line too many times and now there might not be a safety net on which to fall.

But there was always a flip side. Instead of being the end, it could well be a new beginning, an opportunity to go on to greater things. All he had to do was make the right choices, use the right contacts. The situation was difficult, but the fat lady had not yet made her appearance, let alone begun to sing. There was still time to put things right.

Early on in their marriage, his wife had told him that he had a self-destruct button and his hand was permanently hovering over it. When things were running smoothly, he would raise his finger and press, just to upset the momentum of a peaceful life.

What she didn't realise was that if the excitement came in the bending and breaking of the law, then the ultimate ecstasy came in avoiding the consequences. And he was good at that. Sometimes by the skin of his teeth, but every time he had been successful. He'd never been caught, never been bettered, until now. Until Ben Price entered his life.

He did not doubt that he would succeed. It might take a little more effort this time.

*

Suzanna noticed that the two were not quite so attached as they had been earlier on that frost filled morning. She doubted anyone else had noticed. Call it woman's intuition. Doris was excused. It required membership of the same generation to know.

They walked into 'Ask' together, her gloved hand linked to his arm. Smiling, they made their way to the table, where they ordered the same drink: hot chocolate. All very lovey-dovey and nice, but there was something wrong, something that had come between them. It might not be so great that it was irreconcilable, but Suzanna was pleased that it had happened. Maybe they could make decisions now based on logic, rather than on Emma's dubious intuition.

Ben confirmed that he had outlined Delaney's plan and that there were no objections, although plenty of concerns. The main query was which one of them would be the delivery man.

"Wrong sex, I'm afraid," said Delaney. "It's a delivery woman. Doris."

There was a stunned silence around the table, allowing the notion to take effect. None of them believed this to be the correct decision. It would place Doris in too much danger. Anyone of the assembled would be far more suited to the role.

"I'm afraid that would be impossible," said Tom. "I'll go instead."

And all the others voiced their opinions, all proclaiming that they should be chosen. Suzanna was the most vocal. "I've done nothing so far but drive cars and surf the net. Anyway, I'm the fittest of you all and if there's a need to make a break for it, I'm the obvious one."

There was a shake of the head from Delaney. "Doris fits the bill perfectly. I've arranged her cover and she will be the best suited."

"So, we don't get a vote on this. What Delaney says, goes," said Suzanna.

Delaney took a sip from his drink. "Okay. You make the final decision. Take a vote. After all, we do live in a democratic society. But I'm telling you that Doris is the best person. And I have got a few more years' experience in this sort of thing than any of you."

The conversation was suddenly interrupted. "There'll be no need for a vote. I'm fifty-three years of age and you are all talking about me as if I wasn't here. I can make my own mind up, you know. I'm not incapable of doing things. You should all be ashamed of yourselves." Doris was calm and controlled. She looked at them all before focusing her attention on Delaney. "I'll do it, Mr Delaney and that's the end of the matter."

"Thank you, Doris," he said. "I've no doubts you'll pull it off."

"More than can be said for this lot," she replied, throwing a thumb in their direction.

The point had been made. There was nothing more to be said, but Delaney thought it best to consult. "Any objections?" he asked. Of course, there was no response. Doris might well have bitten their heads off had there been.

Just then there was the ringing of a mobile. Ben recognised it as the same ring tone he had heard on the drive to Cambridge. It was Sebastian's phone.

"Now this should be interesting," said Delaney. He clicked the phone on and listened.

It was Ashcroft. "You've failed, you bastard. Anything to say for yourself?" Delaney said nothing. "Haven't you got the guts to own up to it?" No response. "Mr Fucking Organisation. I tell you, you couldn't organise an orgy in a brothel. You're pathetic."

Delaney noticed that Ashcroft was playing it clever. He never mentioned Sebastian's name or his own. He gave no details of the operation, just vague references. He was fishing. He knew something was wrong, just didn't know what it was.

Then the ultimate threat. "Your father will hear of this you know. How you let me down. Me, of all people. A few words here and there and you're finished." Ashcroft knew that Daddy's influence had put Sebastian where he was and he never wanted to let Daddy down. There was no response from the other end of the phone and if he had been talking to Sebastian, there would have been. For Daddy's sake.

There was a long pause before Ashcroft continued, this time more quietly. "Who are you?" he asked. "You're not the owner of this phone, so who are you?" More fishing, but more direct this time. Ashcroft didn't know who had the phone. He could only guess, so he threw caution to the wind. There was nothing to lose. He named names.

"Is that you, Ben? If it is, I want you to know that you are dead. You know how much power I have. If it's the last thing I do, I'll find you and kill you myself if I have to. No-one, and I mean no-one, gets the better of me." A pause for response, then he continued. "Or it could be you Emma. Believe me, you sad little junkie whore, what I've done to you in the past is nothing, nothing to what I will do to you in the future."

Delaney didn't want to hear this. He knew there was nothing more to be gained, so he clicked the phone off and placed it back in his pocket. Ashcroft was as far away from finding them as he ever was.

"Ashcroft," he said. "He hasn't got a clue where we are or who he was talking to. But he's a ruthless man with unlimited resources and he won't be afraid to use them. We have proof of that already, the way he manipulated the Donors for his own purpose. So I suggest we get on our way."

"Just one thing," said Suzanna as the rest made to stand. "You mentioned the Donors. Just how much do you know about them?"

"About as much as you. I had a simple job. I was the bad guy to Sebastian's good guy. I was backup in case things went wrong. That's all. I was well paid for it, in advance. It was Sebastian who was the contact. I didn't know any names until Ben pushed Sebastian for more information, didn't know how or why the Donors were formed. It came as much of a surprise to me as to you, Ben."

Suzanna laughed. "Are you telling me that you were party to God knows how many deaths and you didn't know anything about where the orders and money were coming from?"

"Correct. I know you don't trust me, Suzanna, but it's true. Regard me as a mercenary. I don't exist, I've no National Insurance number, I get my money from whichever way I can. Well paid, no questions asked. Besides, and this will really freak you out, I enjoy it."

Suzanna shook her head. "Delaney, I've never met anyone like you before. And don't take that as a come-on. You live in a different world and I hate it."

Delaney rose from his chair. "So do I. Now let's get off before Ashcroft starts to use what little brain he has. We need a car. How do you fancy a people carrier? We can all travel together, like one big happy family."

*

Randolph Scott sat in his office surrounded by books that had been dusted weekly, but not opened for years. It gave the impression to any infrequent visitor that he was still working, churning out lectures to the constant stream of students that changed each year, all carrying the arrogance of nobility or brilliance.

328

He would need to telephone one of his ex-students now. It was the contact that Delaney required. An average Cambridge student, Timothy Spires had wriggled his way through his four years at university using family influences to ensure examination success. His connections also helped when he was interviewed by Cambridge police about a variety of incidents ranging from drugs to theft of examination papers prior to taking his finals. He was never charged.

Since leaving university, Timothy Spires had been an unqualified success. Rising through the ranks of the Civil Service, his rapid promotion had been accompanied by jibes and accusations of favouritism and nepotism, all of which, under investigation, were proved to be completely unfounded, but all of which were completely true.

He had ridden on the back of his contacts, or rather his father's contacts, for years until one day he became Sir Timothy Spires. The knighthood opened more doors and he actually became quite good at his job. It allowed him to use his devious nature and cutting personality in a more legitimate manner.

Randolph Scott dialled the number. Spires would answer it. It was a number known to only the few and if it rang, then it was important that it was answered. "Sir Timothy here." The voice was laden with dripping honey and just as sickening.

"Professor Scott." He liked to use his title with men like Sir Timothy Spires. He hoped it gave him a little more credence. In Spires' case, he knew it would not, but he used it anyway, just to hear the response.

"Oh, hello," said Spires. What he really meant to say was, 'What's a snivelling, insignificant, ageing Professor doing phoning me during the Christmas break?' Scott smiled at the disappointment that Spires would now be feeling. He was obviously hoping for someone a bit more meaningful like the Pope or the Queen or the Prime Minister.

Spires remained polite. "What can I do for you?"

"I need a favour, Sir Timothy." Always the title when he wanted something from him. It always worked. He just loved being a Sir.

"If I can help, Professor Scott, you know I will," said Spires.

"I know it's family time for you at present, but is there a small possibility that we could meet? Say, in half an hour."

"That would be difficult," Spires replied. Now that was unusual. Family and Spires didn't go together. He would normally use any excuse to get away from them. So, if getting away would be difficult, the only conclusion was that he was with someone more important to him than his family. It must be the mistress. Scott smiled at the thought of interrupting him.

It was more convenient in another respect. She only lived round the corner. Scott pressed home his advantage.

"Shall we make it quarter of an hour then?" asked Scott, which really meant, 'I know you're shagging Bethany Albright right now, so we'd better meet or I might have to go higher and then they would need to know why you'd been bypassed and the answer would be that it was inconvenient for you because you'd rather stay in bed with a young aspiring politics student and that would not look good, Sir Timothy. Not at all.'

"Yes, that would be fine," said Spires. "I'll come straight round." That was even better. No need to don the clothes and trudge through the thronging shoppers to some obscure meeting place.

"I'll be here," said Scott and replaced the phone on the receiver.

*

So now car theft could be added to the list of indiscretions.

For Delaney, it had been as easy as using a key, breaking into the Renault Espace they had found parked along the Backs. In the car park beneath Delaney's flat, they carefully laid the children's toys and buggies by the wall and covered them with a plastic sheet. Delaney promised to return them, with the car, later on.

Unscrewing the number plates, he replaced them with another set that he just happened to have lying around. Informed that there would not be an overnight stop, the group chose their seats and began their journey.

"How long?" asked Suzanna.

Delaney was surprised by her question, thinking the answer was obvious, but then he realised his big happy family had spent little time south of Watford Gap and were unfamiliar with this area. "Let's say an hour and a half, but that could be doubled depending on the traffic."

"So, time for a quick sleep then?"

"Take it. I need you all to be wide awake in a few hours. No sleeping on this job."

They headed south down the M11 and onwards to the capital.

*

In 1732, George II offered a personal gift to the then Prime Minister, Robert Walpole. He thought the gift too generous for one man, but accepted it on the condition that it would be used by future Prime Ministers, a kind of inheritance that had to be relinquished once the Prime Minister found himself out of office.

Downing Street is probably the most famous street in the world and number 10, the gift accepted by Walpole on behalf of the nation, the most famous number. Its black door with lion's head knocker and brass numbers has its letterbox inscribed 'First Lord of the Treasury,' the official title of the Prime Minister. There are two identical front doors, so that when the front door needs to be painted, the external appearance of the house does not change. Just a simple change of doors. One of the golden rules of politics. Appearances do matter.

Ironically, one of the few people working in number 10 who does not possess keys to the house, is the Prime Minister himself but if there's always someone to let you in and out then why bother lugging a set of keys around with you. Not that there is much need for keys nowadays. The wrought iron gates at the entrance to Downing Street provide suitable security.

Amazingly, up until 1989, tourists and anyone else for that matter, could stroll up the street at their leisure. They could click their cameras within touching distance of the front door and the policeman on duty would raise a smile for them, but not too wide in case it questioned his professional duties. Some locals actually used the street as a short cut to get to St James' Park, treating it like any other street in London.

In 1989, Margaret Thatcher, Britain's first female Prime Minister, ordered the gates to be installed. Some thought this was the height of arrogance from a Prime Minister often accused of acting like monarchy, separating herself from her people, but in reality it was an obvious decision given that, at the time, the IRA were conducting a massive bombing campaign around England. What better propaganda than to hurl a bomb through the windows of number 10 as you walked nonchalantly by?

Having caused extensive damage to the Houses of Parliament, car bombed the Sports Minister's family, shattered the front door and windows at the home of former Prime Minister Edward Heath, killed Airey Neave the Shadow Northern Ireland Secretary, whilst he was leaving the car park at the House of Commons and assassinated war hero Lord Mountbatten in a boat blast in Ireland, all in the 1970s, the IRA launched a direct attack on the Government while the Cabinet and others were staying at their hotel during the Conservative Conference in Brighton in 1984. It was the final straw. It was only a question of time before the limited security outside the Prime Minister's front door was breached. The gates were installed.

Huddled together, looking through the gates from the opposite side of the road, they listened as Delaney offered this brief history lesson. Tom and Doris were more acquainted with the facts, having lived through the IRA bombings, but the younger members of the group were astonished that the gates were as recent as they were.

"They weren't the first gates to be erected," said Delaney. "Three metre wooden barricades were built as the movement for Irish independence became increasingly violent, but these were taken down in 1922 after the Irish Free State was created, the Republic of Ireland to you."

"1922?" asked Emma.

"That's right. The struggle of the Irish people has been going on for a long time."

"These gates," said Suzanna, "do they do any good?"

"Yes and no. It made things more secure here, but it didn't stop the bombings around the country. London, Manchester, Warrington, amongst other towns and cities, continued to suffer at the hands of the IRA. And in 1991, while Prime Minister John Major was chairing a cabinet meeting at number 10, the garden was mortar bombed from a van parked outside Downing Street. Life as a politician can never be completely safe."

Given the litany of disaster reaped by the IRA, Delaney thought it wise not to reveal what Randolph Scott already knew: that Delaney held a modicum of sympathy for the cause. It was the indiscriminate nature of their campaign, the killing of innocents, that he detested.

"Forgive me for asking," said Tom, "but given the apparent impregnability of the place, how exactly do you propose to make it safe for my wife to walk to the door of number 10 and deliver an envelope to the Prime Minister?"

Delaney knew the question would be raised at some point. He had his answer ready. They could take it or leave it. "It's best you don't know that. You most certainly would not approve. All I can say is that when the lovely Doris walks up to the security gate, she will be accompanied by a nice policeman who will see her into number 10, where she will leave the envelope on the famous mantelpiece by which all world leaders have been photographed. She will then leave the house, the street and go into the café where you, Tom, will be waiting to greet her with open arms."

"Shit," said Suzanna. "If it's that easy, why doesn't the whole world do it?"

"Because the whole world cannot be as big a bastard as I can be. Given the right circumstances of course."

Tom placed an arm around his wife and kissed her gently on the top of her head. "What do you think?" he whispered.

Doris looked up at Tom, raised her hand and stroked his cheek. "I've always wanted to see behind the door. I'll tell you about it when I get back."

And, she thought, in one of my quieter moments I'll tell Lynn about it too.

333

*

"Sir Timothy, how good of you to come," said Randolph Scott with all the politeness that only the English can bring to a greeting. He offered his hand, which Spires took. "Hope I wasn't interrupting anything important."

"No, nothing that couldn't wait. In fact, some things are worth waiting for. Accentuates the pleasure in the event, don't you agree?"

"I certainly do," Scott replied. "It's so good of your wife to allow you the time to visit an old friend. Please pass on my best wishes."

The two were enacting the usual tit for tat when both of the parties know what they really mean. It was a game of one upmanship which came as second nature to anyone working for the good of the country, a game which could take hours before the real issues were discussed. On this occasion, Spires refused to be drawn. He wanted the discussion finished so that he could be away.

"What can I do for you, professor?" he asked, allowing the impatience to show in his voice.

"Yes of course. Cut to the chase is the expression I believe. If I were in your position, beautiful wife and children waiting for you at home during the Christmas holiday, I wouldn't want to be hanging round some draughty university accommodation. You could catch a real chill." He let the game drift to its silent conclusion before continuing. "The Prime Minister needs to be aware that an envelope will be delivered to him. It's in his best interests to read the contents immediately."

Spires threw a conceited snigger in Scott's direction. "The Prime Minister receives thousands of envelopes a day. You sound like some great member of the British public who actually believes that the PM has the time to read things sent to him. Come on, professor. How can he tell one envelope from another?"

"This one will be hand-delivered."

Spires lifted his head. No-one delivered letters by hand. They either came through the postal system or the internal mail. Secretaries and civil servants ploughed their way through them, sifted out the rubbish, and passed a few onwards. The PM got to read the post after three, four or more pairs of eyes had read them first. If he was presented with a letter by hand, then nobody else would have a chance to read it and that was unheard of within the corridors of power.

If anyone else had told him this, he would have found it difficult to believe. Despite his dislike for Professor Scott, he knew that, as far as the interests of the country were concerned, the man never lied. He also knew that, however this information had got to him, it was correct. Scott would never pass on information without the absolute guarantee that it was genuine.

He also knew that there would be no threat to the Prime Minister. You could rip Scott's nails from his fingers whilst shoving a red hot poker up his arse and he wouldn't betray his country. He was the most loyal citizen Spires had ever come across, a characteristic that sometimes annoyed him intensely.

He chanced his arm. "How do you know this?" he asked.

"I can't tell you that."

"When will it be delivered?"

"I've no idea."

"Who told you?"

"I can't reveal that."

Spires softened his tone. "But you do have to give me a bit of a clue. One person?"

"Two." As far as Scott was aware, there had only been Delaney and the girl involved. At some point in this discussion, he knew he would have to throw Spires a crumb of information. He couldn't reveal anything about his former student, so this little titbit about there being an accomplice was enough for now. If Spires wanted more, he would have to offer more.

"And who were they?"

"Sir Timothy, I have told you all I know. Tell the Prime Minister to expect an envelope, the contents of which he should read. He is at number 10 just now, I believe."

"He is." Sometimes, the PM opted for a break from Westminster during the Christmas break, but this year there were too many important matters that needed addressing and with that plonker of a Deputy PM, it was just not possible to leave him in charge.

"Then please pass this on. I assume the Prime Minister's private personal secretary has his phone number."

"I most certainly do, Professor Scott."

"Then I trust I will not have to break with protocol and approach him myself. Certain pairs of eyes will inevitably see me stepping over the threshold of number 10 and when that happens, you can say goodbye to my work here. The PM and myself never meet."

"And you will have no cause to meet him now," Spires replied. "I will pass on your message." Without another word, he turned and left the room, leaving the cool wind to drift in through the open door.

*

All the sights were around them. Westminster Bridge draped its splendour across the River Thames. Big Ben cast a glowering look over the Houses of Parliament and the most recent of London's attractions, the London Eye, revolved its watchful eyes over them all.

In Caffe Nero, they sat staring into their mugs. None of them knew what they were drinking. All caffeine tastes the same when the tension racks every bone in your body and your skin can't stop bristling and shaking because of the uncertainty. Even Suzanna had relented.

They had said little since Delaney had left. He had told them to wait for the phone call, but had given no indication how long that would be. Of course, if they had been in sound mind, one of them would have asked how long, but they were not. They were like headless, brainless sheep following each other. The problem was their leader was no longer there and they were children in an adult's world.

Before Delaney had left them, he had pointed out Westminster tube station opposite, handed them each an all day ticket for the entire underground system and told them that if any of them got separated, they should make their way via the underground to Oval station where he would be waiting for them.

And they'd sat there and nodded their pathetic little heads.

336

"What the hell are we doing?" asked Suzanna.

The Thames drifted serenely by outside the window and nobody said a word. They just wanted to get it over and done with, no more questions asked. They were tired of thinking for themselves. That's why they had accepted Delaney so readily into their fold. He would do all the work for them. Well, except for the small task that awaited Doris.

Suzanna was not about to let it rest. "Come on, don't let me sound like the only bad apple. I know you're all thinking the same thing. You've all got your doubts about this, even you, Emma, who sees Delaney as some wonder man sent from another planet to fight for the waifs and strays of human debris."

"Steady on, Suzanna," said Tom. "Emma's done nothing wrong here. At this time we just have to stick together and see what happens. There's no other way."

"And that's the problem. We've all gone along with Delaney because there is no other way. Is that a good enough reason to follow him down here like thoughtless zombies and place Doris in danger?"

"What's the alternative?" asked Tom.

"You know I haven't got one, Tom. I'd have voiced it by now. It's just that I've got my doubts about all of this."

Emma, in an apparent daze, had been listening in. Tom had come to her aid before, which was good of him, but she was strong enough to speak for herself now. Her voice was steady and bold. "What you really mean is that you've got your doubts about Delaney. You don't know if you can trust him. Back at your house, I was asked what I thought about Delaney and I said he was on the level. Over the last twenty-four hours or so, I've got to know him better than any of you and, as far as I'm concerned, he's still on the level."

"I wouldn't expect you to say any different," Suzanna said.

Emma gazed back into her mug. "But he's so bloody secretive," she said quietly. "When we arrived at the safe house, he locked himself away for the night. This morning, he met a professor in Cambridge, talked to him, out of my earshot, for about a quarter of an hour. I've been waiting for him to tell you he did that. I've been waiting for him to tell me what was discussed. Nothing. And now, he's gone off somewhere, saying it's best we don't know. Why won't he tell us? After all, it's us that are at risk. He can take care of himself."

"Perhaps that's what he is doing. Looking after his own interests," said Suzanna, surprised at Emma's misgivings.

"Maybe you're right Suzanna," said Emma. "It's just that I know what Mum thought about him in Ireland and I know Mum wouldn't have let someone into her life that was all bad. And I saw the way the professor and him spoke and cared for each other. I just can't believe that Delaney would sell us down the river."

Ben shuffled in his seat. Lifting his shoulders, he took a deep breath. "Here we all are, going merrily along, accepting everything Delaney said and did. Without question. Now, Suzanna, you open a whole can of worms."

Looking into his eyes, she said quietly, "It's what I thought."

"And it's what Lynn and I love you for," Ben said. "Speaking your mind. I think you've made us all take stock, so now it's out in the open, let's go through everything. Work together like we did at the beginning. See if there's another way. It's not too late to back out."

"I agree," said Tom. "Carry on, son."

Ben raced through the initial stages, stopping occasionally for any comment. Ben's initial decision to accept Sebastian and Delaney's offer. "If only I had said no," said Ben. "None of you would have been dragged into this."

"We agreed with your decision, Ben," said Tom. "We supported you all the way."

"Anyway, the clock can't be turned back," reflected Emma.

Sebastian and Delaney, work colleagues, but different, not social friends. "I walked right into their trap," Ben said. "They were waiting for me at Luton Airport. They had evidence that I had killed Buller. They had me hooked."

"Do you think it was a trap?" asked Emma. "Perhaps it was arranged while you were in Germany. Delaney said he was unhappy with the killing of Jennifer. It was different from anything they'd done before."

"We've only Delaney's word for that," said Suzanna.

"But Ben said he noticed the change in Delaney in the car at Luton. Didn't you, Ben?" asked Emma.

Ben nodded his agreement. "There was a definite cooling between the two, but I still had to go along with them. They knew where Tom and Doris lived and threatened they'd do something to them. And thinking selfishly, I could have spent a lifetime in prison." He shook his head. "I still don't know if I'd have killed Jennifer if I hadn't seen the photograph of Emma."

"Irrelevant," said Suzanna sternly. "The fact is you didn't kill her."

"Cast your minds back," said Tom. "If Delaney had not entered Suzanna's bedroom, what would have happened?"

"I would be dead," said Ben.

"And Sebastian would have dragged me off to Ashcroft," said Emma.

"So, Delaney's intervention was, you could say, crucial," said Tom. "Then Delaney offers a solution."

"But we don't know at that time what the solution is," suggested Suzanna.

"Correct, but we go along with him anyway. Why?" asked Tom.

"Because of the Donors," said Suzanna.

"What do you mean?" asked Ben.

"We'd decided that the only way out was to disclose the Donors and the manipulation of its ideals by Ashcroft. For his own purpose and greed. We'd also got proof that Ashcroft had murdered his own daughter. When the truth was out, Ashcroft would spend a long time in prison and the monkey would be off our back." Suzanna shook her head. "It all sounds pretty naïve now."

"You've got to remember that we'd run out of ideas," said Ben. "We were being pursued by a raving lunatic hell bent on having us all killed. So we were happy to welcome someone who seemed to know what he was doing."

"And since killing Sebastian," Emma reminded them, "Delaney has done nothing against any of us. Okay, he may be secretive and mysterious, but if he had wished us harm, he would have done it way before Cambridge and London. His little men in white overalls could have just as easily removed six bodies as one."

"So, Delaney comes along and saves all our lives and offers us a plan. We follow him. What was the alternative?" asked Tom.

The conversation ran dry. Just as there had been back at Suzanna's house, there were no alternatives.

"And anyway, there's no point in talking about alternatives. As Emma so eloquently put it, it's impossible to turn back the clock," said Tom.

"There is one alternative," said Ben, but the manner in which the words were delivered suggested that it was a non-starter. "We could leave now, all of us. Walk away from this café. Ignore Delaney's plan and go."

"What would happen then?" asked Tom.

Suzanna laughed. "Well, Ben and I wouldn't start the new term, that's for sure. And Emma wouldn't see her Mum again." She tailed off, not wanting to say what else she was thinking, that if there was a God above, Tom and Doris would be meeting Lynn sooner rather than later.

"So, we'd all be dead," concluded Tom. "As I said, there is no alternative. Get the letter to the Prime Minister and trust in his judgment."

Was she laughing out of nerves or just to lighten the mood? Suzanna did what Ben so admired her for. She spoke her mind. "When was the last time you trusted a politician?" she asked.

*

When Sir Timothy Spires left Trinity College via the Henry V111 archway, he fully intended to make the call immediately. But the afternoon chill had set in and the jacket he was wearing gave sparse protection from it. He made his way back to the warmth of the accommodation he had recently left and into the loving arms of Bethany Albright.

Of course, when he was in the loving arms of Bethany Albright, thoughts of the phone call requested by the ageing professor drifted from his mind. Prioritise, he thought, and as Bethany slipped the robe from her shoulders, prioritisation became the simplest of tasks.

He glanced at the Rolex on his wrist. It was now two hours since he had left Professor Scott. He really ought to do something about that request. Slipping from between the sheets, being careful not to disturb the sleeping Bethany, he made his way to the bathroom.

He was always a little concerned when he dialled the numbers. He never knew what the response would be. So his breath was a little heavy when there was a connection from the other end. "Yes."

"Sir Timothy Spires here."

"Fuck you, Spires. Don't get all high and mighty with me."

The request had been made six months ago. Well, it was more like an order. And Spires had had to go along with it. A list the length of a gorilla's arm of Spires' conquests had been produced. Most of them were students like sweet Bethany, some of them were younger than that, and there was the occasional more mature lady, all named, all dated, most photographed. It was a list others might have boasted of, but to Sir Timothy Spires, Private Personal Secretary to the Prime Minister, the publication of such a list in the tabloids would signal the end of him. His career, his marriage, his power.

And Daddy would not be able to do a thing about it, even if he had wanted to. If a list of his father's conquests were to be made known, there would be little difference from his own. Shagging Daddy's conquests had become an obsession and if Daddy got to know about it, he would not be pleased.

So, the request was made. "If any internal matter requires the PM's attention, then run it past me first. If I can deal with it, I will. If not, the PM can have it." Of course, Spires knew there was an ulterior motive, but what else could he do? He had his family to think of.

The number he phoned was not the Prime Minister's.

"This had better be important, Spires," said Charles Ashcroft.

Spires lied. "I've just this minute come from a meeting with Professor Scott from Trinity College, Cambridge. He made an unusual request."

"Don't piss around, Spires," shouted Ashcroft. "I'm a busy man."

"He asked me to phone the PM and tell him that an envelope would be hand-delivered to him, the contents of which he must read."

There was silence at the other end of the line.

"Home Secretary?" asked Spires.

"Is that it?" asked Ashcroft, an exasperated sigh audible down the phone.

"Do you know of Professor Scott, Home Secretary?" asked Spires. It always amazed him that politicians never got to meet the important people in Britain. They were either well shielded from them by civil servants who would still be there long after the politician had departed or they simply did not wish to know who was really running the country. He had not expected an answer from Ashcroft and there wasn't one.

"Professor Scott," Spires continued, more confident now, "is the main man who keeps us safe at night. He recruits spies, the people who keep you alive Home Secretary. Professor Scott, in his own way, has saved thousands of lives. His brood foil daily threats to our leading politicians and quash them. So effectively, in fact, that the politician may never get to hear of them. Home Secretary, would it surprise you to know that this year alone, your life has been saved fifty-five times, of which five were serious and two made their way to the operation stage? In other words, the assassins were in position and ready to go when one of Scott's recruits paid a visit and relieved them of the necessity to live. The irony is that not even Scott knows how effective his men and ladies are. Once they're recruited, he never sees them again."

Spires was getting too sure of himself. His last statement was incorrect. But, to be fair to him, he had no idea that Delaney was the one who had made the request of the professor. How was he to know? After all, Delaney did not exist.

Ashcroft put on a brave front. "What's the point of this pissing letter?" he asked.

"I have no idea. Just unusual, that's all. And with Professor Scott being involved, it makes it all the more intriguing."

"Find out who made the request, let me know and then I can decide whether I need to bother myself with it."

"Certainly, Home Secretary," Spires replied and clicked off the phone. Ashcroft was a puffed-up, blustering politician who had a false sense of his own importance. He hated him. It gave him immense pleasure to know that he could make him wait. He raised his two hands palm up and began to move them up and down, alternately. "Scott, Bethany. Bethany, Scott," he said quietly, balancing the choice.

There was no contest.

*

Mrs Eileen Blackshaw checked the time and turned on the oven. The food was already prepared and the table set. She always liked the family to sit down together for their evening meal when the boys returned from school or from their football club, and her husband from work. It was a tradition and even though the boys were now in their teens, they accepted that their mother would never allow beans and toast on their laps in front of the television.

All she had to do was wait for Alan to phone to say he was on his way home and she could start the cooking. So there was time to read a magazine and relax before the house was full and alive. A bit of quiet time to herself.

Evening was the best time of the day. It was when they all got together and in the cold winter months it was not unusual for one of the boys to suggest a game of Monopoly or the like. It would not be something they bragged about to their friends, but it was how they were. How they had been brought up.

Sport was their big thing. Give them a ball and they would be happy. Neither of them had taken to the countless hours other boys spent in front of video games and she was pleased about that. In truth, she didn't want them to grow up, but knew that inevitably, they would and they would leave her nest. What would she do without her boys?

Sitting on the settee with her back to the dining room, she flicked through the pages, stopping at the horoscope page. She didn't believe what they told her. If they were true, she'd have been a millionairess by now, ten times over. They brought a smile to her face, that's all. No-one could tell you what the future held. No-one.

She never got to read her horoscope for the day. Before her eyes could rest on the Gemini section, she was interrupted.

She felt leather across her mouth, tight, suffocating. Instinctively thrusting her head upwards and to the side, struggling with all her strength, she felt it being forced back and then forwards, pushed there with an oppressive force on the top of her head.

Invasive hands held her head in a locked position. Straining against them was impossible, useless. Quickly, she accepted the obvious. She was being attacked in her own home. She ceased to struggle.

Conversation was impossible, so tight was her mouth held by the gloved hand, so she waited for her attacker to speak and tell her what he wanted. And the smell of leather directly beneath her nose was overpowering. Perversely, she thought of the leather thong she had surprised Alan with just a few days ago. It was worth the purchase. But this leather in this context stank of evil and submissiveness and hurt and pain.

Slowly, the pressure eased on the top of her head, but as she straightened, the force was re-applied and held. Put in her place. Seconds later, she remained immobile as the hand was lifted for the second time. With a speed that gave her no time to react, the leather glove left her mouth and was replaced by tape that was pressed tightly into place across her mouth and cheeks.

If she had thought of screaming out loud, she would not have had time to do so, so rapid was the dexterity of movement. He had not finished. Her torso was pushed forward from between her shoulder blades and her hands pulled back and taped so that they lay fixed in the small of her back. She felt hands on her collar bones, each side of her neck, pulling her back against the settee. And there she stayed, immobile.

During the frantic activity of the assault, she had not had time to feel scared, but now, in the quietness that followed, she was overwhelmed by the panic of uncertainty, the fear of the unknown. She could feel the beginnings of an involuntary shaking of her body and tried to control it. She knew she could not. It was no use attempting to clothe her panic. He knew she was scared. It was what he had intended.

Hearing movement from behind, she wanted to look, but did not. She waited until the figure appeared immediately in front of her. Looking up, she noticed the dark trousers and hooded sweatshirt. And the gloves. Black, leather gloves, fitted tight to his hands, that had held her until she had relented.

The mask. Like a balaclava, stretched over his head, black with only the eyes showing. And the eyes blazed into her. Menacing, they spoke of the pain and hurt he would deliver if she did not do exactly as he desired. He did not need to say one word.

In his hand, he held a knife, sharp bright blade shining in the dullness of the day. Like her assailant, it remained calm and still, the more terrifying for it. Slowly, he knelt in front of her, his eyes never leaving hers. And he spoke.

"Mrs Blackshaw, I have killed many times in my life. Guns, rifles, belt, rope, I've used them all. By far my most preferred weapon is the knife. It can be used so effectively in so many different ways. It can be used to cut, each laceration delivering intensive pain to the receiver, like a paper cut multiplied by thousands, cut upon cut. It can carve, slicing flesh from the meatier parts of the body, like the thigh or the forearm. It can stab, relieving the body of its blood, gently, artery by artery, short sharp jabs of pain until the life flows from the body. Or it can kill instantly. One lunge through the ribs or one cut across the throat. One lunge, one cut is all it needs if the knife is in the hands of one who knows. I am an expert in its use. Do you believe me, Mrs Blackshaw?"

Eileen nodded slowly and a tear fell onto the thigh of her beige trousers, causing a dark stain to appear. She felt her neck shake, unsure if she should look down. She should not. The coldness of the blade under her chin raised her head and rested there. Slowly it moved from side to side, passing along the full width of her neck until she felt the sharpness of the blade stop at the centre with each movement.

"I am not a burglar, Mrs Blackshaw, nor a rapist. I am here for a purpose far greater than that and you are going to help me. If you don't or you show any sign of resistance, I will kill you. It may be immediately, or it may be following prolonged use of the knife, but I will kill you, Mrs Blackshaw. Do you understand?"

She felt another tear escape as she blinked her eyes. The wetness slowly made its way down her cheek, coming to rest on the tape that covered her mouth. He reached forwards. Slowly, he lifted a small corner of the tape, allowing the tear access to the corner of her mouth.

"Taste the fear in that tear, Mrs Blackshaw." She looked at his eyes. The point of the knife sent her a reminder. "Go on, taste it." He was all so calm, no shouting or frantic demands, as if this was second nature to him. As if success was inevitable and failure was not an option.

She let her tongue run across the inside of her lips, to the corner, the bitter sweetness of the tear stinging her taste buds.

"That taste will stay with you a long time. It will be a reminder that you should do as I say. I will not be asking, Mrs Blackshaw. I will expect you to do, without hesitation. Do you think that will be possible?"

More tears as her body trembled. She thought of her boys and how she wanted to see them through university and marriage. Maybe even grandchildren. And she thought of Alan who had had enough and was ready for his early retirement. Not long now. Another three months and that would be it. He would spend more time making pottery in the garage and she would return to full time work at the bank. It was all set up. No reduction in income, just a shift in earnings.

"Do you think that will be possible?" the man repeated.

She answered with a single nod of the head.

"Good. Now I can tell you what this is all about." Still kneeling, still staring with those evil eyes that bore through her, he began. "You love your Alan, don't you, Mrs Blackshaw?"

She felt her body jolt and straighten. The very mention of her husband's name had surprised her. This intruder had made a personal reference, one that required research, unless he knew her husband. Could it be someone Alan knew, someone she knew? In a way, that would be more terrifying. Her mind raced off at a tangent, grasping lifelines, finding none. She knew the facts: most attacks, most rapes, are at the hands of someone known to the victim.

Her eyes wide, she looked into his. Clues, evidence, anything. Nothing. Only dark eyes that sank into his sick mind. Whether she did know him or not, one thing was for certain. This was not a random attack. Out of all the women – why just women? – out of all the people, everyone in the whole fucking world, she had been chosen by this depraved monster. Before she could try to understand, he interrupted her thoughts.

"And your boys, Thomas and Joseph, you love them even more than Alan, I think." Becoming more frenzied, she began to struggle against the tape, trying to shout at him, threaten him for what she would do to him if her boys came to any harm, but the only sound that escaped from behind the tape was a muted scream, heard by no-one but the man opposite her.

"I suggest you do not struggle, Mrs Blackshaw," he said calmly, but she continued to do so. He lifted the knife from her throat and held it in front of her, pointed upwards and she watched as the bright red of her blood trickled from the tip down the length of the blade.

"First blood, I believe. It would be a pity if Thomas and Joseph had to live for the rest of their lives without their mother. I suggest you cease to struggle," he said returning the knife to her throat. She felt it prick her skin. She felt the warmth run down her neck and chest until it disappeared behind the blouse and between her breasts.

"Now, if you do as I say, no harm will come to Tom and Joe. They prefer to be called that, don't they?"

Who was this man who seemed to know everything about her and her family? Why was he here? Just tell me what you want and get out of my house. No point in struggling. No escape.

Searching his framed eyes for any sign of humanity, she sat motionless, waiting.

"Now, perhaps, I can tell you what this is all about. You know the meaning of love, Mrs Blackshaw. Do you know what I love more than anything?" he asked rhetorically. He could not receive an answer and was not expecting any reaction, a shrug of the shoulders, a shake of the head, now that the blood had started to flow. "I love my country. More than anything else. Strange, eh? No wife, no kids, just a lifelong service to my country. I saw the fire in you when you thought those you loved were under threat. You would have killed for them. Killed to keep them safe, no matter what the consequences for you. I feel the same for my country. I've killed many times to keep my country safe. And every killing has been a privilege."

Eileen Blackshaw looked in his eyes and knew what he said was the truth. She listened to his words, delivered rationally and emphatically, and was mesmerised by them. They held her, calmed her and she believed them.

"My love is at risk again and you hold the key. I have evidence that, within government, a secret faction has formed. Members of this faction have decided that they are above the law of the land. Because of the power they have and the positions they hold, they believe they can, quite literally, get away with murder. Now, murder isn't a bad thing, given the right circumstances, but when it's solely for the benefit of individuals, then it becomes a disease. And disease spreads." It was a lot to take in, so he gave her time.

She felt the pressure ease around her neck and realised he had taken the knife away. Only a few centimetres, but away. It was a kind of peace offering, to show her he wasn't all bad. She looked down at the knife. A stream of blood lay at rest on the handle at the base of the blade, the beginnings of coagulation in evidence, darkening as she watched.

He continued. "In my life, I've known people such as these, but never before in my own country. I cannot stress how important it is that these people are stopped. Sitting here bound with tape, you will find this difficult to believe, but they are more evil than me. Enough of the explanation. You either help me and live or, well, you know the rest." He placed the knife on the bridge of her nose, the red tip so close to her eye that the man became a blur in the background. "And you are now thinking," he said, "what has this got to do with me?"

Leaving the knife where it was, he stood. Her eyes followed him. "It's simple really," he said. "The evidence has to be delivered to the Prime Minister and you just happen to have a husband who is in the perfect position to help."

*

Spires looked in the mirror. Full frontal and then profile. Not bad. He pulled in his stomach, tightening the abdominals. Even better. His Dad couldn't compete, although Spires had to admit that the old man did look good for his age.

Bethany had served her purpose. He had decided that this would be the last he saw of her. Of course, she didn't know that yet, she'd just get the hint when the phone number he'd given her failed to connect. He didn't expect any trouble from her. He'd chosen her well. She was a good girl with nice parents, regular church goers, who thought she was still the virginal type. She wouldn't want them to know what she was really like.

But if she persisted, after all he was easy to find, she knew who he was, he'd arrange for her to fail a few examinations. Of course, he'd have to let her know that it was he who had the power to do this. He held her future in his hands. All she had to do was forget him. She would.

Fully dressed now, he looked again in the mirror, took a comb from his jacket and straightened his greying hair. Very distinguished. Power, money, looks. He'd have no trouble replacing her.

Enough preening for the present, he had a job to do. Soon, she'd be back with coffee and wraps from Starbucks. He had time to make the call.

"Professor Scott."

"Sir Timothy Spires here."

"Oh, hello Sir Timothy. Good news?"

"You'll be pleased to hear that I made the call. He just wanted a few more details. He has to get the right man, you know. Can't let any Tom, Dick or Harry near him. So, what's the man's name?"

"Sorry, that bit I can't tell you."

"Well, what about the man with him?"

Scott understood. Spires just needed another titbit, something to convince the PM that all this was on the level. He could see his point. He would have done the same in his position.

"Not a man," said Scott. "A girl with the most beautiful blonde hair and creamy complexion. A real English rose. If only I was fifty years younger."

Scott heard the click from the other end of the line.

*

"How's the diabetes nowadays?" asked Delaney. "Pity about the trip to the hospital in September. Good job you've got a husband who looks after you. Must have been quite a shock for him, waking up and finding you in a coma."

He seemed to know everything about her and her family, but by now, she was not surprised by this. He had been in her house for five minutes maximum and she felt she'd known him for years. Ironically, they understood each other. It was simple. She would do what he asked, he would do her no harm, she would get on with her life. She honestly believed that. But what the hell had her husband to do with all of this?

"You look good," he said. "It helps that you can contact Alan whenever the need arises. Contrary to many beliefs about the NHS, the doctors were excellent. They gave you the signs to look for and when you're feeling dizzy or get the pains in the back, all you do is phone Alan and round he comes. Ah, the benefits of mobile phones and good employers."

Removing the knife from her nose and placing it by her eye, tip on the corner, handle horizontal, he knelt down in front of her. He lifted his hand and showed her the telephone he held. She recognised it as one of her own.

"You have to be very calm now, Mrs Blackshaw. Speak to Alan and say there's someone who wants to talk to him. That's all. No hints, no heroics. Do as I say and you will come to no harm. Do you understand?"

She confirmed that she did. "I am going to remove the tape from your mouth, but you will remain silent. Have you ever seen an eye punctured by the tip of a knife? There is no need to reply. I assume you have not, but you can imagine what it would be like."

Slowly, he removed the tape. She stretched her mouth from side to side and opened it, loosening the muscles that had been constricted for too long. There was no temptation to speak, to ask him the questions that had been racing round her head. No point. She knew that the only response would be a seering pain as the knife ripped through her retina.

Delaney began to press the buttons. She noticed that they were all correct and in the right order. He knew Alan's mobile number as well as she did. She heard the ring tone and then the click.

"Eileen? Are you okay?" Alan knew she wouldn't phone unless there was something wrong. His wife was not one to make something out of nothing. His worry was that sometimes she might not contact him when she should.

"Alan, I have someone here who wants to talk to you." And that was all she said, as instructed.

"Mr Blackshaw," said Delaney. "I want you to show no reaction to this phone call, none at all, no matter what I say. Do you understand?"

"Yes," he answered. Of course, he knew that something was desperately wrong. Eileen always began any call by asking him if he was okay. General chit-chat. There was none of that.

"No harm will come to your wife if you do exactly as I say. At the moment, I am holding a knife against her eye. Do you understand?"

"Yes."

"In less than five minutes, a lady will arrive at the gates of Downing Street. She will be wearing a dark coat, but you will see a red scarf around her neck, tucked into the lapels. In her hand, she will be holding a brown bag and in the bag will be an envelope. This envelope needs to be delivered to number 10. There is no time to get permission for this delivery, so her name will not be on the list. When she approaches, tell your colleagues that you have just had a phone call about this, then take her through the security scans like everyone else and accompany her to number 10. Go with her all the way, into number

351

10. She will leave the envelope on the mantelpiece and then leave. You will be with her every step of her way. Do you understand?"

"I'm not sure …"

"Mr Blackshaw, there is a slow trickle of blood emitting from the corner of your wife's eye. Do you understand?"

"Yes."

"At some point, I want you to open the envelope. Inside you will find a sheet of A4 paper and a tape. There is no bomb, no biological matter, nothing to harm the Prime Minister. I want you to see that with your own eyes, to put your mind at a little more ease. The contents of the paper and the tape are gathered evidence that the Prime Minister needs to read and this is the only way we can get them to him. Others in his own government would stop them if they could. Do you understand?"

"Yes."

"After the lady has left, you will stay where you are and await a phone call from your wife. If you follow the lady or anyone else does, then your wife will suffer. You have followed my instructions perfectly so far. You will continue to do exactly as I say. If not, you will return home to find your wife and two sons dead. I am that serious, Mr Blackshaw. Do you believe me?"

"Yes."

"The lady is on her way."

*

Sitting alone with only the roaring fire for company, Charles Ashcroft contemplated the phone call he had received from Timothy Spires. Little shit. It was true that the majority of people did not deserve their knighthood, but Spires would be at the bottom of the pile if Ashcroft had his choice. One day, if things went according to plan, he would be able to make that choice.

He took a sip from the glass. This bloody envelope. It could be something or nothing.

If it was something, something to do with Ben Price, then he needed to know more. That it was, would be highly unlikely. It could be about anything. Given the involvement of this Professor Scott, whom he'd never heard of before, it was most probably a security matter. A serious one with all the fuss Spires was creating.

Professor Scott. Why hadn't he been informed of his existence? He was the Home Secretary, for Christ's sake and he was supposed to know about things like professors who recruited spies. He took a longer swig from the glass and re-filled. The sharp bite on his tongue cleared his head. He had more important things to think about than the security of the country.

The business of the envelope could be entirely coincidental. It probably had nothing to do with a snivelling amateur, out there somewhere, who could throw a dark cloud over his entire career. And his career was all he had left, now that his daughter was dead and his wife no longer shared his bed. It was his career, his position, that gave him the power he had always craved. Just one more step and he would be there. The ultimate goal. That's where the real power lay.

The Prime Minister had been there too long. Even his most ardent supporters were questioning his decisions and rebellion was in the air. Ashcroft suspected that the PM knew himself that his time was up. Why should he have the hassle when he could put his feet up and rake in the money on the American Lecture tour? It was true, he had outlived his usefulness, but Ashcroft would never tell anyone that. He would be loyal to the end and step into the breach that had been created by others.

Timing was the art of good politics and everything had been going like clockwork. There had been a blip when Sebastian fucked up, but he was still confident in retrieving the situation. He always had before. He'd had no problems pushing aside any opposition in the past or hiding anything that could be used against him. Jennifer was like that, with the drugs and the lesbian thing. Too risky. That was why she had to go. Ben Price would be no different. There was too much at stake.

If this envelope was something rather than nothing, he needed to know.

*

Not one of them trusted politicians. Not since Iraq and the fiasco of the weapons of mass destruction that never were. They sat in silence and waited.

Although they were expecting it, all of them jumped when Ben's phone rang. Vibrate was on and the phone danced its jig on the table. Staring at it as if it were some hand grenade, unwilling to touch it for fear it would go off, they let it ring for the third time before Suzanna looked up and said, "Go on, Ben. Pick it up."

He raised it to his ear and heard Delaney's measured tones from the other end. "Go now," he said. "Everything will be okay." The phone clicked off.

Ben placed it back on the table and raised his head to Doris. "There's still time to back out, you know."

Doris stood, wrapped her red scarf around her neck and put on her dark coat, ensuring that the scarf showed above the lapels. She handed her underground ticket to Suzanna, then leaned forward and kissed Tom on the top of the head. "See you soon," she said as if she was popping down to the shops, and made her way out of the café.

At a distance, Tom and Ben followed as planned, leaving Suzanna and Emma to pay the bill and wait by Westminster underground station. Doris walked with a determined stride, which belied the tension that gripped her. This was the most exciting thing she had ever done in her life and the adrenalin was kicking in as she moved closer. She knew the dangers, of course, she wasn't stupid, but nevertheless, it was frighteningly exhilarating. She wondered, as she rounded the corner of Richmond Terrace near the Ministry of Defence, if she could get used to this.

Tom and Ben had difficulty keeping up. Delaney had suggested that they take either side of the street so as not to invite attention. Either that or hold hands and act the gay couple, he'd quipped. There were so many around London that nobody would pay them any attention. They opted for either side of the street. That way if one of them was delayed by pedestrian lights or junctions, the other could always cover Doris.

Before long, the gates of Downing Street came into view. Ben was on the opposite side of the road where there was a constant stream of tourists, clicking cameras, moving on, to be replaced by more. Delaney had mentioned this. He'd told Ben to mingle, then move away if he had to, then come back. Most people came back for a second look. It was nothing unusual. Doris would only be five minutes at the most, so it was highly unlikely that in that time, either he or Tom would attract any special consideration.

Of course, they'd be on CCTV and if the need arose, that could be scrutinised later. But by then, the Prime Minister would appreciate the contents of the envelope and unless he was immensely curious, there would be no reason for further investigation.

Ben's attention was drawn to the three policemen standing at the front of the gates. Doris, about fifty metres in front of Tom, had slowed her walk and was reaching into her bag. As she neared the gates, one policeman stepped forward, placing himself between Doris and the other two officers. Doris looked so tiny standing by his huge frame that it was unlikely her presence had been noted by the other two. The policeman placed his free hand on her shoulder and stopped her.

He cut a menacing figure with his MP5 machine gun resting diagonally across his chest, finger in position on the trigger. The collar of his dark bullet proof vest rose from under his coat, which bore the proud insignia of the Metropolitan Police. Ben saw him flick the red scarf and point a finger towards her eyes.

*

Picking the envelope from her bag, Doris looked up and saw a police officer standing in her way. Stopping her from advancing any further, he flicked her scarf and pointed towards her. In the confined closeness between their bodies, evident only to the two of them, hatred erupted from him, yet he was hesitant, unsure what to do, what action to take. Red faced with anger, eyes on fire and his finger shaking, he struggled to control the rage inside. He was desperate to speak, but afraid to do so. Whatever Delaney had done to engender such a response, she was pleased he had kept the details from her. Like he said, it was best they did not know, they would certainly not approve.

"I have an envelope," she said, which wasn't in the planning, but she was a mature woman used to dealing with crises and improvisation came naturally to her. She thought a few words were needed to calm him, so she said them. The tension abated. His face mellowed.

The policeman turned and made his way the few metres to the gate. "This one's okay," he said. "I had a phone call about her earlier. I've to take her through."

"Okay," said one of his companions.

Leading Doris through the scanner, he motioned that she should put her bag on the conveyor belt. There were no warning bleeps and Doris placed it back over her shoulder.

The policeman walked slowly, deliberately. He had not had time to think about this. The phone call from his house had been less than five minutes ago. He searched for the options.

How long had he been in the Force now? Over thirty years and never a black mark against him. And now, at the eleventh hour with retirement around the corner, he was escorting an unknown woman up to and into 10 Downing Street to deliver an envelope to the Prime Minister. Anything could be in there. He only had the word of the man, who had broken into his house and threatened his wife, that it wasn't a bomb or something else. And what trust could he place in that?

Outside number 11, he stopped and turned to look at the woman behind. Without a word, she handed him the envelope. Delaney said that this would happen. The coppers were too good to let just anybody in.

He opened the envelope and checked its contents. It was just as the man had said. Running his finger around the base and sides, he felt for any small indentation or contusion. There was none. He held the paper up to the light and checked for lines other than the print that ran along the page. None. The cassette. The seal was still intact and the tape showed no signs of interference. There was nothing to suggest that there was anything other than the man had said: one piece of A4 paper and one tape inside an envelope.

There had been no alert when the bag passed through the machine, but he decided to take another look. Rifling through it, he found the usual brush and tissues, but nothing else. No nail files or scissors or lipstick or eyeliner. Nothing that might set alarm bells ringing, nothing to draw attention to herself. She had been well prepared to pass any security checks.

Looking down on this seemingly ordinary woman, he found it difficult to go any further. It was his training, his professionalism. No black marks, not one. Over thirty years. He knew what he should do: call his mates and arrest her. But she was just the messenger, she might not even know the contents of the envelope. The real villain, the bastard he really wanted to get his hands on, was holding a knife next to his wife's eye.

If he called for assistance, his wife would die. He was certain of that. There was something about the man that told him he'd done it before. And would his sons ever forgive him for putting duty before family? Would he forgive himself?

"Follow me," he said quietly.

*

"What do you mean, he wouldn't tell you?" shouted Ashcroft. "You're the Prime Minister's personal secretary. Wield your power, man."

Spires made no attempt to hide his intolerance at Ashcroft's naïvety. He sighed the loudest sigh he could muster before replying. "Home Secretary, I could have spoken with Professor Scott until the American President pulled his troops out of the Middle East and I would still have got no name and no description of the man who made the request. Some people become stubborn with age. Scott was born that way."

He heard a protracted snort from the other end of the phone. He had sensed it from Ashcroft's initial remarks, but following the almost perfect impersonation of a fat pig ready for slaughter, an apt allegory, he was now certain that Ashcroft had been drinking. He could practically smell the alcohol down the phone. The Right Honourable's voice slurred into action. "Then we're no further fucking forward."

Spires barely contained his amusement. It was a tongue twister at the best of times, but the three alliterative 'F' words took some time to escape from his mouth. Pissed to high heaven. Or the development of a stammer that would put him out of politics for good. Spires hoped it was the latter.

After a long pause for effect, in which he had time to revel in the demise of the bewildered Home Secretary, Spires took a modicum of pity and offered Ashcroft the crumb of information that Scott had given him. "There was, Home Secretary, a short description of the man's accomplice."

Spires heard the leather creak as Ashcroft shifted his fat backside across the armchair. Sitting up, more alert, his attention had been grabbed. "Well, get on with it, man," he shouted.

"A young lady, apparently. An English rose, to quote Professor Scott. If he was only fifty years younger and all that."

"Yes, yes. I don't need to know the ramblings of a letchy old professor. Get on with it."

"Well, there's not much more, I'm afraid. Beautiful blonde hair and creamy complexion. That's all."

That was enough. Ashcroft pictured the girl kneeling in front of him. He had his hand in her hair, beautiful blonde hair, and when she had finished, he gave her a packet full of the white powder as her prize. He'd enjoyed it in the beginning, but as her life disintegrated, the grease in her hair and the pockmarks on her face made him sick, repulsed him to think that this whore could have slept next to his Jennifer.

When he spoke, his words were measured and strong. Gone was the slurred speech and the confused state. His mind was acute and fully aware. "Phone the Prime Minister. Tell him about the envelope and tell him that when it arrives, he must not open it on any account. I'll wait here for your call. Have you got that, Spires?"

"I have, Home Secretary."

"And Spires?"

"Yes, Home Secretary."

"You do it now. Right fucking now. Don't you dare wait until you've shagged Bethany Albright. Got it?"

"Yes, Home Secretary."

Ashcroft rammed the phone down in its place.

*

Emma Parker, the bitch.

But who was with her? It had to be Ben Price. But that was ridiculous. How would Ben Price know Professor Scott of Trinity College, Cambridge? Surely he wasn't there in his student days. He was a teacher in a state school. That's all he was. Did any Cambridge students become teachers? Of course they didn't. They were destined for higher things than that.

Questions and answers flooded his mind, but they were all guesswork. He actually knew nothing about Ben Price. Ashcroft had seen no CV, no records, no details. He'd left all that to Sebastian and now it was too late to find out. Sebastian could no longer help him. After those useless calls to Sebastian's phone, he'd come to the conclusion that Sebastian was no longer alive.

Which opened another tirade of questions. If Sebastian was dead, who had killed him? Ben Price was the obvious candidate again. But that was ridiculous too. How could he kill an ex-army officer with a string of citations to his name? So if it wasn't Price, who was it? Who had the capability to kill Sebastian? He drew a blank.

Time. How much time did he have? If he knew he had weeks, even days, then a visit to Professor Scott would have been necessary, but he had to assume that the envelope was on its way. Now. If it was, what was inside? How could there be proof that he was involved in anything untoward? They had no evidence, not that he knew about. Only Emma Parker, and probably Ben Price now, knew the facts about his daughter's death. Only they knew that he had been responsible for Jennifer's death. And if it came down to their word against his, who would believe them when the Home Secretary said different?

His thoughts returned to Emma. Why was she visiting a Cambridge University professor famed, apparently, for recruiting spies for British intelligence? Ridiculous again. None of it made sense, but there was no denying that in some way, Emma Parker was linked to the envelope that was on its way to the Prime Minister.

Getting to the envelope before the Prime Minister was crucial, even if it was nothing rather than something. It would put his mind at ease. He could only hope that Sir Timothy Bloody Spires didn't mess up again like he usually did.

*

As they stepped up between the railings, the black door swung magically open. It was so smooth, Doris thought it must have been electronically controlled. Either that or someone had spent a long time perfecting the art of perfectly timed door opening.

The black and white chequered floor appeared before them. Doris stepped inside and heard the faint click of her footsteps. She guessed the floor was made of marble. Of course, it would have to be. Only the best to welcome Heads of State from around the globe.

As she glanced around taking in the splendour, the only thought that ran through her mind, rebelliously, was that she had paid for all of this. If not the fitting, then the upkeep. The leather chair, Chippendale at a guess, the alcove with some fancy modern sculpture, the painting of Horse Guards Parade, it was all there to impress First World Premiers and to remind Third World Premiers of their rightful place in the pecking order.

Clicking her way across the room, she reached out to the clock on the white mantelpiece. Carefully, she placed the envelope against it so that it could be clearly seen and turned to leave.

The policeman was directly in front of her, blocking her path to the door. "One minute," he said.

*

Ben had seen Doris disappear up the steps. From where he was, he couldn't tell if the door was closed or open, but she should only be in there a short time, so Delaney said. All she had to do was put an envelope on the mantelpiece and leave. How long did that take? One minute at the most.

"She can be an inquisitive little devil," came a voice from his side. There was no need to look. Tom had joined him. Which meant that Ben should move on. Shouldn't be seen together. Especially not now, with Doris inside. But he couldn't. Not till he knew Doris was safe. One minute, that's all.

It was like Houston waiting for sight of the Lunar Module as it tracked round the dark side of the moon. The greatest scientists in the world knew exactly where it should have been, but when sight is lost, there is always an element of doubt. Ben refrained from raising his nails to his teeth and taking a nibble.

"I hope she doesn't start nosing around," Tom continued. "If there's any artwork or pictures in there, you should make yourself comfortable. We go to museums and I take the newspaper, find a chair and do the only thing a man can do at times like that. I wait."

"We're experts at it," said Ben, his eyes scanning the street for movement. He remembered Lynn's shopping trips. Thank goodness she'd got on with Suzanna. The two of them were quite happy to go off together and leave Ben to do what men do.

He sensed movement by his side and glanced left to see Tom drifting off up the street, nonchalantly stopping now and again to view the sights. He was so calm about it all. His wife was trespassing in 10 Downing Street, accompanied by a policeman who had been cajoled, somehow, into walking with her. She had disappeared inside and could no longer be seen. And Tom was strolling away without an apparent care in the world. Either he knew something Ben didn't or he had complete faith in the workings of his wife. It was, of course, the latter. He knew her better than she knew herself.

Ben only wished he was as confident.

*

361

Lifting the envelope, Alan Blackshaw brushed the mantelpiece with the palm of his other hand and checked behind the clock. Satisfied that nothing else had been left behind, he replaced the envelope in the exact spot, took hold of Doris' arm and led her to the door. Before they left, he rummaged through the emptiness that surrounded the brush and tissues, the only occupants of the brown bag. Nothing had been added.

Doris could feel the tightening grip of his hand on her arm as they walked the short distance to the gates. His breathing had become more laboured and his pace had quickened. As he walked, staring straight ahead, he spoke.

"If anything happens to my wife, I swear …." He could not finish the sentence.

*

Ashcroft could be ignored most of the time, but this was not one of those times.

Spires knew that. Despite what people thought of him and how he had risen to such a position, Spires had developed an inbuilt protection system which could syphon the mundane from the important issues, either for the country's good or, mainly, his own. He was now a master at differentiating the relevant from the irrelevant, both in material and manner. It was Ashcroft's reaction that had convinced him. How he had switched at an instant from drunkenness to sobriety. How he had thrown in the name of Bethany Albright, meaning that it would not be the last time he would use her name if Spires didn't do what he asked. Bethany, sweet innocent Bethany, had been one of his father's conquests.

This was serious. Serious for Spires. Serious for Ashcroft.

Ashcroft had changed as soon as Spires had mentioned the girl with the blonde hair and creamy complexion. That's when he had changed. Ashcroft either knew her or knew of her or knew what she was doing. Was she that dangerous, this English rose, as Professor Scott had called her?

Scott would not have given her that moniker, would not have revealed the remotest description of her, if she had been one of his recruits, so she was unlikely to be a professional contact either for Scott or for Ashcroft. Most likely, it was personal. The obvious answer was that she was Ashcroft's mistress. Everyone had one after all. Ashcroft was nothing special to look at and he had a revolting temper, but he would be no different from the rest. But who was the girl, Spires knew most of the mistresses, and why would she want to deliver an envelope to the PM? There was something in the contents that had made Ashcroft jump. He was either protecting himself or someone dear to him.

His wife maybe, but it was unlikely she had done anything that required his protection. She was a totally independent lady, loyal to the point of lunacy and worth a hundred of him. What about his recently deceased daughter? Wasn't there something in the past about her being a lesbian, and of course she had died from an overdose. Not the finest daughter a Home Secretary could wish for. But that was mostly out in the open now, and she was dead. No protection required.

So it must be the man himself. Charles Ashcroft shitting himself over an envelope that was being delivered to the Prime Minister. This could be fun. It could also place another very large feather in the Spires' cap.

Wasting no more time, Spires phoned the Prime Minister.

"Timothy, you're supposed to be enjoying a well-earned rest, not contacting your boss during recess. What can I do for you?" Straight to the point as usual.

Spires often wondered how the Prime Minister could be so upbeat about everything. He'd made enemies both outside and within his own party, been criticised and blamed for everything from education to asylum seekers and yet every day, he sounded as enthusiastic about the job as when he had first come to power.

Probably closer to him than anyone else, professionally, Spires knew the stress he had been under and how his health had suffered, but he was a stubborn man. He knew what he believed in and was determined to push things through. Some said he just liked the power and it would be difficult to give that up, but Spires knew that deep down, all his decisions were made for the right reasons. His critics should try the job for a day or two. Then they would realise what an extraordinary man the Prime Minister was.

Anyway, who were the alternatives? Charles Ashcroft?

"Prime Minister, I have a rather unusual request."

"Is it your request or someone else's?"

"I have been asked by someone else."

"And who would that be?"

"I'd rather not say, if you don't mind."

"Not like you to be cagey, Timothy."

"I'll take that as a compliment, Prime Minister."

"And the request?"

"Apparently an envelope is on its way to number 10. I have it on good authority from Professor Scott of Trinity .."

"Professor Scott. How is the old guy?"

"Fine. He's fine, Prime Minister."

"Well, if it's Professor Scott with the request, then the answer is yes."

"But you don't know what the request is yet."

"With some people, Timothy, you don't need to know."

"Prime Minister, I have actually had two requests. The first was from Professor Scott. He asked that when you receive a hand-delivered letter addressed to you personally, then you should open it."

"All very mysterious, Timothy."

"The second request was that you should not open it."

"Even more intriguing. I take it that the second request did not come from Professor Scott."

"I feel a little embarrassed naming the second requester. It puts me in an uncomfortable, almost difficult, position."

"And I would never wish you to feel uncomfortable, Timothy. So let me inform you. The second request came from Charles Ashcroft, did it not?"

How the hell did the Prime Minister know that? Spires had spoken to Ashcroft just a few minutes ago and it was only then that Ashcroft had made the request.

"I can tell by the silence that you're a little baffled. Your silence also tells me that I have the right name. Let me ask you, Timothy, if you know anything about this envelope."

"Nothing, Prime Minister. Nothing at all. I am merely the go-between, the messenger."

"For once in our association, Timothy, I believe you. You see, your name is not mentioned in the letter."

"What letter is that, Prime Minister?"

"The letter in the envelope. I am reading it now."

*

Doris looked across at him. There were tears in his eyes. She wondered what Delaney had done to make the walk down Downing Street so possible. So easy. They'd just walked right up to the front door and delivered the envelope, more easily than a postman would have been able to.

Doris spoke with compassion. "I don't know anything about your wife, officer. I'm sure everything will be fine." It was all she could muster. She just wanted out to be out of the street and back home with Tom.

They had all agreed to let Delaney get on with his part of the operation. After all, ignorance can be bliss. But now she knew that this policeman, who had been witness to vile killings and devastating bombings in the line of duty, was terrified beyond belief that he would never see his wife again. The thought that she was party to whatever Delaney had done turned her stomach.

As she walked through the gates, she looked back at the officer. "Thank you," she said and quickly disappeared down the street.

*

Dear Prime Minister,

A number of years ago, an idea was muted in private by a former Prime Minister that one way to resolve the increasing number of guilty

365

people walking free on technicalities, either before or after court appearance, was to create an association that would finance the required punishment. If this resulted in the death of the guilty person, then so be it.

Without knowledge of the Prime Minister, the idea gained credence and a secret association was formed. Unknown to successive Governments, the Donors (not known if this name is fictitious) operated on Government money to serve justice where the police or courts could not.

Relatives of victims were approached and asked to sanction the death of the victim's murderer. If an agreement was reached, then the death was arranged by highly professional organisers. The relative was then told that they would have to execute the task themselves. Most agreed.

Recently, the Donors have been manipulated from within the organisation. Relatives are now being blackmailed into performing other killings, victims unknown to them. The organisation has taken a more sinister direction. Individuals are using their power and Government money for their own purposes.

No written proof of the above is available.
Contact Oscar Baker for confirmation that the Donors exist.
Listen to the enclosed tape for confirmation of manipulation.

Prime Minister, this information has been sent in complete secrecy. The senders do not wish to profit and wish to remain anonymous. The only custodians of this information are the senders and you, Prime Minister. It is hoped that the matter will be resolved from within.

However, if there is no indication of this, then the information will be forwarded to the newspapers, not for financial gain, but for the benefit of the nation. When the tape reveals Charles Ashcroft, possible future Prime Minister, endorsing the murder of his own daughter, the resolution of the matter becomes paramount. Hopefully this can be done effectively and without fuss.

An appropriate announcement will be expected within two days.

It was an extraordinary letter. The Prime Minister read it for a second time.

If any of the accusations had the remotest of truth attached to them, then immediate action was necessary. Of course, he could dismiss it as another crank letter. He knew he received thousands of them in a year, but never saw them. They were sifted out before they got to him. It was the same with the threats on his life and those of his family. The less he knew about them the better.

But this was different. Why not send it through the normal postal system like all the other crank letters? Someone had gone to the trouble of passing through security and delivering this inside number 10. It was meant for his eyes only.

Of course, the delivery man might be an insider, one who had access to the building. If he had the right security, then placing an envelope on the mantelpiece would have been no problem. He should make a check on the list. He'd do it personally. Christ, if the Home Secretary was implicated, then who could he trust?

He read it again. Although it was not signed and there was no indication as to who had sent it, he had a gut feeling about it. There was a realism to it and more than that, standing in the alcove off the main entrance hall, he could think of no reason why it had been sent to him, other than the one in the letter.

The information had been kept to a minimum. He liked that. Short and to the point. But it was strange that Oscar Baker had been named specifically. Maybe they knew that he respected Oscar Baker more than any other politician. If Oscar Baker spoke, he listened. If Oscar could confirm the existence of this group, the Donors, then he would have to take the remainder of the letter very seriously.

He knew there was more than one person involved, the letter had mentioned senders rather than sender, but apart from that there were no other meaningful clues. Well written, no spelling mistakes, which suggested an educated person. British, he was sure, and patriotic. 'For the benefit of the nation' was an unusual phrase, even old-fashioned, but still good to see.

All this conjecture was delaying the inevitable. It didn't really matter where it had come from or who had sent it. What mattered was whether there was any truth in all of it. There was only one thing to do. Something he had been putting off for fear the information in the letter was correct. Listen to the tape.

He moved towards his private office and closed the door behind him.

Listen to the tape.

Then phone Oscar Baker.

*

It was all very amenable. Apart from the lack of circulation in the arms and the smell of the tape round her mouth.

They sat together on the settee, she in the same position as he had placed her and he nestling against the corner of arm and back, resting on the cushion that was there. Angled towards her, he held the knife against his thigh, blade pointing in her direction.

Peaceful silence had invaded the room. If it hadn't been for the balaclava and the knife and the tape and the blood on Eileen's face and throat and chest, an observer would have said that the two were comfortable in each other's company. Best of friends almost.

When the phone rang, neither of them showed any sign of alarm. They both knew.

It was four rings before Delaney clicked the receiver on. "Yes," he said.

"She's on her way back," said Ben. "Everything seems to be okay. She took her scarf from inside her coat and wrapped it around her neck."

"Good. See you soon."

Delaney rose from the settee and looked at his hostage. "You have a remarkable husband, Mrs Blackshaw." He stroked her hair and ran the back of his hand against her cheek. "And you are a remarkable lady. I apologise for the hurt I have caused you. In my twisted mind, it was necessary. The only consolation for you was that it was for a good cause."

He moved across to the wall behind the door. Photographs of the two boys and a couple of Eileen and Alan, at their wedding and a more recent one, hung perfectly in an orderly manner. Thinking briefly of what might have been, he turned back to the settee.

"You realise I can't remove the tape. Your sons are due back from their football club in half an hour and they will release you. It will be a terrible shock for them to find you like this, but they're tough lads, they'll get over it. By that time, I will be long gone. Phone your husband to tell him you are okay. He'll be waiting for the call."

He moved around the settee and into the kitchen. Opening the cupboards, he found the largest pan, an old pressure cooker, and took it into the lounge. Sitting beside her, holding the handle, he said, "A couple of days ago, I was asked to do a job which appalled me." He smiled. "You see, even I have some morals. I was supposed to kill a man. We are now on the same side."

He reached into his coat, retrieved a brown envelope from the inside pocket and threw it into the pressure cooker. Placing the lid on the top and screwing it tight shut, he returned it to the cupboard. "I never accept payment for a job I don't do. Treat your family to a few luxuries, Mrs Blackshaw. And I'm sorry about the cuts. In a few days' time, there won't be a single mark to show the pain you have suffered. The wounds don't look so good now, but they're superficial. I told you, I'm an expert with a knife. If I had wanted to do you serious damage, I would have."

Then there was silence.

*

If they ever found out, the security men would go ballistic, but he'd been told what to look out for and had been constantly updated on the matter. He'd had a good look round the tape. The seal was tight and showed no signs of interference. He carefully wound the tape round a little with the tip of his pen. Everything normal.

He placed the tape into the machine, special and few of its kind in existence, and closed the surrounding lid which would contain any emission of gas and limit any explosion. Retreating to the farthest corner of the room, he pressed the play button on the remote control and listened.

Although he had been warned in the letter that Charles Ashcroft would be revealed as orchestrating the death of his own daughter, the tone of the recorded conversation shocked him. He'd heard his Home Secretary get annoyed in Cabinet meetings, but the ferocity of the onslaught and the abusive language aimed at the girl on the other end of the line appalled him.

Undoubtedly, the distinctive voice on the tape was that of Charles Ashcroft. The girl had even called him Charles and he had not denied it.

And then he heard it. "If I can have my own daughter murdered, then killing you will be easy. Look around every corner, you bitch. They're coming to get you."

A confession and a threat all rolled into one. The information in the letter had been correct.

Now for Oscar Baker.

*

It was a distinctive sound. One she had heard many times before. A repetitious thud at regular intervals with a few short, sharp thuds intermittently breaking the constant rhythm. Then the delay of a few seconds before one louder thud. And then their voices.

"Yo, man. Two points to the Tom Man. He could have taken the three pointer, but with only two needed to win the game, the Tom Man used his brain and took on the easier shot. What has the Joe Man got to say about that then?"

The back door flung open. "Yo, Mum. Tom Man is the man. He wins the basketball game with perfect timing."

The right expression, thought his Mum. Perfect timing. But only if the man in the balaclava had left the house. It had been only a couple of minutes since she had heard the silence. If he was still in the kitchen, her sons were at his mercy and he had already proven that mercy did not come easily to him. Given the right circumstances.

She began to struggle against the tape. It was useless.

Listening hard, she was relieved to hear the sounds of normality from the other side of the door. The fridge door opened, wrappers from chocolate bars were ripped apart, the bin closed with a bang and the laughter raced through to the lounge.

As the door opened, she heard Joe shout, "Hey, Mum. Football club cancelled so we had a bit of a kick around and then ... what the fuck ... ?"

Joe was the oldest of her two sons, the more serious, the more responsible, so she was pleased it was he who saw her first. His would be the more appropriate response. Tom, the more extrovert yet the more emotional, would have gone into hysterics and burst out crying.

It was a surprise to hear her Joe swear. The first time ever in her earshot. Tom was different. He had been a little embarrassed the previous football season when he had had to explain to his mother that he had been sent off for foul and abusive language. His only defence was that it was all aimed at Joe, so it didn't warrant a sending off. Brotherly love.

"Stay there," Joe shouted to Tom. He raced round the front of the settee and looked at the bloodied face of his mother. There were tears in his eyes, but at that moment, he knew there were other priorities. He had always had a bit of his Dad in him, calm in a crisis. Slowly he pulled the tape from her mouth and held a finger over her mouth.

"Is there anybody in the house?" he whispered.

"I don't think so," his Mum replied.

"Upstairs?"

"No, definitely not."

Joe eased himself up and made his way to the hallway. Slowly, he opened the door to the downstairs toilet and looked inside. Nobody there. Upstairs was clear and now he knew downstairs was too. He returned to the lounge.

Tom was sitting next to his Mum, quietly sobbing. "Tom, get a towel, soak it in warm water and bring it here," said Joe and without a moment's hesitation, Tom was gone. He may have had the biggest mouth, bragging about this, that and the other, but he knew his brother was the man in charge. Now and always.

"Joe, tell me. Did you see anyone in the street when you were coming home? Outside the house I mean."

He shook his head. "Think, Joe."

"Nobody in the street, Mum. Just a man in a people carrier who drove past us."

"Was he in a rush?" asked Eileen.

"No. Nice and steady."

"Did you see what he looked like?" Joe shook his head again. "This time I'm certain, Mum." Eileen knew they were silly questions when she asked them. Of course, he would be driving off nice and steady. Anything else and he'd draw attention to himself.

"Did he see you?" she asked.

"Yes, he did."

"How do you know?"

"Well, that's how I noticed him, but couldn't see what he looked like. He waved to us with his hand in front of his face. I remember wondering if he knew us."

Eileen smiled. "I suppose he does, in a way," she said.

As Joe leaned his mother forward to remove the tape from her wrists, she said, "The phone, Joe. I need to call your Dad." He rolled the tape off and picked the phone from its stand. When he turned back, Eileen was massaging her wrists. He handed her the phone. Quickly, she dialled the numbers.

The first ring hardly had time to finish. "Eileen?"

"Yes, Alan. I'm okay. The boys are here and they're doing a fine job of looking after me. Just a few cuts, but honestly, Alan, I'm okay."

"I tell you, if I ever get my hands on ..."

"Come home, Alan. Come home."

"I'll be there as soon as I can be." He rang off.

Eileen gave the phone back to Joe, took the damp towel from Tom and burst into tears.

*

Ben and Tom, on opposite sides of Richmond Terrace, headed towards Caffe Nero. If Delaney had managed to get back, he would be there to pick them up. If there was no sign of him, they were to take the underground and make their way to Oval station. Not one of the busiest stations, but Ben supposed that was the point.

Doris had already turned the corner at the end of the street and was walking alongside the River Thames in the direction of the Houses of Parliament. Westminster underground was opposite Caffe Nero, not two hundred metres away.

For the first time in days, Ben was beginning to feel more confident. As he glanced around, walking nonchalantly down the road, he felt a spring return to his step. He even dared to have a five second moment when he thought that this nightmare could be over. Under Delaney's guidance, they'd done their bit. The envelope had been delivered. All that was needed now was a positive response from the Prime Minister. If not, the newspapers would have a field day.

But confidence is a terrible enemy. It can lift you up and then drop you into depths lower than you have ever experienced, all in the time it takes to breathe a solitary breath.

Hearing a commotion behind him, Ben turned to see passers-by parting as a police officer came hurtling down the street, his machine gun unslung. Leaving a glancing blow on Ben's shoulder, he was past before Ben could bat an eye.

Quickly, he looked across at Tom, who was now crossing the road, walking much more quickly than before. While Ben dithered, not wishing to attract attention, in two minds as to whether to run after the policeman, Tom had increased his pace. The older man had reacted quickly again, but even he had been surprised by the threat of renewed danger. They had lost valuable seconds. Already they were some distance behind.

373

Tom raised his pace again and began to run, closely followed by Ben. Attracting attention had taken second place to helping Doris. Pushing their way past people still alarmed by the policeman's charge, they were running side by side. By now, Ben had regained much of his composure and thought of the officer's colleagues. Taking a moment to glance round, he searched the gaps between dispersed bodies, but was relieved to see no-one was trailing them.

The policeman was fast reaching the end of the street where Doris had turned. He had only a few more people to push past. Ben was willing them to offer more resistance, but they stepped aside, allowing the policeman to turn the corner and disappear from view.

Ben could not be certain just how much of a lead Doris had got.

He prayed that Delaney was waiting.

*

The Embankment looked the charming picture postcard with the Christmas lights adding their own brand of brilliance to the festivities. Dusk was closing in and, if she had a mind to, Doris could stay awhile and watch the transition of day to night. It brought with it that special kind of atmosphere which only occurred at this time of year when the winter chill bit through the coat and the nose began to stream with the cold.

But there was no time for that. There was work to do. Doris looked around for a sight of Delaney. She was certain she would not have to look too hard. He would be there at her side if he had to be, but if he wasn't, she would catch the tube as planned. Although she had been worried by the anger of the policeman, the calmness had returned as she had walked away from him. She had convinced herself that Delaney had only done what he felt necessary.

Looking over her shoulder, she scanned the throng of people milling around the entrance to Westminster station, but there was no sign of him. Taking one last look up Victoria Embankment, she began to turn towards the turnstiles that would allow her access to the escalators, but she was drawn back as her brain threw her a replayed picture of what she had just seen.

In the distance, by the corner of Richmond Terrace, pedestrians were standing to one side and through them, brandishing a gun, came a solitary uniformed officer. Doris thought it could only be one man, the man who had escorted her to number 10. It was too coincidental to be anything else.

For some reason, the plan had gone wrong. The co-operation squeezed out of the policeman had been replaced by a sense of duty. Doris presumed that this was because his wife was no longer in any danger and if that was the case, he was looking for only one person and when he found her, he would want answers and fast.

Leaning against the wall, she glanced round and saw that he was beginning to slow so that he could check each entrance, each doorway at a more deliberate pace. There was no time to waste. She must take advantage of his uncertainty.

Turning once more, she was immediately flanked on either side. She felt a hand at her neck and the red scarf was removed with remarkable speed while the bag was taken from around her arm. Some kind of headwear was tugged into place and her hand opened, palm up. Something was pressed into it. Looking down, she saw a ticket.

"Ticket in the turnstile, down the escalator, follow signs for the District line. Take one stop east and get off at Embankment. Take the Northern line south to the Oval. Got it?"

"Yes."

"Sure?"

"Yes. District, Embankment, Northern, Oval."

"You're fantastic, Doris. See you there."

Without a moment's hesitation, Doris inserted and retrieved her ticket from the turnstile and stepped onto the escalator. As she descended, she looked back to see that Suzanna and Emma had already turned their backs and were walking back to the entrance.

Following the signs, she made her way to the District line. The information boards showed her that she had three minutes to wait before the train arrived for the Embankment. The only question was, was that too long to wait?

*

It seemed to have taken forever, but it was necessary to check every possible hiding place just off Victoria Embankment. Since turning the corner by Richmond Terrace, Alan Bradshaw had seen no sign of the lady in the dark coat and the red scarf. And now here he was outside one of the two entrances to Westminster underground. He should check inside and quickly. It would be the logical thing to do: get speedily away from the area and the best way to do that was by tube. If she had gone down and caught a train, she might still be waiting.

Picking up speed, he headed for the turnstiles. No ticket was required. He'd slide across the top on his backside and place his feet down on the other side. Barely a moment lost. He'd done it many times before. It was automatic.

But before he got there, he was felled by an impact of such force that for a moment he lost the grip on his gun. It was still attached around his neck, but he felt the strap dig into the flesh, burning his skin as the edge dragged across his hairline. His first thought was for the public, but he was aware that the safety catch was still on and there was no danger of accidental discharge.

His second thought was more complicated. What the hell had just happened?

He'd landed on the floor, on his shoulder before turning half on his back, supported by his elbow. All he could see above him was the internal space age structure of the station which had won national architectural prizes. Dizziness hit him as each light merged with another and each metallic escalator crisscrossed with the next, shining like new pins.

Shaking his head, he began to push himself from the ground, only to be slapped down again by the palm of a hand in his chest.

A voice coming from above screeched at him. "You pig. You fucking pig. Look at the blood, you pig."

Lifting his head, he blinked his eyes, trying to clear the haze, but his head only managed to jerk from side to side in slow motion as if he was returning home after a night out with the lads and trying to make sense of the questions Eileen was throwing at him.

More insults were hurled in his direction and he felt the hand in his chest again, pushing him against the floor. "Think you can barge into me, do you? Well, you fucking can't. I'm going to have you for this. I know what compensation is all about."

Slowly his vision was returning. Removing the hand from his chest and holding it in his, he pushed himself to his knees and then onto his feet, all the time his ears echoing with an endless stream of abuse. One word collided into the next until he no longer heard the individual words. He shook his head, clearing it.

"Listen," he shouted above the insults. Reaching out, he gripped two shoulders with his hands and steadied the body in front of him. Standing in front of him was a mess of a female. Mascara ran in rivers down her cheeks, dishevelled hair hung over her eyes, her head leaned forward against her chest. Bending down, then looking up under the mass of hair, he saw that she was bleeding from beneath her eye. It must have been the collision with his radio or his gun, something sharp.

As gently as he could, he shook her until the screeching stopped. "Listen," he said quietly. "Stay here. I've got to go downstairs, but I'll be back. I promise."

"No you won't," she shouted. "You're a pig and pigs get away with anything."

"Look, I have to go. Stay here." He pushed her grasping hands aside and launched himself over the turnstiles and down the escalator.

*

"You've been wanting to do that from the moment you first met me, haven't you?" asked Emma.

"Before that," Suzanna replied. "I hated you from the time you entered Lynn's life."

377

Emma stroked her own cheek. Rubbing her thumb across the blood on her fingers, she said, "You pack one hell of a punch. Feel better for it?"

"Strangely, no. I suppose in some masochistic way, I've come to like you."

Walking away in the direction of the river, Suzanna asked, "Do you think she had enough time?"

"Dunno, but I hope the delay helped a little bit."

*

Running down the escalator, Alan Bradshaw could hear the rumble of trains below him. If the lady had escaped down here, she had three lines to choose from. Out of the three, Circle, District or Jubilee, he thought she might have gone for the earliest train, no matter what line. But that would only be if she knew he was following her. He had not seen her, so he had to assume she had not seen him and was oblivious to his pursuit.

So, he thought, she thinks she has time. There would have been an advance plan and she would have stuck to it. Everything she had done had been meticulous. Not everyone gets to see the inside of the Prime Minister's residence, yet she was in and out of there as quickly as she could be. No loitering. Stick to the plan. It was he who had delayed the operation by checking the mantelpiece and before that, the envelope.

Another scenario flicked through his mind. One that frightened him even more. Maybe she was carrying the envelope because she had to. Just like he had had to accompany her, even when he hadn't wanted to. Did she have a loved one, a husband, at home with a knife against his throat? And if that was the case, then she was as innocent as he was. And if he caught her and arrested her, then her husband would die and he would be responsible.

Oh, shit. He stopped running and allowed the escalator to drift towards its destination, giving him more thinking time. What about his own family? The man on the phone knew where he lived. If he stopped the woman, then the man might know about it. And if he did, he would carry out his threat. He would return to the house and Eileen and the boys were there. He would kill them.

Four deaths because Alan Bradshaw felt obliged to do his bloody professional duty.

The escalator dropped him off. Sifting through the options, he decided to check the platforms, just the Circle and District lines. The Jubilee line was down another level. He might check that later, but he could feel his initial enthusiasm draining from him.

If he found her, he would stop her, but now he would treat her as an innocent. He wanted to talk to her, find the facts. He knew what he'd been through since Eileen phoned him and told him there was someone who wanted to talk to him. How must she have felt if the same threats had been made against her?

He glanced round the corner. The Circle line platform was busy, full of passengers ignorant of what had gone on above ground. He strolled though them. Just another security patrol. It made everyone feel better. A slight variation on 'bobby on the beat.' He even got a few smiles thrown in his direction. He threw some back.

The air was full of the loud continuous beat of a ghetto blaster resting on the shoulder of a slouched teenager, baseball cap tilted at an angle on his head. Bradshaw made his way towards the youth, slowly meandering through the crowd, the noise rising to a crescendo as he got closer. To be honest, Alan could only hear the base line thumping a hard, regular beat. Anything in between was lost. A sign of age, he supposed.

Turning his head in time to the music, the teenager caught a glimpse of the policeman in full uniform, carrying a machine gun. Surprise turned to shock. Tough teenager turned to pliable youth. His hand reached up and turned. The volume decreased immediately. Maybe there was respect for the law after all. Alan smiled and got one in return.

Then he heard the train. Not on this platform. Arriving or departing? He wasn't sure. Couldn't make it out over the lowered tones of the ghetto blaster. He made his way towards the District line. He found himself walking, not running as before. He wasn't sure if he wanted to find her anymore. It would be simpler if he didn't.

Arriving on the platform, he caught a glimpse of the back of the last carriage disappearing from view down the tunnel. Not even sure that she was on that train, not caring much anymore, he felt his body relax. There were no decisions to be made. All he wanted was to be at home with his wife and kids.

Looking around the empty platform, more out of habit than anything else, he walked towards the exit and decided to call his colleagues and let them know he was okay. They might be getting a bit worried by now. He lifted the radio to his mouth. God knows if it would work down here.

He didn't make the call.

*

Hearing the whistle, Ben looked around. It wasn't the first time he'd heard it. He'd often laughed during games lessons when he taught the boys football and Suzanna taught the girls netball. She was the only teacher he'd known to referee a match without the aid of the silver Thunderer blasting out from between the lips.

Suzanna had once said that she preferred things 'au naturel,' which had Lynn in hysterics. The upshot was that she could whistle without any aid, in various tones, and that was what he could hear now.

He spotted her waving from behind a tree, motioning him to cross the road. Tapping Tom on the shoulder, he coaxed him across.

"What the hell happened to you?" asked Ben pointing at the blood still trickling from the wound on Emma's cheek.

"Bumped into Suzanna's fist," she answered, but before the conversation could develop, she added, "I'll tell you later."

"We think Doris is okay," said Suzanna, more out of optimism than belief. It was an attempt at reassuring Tom. Of course, he didn't buy it.

"I'm going down," he said.

"Just a minute," said Emma. "I think that's a good idea Tom, but there's no point in us all charging after Doris. I suggest we split up. Tom, go down. If Doris is nowhere to be seen, then you can presume she has gone to the Oval. Get on the next train and meet up with her. Suzanna, follow Tom, look out for our friendly policeman on the way down, he may have caught a glimpse of you, then take the Jubilee line. Go anywhere for half an hour and then head for the Oval. Ben, stroll over to Embankment Station, then take the Circle line for half an hour, then meet at the Oval. I'll take a stroll around here, check on activity around Downing Street gates and then head for the Oval. How does that sound?"

"Good," Tom said. He reached forward and stroked Emma's cheek. "Take care of that," he said and left.

They watched him disappear through the entrance before Suzanna followed, crossing the road, not looking back.

"Enjoy your walk," Emma said and headed off up Victoria Embankment towards Downing Street, leaving Ben alone. Feeling isolated for the first time in days, he lifted the collar up around his neck and looked in admiration at each disappearing figure. They had put their lives on hold for him. They had snatched him away from his morose existence and tried to put his life back together. With a little help from Delaney, of course.

Which made him think. If Delaney wasn't here, where the hell was he?

*

If connection is made with the back of the knee at the correct point, then only a limited amount of force is necessary to take a man down. And Alan Bradshaw was down.

Falling backwards, his elbow bore the brunt for the second time in the last few minutes. He knew he was heading for the tracks, but was stopped by a hand on the top of his head. Another hand reached forward and took hold of his mouth, covering it, restricting his breathing. He felt the hand release on his head and take hold of his armpit, dragging him backwards till the weight of his body plummeted hopelessly into thin air.

He was twisted and turned so that he faced the advertisement hoardings that reached the length of the wall opposite the platform.

Suddenly his torso stopped, held in position by a knee that had wedged into the base of his spine. His legs continued their fall until they landed, almost balletically, by the tracks.

There was no hope of struggle. He was held tightly by hands, knees and body and semi-dragged away from the platform and into the darkness of the tunnel. Only a few metres, that was all, far enough to escape prying eyes.

His attacker's hand left his mouth and pushed his face against the wall so that the grit from the bricks squeezed against him, pricking his skin. Mouth distorted against it, unable to move, he could smell the dirt and grime in the confinement of the airless tunnel.

It had all happened so quickly. Even if he had wanted to offer resistance, it would have been impossible. He was being held by someone who knew what he was doing, a professional. Besides, he still had a picture in his mind of his wife and kids at home. He wanted to be there.

He was aware of the closeness of breathing by his ear. When they came, the words were whispered and slow. "Alan, your wife's been through too much to have it spoiled by one stupid decision made by you. I just want to make sure you don't do anything foolish. I know it was difficult for you. I know how conscientious you are, but there was never any danger to the Prime Minister. He will be pleased to receive the envelope. Go back to your colleagues. Tell them you thought you saw someone you recognised. But, false alarm."

Alan pulled his face from the wall. "They'll never believe me," he said.

"Yes, they will. Same thing happened to Jeff a couple of months ago. Left his post. Mistaken identity. Remember?"

"How did you know that?"

"Kept it between the three of you, didn't you? You're a good team. They'll believe you."

They felt the vibration first, then the sound. It was difficult to tell if it was on their line, but the vibrations were getting stronger and the sound louder. Metres away, a different sound drifted to their ears. The platform was beginning to fill with people, making their way home after another boring day at the office. A sudden stillness hit the air.

"Eileen has come to no harm, I can promise you that. Go home and in a few months, enjoy your retirement. You've earned it. All you have to do is remain quiet about all of this. It didn't happen."

There was no doubt now that the train was on their line, coming closer. The noise was speeding towards them, wrapping itself around the curves in the darkness, before thrusting forward in their direction. Alan began to struggle. Not to harm his attacker. His needs were more basic. Survival. See the kids again.

He heard words, shouted above the deafening rumble of the approaching train. "Take this no further, Alan. If you do, there will be problems. I know where you live." And he was dragged and lifted and found himself rolling onto the platform, coming to rest by the retreating legs of a surprised and shapely young lady. Such were her priorities, that she stepped over him and passed through the doors that slid open before her, not once looking back.

Alan picked himself up and looked around. No-one came towards him. There were no offers of help or enquiries about his well being. No words of commiseration from Joe Public. This is what policing in London had come to. You could be thrown out of a tunnel and rolled onto a platform by an unknown source and everyone was too preoccupied, too scared, too bloody apathetic, to help. Roll on retirement.

Dusting himself down, he allowed the train to leave with its passengers on board before leaning over the edge and searching the darkness for signs of his assailant. He didn't know why. He wouldn't have done anything. He wanted to go home.

There was nobody there.

*

Walking alongside a very shapely young lady, Tom ignored the prostrate policeman who had emerged from the tracks. He accompanied his new companion onto the train. Holding on tight as the train picked up speed, he scanned the platform. Only the policeman was visible, dusting himself down, but there was someone else, somewhere close. He knew it.

In the unreal light of the carriage, he drifted into his own world. He never even noticed the young lady return his smile. The smile was not intended for her. It was simply a natural reaction to his latest rumination. If the policeman was there on the platform, then the chances were that Doris had managed to avoid detection.

It would be nice to see her again.

*

Ben Price. The name was beginning to haunt him.

He thought of his family and his career. One long since over and the other in the balance. Ben Price was to blame for everything.

Looking down, he saw his hands twisting the glass. The contents gave off the most beautiful colour, accentuated by the reflections thrown out by the crystal pattern that ran round the circumference.

How many glasses had been twisted between fingers and thumb? How many hours of reflection had his great friend witnessed? Perhaps his liver was keeping count.

Whiskey gave him the most remarkable pleasure and repaid him in full for all the hours he spent with it. Sometimes an occasional doubt crept into his mind, a hint of conscience behind the stern exterior, a touch of guilt over the latest manipulation, but the contents of the glass soon convinced him otherwise. The blame never lay at the feet of Charles Ashcroft.

Throughout all the misdemeanours, the bullying, the abuse of power, the plethora of criminal activities, the whiskey heard the confessions and administered total absolution. It was a friend indeed. The one friend he had. Permanent, never wavering, through thick and thin.

And now Ben Price had infiltrated the friendship. He had driven a wedge between them. For the first time, his friend could not provide an answer and the problem remained.

The telephone rang. Operating the receiver, he listened in silence to the insipid, lamentable voice of Timothy Spires and when he had finished, he clicked the phone off without a word. Ashcroft could sense that Spires' voice was laden with gleeful undertones when dispatching the news that the PM had already received the envelope. He felt no compulsion to respond. They had never liked each other. Let Spires have his moment of satisfaction. His undying optimism in his own powers of recovery led him to believe that one day, the tables would be turned, and on that day he would drive a spike through the aspirations of Timothy Spires.

Lifting the glass to his lips, he allowed the entire contents to scorch its way down his throat. Raising the glass in the air, he reflected on the beautiful design and craftsmanship. Turning it to take in the light, he lifted it higher, each crystal line throwing a different pattern back to him. Such beauty.

And when beauty failed you, there was only one course of action.

Launching the glass forward, it sped towards the open fire and smashed against the marble surround, the remnant drops of whiskey fuelling the fire, each shard of crystal pursuing its individual path. Charles Ashcroft stared into the merging flames, out of focus as his head swam in a quicksand of depression.

Only one thought was clear.

He would have to meet him. Face to face. Ben Price.

*

A degree of euphoria might have been expected, but there was none. Maybe sheer exhaustion had swamped them, maybe they realised it was not yet over. Whatever it was, the journey back to Cambridge had been quiet with hardly a word passing between them.

It could have been anti-climax, a realisation of what they had been through, and now there was a feeling of emptiness. They had rubbed shoulders with the seat of power, felt highs of exhilaration and depths of hopelessness, and now there was the possibility that they were en route back to normality.

Suzanna closed her eyes as the doors closed and opened them when the doors opened, as if the doors and her eyelids were attached by string. She was either overcome with tiredness or she wanted her own space to reflect on what she had been through. Only she could know her own thoughts.

Doris held a satisfied, permanent grin on her face while Tom held her hand and rested it on her lap. Ben wondered if he would ever let go of it again. The three of them were unable to sleep.

Emma sat up front with Delaney. Although there were questions that still needed answers, they had formed an unbreakable bond. Their link with Ireland had started their relationship, but this mission had cemented it. Mission? New vocabulary had ingrained itself into Ben's mind. He often referred to work he set the children as tasks as in 'Your task today is …' He imagined himself dropping automatically into 'Your mission today is …'

My God, would any of them ever be the same again?

He doubted Emma would be. He thought back to her on the Embankment and how she took control. You do this, you do that. She gave the orders and they obeyed them. Even Suzanna, who distrusted her more than anyone. Emma was a natural. It was only right that she sat up front with Delaney.

The garage door opened and the people carrier eased its way beneath the apartments. Delaney punched in the security code and, on instructions, they mounted the stairs. Emma and Delaney remained, ensuring that nothing was left in the vehicle, nothing could be linked to them, before changing the plates, loading the previous contents and returning it to the Backs where, at some stage, a bemused owner would find it unscathed and full of petrol. It was the least Delaney could do.

Back at the flat, with everyone fed and in their beds, Delaney and Emma sat on the twin beds in his room. Emma was not yet ready for sleep. Delaney never seemed to need any.

"What do you want to know?" asked Delaney, sensing Emma's restlessness.

She was straight out with it. "Last night, you shut yourself away in here, not letting any of us know what you were doing. This morning, you met Professor Scott, but never mentioned it to any of the others. You never even told me what was discussed just a few metres away from me. Then this afternoon, you go scooting off on your own, leaving us in the café. Why so secretive, Delaney? That's what I want to know. Why so bloody secretive?"

Leaning back against the headboard, Delaney looked across at Emma. He was reluctant to answer, fearing that he might be encouraging her into his world, giving her more of an insight, but he knew there was no alternative. Emma would keep asking until he told her.

"Simple really," he replied. "To keep my activities separate from yours. On a much larger scale, it was a method used with great success by the IRA who operated different cells, each cell knowing nothing about the others. No names, no places, no plans. Nothing. Only the very top people knew what was happening and even then, there was separation. You know, London from Birmingham from Belfast and so on. It was a system so successful that it has been copied by Al Qaeda and other terrorist groups. That way, if one cell was infiltrated, they couldn't give information about other cells, either by loose tongues or under torture. What they didn't know, they couldn't reveal."

"I thought torture was banned under the Geneva Convention or something like that."

"Absolutely. And driving over 70 mph on British motorways is banned, but it still happens. Anyway, I don't think any of you would have been tortured if caught. Interviewed, certainly. Interrogated, probably."

"There's a difference?"

Delaney nodded and smiled. He continued. "Our problem was that all six of us knew most of what had happened. Only when I entered the equation did I try to cloud it a little. Still, better late than never."

"Which brings me to our nice friendly policeman," said Emma. "How did you manage to get him to escort Doris into 10 Downing Street?"

"Ah, now that would be telling. Perhaps later, when you're more experienced."

"What do you mean?"

387

"Well, I was wondering. What are you going to do with yourself now?"

"I've got a nursing course to finish, remember?" Emma replied. She looked out of the window, knowing the prolonged pause was teasing Delaney. Delaney had wanted a different answer, she was sure. "Then," she said, turning back to face him. "I may pay a visit to Professor Scott at Trinity College. Do you know him?"

Delaney smiled.

"Like I said, when you're more experienced."

*

30th December

Water cascaded over Ben's head. To no effect. During the darkest of days since Lynn's death, an early morning shower had somehow managed to clear the head and make him more prepared to face the day. Yet today, after the success of yesterday, his body refused to believe it was all over. An ugly cloud of doubt still hung over him.

He had woken early. Throwing the duvet back over his head, he had visited the events of previous days, but refused to linger over any of them. He still blamed himself for everything. If only he had not agreed to Sebastian's offer, the occupants of the flat would be elsewhere, getting on with whatever they had to do. A feeling of overwhelming guilt shuddered through his body. It had been with him since the whole thing started.

But then Lynn visited him, as she often did, and told him he couldn't turn the clock back, so get out of bed and get on with life.

Raising his head, he heard the sound of stifled giggles from the next room. The bedroom, he thought, but on the other side of his room was the kitchen and when he heard the clinking of mugs and Emma's giggles turning to laughter, for some reason he felt more comfortable. He didn't know why. They were both adults.

Hearing the opening of the lock on the bathroom door, he swung from the bed, took a look in the mirror, grimaced at what he saw, and made his way to the shower. It failed miserably. All the old worries clung to him, refusing to let him live.

The problem was that he was not in control. Neither was Delaney. Someone else held the final piece of the jigsaw and he wasn't certain if it would ever be put in the right place. Only then would there be completion.

"Ben, Ben, get in here now," shouted Suzanna.

Sensing the urgency in her voice, Ben quickly wrapped a towel round his waist and ran into the lounge. They were all standing round the television. Joining them, he saw the scroll bar across the bottom of the screen declaring that the Prime Minister was to make an announcement.

Out he came, striding from the door of number 10 across the road to the waiting press.

"I've been in there," said Doris, but no-one really heard her.

The Prime Minister reached into his inside pocket and took out his prepared speech, like Ben had seen him do a thousand times before. Yet now, there was an expectation about it. This could only be about one thing, couldn't it? Of course, he couldn't just come out and say that Charles Ashcroft was guilty of his daughter's death and had used government money to finance it. It would all be cloaked in vagueness. They would have to listen for the clues.

The Prime Minister began.

"I have an announcement to make and there will be no questions taken. It is with deep regret that today the Home Secretary has tendered his resignation. I have accepted. Following the death of his daughter, the Home Secretary has found it increasingly difficult to devote the required time to his duties. Of course, he will be afforded the privilege of a full time bodyguard who will be with him at all times."

"That's it then," said Delaney, throwing his arms around Emma and hugging her tight. In return, she jumped up and wrapped her legs around his waist as she would have done all those years ago if she had been given the chance. But only the two of them were celebrating. The others had missed something. Must have done.

"What do you mean?" asked Ben, allowing his frustration to melt into his question. "I can't see how this means that we will be safe and that we won't have to look around every corner for some hired assassin."

Delaney began the explanation. "Well, we know he got the envelope. He's acted on that by sacking Ashcroft."

"Sacking? What's all this about 'tendering his resignation' and 'deep regret'?"

"Political talk, Ben, but the interesting bit is the last sentence. It wouldn't have been noticed by those not looking for it. Look, he's still talking," he said pointing at the screen, "he's glossed over it. He slipped the sentence in and has carried on. Ashcroft will have someone with him 'at all times.' Notice how he looked straight at the camera when he said those last three words. He was speaking directly to us and only us. He was telling us that Ashcroft will be under permanent house arrest. For 'bodyguard' read 'jailer.' Anyway, he's getting over the death of his daughter and remember, outside our little circle, he's respected by one and all. Not even the press will go near him. They'll give him space."

"I see what you mean, but it all sounded too, well … normal to me. Like any other politician resigning."

"Good. And that's how it will seem to everyone else. There'll be a great deal of sympathy for Charles Ashcroft and we're going to have to put up with all the eulogies he gets. Two things are more important than that. We know we've done all we can and the Prime Minister knows what the real Charles Ashcroft is like. He couldn't even bring himself to use his name. Always the Home Secretary. Never Charles Ashcroft. And he's worked with him for years."

Emma cut in. "I know that man."

They all looked towards the television again. The Prime Minister was still talking, but a small photograph had appeared in the corner of the screen.

"I am delighted to say that I have managed to persuade the highly respected Oscar Baker to emerge from his retirement. He has been tasked with looking for any inadequacies within government regarding use of public money." He allowed a smile to grace the screen, a weapon he used to the greatest effect. "Of course, we don't expect him to find any, but it will be good to have someone so talented return to the political fold. And then, who knows, once that job is done, maybe I can persuade him to join our party and be part of government, an honour he has so rightly deserved for so long. Thank you." With questions ringing in his ears, he turned and returned to the sanctuary of number 10.

"The man's a bloody genius with words," said Delaney. "The headlines across the globe will all be about the return of Oscar Baker to the political frontline and, even more important, his possible defection. The PM practically promised him a Cabinet position."

"I do believe," said Tom quietly, looking around the intimate group, "that Delaney is right. It is all over. The Prime Minister has sacked Ashcroft. As much as we can be, we are protected from him. He has recruited Oscar Baker to seek out the Donors and disband them."

In his rational way, Tom had said the words they all wanted to hear.

He took hold of his wife and held her tight. Her face was against his chest, the tears wetting his shirt. Neither of them said a word. They were thinking of their daughter and of her death and of the separation that it had brought. Now it was over and they were together again. As Lynn would have wanted. Would have demanded.

Delaney and Emma. Tom and Doris. Ben afforded himself a smile. Turning towards Suzanna, he shrugged his shoulders and held out his hands in front of him. She walked the short distance to him and stepped in between, slipping one arm around his waist and the other around his neck, slowly stroking the base of his hair.

For a moment, he froze in this position, unsure of what his response should be. Unsure of what Lynn's response would be. She would only want what was best for him. Live your life, Ben. Slowly, he closed his arms around her. And then he pulled her closer, placing the palms of his hands on the small of her back and between her shoulders.

He held her and smelt her.

And he sobbed like he had been unable to for a long time.

*

Delaney suggested that they might wish to stay in Cambridge for a few days and then return north in the New Year. They all agreed.

They were given the grand tour. Every College, all the history. Access all areas. Delaney seemed to be allowed to go anywhere. All he did was flash a pass at every entrance and they were in. If Delaney was with them, then it was assumed that they were all to be trusted. Privileged is what they all felt. It kind of fitted in with the place.

Delaney noticed that, as they were leaving Trinity College, Emma lingered awhile, staring at the grand entrance topped by the statue of Henry V111. Of all the Colleges, Trinity held the most significance for her. Only she out of the group had witnessed what lay within.

"Coffee?" Delaney asked. He led them to the corner of the street and pointed out Starbucks just off the market square.

"Forgive us for a moment. Emma and I have to take a look in here," said Delaney. He watched as four figures swathed in coats and scarves and hats made their way down the street, never looking back, accepting that Emma and Delaney were different from them. If they had things to do, then it was none of their business and they were happy with that.

Delaney entered the Press' bookshop and made his way to the history section. He pointed out a number of books. They were all various publications on the Cambridge spies.

"Remember them?" he asked.

"Blunt, Philby, Burgess and Maclean."

"Well done. Have a quick look, then we'll purchase any you fancy." He offered her a seat by the window. She accepted. He drifted away from her.

She did not look up from her books immediately, but when she did, she noticed that Delaney was thumbing his way through a few books in the law section. Carefully, he lifted them individually from the shelf, treating them with a kind of reverence, checking the author, reading the summary. It was all a game. She guessed that he never read a single word.

Neither did the old man standing next to him, perusing the shelf above.

The dark overcoat, the hat that could be so easily lifted and the scarf lying loose around his neck. The grey ponytail, neatly tied back, hanging over the scarf. She returned to her reading.

When Delaney returned, she had chosen her book. Paying for it, he lifted the bag from the desk and made his way out, placing an arm around her shoulders as he went.

"What did you say to him?" she asked.

"Thank you."

"Is that all?"

"That was enough."

1st January

It had been a New Year's Eve like no other.

Exhaustion finally kicked in. They all succumbed to how little they had slept over the last few days. Over a week in Ben's case. Bed called at six o'clock for Tom and Doris, a couple of hours later for Emma and Suzanna and a few minutes later for Delaney and Ben.

In those few minutes when they sat alone on the same settee, Ben had many more questions to ask and so much gratitude to give, but couldn't find the words. There was a silence between them. Strangers, thrown together to become friends, who would never see each other again after the following day.

Delaney had saved his life and maybe, just maybe, placed his life firmly back on track. What else could a stranger do for him? Indebted was not enough. Yet, he could not speak.

If the man sitting beside him knew what he was thinking, he gave no indication. Draining the last of the tea from his mug, he rose, yawned and threw out a nonchalant, "See you in the morning" as he made his way to his room.

A New Year's Eve like no other. No party, no alcohol, just absolute fatigue.

As they waited for the others at breakfast, Suzanna broached a tricky request with Ben. She was terrified about returning to her house. After all, the last time she was there, there had been the unnerving sight of Sebastian being shot through the head in her bedroom. Sleeping there would be impossible. Was there any chance that she could stay at Ben's house for a few days? Everything above board. Separate bedrooms of course.

There was no hesitation from Ben. No problem at all, but best to keep it from Tom and Doris for now. It would save any embarrassment, even though it was all completely innocent.

Ben found it difficult when they said their goodbyes in the car park beneath Delaney's apartment. He would see all of them again at some point, except Delaney. Yet the only formality Delaney offered him was a shake of the hand and his best wishes for the future.

After all they'd been through. It had to be his way, Ben supposed. He couldn't get too close to anyone, show his true feelings. Ben was not in his trade. He was an outsider.

Which was why Emma shared the car with Delaney on the return journey.

Suzanna drove Ben back to his house. Then she would deliver Tom and Doris safely back to theirs before briefly returning to her own house to quickly pack a case and get out.

As Suzanna pulled away, Ben could sense there was a welcoming party. Turning round, he was greeted by Mrs Robinson and a beaming smile that stretched across the whole width of her face.

"Happy New Year," she said, grabbing firm hold of his cheeks and delivering a proper New Year kiss on both of them.

"Happy New Year," Ben replied. He decided to take the bull by the horns and let Mrs Robinson know exactly what would be happening. "You see the young girl driving away," he said, "she's coming to stay with me for a while."

Waving after the car as it went, Mrs Robinson could not contain her excitement. "I'm so pleased for you, Ben. Suzanna is a lovely girl. I met her when she came to stock up your fridge. I'm very happy for you. You make a lovely couple."

Ben had had the wind taken from his sails. "No, no," he tried to explain, "There's nothing between us. It's just that …" Just that what? She's frightened because a hired agent had been shot by a hired killer in her bedroom? And how did it go from there? Oh, yes, the Home Secretary had his daughter killed and proof of that had to be delivered to the Prime Minister. 'So that's what you've been up to,' Mrs Robinson would calmly say. 'Yes, just the usual Christmas, Mrs Robinson,' Ben would reply.

It was easier to let her have her own thoughts. "I agree," said Ben. "She's a lovely girl."

They parted on the driveway, each disappearing through their own front doors. They faced each other again as they drew the front curtains, each waving a goodnight to the other from their bay windows. Things were beginning to feel normal again.

Not quite.

Leaving the lights off, moving by the greyness of the streetlight alone, he checked the lounge and kitchen first, before moving upstairs to give it the once over. Make sure he didn't have any unwanted guests. You know, the sort that might want him to carry out the odd killing or two. He imagined that this would also be part of normality from now on. Wave goodnight to Mrs Robinson. Check the house for intruders.

All was well.

Opening the fridge, shielding his eyes from the interior light, he found a bottle of coke. Twisting the cap off and throwing it into the bin, he made his way to the front room. Mrs Robinson was settled in for the night. He could hear the sound of singing from the television next door. Good idea. Switch on the television. Catch up on the day's sport. There was always a full programme on New Year's Day.

He walked across the room towards the television.

The first blow was to the stomach, the second and third followed in rapid succession, one to the chin driven upwards and another on the same spot from the side. He couldn't remember hitting the ground.

Through the daze, he could feel himself being lifted and dumped onto a chair, a hard one. His legs were pulled back and tightly tied together at the ankles, then secured against the chair legs, the rope biting into his skin where his socks had fallen. His arms were pulled back by the hands, one at a time, and thrust together behind him, held in place by more searing pain as the skin was ripped from his wrists. A hand from behind grabbed at the front of his hair, yanking his head backwards until it was leaning over the back of the chair. Tape was stretched across his mouth. Two fingers inserted into his nostrils pulled his head further back and one last fist hammered onto the top of his head, rendering him senseless.

One second? One minute? One hour? He had no idea how long he was out.

His torso was upright, pinned against the back of the chair by more rope across his chest, but his head lolled forward, refusing to rise when his brain requested it to. His heart was still beating and his lungs, though laboured, rose and fell against the constriction around his chest. He had a functioning body; it was just that its various components had their own agenda. Each part of the puppet wanted to dance, but the strings had become entangled.

Instinct tried to move his aching limbs from the chair, but the slightest adjustment was brought to a sudden halt as pain scorched and tore through his skin. Legs and arms were helpless. His whole body was held in a vice. Struggle was pointless. He gave up.

Slowly, the carpet became more distinct as his eyes focused. He noticed a damp stain beginning to form and the Coke bottle lying on its side, the remnants settling to the horizontal. So he had not been out for too long. Seconds maybe, and in that time he had been completely immobilised.

Shit. He'd dared to believe it was all over.

It is said that the human brain is the fastest computer in the world. It can assess situations and offer solutions within milli-seconds. On rare occasions, the brain fails us, but in the majority of cases, it will make the right decision and recommend the correct course of action. Within milli-seconds. It is up to the human whether he complies with the brain's recommendations. And that's where most things take a turn for the worst. Human error.

Occasionally, there is such a vast amount of information thrust upon it that it takes a little longer to negotiate the maze. And even more occasionally, the maze seems overwhelming and each detail gets battered around between the myriad of hedges and never seems to get close to the exit. Panic ensues. The solution gets lost within it.

Ben's brain was in overdrive.

Two weeks of information. So many contenders. One question. Who was in the room with him?

Ashcroft. It had to be him. Talk of resignations and permanent bodyguards had thrown a veil over reality. They had all been convinced that the Prime Minister had dealt with the evidence in the envelope, but now it was transparent that he had failed. Ben was struggling to control the chill that was reaching through his body. Ashcroft's power was strong enough to withstand anything and anyone. His activities had not been curtailed. And soon, he would be in front of the cameras again, lying to the great British public, while in private he would be back to his bullish self, delivering his own brand of punishment.

Now, he was here. In Ben's front room.

Ben had set out to destroy him and failed. There would be a serious price to pay.

Able now, but unwilling, to lift his head, he stared at the Coke bottle, gathering his thoughts. There had to be some logic to what was happening. The Prime Minister knew that there were duplicates of the evidence in the envelope which could be delivered to the newspapers and when published, it would mean the end of his premiership. Earlier than he had planned. To have his reputation, his legacy, destroyed in the final hours. Why? There was too much to lose. Why had he allowed Ashcroft his freedom?

Unless … . No, the thought was preposterous. Ben tried to sweep it from his mind, but it wouldn't go away. It was the only thing that made sense.

Come on brain. Think. There must be other possibilities. But it wouldn't go away.

Preposterous idea. Had the Prime Minister known about the Donors all along? If he had, he must surely know of their activities and their purpose. And another thought battered his mind which was too absurd. But why not? Rationality had long since disappeared.

Absurd. The Prime Minister might be a member of the Donors himself. If either thought, whether preposterous or absurd, was true, then the Prime Minister must know of Ashcroft's involvement. Mind racing, Ben imagined them as associates in the same group, the same club, seated at a large round wooden table, facing each other, disposing of public money to approve the finance of vigilante killings so that vermin would receive appropriate punishment.

The contents of the envelope had been no surprise to the PM, except perhaps the evidence on the tape. Ben shivered. He might have known about that too. First Ashcroft and now the Prime Minister. Both above the law. Both able to use their influence for their own gains, each accepting and ignoring the other's foibles, the other's needs.

Ben Price stood in their way. He assumed that they had no knowledge of Tom and Doris or Suzanna and Delaney and their involvement. Neither the Prime Minister nor the Home Secretary had met them or heard from them. So they had to believe that the duplicate evidence was with either Ben or Emma. And if Ashcroft didn't find the duplicates here, and if he couldn't get Ben to talk, then Ben would be killed and then he would pay Emma a visit.

He knew it wouldn't come to that. The house would be searched and the evidence found upstairs, in the wardrobe of all places where it had been placed neatly and tidily on a shelf. Ben would not be allowed his freedom. He was living his final day on Earth and, no matter what happened here, so was Emma.

Things got worse. Another random thought. Ashcroft couldn't have done this on his own, couldn't batter him as he had been, couldn't tie him with such expertise, couldn't render him unconscious with that final blow. He hadn't the skill nor, Ben believed, the ability. Hiring someone else was his style. He would do that. Couldn't do this himself. Hadn't the guts. Get someone else to do his dirty work. That's what he'd done all his life. Why change now when his whole life was at stake?

His minder. He might have got to him. He had enough money and who on this planet didn't have his price? One thing was certain. Ashcroft would want to be there in person, to witness the harm inflicted and the death of Ben Price. So there were two of them in the room. It didn't really matter who was with Ashcroft. He was at their mercy.

Slightly longer than milli-seconds, but quick enough.

It was time to face his future.

He raised his pounding head and faced his attackers.

Not for the first time, he was wrong. Only one person sat opposite. One person with a gun in his hand, silencer fitted, resting across his lap. Bloodied fingers held the gun loosely, forefinger on the trigger. He noticed that his jeans wore the occasional splattering of red. Ben guessed the blood was his.

Looking round to check for another person, he saw no-one. There had only been one assailant and he was sitting directly in front of him, out of reach.

Wrong clothes, wrong build, too athletic. The figure in front of him was not Charles Ashcroft.

Ben looked more closely. The top part of the man's body was in total darkness, the rest was lit serenely, obscenely, by the light that filtered from the streetlight through the hallway. The gun began to twitch, the barrel tapping lightly against the thigh. Slowly, in rhythm, while the handle stayed firm in the palm of his hand. His finger never left the trigger.

The maze was all consuming. Think straight, Ben.

Sebastian. It could be Sebastian. Okay, Ben had seen Sebastian shot in the forehead, he'd seen the blood trailing down the wall, seen the painters at work, but that could have all been faked. If he had learnt anything in these last days, it was that anything was possible. And if it was faked, oh shit, one other person must be in on it.

Delaney. He had appeared in the room with perfect timing. He had pulled the trigger. He had taken control, led them through the rest of the operation and brought them back home. Delaney knew where Ben was every second and he knew where he would be now: settling back at the house, believing the danger had gone away.

He'd been an idiot. If only he'd listened to Suzanna. She was never sure of Delaney. There were doubts. She even voiced them when the rest of them followed like sheep. He'd known her long enough, for Christ's sake. She had great instinct, could quickly evaluate the good and bad in people. It was what he and Lynn often said. They could trust Suzanna's judgment more than anyone else they knew. And he hadn't listened to her.

The two strangers who had got him into this were there at the end. They'd been in his house before. They knew their way around. It would have been no problem for either of them to break into the house and switch rooms as Ben made that cursory search.

They were professionals. That was what they had told him time and again. Trust us, they had said. And he had.

Ben shook his head. Too many thoughts. Not enough answers.

It couldn't be Sebastian. He couldn't kill people. Couldn't shoot when he needed to in Ireland. Couldn't shoot Ben when he was at his mercy. But then, there was only Delaney's word for Sebastian's inability to kill. And it was Delaney who had stopped him shooting Ben. And if the whole killing of Sebastian was a charade, then what the hell could you believe?

Suddenly, the darkness spoke. "Who's been a naughty boy then, Ben?"

Rule out Sebastian. He couldn't hide his roots, too ingrained, and this voice was more rugged, more working class. The type of dialect that Delaney would have no problems with. Emma had said he was a genius with languages.

Not enough answers. Why go to the trouble of faking Sebastian's death? Why go to the trouble of dragging them off to London to deliver evidence to the Prime Minister? Why not just shoot Ben dead back at Suzanna's house, along with the rest of them. The two of them were working for the Prime Minister and the Home Secretary, weren't they? They could get away with anything.

All his disconnected thoughts merged into each other. Confusion reigned in his mind. No answers. Which one of them was sitting opposite with his finger on the trigger and the barrel tapping against his thigh?

With no warning, the figure glided up from the chair and drifted into the eerie light.

Ben stared hard, eyes narrowing, dragging images from his memory of the man he had seen before. Liquid filled his eyes as he blinked them hard to get a better look. Frantically shaking his head, pain etched on every line, eyes tight shut, then opening them, searching for his features, hoping the image dragged from his memory did not match the face looking down at him.

There was a mistake. There had to be. It must be someone who looked like him.

A dead man stood above him.

Delayed by Sebastian outside the Mess before he went into his room, he drank his water and within hours, he was dead. Sebastian met Ben at Luton and told him, more than once, that the operation had been a success. More than once. Emphasising it. Ramming home the fact.

Sebastian had told him.

Jimmy Buller was dead.

The man laughed quietly, an arrogant snigger that rang around Ben's ears. There was no mistake. It was Buller who had knocked him senseless, taped his mouth and tied him to the chair. It was Buller who stood over him with his finger on the trigger of the gun.

Ben couldn't move. Paralysed by the shock, he closed his eyes and prayed that all this was some side effect from the beating his head had received. But when he allowed his eyes to open, he saw that it was all true. His despairing body succumbed to the hopelessness, collapsing as far as it could against the restraints of the flesh tearing rope, like some discarded rag doll.

"Bit of a surprise, eh, Ben?" Buller said. "Thought I was dead? I would have been if you'd had your way." He nudged the tape around Ben's mouth with the end of the silencer. "Cat got your tongue?"

Beneath the agitated movements of his eyelids, he saw a hand grasping his chin, taking firm hold, its nails burying themselves into the skin of his jowls. His head was wrenched backwards. Looking forwards, he caught sight of the silencer of the gun in front of his eye, but he had no strength to react. It forced its path between the eyelids, forcing them open until the coldness of steel prodded against his pupil, where it wriggled and twisted, sending immeasurable pain throughout his body.

"Can't say a fucking word, Price, can you? You want to shout for help, you fucking excuse for a human being, but you can't. Feel the pain, Price and remember it, 'cos one thing's for fucking sure. It's going to be the least pain you feel for the next few minutes."

He sucked the barrel out of his eye. Ben felt burning pain from where it had been, hot fluid streaming out of the socket and down his cheek. Vessels popped, each one more painful than the last.

Head lolling forward, the carpet was indistinct again, viewed through a frequently changing haze as he continuously blinked in involuntary spasms. Grabbed by the hair, he was pulled back until the chair rocked on its legs and then dragged until it leant against the arm of the settee, perched on its two hind legs.

His angled body had only one place to look. Directly at Jimmy Buller.

Despite the violence and the aggressive shouting, the figure above him was perfectly calm. It was what Ben was beginning to realise. Professional killers, the real ones, not the occasional ones who killed the old lady down the road for fifty pence for the next hit, the real ones were comfortable when they were killing. It was what they did. They were in control. They knew what they were doing, knew when and how to inflict pain without the frantic brutality that an amateur would resort to. Every action was measured and planned, with alternatives in place just in case. They were rarely required.

His voice. Controlled now. Still rough with dialect, but calm.

"I can't let you die, Price, with so many unanswered questions going through your mind. Maybe an explanation will allow you to rest in peace. Is that what you would like to hear, Price?"

Of course he would, but he was too drained to nod his head. He had lost the will to fight.

His face was forcefully covered by the palm of Buller's hand, fingers pressing down against his eyebrows, chin forced upwards, suffocating hand tight against his nose, forcing his breathing to quicken, more frantic against the tape, head reluctantly nodding within the man's grasp.

"I thought you would," said Buller. "Let's start with why I'm not dead. Ironically, it was all your fault, Price. You see, you were too inquisitive, wanted to know too much about the operation, the whys, the wherefores. It made Sebastian a bit suspicious of you. He had another job for you, but wasn't sure you would pull it off. I'd never met Sebastian before I bumped into him outside the Mess, but he knew a hell of a lot about me. You ran out of the barracks with his partner and he explained the whole story to me, the reasons you wanted me dead, the drugged water that would stimulate a heart attack and how he had organised it all. He said he had a proposition for me. He wanted me to fly to England and do the job if you backed out. A sort of trial run for me, with more to come if I was successful. I thought, why not? The army didn't want me anymore and I didn't want them. So, when you chickened out of killing the bitch in the flat, in I went and did the job. All women are bitches, don't you think, Price. Oh, no, you don't, but we'll get to that in a minute.

"Then he's telling me that, no matter whether he kills the bitch or not, Ben Price is a dead man. He knows too much. Too bloody inquisitive. He's got morals and morals are no good to him. So I fly to England and I kill the bitch 'cos you hadn't the guts. I sit by the phone and wait for his phone call. Day after day, waiting. I wipe the grains of toast from my lips and think of this new chance. A new beginning. My whole life filled with the rush of adrenalin, tiptoeing the thin line between success and failure, but never caught, never bettered. I've always bent and broken the rules, but what fucking ecstasy when I avoided the consequences. And now this guy tells me how much he appreciates what I do. Admires me.

"The phone never rings to tell me that you're dead. So when the days drift along and New Year comes and the phone doesn't ring, I stick by the agreement. Perhaps that's why he didn't phone. Checking to see if I'd stick by what I said. A man of principle. That's what I am. And that's why I'm here, Price. Sebastian says, if I don't hear from him by the New Year, then earn the money he's already given me and kill Ben Price. So, I'm here, Price. To kill you."

All the questions had been answered.

Ben had allowed his imagination to run wild. Charles Ashcroft, evil and vicious though he was, was not involved in these latest events. Neither was the Prime Minister. It was all organised as backup, in advance, by Sebastian. The master, as Delaney had called him.

Delaney. Buller had not mentioned him at all. That was good. Confirmation, for Ben, that he wasn't involved.

Ben only saw a blurred image of Buller through his blood filled eye, but he was able to listen to his every word. It all made sense. Sebastian was not a man to be outwitted by some curious amateur. He would have the last word, the final action, even after he was dead. The master.

He wondered if Delaney was still with Emma. If he was, then she was safe. If he wasn't, then she would be next on Buller's list. Sebastian knew that Ashcroft wanted Emma delivered to him, but if that was not possible, then she had to be killed. Sebastian would have left no stone unturned. Buller would have been given his instructions. It was inevitable and Ben could do nothing to prevent it.

Tom and Doris were safe. That was for sure. Neither Sebastian nor Ashcroft knew of their involvement, save that of Tom being used as the alibi when Ben flew to Germany. Unless Delaney was in on it. The greatest conundrum. Delaney. But he couldn't be involved. The old chestnut again. If he had been, why did he help them? Why not just clear the decks and kill them all? He had had the opportunity. Many times over.

And no-one, other than Delaney, knew of Suzanna's participation. She was safe. She'd be home now and settling in, looking out for the day's football results to see how her beloved Manchester United had gone on.

The sudden hot flush ran through his body as realisation exploded within him. Suzanna wasn't at home. She was on her way here. To stay with him. She didn't feel safe in her own house, so she was coming here. To be safe. Shit, this was the least safe place on earth right now.

One way or another, he had to get this over with. Before she arrived. Better she find Ben's body than walk in on this. If she was seen by Buller, he would kill her too. He would have no guilt. He would have no alternative.

But before Ben could engage his brain, Buller was talking again. Ben shook his head, liquid flicking across his cheeks. His vision cleared. He listened.

"I'm going to enjoy this bit Ben," said Buller, eyes sparkling with excitement. And he went off at a tangent, Ben wondering what it had to do with him. "Fucking IRA. Got away with anything. Could blow the limbs off innocent folk, some Catholics even, and they didn't give a shit. For the good of a united Ireland, they'd shout. Fuck that. For the good of themselves, more like. And they got away with it. We knew who they were. Bastards. We could have picked 'em up no problem. Any time. Any day. But there they were, strolling the streets, taking the piss as we walked past. Unfucking touchables. That's what they were. But we got a few of them back. On the quiet, you know. We made a pact, me and two of my men, that if any of them took the piss out of us, then his card was marked. We'd wait till he was on his own and we'd get him. Dragged one of them out of his own bed, we did. Tied him up and told him what we were going to do to him. Every fucking detail. Let him know it was the British Army doing this. No-one took the piss out of the British Army. And before long, he'd be sweating and crying and pissing his pants and all we'd do was laugh. They were okay when they had their mates with them, but on their own they were fucking cowards. Every last one of them. And when they were so shit scared they were fucking pleading with us, we'd say okay, enough was enough and they'd smile and thank God. Then we'd place the handkerchief over their mouths and noses and watch 'em struggle till the last breath of life was out of them. I tell you, Price, it was fucking great."

And all the time, his laughter was more frantic, turning to hysteria. Uncontrollable, like a teenager high on his first hit. There was nothing like it. The feeling of power, of getting your own back. Of not letting them get away with taking the piss when they thought they had. He was reliving those moments when he was in control, when no-one would refuse him.

Slowly, his body ceased to shake and his breathing returned to normal. He wiped the phlegm from his lips and grinned.

"And guess what we did next, Ben Price. We took them outside and we put 'em in the fucking car and we took 'em out of town and, guess what, it's so fucking easy to fake a road crash."

His face was close to Ben's now, noses touching as he allowed his words to flood Ben's mind. His manic eyes stared at him, waiting for a reaction and when it came, Ben rocked the chair just once and threw his body forward, aiming a blow with his forehead towards Buller's.

Buller was too quick. Sidestepping Ben's momentum, he caught Ben a glancing blow across the cheek sending him, still attached to the chair, onto the floor. His ankles were still rigid against the legs of the chair, his hands still tied behind. The tape was still across his mouth. He had simply moved from the vertical to the horizontal, lying on his side on the carpet.

Expecting some kind of follow-up from Buller, Ben looked out of the corner of his blood-soaked eye. Buller was motionless, staring at the adjoining wall. Ben hoped that Mrs Robinson had heard the landing of the chair on the carpet, but it was all too gentle. If only he'd had the wooden floorboards that Lynn was always talking about. There was no discernible change in the television's volume next door. Nothing to suggest that Mrs Robinson had the slightest idea what was happening a few metres away from her. But then it was best she didn't know. She might try to help.

Buller knelt down by Ben's side. "There just wasn't enough time to do it right," Buller said, almost apologetically. "I had to get back to base. Back my men up just in case the bitch talked. Stick together. It's the only way. Pity, I could have had such a time with your bitch, Price. Struggled like fuck, she did. More than any of them IRA trouser-pissing cowards. All I could do to keep her fingernails from my face. Now that would have taken some explaining. Scratches across my face when I was defending my men accused of rape. Wouldn't have looked good. So, it was the only thing I could do. Handkerchief over her mouth and she was gone. Dead, Price. Fucking dead."

He lay on the floor, placed his cheek on the carpet and stroked it with the barrel of the gun. He was so close that Ben could hear his escaping breath panting in rapid succession and smell the toothpaste on it. Ben remembered Buller's room at the Mess and the tidiness. Shoes laid neatly out, bed folded perfectly. And now the toothpaste. Pride even when he was killing.

So close, yet Ben could do nothing. Remembering that Suzanna would be here at any time, he made a futile attempt to shuffle closer, but it was useless. His body was in a vice-like grip of excruciating pain, the rope chafing more skin from his joints with each miniscule movement.

The steely hardness of the end of the barrel poked him in the eye. Just the once, sudden and sharp. A reminder to behave.

They lay for a while, looking at each other, side by side, like two lovers, before Buller pushed himself up and stood over him. Raising the gun, he pointed it directly at Ben's forehead. "D'you want to know her last words, Price? She said, 'If only I'd met you before I met that snivelling coward Ben Price. No good when the going gets tough. No good at all.'" His finger began to squeeze the trigger and there was that arrogant snigger again, followed by subdued, hysterical laughter, forced through clenched teeth.

Ben could only watch as the encroaching light from the doorway was blocked by Buller's shadow, a shadow that grew larger as he leaned closer, spreading either side of his arms and torso. And out of the shadow he saw a hand reach round Buller's waist. Then another hand reaching over his shoulder. Hands working with such speed and in such unison, it was impossible to believe.

Buller's wrist was held and wrenched upwards, the gun silently emptying a chamber into the ceiling, before being released from his grasp, falling to the floor. As expertly as any pickpocket, the second hand stole Buller's belt, which was swiftly wrapped around his neck, passed through the buckle and tightened.

He fell. Landed next to Ben. Face to face again. And his hands were pulled behind him and up between his shoulder blades. Ben heard the double sound of cracking, but was unsure whether it was the breaking of the forearms or the dislocation of the shoulders. He didn't care. Buller could not shout, could not make a sound as the belt tightened around his neck. Two knees landed on his back, expelling more air, so that even the thought of shouting disappeared from Buller's mind. He was gasping for oxygen, but the belt grew taut, constricting what little breath could enter or escape.

Looking away from Buller's contorted face, Ben saw a dark shadow kneeling on Buller's back, leaning away from him, belt held tight in one hand, the other in the middle of his back pressing his torso to the ground. He was riding him like a bucking bronco, the pull on the belt lifting his head off the carpet. Except, unlike the horse, there was no resistance from below.

The shadow glanced at Ben, his face becoming clear as he turned into the light. He threw a smile at him and winked, before looking down at the figure beneath him.

"Sergeant Jimmy Buller," he said quietly. "We meet at last. Allow me to introduce myself. I am Delaney, Sebastian's partner. Well, I was until I shot him in the forehead from close range."

Wrapping the end of the belt around his hand, Delaney gently pulled it tighter, lifting Buller's head further from the ground so that his chin hovered over the carpet. Uncontrollable gasps of air squirmed from his open mouth. Saliva crept from its corners till it hung, dangling from the end of his chin until it delicately touched the carpet, creating globular domes which grew larger as Delaney rocked his head back and forth.

"We had a disagreement on future policy," Delaney continued. "I wasn't keen on getting people killed who had no reason to die. He was, so he found someone as lowlife as himself to do the dirty work for him. In normal circumstances, I'd let you get on with it. I've learnt to let people get on with things as long as it doesn't affect me. When it's personal, it's different. I once told Ben that he was the one who had to kill you because it was personal to him. You'd killed Lynn. He'd feel much better for it afterwards. Of course, in a straight fight, you would win hands down, so we stacked the odds in his favour. Lethal drug in the water. Easy. But Sebastian spoiled all that because he saw you as his next assassin. You were just the man Sebastian needed because times were changing and he needed someone like you who would kill anytime, anywhere, for the right money."

Delaney leaned back. The belt tightened. Buller's breathing, such as it was, became so laboured that he took chunks of air when he could. His head wrestled with the belt, searching a modicum of freedom that would allow his air passages to expand, but he was held rigid. Delaney was only allowing him to breathe when he wanted him to. He was toying with him, tightening and relaxing the belt with expert dexterity.

Delaney carried on where he had left off, as if in ordinary conversation. "It will come as some surprise to you that some human beings have still got morals. And that's where you have a problem, Buller. You see, somewhere in this sorry tale, it became personal for me. And I'm a different proposition to our Ben here. Head to head, you haven't got a cat in hell's chance of defeating me. That's why you're on your face and I'm slowly drawing the breath from your body. I could kill you now, snap your neck. No problem. Over and done with in the time it takes you to say Iraq or the Balkans or Ireland. But this is so much better. It's nice to see the bad guy squirm once in a while."

Sliding a hand up his spine until it rested on the vertebrae below the belt, he pressed down hard, forcing the torso further into the ground. The belt remained in place. The neck stretched further. Ben heard the popping and cracking as the vertebrae were stretched to their limit, unnaturally backwards.

Lying on his side, peering upwards, Ben saw Buller's eyes rolling and disappearing under his eyelids. White balls stared forward aimlessly, unseeing. Flickering eyelashes dashed across them, paying them infrequent visits, never covering them. And it struck Ben that he was watching a man die by his side.

Looking up, he saw a calm Delaney in perfect control. Comfortable. It came as easily to him as standing in front of a class full of eleven-year-olds did to Ben. Ben knew how good it felt to be at the top of your game. You could do your job and you knew the outcome before you began. There was no uncertainty, no doubt. Like playing the eighteenth hole in the Open Championship with a five shot lead. Comfortable.

Delaney relaxed the pressure on Buller's back and the vertebrae popped back into place and the restriction on his windpipe disappeared and he was gasping for air, filling his lungs and hanging onto life. But he couldn't function. His brain had been starved of oxygen and his befuddled mind refused to operate.

Allowing Buller a few seconds of respite, Delaney then moved his hand to the buckle that rested on the back of Buller's neck, slowly

410

feeding more of the belt through it, tightening it, tighter than a collar round a dog's neck, ripples of flesh beginning to spill over the edges.

"I don't know if you're capable of love, Buller, but I am. I loved a woman in Ireland so much I would have died for her. At the drop of a hat. She had a daughter. That daughter also loved. She loved Jennifer Ashcroft. The girl you poisoned for no reason at all. You didn't know her. You had no reason to kill her. But you did. Because Sebastian told you to."

He pushed the belt further through the buckle. The increasing constriction of the tightening collar round Buller's neck immediately affected his breathing and once again his lungs desperately searched for air. "That's when it became personal for me. You see, the daughter of the woman I loved was the girl you allowed one of your men to rape behind the club that night. You could have stopped him, but you didn't. It was probably your idea. You'd have had your little turn as well if it wasn't for the appearance of Lynn Thomas."

For a brief moment, Buller's legs kicked upwards in a despairing act of self-preservation, but the collar became smaller as the belt was pulled. The mouth opened and the saliva flowed and the eyes rolled and disappeared and the gasping became frantic, each rasping breath getting shorter. The torso was pushed into the floor, the head pulled back and the popping began again. Both hands working in unison, as they had began, one driving downwards on the spine and the other straining upwards, prising the vertebrae apart.

"I would like you to know, Sergeant Jimmy Buller, who is an insult to the rank and to the good men and women serving in the British Army, that you are about three centimetres from death. A gentle push with the palm of my hand and you're gone. No-one will be sorry. Not your colleagues, not your wife and not your children. At this moment, Ben Price is lying beside you. His conscience may be telling him that it's wrong for one human to take the life of another and you should live. He's a good man. He thinks that way. So it's a good job I'm here. Because I'm a bad guy and I don't think like that. If it's the right cause, I take life. Without a second thought. With no regrets. So, it's the end, Jimmy Buller. May you have no rest in hell."

The movement was indeterminable. Then all was quiet and Ben looked at the face of the man who had killed Lynn as it was laid gently onto the carpet.

*

Delaney left them there.

Ben heard the sound of water gushing from the tap in the kitchen, then the filling of a bowl, and all the time, he looked at Jimmy Buller lying by him. Surprisingly, he felt no remorse. He would not have believed it two weeks ago, but Ben had changed. Delaney had been wrong. Ben now believed that there is reason to take another human's life. If the cause is right.

"This is going to hurt," said Delaney, "but there's no other way."

Reaching down, he took hold of the back of the chair and tilted it upwards until the four legs sat evenly on the carpet. He was right. It hurt like hell. His ankles, his wrists, his eye, the list was endless. His whole body. But he didn't cry out beneath the tape or writhe in agony. He accepted the pain. It was necessary.

Whatever physical agonies he felt, were overwhelmed by sensations of relief and gratitude. As first his wrists and then his ankles were released from the rope, he formulated words behind the tape, words that he should have uttered when he was sitting next to Delaney the previous evening. For the second time, Delaney had saved his life and he was not prepared to let the moment pass again.

And he felt the cold. Easing its way amongst the chafing and the tears and the burns. Gently wiping his cheeks and invading his eye. Loosely wrapping around where the skin had been destroyed before being removed and cooled and applied again.

The tape was carefully removed and he was lifted from the chair and placed on the settee. Delaney sat beside him and handed him a glass of water.

"Drink," he said. "Slowly."

Ben did as he was told. He stretched his mouth and ran the water round his lips, before wiping it away with his fingertips. He left his hand

412

there. It was the first time he had seen the damage at his wrists. It was considerable, enough to make you vomit. But he was alive and that was more important than a few cuts and bruises. He had rationalised the damage to that.

He amazed himself. This feeling of wanting to be alive. The desperation of wanting to live the next day and the one after that. It was the first time he had felt that way since Lynn had died.

Opening his mouth to speak, he was stopped by the interruption of Delaney. "Don't you dare thank me or I'll put the bloody rope back round your ankles, laddie. Remember, I got you into this mess. It was the least I could do to get you out of it."

Ben took another sip of water. "If you won't let me thank you, then tell me this. What the hell are you doing here?"

"I told you once before. I'm your guardian angel, Ben. Not that you'll need one from now on. It's all over."

"We thought that this morning," Ben replied.

"You might have done. I wasn't so sure. There was one question I couldn't find an answer to."

"Which was?"

"Who killed Jennifer? The odds were that Sebastian wouldn't have done it himself. He found killing difficult as you know, even if he had drugged her. This was the Home Secretary's daughter, a reasonably unstable Home Secretary at that, and so he would find it easier, safer even, to delegate responsibility. Find someone else to do it. Before I killed him, I accused him of all sorts to belittle him. Not once did he come back at me and say he'd killed Jennifer, just to prove he was capable of it. So, if it wasn't Sebastian, who was it?"

"You could have thought it was Ashcroft," Ben said.

Delaney shook his head. "Another fixer. Never got his hands dirty himself. And then there was the taped conversation with Emma."

"The tape?" asked Ben. He couldn't remember Ashcroft pleading his innocence.

"Emma had wound him up so he was almost completely out of control. He was losing it big time. Yet when he mentioned Jennifer he said, 'If I could have my own daughter murdered.' If he really wanted to frighten Emma, and he had killed Jennifer, then he would have told her straight, 'If I could kill my own daughter,' but he didn't. He knew his daughter was dead. He knew someone other than he had done it."

"Couldn't Sebastian have got anybody to do it?" asked Ben. "After all, he was the great organiser. He must have known lots of people."

"Not at such short notice. He had a small team working for him. The fewer people who knew about our little ventures the better. When he got the team together to hunt for you, they all looked as if they had spent a normal Christmas. Hangovers, the lot. His chief assassin, the man who always hovered in case things didn't work out, had been killed by Emma. All the others were actors playing roles."

"So you thought of Buller."

Delaney smiled and shook his head. "Not once. Sorry to disappoint you, but I thought he was dead and gone like you did. The only thing I knew was that whoever killed Jennifer was still out there and if that was the case, you might still be at risk."

"So being here was just a coincidence."

"Yes and no. I dropped Emma off and thought I'd take a drive round. I saw you with Mrs Robinson and saw you draw the curtains. Liked the quick inspection of the house by the way. Well done. I gave it a few minutes for the light to come on, but it didn't. Then I caught a brief glimpse of a shadow stand up in front of the curtains, then move further into the room. In a way I was pleased about that."

"What do you mean, pleased?" asked Ben, a little indignantly.

"Well, that meant that you had a visitor and I knew it wasn't Suzanna."

"If it had been Suzanna, the lights would have definitely been on, I can assure you."

"If you say so," Delaney replied with a smirk running across his face.

"So, you were pleased I had a visitor. Why?"

"Well, for one thing, it meant my hunch was right and you were in danger. And secondly, it had happened quickly. He'd come in for the kill sooner rather than later. That meant I didn't have to keep watch over you day and night. The rest was easy."

"Shit Delaney, I'll never work you out."

"Don't ever try, laddie. Now, we'd better move the body before Suzanna comes to stay. She'd freak out if she knew someone had died in this house as well. I'll reverse the van down the side of the house. Mrs Robinson can't spy on you there. If she hears the van, you can tell her that Suzanna had a few more things than you were expecting."

He stood up and made his way towards the back door, but was stopped by Ben. "Delaney," he said with a touch of alarm in his voice. Delaney spun round, taking in the whole room. There was nothing untoward.

"What?" he asked.

"Thanks," said Ben.

Delaney raised his fists in mock attack. "Where's that fucking rope?" he said.

*

"Did you ever think I was still with the bad guys?" asked Delaney.

"Once or twice," answered Ben.

"Don't blame you for thinking that."

Delaney placed the bowl of cold water on the rug that covered the odd graze of blood on the carpet. Delaney explained that ropes and belts cause damage, but little blood, not like a knife attack might. "Suzanna will be here soon. She can act the Florence Nightingale from now on. Tell her it was Buller who did these things to you. The blood on the carpet, the hole in the ceiling, it was all Buller's fault. Tell her I carted him off and you don't care what happened to him. That way, she'll feel better knowing she's not moving in with a murderer."

The thought had never occurred to him. Delaney was right. Ben was in the clear. He was not guilty of any crime. A few misdemeanours maybe, but no real crime. Not murder. Not anymore.

"Time to go," said Delaney. "I've said this to you before, but this time, I mean it. We'll never see each other again."

He held out his hand. Ben took it, covered it with his other hand and held tight, not wanting the moment to pass. Gradually, Delaney slid his hand away and left through the back door.

Ben heard the engine of the van kick into life and listened until the very last sound drifted away down the road. He had not even asked where the van came from. There was no need.

26th May

There was another photograph on the wall.

Tired father, concerned mother, proud teenage sons. The photograph only showed the pride. On all four faces.

It is easier for children to push aside bad memories. They remain, but only surface when reminded. Alan and Eileen Blackshaw never reminded their children of the day they had returned home to find their mother tied up. An explanation was offered and accepted. It was accepted because it was the truth they were told. They were sworn to secrecy.

The note helped. It arrived the following day. Simple paper, not headed notepaper, with few words. Sometimes, least is best.

Alan, Eileen, Tom and Joe,

Alan, you have been an outstanding member of the police force, respected by all your colleagues. I wish you all the best in your forthcoming retirement. It has been thoroughly deserved. In our chosen professions, we sometimes have to make difficult choices. Just as you did yesterday. You have performed your duty impeccably,

PM

PS In your circumstances, I would have done the same thing.

"Never a black mark," said the Chief Inspector at his award ceremony and Alan's eyes twitched momentarily at that remark. Only Eileen noticed. She knew he'd never quite get over the day he escorted a lady with an envelope into 10 Downing Street.

But he was getting there.

Eileen dusted the photographs, called the boys from upstairs and Alan from the garage where he was placing his pottery in the kiln. They sat round the table and chatted the day's events away. Football club – it hadn't been cancelled that week. The deeper grooves Alan was putting in his new line of vases. Eileen getting more accustomed to full working days. Normal events.

Out of the blue, Eileen threw out a remark which grabbed all their attention.

"How about a trip to America?" she asked.

The boys laughed and got all excited. Alan thought about the salary he had just relinquished. "And just how are we going to be able to afford that?" he asked.

"I've been saving," she replied. "And there's your pension and my wage. I think it's about time we treated ourselves to a few luxuries."

There was a stunned silence when they realised that she was serious and then a sudden agreement in case the offer was withdrawn.

'Luxuries,' the man in the balaclava had said as he had left the house.

Luxuries it would be.

*

Down to fourth, then third and finally second. He reached the cone, slid the car round the hairpin and accelerated away, shifting back up the gears.

The small metal gear stick had given him problems at first, so little room between the gear positions, but he had quickly got used to it and was now flicking through them with grace and precision.

Another bend. Easily enough time to overtake on the outside before easing through the bend and dashing through on the inside of the car that had drifted too wide. A natural. Comfortable.

Flashing past the pit lane, he saw his number displayed, indicating that this was to be his last lap. Three quarters of the lap and then he would have to ease off. He was determined to make the most of it.

There were other cars on the track. He liked that. It gave him the feeling of proper racing, even though there was a constrictor on the accelerator. Pressing the car to its absolute maximum, he left others behind, passing on the outside and the inside, whichever was the most opportune. He seemed to be able to spot the gaps before they appeared.

Never a danger to himself or others. Always in complete control. He valued life too much to allow any moments of madness to occur.

It was the same as road driving, only quicker. Mirror, manoeuvre, but not signal. Just go like hell. He loved it.

Lynn knew he would. The best birthday present he could have received.

He slowed the car and pulled into the pit lane. Pushed back into the bay, he killed the engine, removed his helmet and eased his way out of the narrow cockpit. His instructor was waiting for him.

"Great driving, Ben," he said. "There's a weekend course I'd like you to come on. Take it a step further. Faster. You can do it. You've got the talent."

Ben smiled and handed back his helmet. "Thanks, but no thanks. This was a one off, a special treat. I loved every minute of it, but that's it for me. It's done. It's out of my system now."

The instructor returned the smile. He'd heard it all before. Those offered the chance came back. They shook hands. "Well, if it ever gets back into your system, you know where we are."

Ben walked through the pit lane and over the bridge. He stopped for a while watching the cars thunder by beneath him. He paid them scant attention. His mind was elsewhere, reliving the past months that had brought him back.

The wounds had been too painful. He could hardly walk. Could hardly write. Could hardly see. Emma knew a doctor who was stealing hurried liaisons with the chief registrar in whatever room could be found. If her husband found out, he would not be pleased. Neither would the wife of the chief registrar. It would be even worse if Emma fabricated the notion that the doctor was also Emma's lover and with it the tales of unadulterated passion between them.

The doctor wrote the sick note. Ben was signed off work until the end of February.

Everyone at school assumed it was the backlash of Lynn's death. He was taking time out for counselling, something he should have done immediately after the event, but which he refused.

Edward Holton, who like the others did not know the real reason for Ben's absence, supported the counselling theory with stories of an amicable Ben having a drink with him and the two children in Starbucks just after Christmas before suddenly departing without warning. A little irrational, but when Ben returned to work, he told his staff, they would all have to be supportive. Ben was just too good a man to lose. Too good a friend.

He was welcomed back with open arms. It was as if the last seven months had never happened. Straight into the job. As good as ever.

The sun was high in the spring sky. No clouds disturbed the day. As cars raced below him, the smell drifting up to fill his nostrils, he relived some of the overtaking manoeuvres, proud of his ability. Maybe he would be back after all.

It had been a perfect day.

Only one thing was missing.

There were no tears. He had shed enough of those. Seven months of tears had drained him. He had no more to give.

Anyway, there was nothing missing. She would be with him always.

"Great drive," he heard.

"Thanks."

"It was a perfect present for you."

"The only word for it. Perfect."

The roar of the cars drowned their words and they made their way across the bridge. They sat outside the café and drank their cool drinks. The silence between the two was not unusual. Sometimes, he needed time.

It was Ben who spoke. "Thanks for coming," he said.

"No need for thanks. I wouldn't have come if I didn't want to." Always the same. Always direct and to the point. She placed a newspaper on the table. "I bought this for you. I think you may find page six, bottom left hand corner interesting."

She rose from the table. He would want to read this on his own. She would keep her distance and be there for him when she was needed.

He needed less looking after nowadays. She knew the relationship was changing. It was becoming more intimate, yet more open. The occasional hold of the hand, the leaning of their heads towards each other as they laughed, the visits to see Tom and Doris. She didn't want to rush it. She would wait and if there was something between them, then it would happen. And if it didn't, then it was never meant to be. She also knew that if it was not to be, Ben would not live his life alone. Lynn would always be there.

She looked across at him as he opened the newspaper.

Six paragraphs. That was all. Six months ago, the story would have been splashed across the front pages around the globe.

Ben read slowly, savouring every word. And as he read, one unwritten word invaded the entire report. He could not read without his mind throwing the word into each sentence, each word, each letter and by the time he had finished reading, the entire article was consumed by it. There were no other words there. Only one.

He read again. Of the habit of walking the dogs three or four times a day and of that afternoon when he had been running with them. Whether that was the right move for a man of his age, his condition. He read of him standing, sweating, in the kitchen and drinking the water from the fridge. He read of the shower and the relaxation by the fire and of the whiskey that he took that night. A habit he had picked up when relaxing from the strains of work. He read of the sudden seizure witnessed by his bodyguard who never left his side and the frantic efforts to resuscitate him. And of the hopelessness of it all. And of the death by heart attack of the former Home Secretary, Charles Ashcroft.

He had been a loyal servant, the report read, but, Ben thought, only loyal enough to warrant six paragraphs on page six.

He read it again as Suzanna watched from the distance.

If the cause was right.

One word infiltrating every detail.

Delaney.